USURPERS

ROBB PRITCHARD

Foundation of the Dragon

Book II

To Ray Stevenson

For Pullo

Usurpers: Dragon Foundation Book 2 by Robb Pritchard

Published by Robb Pritchard

www.robbpritchard.co.uk

Copyright © 2023 Robb Pritchard

All rights reserved. No portion of this book may be reproduced in any form without permission from the publisher, except as permitted by U.S. copyright law. For permissions contact: robb@robbpritchard.co.uk

ISBN: 979-8-8573-1992-5

Cover and map by Sasa Juric (www.sassch.com)

If you must break the law, do it to seize power: in all other cases observe it.

> Julius Caesar

Segontium	Caernarfon
Deva	Chester
Rutupiae	Richbourough, Kent
Eboracum	York
The Wall	Hadrian's Wall, northern England
Canovium	Caerhum, near Conwy
Mediolanum	Milan, Italy
Treverorum	Trier, Germany

PROLOGUE

The voice dragged Magnus along as helplessly as though the words had turned into thick ropes that had wrapped themselves around him. Where they were leading him, he didn't want to go, and the panic rose. It was the feeling of leading a detachment to where he knew an ambush lay, yet couldn't prevent his men from getting killed.

They were pulling him to the edge. Closer and closer. His feet scraping little cascades of gravel off the edge of the cliff. He began to scream...but couldn't hear himself as his cry was drowned out by the raging din of every battle he'd ever fought in over the long years of his military life. He heard the thudding of swords on shields, of horses against man, spears piercing chests, axes crashing into the backs of necks. A hundred more dead in the count of every heartbeat.

The screams were from all the men he'd sent to their deaths over the years, all braying to be the first to rip him to shreds.

The voice came again, the words saving him from the mindless slaughter, carrying him across the mountains and rivers, to stand him before a girl.

Sounds of battle suddenly silent, he looked at her. Young and shy, she slipped away from him in fear and tried to hide behind a portico column. Despite being so bemused about where he found himself, knowing his appearance frightened her so much, shamed him.

He looked down to see what was terrifying her. The scaled armour plates over his chest were dented, dusty, and covered in the spatter of other men's blood. Next to her, in her delicate purity, he seemed a monster...but she didn't run away screaming as she should have. And at the thought that she could be as intrigued by him as he was of her, a warmth as though a brazier had just been lit in a dark empty room welled from the centre of his chest. Her innocence seemed so pure. He'd seen so much of the blood and brutality of war for so long he'd forgotten that there were some people in the world untouched by such horrors. But like a young child that didn't know to be frightened of a wolf, she needed to be protected from dangers she couldn't even imagine.

Tentatively, so she wouldn't take flight, he tried to take a step closer, but suddenly the distance between them opened into an immeasurable gulf, and he might as well have tried to walk to the stars.

With a surge of nausea, head feeling as though it was full of sewer water, he threw up at the side of the bed, splashing one of his slaves who knelt next to him.

"Dominus!" she cried and hearing her voice, for a moment Magnus thought he'd reached the girl after all. She was a sweet one, adept at using her feminine wiles to make her life of collared servitude a little easier. He'd used her enough times to appreciate those charms, but in the dream he hadn't felt lust for the girl. Strangely, it had been a deep love. The thought that a man of his standing, a general in his late forties, his name known by almost every soldier in the empire, could fawn over a girl young enough to be his daughter, and one he *owned*, made him retch again.

"I will bring water," she gasped, concerned. Despite feeling so sick, Magnus still caught the inflection in her voice, yet wasn't sure if that was because she was afraid for him or more for herself.

His head span and for a moment he wondered if her voice was familiar. But no. If he was having such dreams of a slave, then he really was a sick man.

He tried to sit up. It didn't feel like a fever, nor like the morning after eating some bad oysters. In the nightmare, he'd been young and full of a vitality long lost to him now. More than twenty years of soldiering had taken a cruel toll on his body and it felt like a ship that had barely survived a storm, all tattered sails, creaking timbers and starting to list slightly to the side.

He looked at a hunting scene painted on the wall. The wolf was about to be struck by the spears and knowing it was fighting for its life, it seemed to swirl and paws padded on the damp earth of the forest floor and he was pushing through the undergrowth, mouth dripping with saliva at the scent of wounded prey.

When the slave came back with water, he snapped back to the room. Her eyes were full of terror, as though she was expecting him to harshly flog her. He wanted to ask what she was so frightened of, and why she looked so guilty, but he didn't have the strength to speak the words, never mind to raise a whip. She had to hold the cup to his lips.

The water was cool and fresh and for a moment, he was scooping handfuls of it out of a lake of impossibly clear water at the foot of a jagged, snow-covered mountain. He saw it, and smelled the soft scent of elderflower blossoms as though he was really there. And up the valley, voices as clear and piercing as a songbird, a girl called out his name, imploring him to follow.

I

Summer AD 380

Segontium, Britannia Secunda

"I want his cock!"

The angry voice of the harbourmaster echoing around the preatorium courtyard startled Elen so much she almost dropped her father's cloak.

With shaking fingers, she struggled with the ornate boar-shaped hasp at his shoulder.

Dear God above, she silently pleaded to the grey sky. *Please, I beg of you, don't let it be Eugenius...anyone but Eugenius.* The two of them hadn't spent much time sleeping in the last few nights, and he'd said he hoped to find some strong posca to drink before taking his post on dawn patrol...*Please God no!* If it was his blood on her hands..."Why did you have to kill him?" she whispered. Monster or man, she wanted to know how Father could put a man so young to death. Not even twenty. His whole life ahead of him. Only a couple of years older than her brother, and Kenon was certainly no man!

A vein throbbed at Father's temple and his face was almost as red as his cloak. "Discipline," he said with a set jaw.

For a painful moment, Elen's heart stopped. Had she angered him? Was he going to lash her for asking such a question?

"You're just a girl, so you can't know what it is to be a soldier," he continued. "Discipline is the mortar between the stones that holds them together and makes them a wall. The stronger it is, the stronger the wall."

Finally, the clasp came undone and she bundled the dirty cloak up, trying not to get any of the revolting blood on her hands.

"And he was no *boy*. He was a soldier! Asleep on watch duty. If I didn't punish him, anyone on guard at night would feel as though they could just take a nap whenever they felt like. And then where would we be? The raiders from the sea could just dock their ships and walk straight into the fort."

Elen could still feel Eugenius' rough hands on her body, his hot, urgent breath on her neck. So desperate to know if he lived or not, she was almost ready to run to his barracks and bang her fists on the door, uncaring about who saw and what they would think.

The harbourmaster pounded on the gate again this time with something hard. Servants and slaves scattered around the courtyard like a flock of startled birds. The thudding was so loud it was impossible to ignore. "I want his balls as well!"

"Where is that cock-proud brother of yours? Kenon!" Father bellowed, his voice laden with such authority that the pounding on the gate stopped.

There was no love lost between Elen and her arrogant, bullying brother, but Father's wrath was too much to wish on anyone.

Hoping it would be a calming gesture, she offered a glass of wine. "Have mercy," she pleaded and readied herself for the rebuke.

"You think I'll execute him as well, child?" he scoffed.

At his harsh words, she bowed her head in deference, but at least he'd called her child. What she got up to in the hayloft at the end of the vicus with Eugenius certainly wasn't childish, so perhaps she could hope what they did together was still a secret. But if it was her lover's blood spattered over the cloak and her hands, she didn't know what she'd do. Just kill herself, or try to kill Father first?

He drowned the wine in one go. "Being merciful is the *problem*. Men perform at their best once a rigid discipline has been instilled from routine, hardship and strict *punishment*. Indulging your brother and you as I have, letting you believe you're special, above others, just because I am the Governor of Britannia...it was a sure way to spoil you. But that will be no more."

If her upbringing had been easy, she couldn't imagine what a harsh one would have been like. Bruises still dotted the back of her legs from the last time she'd displeased him, nearly a month ago.

"Father," Kenon said as he strode confidently across the courtyard. Outwardly, he sounded respectful, but Elen could clearly hear the spite in his voice.

She picked the bloodied cloak up and began to back nervously away. Maybe with Father's attention taken with Kenon, she would have a chance to slip away and find out which soldier had just been killed.

"Stay!" he ordered and the single word was enough to make her stand as still as a statue, or a soldier standing to attention before the governor. To Kenon, he spat, "And what do you have to say for yourself, boy?"

"*Me?*" her brother asked, feigning innocence. "Nothing!"

"So you didn't deflower the harbourmaster's daughter?"

Elen felt her cheeks blush. If Father knew what she'd been getting up to in the hayloft with Eugenius she wouldn't be able to walk for a week from the whipping she'd get.

Kenon, though, didn't even try to hide the look of boyish pride.

Father seemed sickened. "You think that's something to be proud of?"

"Who cares," Kenon shrugged with a nonchalance none of the thousands of men under Father's command would have ever dared. "She's just a low girl. A slut."

Elen watched as Father's fists clenched into a pair of white-knuckled battering rams. Even though it was Kenon in trouble, not her, she'd been at the receiving end of enough of his disciplining that her knees began to tremble on her brother's behalf.

"How many times have I tried to explain," he sighed. "The power you think I have is not that of an emperor."

He spoke in a growl now. Elen wondered if that was the tone the executed soldier had heard before the cudgel smashed into the side of his head for the first time.

"*Real* ruling is not like that. You can't simply bark an order and have men obey. Not here at the end of the world. Here it's all about *alliances*, getting what you need by giving men what *they* want and need."

"You're the Governor of Britannia," Kenon said dismissively. "You hold power over the whole land. No one would challenge your command. You shouldn't be so afraid of your power, Father."

Elen saw the amount of strain Father needed to control himself and took a step back. She wondered if she should try and save the ornate wine decanter before the violence that was surely coming, erupted.

In a tone that couldn't be misunderstood as anything other than a warning, Father said, "I've just put a better lad than you to death for nothing more than nodding off on duty. The scorn of a petulant child, I do not need."

"Octavius!" the harbourmaster shouted from outside. "I would have words with that boy of yours!"

"The girl you deflowered is the same age as your sister." He pointed a blood-stained finger right at Elen's chest. "What would you do to a man you found rutting her?"

Again, Elen's first reaction was to fear for Eugenius, but was dismayed at how Kenon looked her up and down as if he was deciding if she was a brothel wench worthy of his coin. "He'd be welcome to her," he said.

Never mind what her father was planning to do with him, if she hadn't been encumbered with the cloak, she would have slapped his smug face. Father didn't react to the insult though, and that was worrying. Did he know about Eugenius and the hayloft? The terror of not knowing if he was dead or alive made it hard to breathe.

The heavy silence was cut by the high-pitched cries of seagulls.

"Will you speak with the harbour master?" Father asked, calmer than Elen thought possible.

"I would sooner run him through with a pilum."

Elen saw how Father's shoulders sagged, as though he had given up on something important. Old enough to have a head of white hair, he may have been, but he was still as hard as an oak tree. Elen couldn't help a scream as the back-handed slap across Kenon's face sent him sprawling across the floor. For a brief moment, she saw sorrow and pain on Father's face, but both were held in check by an iron determination.

As Kenon pushed himself back to his feet and stood up, Elen saw his fingers twitch on the hilt of his pugio at his hip. The short knife with the jewelled handle had been a birthday gift a few years ago. She was about to cry out that he intended his father harm, but a man who commanded legions didn't have anything to fear from his own son.

"You want to use that blade? Let it be. We'll see how much of a man you are. Open the gates," he called to any slave in earshot. "Let him in."

A primal fear flashed in Kenon's eyes. "You can't!" he gasped.

"Why not?"

"He'll *kill* me!"

"Maybe," Father shrugged. "I suspect, however, he will be satisfied with a simple gelding."

"*What?*" Kenon wailed.

In a single fluid movement, Father reached down and twisted Kenon's knife hand so savagely that Kenon probably didn't even realise how he was folded to his knees like a straw doll.

"Where is he?" the harbourmaster boomed, no less enraged now that he was inside.

"Futou!" Kenon cursed, futilely trying to pull himself free of Father's grip. But the more he squirmed, the tighter he was held.

Elen was torn between trying to intercede and the raw fear she had of Father's temper.

"You wish me to defend you?" he snarled. "Perhaps some responsibility for your actions is something you should have learned a long time ago."

Elen had no idea what he planned, but she was sure she didn't want to witness it. She hadn't been dismissed though, so his command still held her rooted to the spot, just as if she was a house slave.

"You will witness this," he said to her, as though he could hear her thoughts. "And then we will talk of the future."

She had no idea what he meant and watched mutely and helplessly as the harbourmaster strode up to them. Red-faced, a few specks of white spittle on his chin, the wild look in his eye made Elen want to hide behind one of the colonnade posts of the inner roof at the side of the courtyard.

"Sabinus," Father nodded in greeting.

"Octavius, may I speak my mind to this son of yours?"

"You may."

"My daughter is but a child..." he started, voice wavering from the rage he was trying to subdue.

When Father released Kenon, at least he had the acuity to stay on his knees and Elen was relieved he wasn't as arrogant and flippant with the harbourmaster as he was with his own father. Maybe he could talk his way out of the situation after all.

"Will you do the honourable thing and marry her?"

"What?" Kenon stuttered. "She's just a..." Fortunately, he stopped himself before speaking the insult. Elen wondered if he'd just saved his life by biting his tongue and not letting the words out.

"*Beneath* you, is she?" Sabinus grinned. "Wishing for a daughter of a more powerful man to bring you land and riches as dowry, are you?"

Elen watched Kenon squirm.

"Well then..." Sabinus sighed with a terrible finality.

"Before we get to blood," Father interjected. "Perhaps we can come to some other bargain?"

"What do you suggest?" Sabinus asked. His fist hovering near the hilt of his spatha indicated how unlikely he was to agree to any punishment he didn't deem severe enough.

Kenon was shaking now, either with anger or fear, but at least kept his hand away from his pugio. With two battle-hardened men looming over him, there was no scenario where a seventeen-year-old boy drawing a weapon would end well.

She dared to take a little step back not wanting to be anywhere near what was about to happen.

"Carry on," Sabinus said.

"Your misdeeds are grievous," Father said to her trembling brother. "And it is known that it is far from the first transgression."

"And far from the last, I don't doubt," Sabinus interjected.

"With everything you do so mindlessly, so arrogantly, you piss on my name with dishonour. I have fought in many wars, killed many men with spear, sword and command. More men than you can count. Now I have an entire *province* under my rule and *own* a damn good part of it, as well. You think that when I die it will all be yours, to do with what you will? My estates a giant playground for you to drink, fuck and have slaves place fruits on your tongue by for the rest of your days?"

The acceptable answer would have been 'no, Father' but with a sneer that assured Elen of some fast-approaching finality, Kenon spat, "You are old."

Sabinus coughed with disbelief at the insult and Elen took another step back. Such words spoken to a father were a much more grievous offence than what he'd done to the harbourmaster's daughter. Kenon could have been consumed by plague, or cut down by Scotti raiders, but with those words, Elen knew his loss to the family could not have been any more complete.

"I will not flog you," Father said.

As she saw the triumphant grin spread across Kenon's face, Elen wondered why her brother couldn't see that what was coming was going to be so much worse than a mere whipping. She thought about running for Mother. Surely Gula wouldn't stand to see harm come to her son, whether he'd brought it on himself or not. Sabinus blocked the way to the rooms at the far side of the courtyard though.

In a formal voice, her father addressed the aggrieved harbourmaster. "Friend, I have known you for more years than I care to recall. I consider you a man whose honour anchors him as secure as the ships in the harbour he administers. For his misdeeds, would you accept my son's banishment and conscription?"

"Put him into training as a soldier?"

Father nodded.

"Without your name for him to wear as armour."

"Without my name," her father sighed.

"Father!" Kenon gasped.

"Agreed," the harbourmaster nodded and held out his arm for Father to grip. In the shake, Kenon's fate was sealed.

Kenon, still on his knees, shouted, "You're *banishing* me!?"

Father turned to the boy who had been his son. "You will train in the army. At the lowest rank. Four months of training, maybe more, as a new recruit. Without my name to shield you."

"You can't do this!" Kenon wailed.

"I just did."

"You're sentencing me to *death*!" he cried, which amused the harbourmaster.

"Such may well be your fate. But if the last thing you see is a centurion's cudgel coming at your forehead, know that you brought it on yourself."

Neither man smiled at how Kenon seemed to shrink. They had both just lost a child, as a daughter's poor reputation was as much a banishment for her in her own life prospects as Kenon being sent away.

"I will pray for a month that her cycle comes again," Sabinus said with gravitas.

Father nodded. "If not...come and see me again and we will talk some more. I will honour such a child as of my line."

"Even though the boy no longer bares your name?"

"Even though."

"A great honour you do me."

"Nothing less than is warranted," Father said, holding his hand out.

The two men clasped wrists again and agreement made, Sabinus strode away.

In the silence, as his footsteps receded, Elen tried to calm herself down, but Kenon stayed prone on the floor, all fight gone from him.

"Attend me," Father snapped and she skipped to follow him, not reacting to Kenon's hate-filled glare as she passed him.

In the dining room, a soft warmth radiating from the floor and walls from the hypocaust, Father slumped wearily into his chair. She set the cloak aside and knelt before him to begin unbinding the thongs of his sandals.

"In truth, his fate was sealed more than a month ago," he sighed. He took his knife from his hip and began scraping thoughtfully away at a little piece of wood which after a while would become a ludus counter. It took long hours of a patience that to her seemed infinite, but he could whittle cuts of oak down into perfectly shaped pieces. As little chips fell across the mosaic-like flakes of snow, she was dumbfounded that despite what had just happened, his hands were as still as a scribe's.

"Game pieces are made from wood by the repeated intelligent application of the knife," he mused, sounding terribly sad. "In a similar way, real men are carved from boys by *discipline*." He carried on scraping the counter. "And discipline comes from respecting your superiors! Spoilt, he was. But I blame myself for it. He'd bring all of my estates to absolute ruin in just a few short years, I am sure of it." He was concentrating on the counter so much that his speech was slow. "Too soft. Too soft," he sighed.

Elen heard him speak, but couldn't really listen. He'd said Kenon's fate had been sealed a month ago...so she wondered what arrangements he'd been making in that time. Certainty settled on her as heavy and unyielding as concrete. If Kennen truly was banished, she was now heir to Father's lands...and that meant a husband would be chosen for her. And if he'd been considering it for weeks...

Every girl of a good family from the Wall to the Pyramids knew that one day the time would come when the absolute joy of choosing a partner for a dalliance was ripped away and replaced by a man imposed on her. One she'd have to serve in the same way as she did Father... and in much more unpleasant ways. The thought of not being able to be with Eugenius, to share a life and family with on some quiet farm in the country, made it feel as though she was drowning...her body, just like her hope for the future, lifeless, bloated, bobbling face down in the murky waters of the harbour.

She wondered how long they had left together. Another month? A week? Did Father already know the name of the man she was to marry? To bear the children of? She struggled to keep her belly from heaving.

With the laces of one of his sandals finally free, she began to tease the knots of the other. She had to do it by touch though, as her eyes had become blurry with tears.

"Don't worry about your precious Eugenius," he said. The words were spoken softly, but it was as though he'd lashed her legs with his hardest whip. Not least because it seemed he was reading her mind as though it was an unwound scroll.

"It wasn't him. I wouldn't do that to you. Not without warning you first. Probably not even if he was sleeping on watch. But..."

In a flood of relief that Eugenius was alive, her heart pounded like the footsteps of a cohort's march. But Father knew her deepest secret and it was as if he'd reached into her chest and was gripping her heart in his fist.

"You will have to say your goodbyes to him soon. You are worth much more to your family than fooling around with a common soldier. With Kenon gone, my lands will go to you now, daughter.

You will have the grandest dowry in the whole of Britannia. And so, I will choose a suitable husband."

He spoke gently, respectfully, as though he was arranging a great honour for her, but she felt as though she was listening to a brothel owner ushering her through to the back room to serve another client.

"And don't worry about your brother, either. He will only be gone for a year or so. No more. He needs to learn how to be a man, and being sent to the army as a fresh recruit will do that for him. He will be forged into a man like an ingot into a sword. But in a year you will have a child who will in turn come to inherit my lands. If he makes it to next summer alive, Kenon can have my name back again. I meant what I said about him not ruining my estates, though. He is...unsuitable." He looked at the little counter in his hands, already roughly rounded. "I don't know where I went wrong with him," he said with another deep sigh. "Not enough discipline."

For Elen, it wasn't too hard to understand how Father's corruption in swindling locals to sell their land and farms cheaply under the threat of using the army to seize their harvest, coupled with his inclination to brutality, had washed off on his son. He was either too short-sighted to see himself properly, or believed himself so perfect, but it was obvious to Elen that Kenon had become his mirror. The fact that Father detested in Kenon what he wasn't aware of in himself almost made her laugh. But like every girl in the empire, she was as helpless to her father's plans for her as a guard dog kept on a short chain.

"You think yours is a cruel fate? Don't worry daughter, I will choose wisely for you. A strong man. One capable of running my estates at a profit."

It took a lot of effort not to roll her eyes. She couldn't imagine how he could believe she was interested in such things.

A young slave boy brought a bowl of gently steaming water and set it down at his master's feet.

"Fetch a scribe," Father told him. "With parchments and a pen."

As Elen lifted Father's feet into the bowl, she wished it was her he'd banished instead of Kenon. As she began gently washing them she tried not to think that as he whittled away at the wood he was probably thinking about which man he deemed best to impregnate his daughter.

II

Kenon's horse, almost as impatient as he was, tossed its mane to brush away the files. Kenon did the same with his hand. The smells of various industries mixed with human functions made him want to visit the bathhouse to scrape himself clean as soon as this nonsense was over. To the curious onlookers, he, with the five other riders, saddlebags full of provisions, would have looked like a group about to head out on some journey that would take a few days. He had to admit that the charade seemed very authentic. But Father never did things by half measures, and if Kenon wasn't aware it was all just a show to frighten him, he could have believed he was really about to be sent away.

He slapped another fly from his cheek, angry that the stupid insects couldn't tell the difference between the filthy plebs from the vicus and the civilised men from the fort.

He didn't like the sight of Sabinus standing by the twin gate towers, gloating at the little display of discipline. Prigging the harbourmaster's bint had been a nice way to pass a few moments of a summer afternoon, but was hardly worth this and he was impatient to the point of annoyance for the tiring jest to be at an end.

The others didn't look too amused either. Four of them were young soldiers, but a few years older than Kenon. Early twenties. Another two decades in the army to look forward to, at least before they would be granted citizenship and a plot of land. Kenon shuddered at the thought. He wondered what their officer had told them they were going to be doing this morning, but wouldn't lower himself to ask.

A fifth rider was older, flashes of grey at the sides of his short beard, and he looked so pissed off that Kenon wondered if he was being disciplined for something as well.

His arm still hurt from how Father had twisted it and he flushed with anger again at how his sister and slaves had seen him treated like a green recruit in the training yard.

The fort stood on a hill overlooking the harbour. A dozen ships of varying sizes nestled there safe from the famously dangerous currents of the straits between the mainland and the isle the locals called Mona. Kenon wished that the ships were engulfed in leaping flames as once, legend said, had been the sacred groves of the druids.

He wondered if it was a look of amusement on the face of one of the guards in front of the perimeter ditch. He sighed loudly so that those around knew how frustrated he was. The point was proven; Father unquestioningly held true power over the soldiers of the fort and the farmers of the lands further than Kenon could see. Further than he could ride for days. He decided that from now on he'd be careful whose daughters he fucked in the abandoned mithraeum. More careful not to get caught, at least. And when the miserable old bastard smiled and told him he could return to the praetorium, Kenon swore to himself that he'd not speak to him for days.

At last, short, snow white hair seeming to glow like a halo in the morning sun, his aged father came out, hobnailed boots loud on the cobbles, the end of his blood red cloak flowing out behind him in the breeze. Kenon had been waiting outside long enough that curses and insults were ready to spew off his tongue in a torrent. He wanted the farce over and done with though, so kept silent. He'd find an unsuspecting slave later to take his wrath out on, although with a sigh, he recalled that Father had warned him about that as well.

Octavius came to stand near the horse's head. "Kenon," he said, a sad smile on his weather-beaten face. There was no mirth in his eyes, no indication he was about to smile and tell him to run like a chastised child back to the praetorium. "I am sorry it has to come to this. Truly, I am. Maybe one day you will understand that far from ruining your life, I do this in the hope of saving it. You are lucky that Sabinus would never draw the blood of my family in my walls, but with the path you are on, one day it would have been another man with a defiled daughter who seeks recompense. And he may not be so reserved."

"Father, you don't have to..." Kenon started, bored now to the point of exasperation.

"Write and let your mother know you have arrived safely," he said and held out his hand as though he wanted Kenon to grip his wrist in farewell. His palm was open though. Kenon was confused. "Your pugio," Octavius sighed, and suddenly Kenon saw the pain in his father's eyes. With a shock, he understood it was all real; he really was being sent away. The horse shuffled under him, unsure if the movement it felt of Kenon squirming was a command to start walking.

Numbly, Kenon took the small weapon from his belt. "It is my grandfather's blade," he said, trying to sound defiant. "And his before that."

"Don't worry," Octavius said. "I shall find a worthy man to pass it to. Write to your mother." And with that, his father turned his back.

Kenon stared at the old man as he strolled away. Next step, he thought. The next step and he will turn around and ask if the lesson has been learned. But he watched in a white hot rage as Father shared an understanding nod with Sabinus and strode back into the fort without turning back. Kenon made a silent vow to cut the tongue from whichever rider was chuckling behind him.

"Right then," one of the young soldiers called as he kicked his horse into a canter. The others followed.

Kenon cursed. Not one the gods usually heard directed at a father, and turned his mount ready to follow them, but before it had taken a few steps, the older man blocked his way. "Easy," he said, hand out in a gesture that was meant to be calming. His demeanour was so effortlessly dominant, Kenon pulled the reins back before he even realised he was doing it.

"You don't know me, but what you *need* to know is that I don't trust those others. That means you shouldn't either. Be on your guard!"

Kenon had no idea what the man meant, and all he wanted was to run from the fort as fast as he could. But riding away at least he was glad of the small mercy afforded by the air becoming fresher away from the vicus.

The fort of Canovium was the best part of a day's ride away, if they were going to thrash the horses, and as he felt the addictive power of the beast under him, he wondered if his punishment would be a night or two in the rotten old fort before being called home. Or maybe they'd march all the way to see the Twentieth Legion's fortress at Deva long enough to shock him into seeing the error of his ways. Maybe the real point of him being sent away for a little while was just to let the harbourmaster's blood cool. But whatever Father had planned, riding in the fresh air was better than a beating, so maybe he should be thankful for that. And some of the best brothels outside Londinium were in Deva's sprawling vicus. Maybe he'd stay there for a week or two waiting until the girl, whatever her name was, had her moon blood again. Feeling the sun warming his face, he decided it wouldn't be so bad at all. It was also much better to think of soft flesh and moist places than how Father had walked away with the pugio in his hand.

The cold wind pulled Kenon out of his pleasant reverie and he looked around to see where he was. No sprawling villas or farms here, just rugged mountains and empty moorland. But every slope was dotted with little white flecks. Each one gave a lamb and a fleece of wool every spring. It meant nothing individually, but multiplied by the tens, the hundreds of thousands, and it was why Father was one of the wealthiest men in Britannia, never mind the power and status he held as governor of the whole province. His lands extended all over the next range of hills and he also held vast estates in the fertile plains south of Deva with dozens of farms, lakes full of fish and endless fields of wheat, barley and flax.

And all Kenon had to do to get it for himself was to wait for Father to die.

With a familiar thrill of anticipation, he imagined the hundreds of workers and thousands of slaves which would be his to do with as he pleased. He'd choose the most well-appointed villa, stock it with the most nubile slaves, get the best wines and fruits imported...and he'd never have to leave for the rest of his days.

The surge of excitement from thinking of such a future welled up on a wave like the promise of an orgasm, but it was swiftly quashed by another surge of anger that Father had made him take this pointless ride. And why had he taken the pugio back? That was a deep insult and had left a taste in his mouth like he'd swigged a mouthful of posca instead of Falernian wine.

The four young soldiers clearly rejoiced in their temporary freedom from the drudgery of the fort, the daily drills and marches and endless polishing of never used weapons and equipment. A couple wanted to gallop off, but their leader, the eldest of them, was holding them back with harsh words.

The way the older man rode close and kept a hawk-like eye on the others gave Kenon the impression that he was protecting him, but that made no sense, and so he tried to dismiss it. He was burning to ask where they were going, but he didn't know how to phrase the question without tacitly admitting he had no idea.

Around midday, Kenon was more than ready to eat. On the sloping plain with heather-covered mountains to their south and the murky coast to the north, they were at the site of an old battlefield. He'd heard lads about his own age being curious about the blanched bones poking out of the thin soil and told tales of some forgotten slaughter of savages. It was a history he cared absolutely nothing about.

The others, all well used to long days in the saddle, ate on the go, but the bread and dried strips of meat weren't enough for Kenon, so by the time they got to Canovium, he was desperate for some proper food. Even more so than the beggars on the road leading into the vicus who thrust up their filthy hands, thinking they'd be given what was Kenon's own.

Inside the rough settlement hawkers called out vivid, and probably wildly exaggerated, descriptions of their wares. Supposedly fresh oysters and scallops from the estuary a little to the north were crammed into buckets and rabbits dangled from hooks. His stomach rumbled, but they rode straight through to the main gate and passed the guards tasked with blocking the way for the native-born rabble.

Canovium was just an auxiliary fort in the middle of nowhere. Three centuries ago, some local tribe had managed to storm it and burn it to the ground. No trace of that assault was left now, as the walls had been rebuilt in stone, but in the mood he was in, he wished the barbarians had done a better job.

It was the same size as Segontium, but manned by much rougher soldiers, ones sent here to rule over the flocks of sheep as a form of punishment, Kenon didn't wonder. One look around at the men who were stationed here and he was sure the natives knew to keep their daughters far from this place. And for that, he judged himself to perhaps be in good company.

Eye watering from the miasma of smoke from countless cooking fires, he had to force himself to keep his mouth shut when the others stopped their horses outside a long barrack hut rather than the praetorium of the fort commander. Silently fuming that Father had ordered yet another pointless humiliation for him to endure, he got stiffly down from the saddle. Blanket unstrapped, he stormed inside and in one of the smokiest and crossed tossed it onto the nearest bunk.

"Not what you're used to, huh?" one of his travel companions smirked, barely able to contain his laughter. Straight away, the four of them squatted down and crowded around a dice tower. A few shouts, some groans and curses, then mocking laughter as it was decided who would be cooking for the group.

One of them held the die out for Kenon. "Want to know what cursed future Fortuna has for you?"

Kenon took them, but after a day of suffering their company, the last thing he wanted was to spend any more time with them. He looked at the tower that they used to be sure no one was cheating by sleight of hand. It was covered in thin strips of bone intricately carved in circular geometric patterns. It was exquisite, and Kenon wanted it for himself.

"So, me and the lads, what we were thinking is...Seeing what your father said to you this morning...do we call you 'bastard' now?"

Kenon's finger was pointing at the lad's eye socket, a gesture that had it been made by his father, the lad would have dropped to his knees, begging forgiveness. He didn't even flinch though. And that wasn't just enraging, it was unnerving. "Do you know who I am?" Kenon snarled.

"Leave him!" the eldest snapped. "He's the governor's son!"

"Aye, and just got himself disinherited in front of us, so he probably hates him as much as the rest of us."

"Enough!" the one who seemed to have the most authority snapped.

"You can kill him tomorrow," another said under his breath, but despite being in the middle of a fort, a place where discipline had the same importance as air and grain, Kenon couldn't contain himself and barrelled into the mouthy lad...but he was quick, and twisted easily away, and the foot he stuck out tripped Kenon face-first to the floor. Before he could get his wits back, the lad was on top of him, pummelling his head and face so hard all Kenon could do was curl up in the vain hope of protecting himself. And he stayed lying there even after the blows had stopped. His friends pulled the lad away, but he was laughing and didn't protest being held by them.

"What's going on!" someone bellowed and at the voice of a stern superior and all four of them stood to attention so quickly it was as though they'd been struck by lightning.

Kenon felt hands on him and he was dragged to his feet and his tunic was patted down to make him look more presentable.

"*Fighting?*" the decanus shouted, outraged, and stepped over to pull Kenon to his feet.

Kenon had never been handled in such a way by a lowly decanus, a soldier in charge of just ten men. His father commanded fifty thousand.

"No, no," one of the others said, "He just fell over. We were just helping him up."

Kenon touched a painful cheek and wasn't surprised to see blood on his fingers. His left eye was beginning to swell and his jaw hurt so much that dinner wasn't going to be the joy he'd spent most of the day imagining. But much worse than the pain was the humiliation of how easily he'd been bested.

He grasped the hilt of his gladius, but a strong hand on his wrist stopped him pulling it free of the scabbard. "You do not want to do that," the decanus warned. "A bout of fisticuffs works wonders to clear the air every now and then, but draw steel here and I'll stripe your back for it." He looked at the other lads. "He fell, did he?"

"Yes, sir."

"Are you Octavius' boy?"

"I am."

"He *was*," the lad who'd hit him smirked...but the smile was wiped off his face by the decanus' scornful look.

"Well..." he said. "You have a long ride ahead of you. Better get some rest."

The outrage that the decanus knew where Kenon was going was tempered slightly by the knowledge that the next stop would be Deva. Father could leave him there for a month if he wanted, that would suit him just fine.

"It don't matter," one of the other lads said cheerfully. "We've all been away from our families so long, none of us remember what our father's faces look like any more. So we're *all* bastards."

Kenon didn't know if that was meant to be a consolation, or another insult.

"But you're *the* bastard," the one who'd beaten him growled and got a slap in the head from the decanus.

The decanus pushed Kenon out into the evening air. "Go and find a doctor and get yourself cleaned up."

Kenon was about to do as instructed but saw one of the dice on the ground. A battered old thing, it must have been rolled through the box and over the floor more times than even God knew. They were the soldier's way of divining what future awaited them, how Fortuna communicated her favour or not, and it was so old it would probably be a precious belonging for one of them. Instead of tossing it back through the barrack door, he slipped it into a pouch. And if God favoured him, he'd somehow get the beautiful tower for himself as well.

As he walked away, the words he'd heard one say before the first punch had landed, came back. Kill him tomorrow. Although it didn't make much sense, he was sure it hadn't been meant as a joke...more as a way to stop the fight. But more urgent than getting someone to look at his eye, was his need for the latrine. The others had been happy to squat at the side of the road to do their business but Kenon's bowels had clenched themselves as tight as a fist until he came across some more sophisticated surroundings. The older soldier was sitting down looking pensive. Kenon hiked his tunic up and sat over the hole next to him.

The man looked at his bruised face for a moment and rolled his eyes. "I warned you."

"What did I do to them? I gave them no reason to hate me," Kenon blurted out.

"They hate what you stand for," was the matter-of-fact reply.

"And what's that?"

"Inherited wealth. Inherited status."

"That's not my fault!"

"Maybe not. But you embrace it wholeheartedly. You can't deny that."

"And why wouldn't I?"

He just shrugged.

"Why did you tell me not to trust them?" Kenon asked.

He sighed. It was like a tired old teacher giving up on trying to instruct a dull child. "They have their minds on other things."

"Like what?"

"It might not mean anything to you, but yesterday your father executed one of their friends. Right in front of them. And, as though it meant nothing to him, the very next day he put them in charge of escorting his son. Can you see how perhaps their frustrations could find a target in you?"

And so they'd have their minds on beating him up the next day, as soon as they were far enough from the fort that the sentries wouldn't hear his cries. Kenon decided it would be a good idea to know the name of the man he hoped would protect him.

"You don't need to know my name," was the unexpected reply. It was clearly insubordinate, but before Kenon demanded a clear answer, he stopped himself. After what had happened that morning, he wasn't entirely sure of his current status.

"Some call me the Areani," he offered a little reluctantly.

That made no sense. The mythical trackers and scouts who'd spent so much of their lives outside they become part animal, and consequently less human, had been disbanded in disgrace after the Conspiracy. With the man's demeanour so frosty, Kenon didn't want to push, but he did want to know how long he was going to be away from Segontium. "So..." he began uncertainly. "How many nights will we be enjoying the fort of Deva for?"

The Areani looked at him with a quizzical expression. "One."

"One?" Kenon spat in surprise.

"You don't know where you're going?" He sounded genuinely surprised. "Our destination is Rutupiae."

Kenon's head span. Rutupiae was on the coast at the far end of the land, almost as far away from Segontium as it was possible to get without boarding a ship. A week's ride at least, maybe two. But then he was sure that it must be another part of Father's ploy to scare him. "All I did was fuck the harbourmaster's girl. Why does everyone insist on mocking me?"

The Areani didn't reply, just wiped his ass with the sponge, dipped it in the big jar of vinegar, and handed it to Kenon to use.

Rutupiae, he chuckled. If he ever spoke a polite word to Father again, he'd tell him how much of a fright that had given him. For a heartbeat at least. Of course, it couldn't be true.

III

Rome

Magnus' palfrey moved under him with grace and confidence. Lithe. It was an animal with pedigree enough to make an emperor sore with jealousy.

A nudge to the flanks with his heels and she sped up to a trot. A call of, "Gaa!" and she wilfully broke into a gallop. As the wind whipped into his face and pulled at his hair, the familiar thrill of the ride coursed through his blood. The barks of the hunting dogs came from behind, excited at the sudden change of pace, thinking prey was near.

She checked her step then sprang over a small brook, and Magnus was taken back to his childhood, mornings and nights in the stables, the absolute wonder of assisting with a birth and watching the foal get straight to its feet, eager to run from its very first breath. Days in the hot sun training colts and fillies in the longeing circle, breaking it in to the bridle and saddle and watching the farrier change its shoes. Those long days were simple and it was a life he often missed.

Leaning forwards, gripping the pommel, arms dampening the ride, he remembered the day he was first allowed to take out one of his family's thoroughbreds on his own. Tearing away on such a beast, he'd felt that the four corners of the empire were suddenly but a day's ride away. It was a memory he would treasure forever.

He pushed her harder until they were charging fast enough to rouse him from the fatigue that clung to him like wet clothes, so fast he came close to the exhilarating feeling of becoming one with the horse, its will bent to his. She tossed her head and neighed, enjoying the fresh air as much as he was. The deep thumping of the hooves on the ground, the heady feeling of the animal under him, so much bigger and stronger than he was, yet completely at his control, was something only a very experienced rider could feel.

Charging along the edge of the last of the farmland, the dark line of forest lay ahead. With no direction from the reins or his legs the horse seemed to know instinctively where he wanted to go and he could almost dream about running with her forever and ever.

Above the quickly approaching trees, a ridge of distant mountains lined the horizon...but as he looked at them, they seemed to soften, then dissolve to become a cloud of desert dust kicked up by an undisciplined line of Berbers as they charged.

He came back to where he was with a shock, and wiping a trail of drool from the side of his mouth, realised he'd been dreaming in the saddle. The horse twisted her ears back at the curse he shouted at the strange lethargy which had been plaguing him for the last few weeks. All the exhilaration of the ride spent like his seed in a cheap whore, and all he wanted to do was lay down and sleep. The horse, trained to perfection, slowed in response to Magnus' change and began to canter.

He looked back and saw his brother trying to keep up, a wide grin on his face. They'd left the others far behind. The Tiber, this close to the city, was wide, lazy, and dirt brown after the last day's rains and didn't look too inviting for a reviving dip. Marcellinus reined in alongside. From riding at such a speed, his face was flustered and his eyes were watering. "Spotted one?" he asked enthusiastically.

His eagerness was unsettling. The thrill of the hunt, the terrified squeals and thrashing as the boar fought for life against the sharp spear tips, tusks ready to gorge those careless with their weapons... it was a passion that should have been pumping through Magnus' veins. He didn't want to say it wasn't a boar he was searching for but a place to curl up and doze. He'd spent weeks trying to convince himself it was just worry, the burden of intrigue and politics where a man didn't know in what regard any of the three emperors held him, or planned to do with him. But now he wondered if it was time to consult a doctor. "You ride on," he said. "It was an early morning and that girl last night was especially energetic." He tried to give a confident smile to go with the lie, but felt how strained it was.

It was no whore who'd been haunting his dreams for nearly half a month. On the back of his neck, he felt her breath, saw her green eyes staring at him again. Dog tired, he was ready to go to her right now. "It's hot and I didn't sleep well," he lied. The truth was that he'd been sleeping deeper since the dreams had started than he had when he was a babe. And when he was awake, going back to sleep was all he wanted to do. The need for it was so heavy he was beginning to wonder if he was slipping slowly away from the world. The mysterious maiden in a far away fort in a far away land was always waiting. For falling in love with a girl from a dream, he'd never felt such a fool, and knew how mercilessly he'd be ridiculed if anyone was to find out.

Before he began noticeably swaying in the saddle, he dismounted and led the horse to the sparse shade of a willow tree near the bank of the river. The rest of the contingent gradually arrived with the weapons needed for the hunt, and behind them came the slaves with everything else.

"I wish to take a rest," he called.

"In the sun?" Marcellinus asked.

Magnus threw his cloak down, his head starting to spin alarmingly and dropped to a knee. It felt as though he'd drunk a whole amphora of wine and he didn't care about lying down in front of the men. And appearing to sleep was better than simply keeling over on useless legs.

"Bring your shields," Marcellinus shouted. "Stand them up together to make shade!"

With the sound of the wooden shields scuffing together over him, clinking and thudding near his head, Magnus was back in the testudo, men closer than brothers fighting shoulder to shoulder. The shouts of the decanus' and whistles of the centurions rang in his ears as the first row shuffled to the back and the next took the line, but he couldn't work out if he was commanding the offensive, or was bracing the front. Against the chaos, as their foe threw themselves at the wall of shields to die on the short thrusts of the gladius, Magnus stabbed for all he was worth.

"I will care for him," he heard a voice say and he felt a slight breeze on his forehead as the girl wafted him with something. A good slave, she was. She performed her duties with the right mix of attention and fear. Although he was beginning to dislike how terrified she looked every time he caught her eye.

He felt himself slipping away again. He was so tired it could only be a sickness. It was such a struggle to keep his eyes open, he wondered if he would even wake again or whether he would see Lydia once more. She had been smiling in the morning as though she had no worries in the world and was dead of fever before he'd got back to her that evening. Her loss had hit him hard and he hadn't wanted to marry again since. Not until the green-eyed girl had come to him in his dream.

As he drifted off, he heard the sweet whispering of the story of his dreams…the river…His last waking thought was that such a thing couldn't be right, but unfettered of worldly concerns and an ailing body, he floated along on words he could see but not hear.

At first, the Tiber wound into countless lazy bends meandering through vineyards full of succulent grapes and olive groves that were already ancient. Eventually, the land became more hilly, then rugged until the river turned into churning white rapids, before diminishing to streams and springs trickling down the sides of mountains so high they touched the sky. Like an eagle, he soared on the rising air and glided effortlessly over the snow-capped high ridges, looking down at how the land on the other side fell away from bare rock faces into foothills…that became rolling vistas of dense forests and wide sweeping meadows. So many buck and boar to hunt. A land to make his own.

Another river, and again he followed its course as it wound through endless plains gradually widening until at its wide estuary he came to a huge fort surrounded by a vast town. Flags and banners of all colours and designs fluttered gaily in the breeze on the towers. He'd travelled and fought from one end of the empire to the other, but had no idea such a place existed.

The harbour was full of a fleet of huge ships, the biggest of which was fit for an emperor. But then he saw that it was made with planks of gold and silver. He stared at it enthralled, amazed by the sheer opulence, enough even to make Caligula jealous. He had no idea how such a ship could stay afloat, but equally incredible was the long pontoon which somehow had been crafted from white whale bone. And as soon as he was on the ship's deck, it raised itself.

They sailed north for days, but to where, Magnus had no idea. After a while, a new land reared from over the horizon, and without realising it, he was flying again and he glided over rich forests, deep valleys, and mountains and moors that stretched from coast to coast. It was the most beautiful place he had ever seen. At the mouth of the river, a fort on a hill looked out over the sea. Through the sturdy gates, he walked along the via principialis to the praetorium which was the most well-adorned he'd ever imagined. Gems were set into the walls, the roof was covered in gold tiles, gleaming so much in the sun that he had to squint.

At the far end of the courtyard, past a fountain, two young men played a game of ludus, their black and white counters spread out over an ornate board, locked in a mortal battle. Near them, watching the game with rheumy yet alert eyes, was an old man, with rather unkempt white hair framing a weathered face. A gleaming diadem was set on his head and around his throat was a torq of gold in the style of the ancients. Magnus watched the rubies of his rings flashing as he whittled away at the rough edges of a ludus counter with a small knife.

But it was the girl Magnus knew he was here for. She approached from the side, and as he turned to look at her, he was astounded by her beauty. She was more dazzling than the sun, and this time she didn't seem so afraid. She took a timid step towards him, eyes tearing up as though she was greeting a friend she'd thought long lost, or husband home from battle unscathed. They slipped into each other's arms and faces close, her lips were about to touch his...

The din that disturbed him was the melee of a pitched battle. Dogs barked amidst the shrieking neighs of the horses and spears crashed against shields. Panicked, especially as he was unsure where he was or what was happening, Magnus tried to roll to his feet but was pinned to the ground by half a dozen shields. His unknown enemy had overwhelmed him, he had no chance to fight, and he called out for his men to retreat to try and regroup or save themselves.

A girl screamed, but it wasn't the maiden from his dream, just the slave, and with a sense of dismay, he came back to the bank of the lazy Tiber and the abandoned hunt. Marcellinus pulled the shields off him and helped him to his feet, but standing only made the feeling of weakness and nausea worse and he doubled over to retch.

"Bring water!" his brother shouted and the girl scarpered off to the baggage horse. With eyes full of terror, she returned with a flask. It wasn't just the fright of her master having some kind of a turn he saw in her. As he took a long swig, he knew it was real fear and for a moment, he was utterly convinced she was casting some dark barbarian magic over him to pull him from the waking world into the one of his dreams. He didn't remember where she was from, it had never concerned him, but in the depths of their vast forests beyond the empire's borders, tribes still practised such ungodly arts. He wondered if she'd been taught such things before she'd been captured or traded.

Who had paid her to do it to him, he burned to find out and in a rage was about to reach out and grab her hair, tie it to the horse's harness and slap its rump. But down in the cellar would be better. There he could break her and bleed her to find out exactly what she'd done, and at whose order. The next moment though, he dispelled the idea. Not because it would be a pity to destroy such a fine specimen, one he'd used for his pleasure many times, but because she was a young slave, and a girl like that couldn't possibly have such power over a man. Especially one such as he. To accuse her, he wouldn't have to admit how pathetically weak he was.

He forced himself to stand without Marcellinus' help and as he gathered his wits about him, he noticed that some of those watching him looked sheepish. They'd made the noise to wake him and now they didn't know what to think about the strong man who could barely stand.

"We return," he croaked. To Marcellinus, he said, "It's time to fetch a doctor."

He looked for the slave's reaction and wasn't surprised at how she paled at the thought of a man trained in the body's processes investigating what was wrong. Maybe he should order the irons heated in the fire to see what she had to say after all...but again he was torn. If the news that he'd allowed a mere slave to have power to pull him almost to the point of madness, he'd have to go back to Hispania and be satisfied with running a horse farm for the rest of his life.

He retched again.

IV

Segontium, Britannia Secunda

Elen came slowly awake and smiled at the memory of the breathless ecstasy Eugenius had brought her to. The afterglow, like embers in a fire pit, lingered all through her body like the day's heat on the stones of the fort wall.

To her side, her lover lay breathing softly, naked as the day he was born. She couldn't imagine how such pleasure, such a deep connection to another human, could be prohibited, so harshly punished, just because there was no piece of parchment to say that they were man and wife. She was sure nothing on earth was as heavenly as Eugenius' touch and at the point he was bringing her to the edge, Elen was sure that not even the Bishop of Milan could get her any closer to God.

But as soon as she remembered Father's letters the loving warmth turned to a sudden chill. They were probably signed and sealed and on their way to whomever he was considering marrying her off to. He hadn't deigned to tell her their names. Not for the first time she shuddered with revulsion at the thought of a strange and unwanted man entering her chamber. Entering *her*.

She gazed longingly at Eugenius' perfect body again. In his embrace, there was so much tenderness and softness, love and mutual affection, where the idea of men signing documents bestowing themselves rights over her body was abhorrent. More than she'd ever wished for anything before, she wanted for this moment to last forever.

She leaned closer to Eugenius' chest, about to blow gently on his nipples so he'd wake, as another round of pleasure would be the perfect way to forget the harshness of the world for a while. But cutting through her reverie as a sword through flesh, a man's voice came from below. Heart frozen, desire doused like a pale of water on the fire, she lay as tense as a mouse startled by a buzzard's shadow. If they were discovered in such a state, she'd be tied to a post and lashed like a slave until her legs gave way. Even worse, she'd probably never be allowed to see him again. And then the recollection that Father knew about Eugenius hit her once more. If he wasn't a secret, he couldn't be safe.

"It has to be so," the man said, and the unmistakable lilt in his voice stabbed such a bolt of terror through Elen that her breath caught in her throat. He was from Hibernia! The land over the sea to the west, where the most savage raiders came from. She held her breath and strained to hear what a sworn enemy of the empire was saying and whom he was speaking to. Surprisingly, he was talking to a woman. "Rome will soon consume itself and another time will come," she said. "And when it does, we'll be left to fend for ourselves like lambs in a storm, soft prey for the teeth of those who wish us harm." The words were a dire warning, which was worrying enough, but much worse, was that Elen recognised Mother's voice. Hearing her speak in hushed tones to a Scotti hidden in the barn caused a chill of foreboding that set her skin to a flood of goosebumps.

"And what about your husband?" the man asked.

Cold with fear to the point of shivering, Elen carefully reached out for her tunic, but the movement woke Eugenius. He yawned so loudly Elen jumped to put her hand over his mouth. But still mostly asleep, he protested.

The voices below were silent.

"Shh…" Elen pleaded and with the look of wild fright, Eugenius understood they were close to being discovered and reached out for his sword. He wasn't on duty though, so it was in his barracks.

"Who is there?" her mother asked, voice stern.

Elen thought about staying silent, but heard the unmistakable metallic hiss of a sword being drawn from its scabbard. She motioned for Eugenius to stay still and pulled her long tunic over her head. "It's just me. A girl," she said as she pulled the tunic down to her ankles. She crawled meekly to the top of the rickety ladder, looked down and saw the sword. "There's no need for weapons."

"I think I'll be the judge of that," the Scotti growled.

"Elen!" her mother gasped.

"You know her?" the man asked.

"Of course," Gula said, waving her hand at him to resheath his sword.

"Your *daughter*?" he asked, surprised and Gula nodded. "The very one we've come to speak about?"

Talking about her? Elen was sure she'd heard wrong, but once she'd got to the bottom of the ladder, she turned around and saw the look of surprise on his rough and scarred face.

"A good omen it must be that we three find the same barn for our dalliances. Mayhap the gods smile on us!" he beamed.

Gula pressed on his arm and he put his sword partly back in its scabbard, but kept a hold of the pommel and the steel of the top part of it gleamed menacingly.

"What did you hear?" he asked cautiously, the sound of his strange accent quickening her heart. She backed against the ladder and held onto it for support. If being found with Eugenius would be bad enough, she didn't want to imagine what would happen if she was discovered with a Scotti. If the soldiers of the fort knew such a man was in the vicus, they'd be out searching house to hovel, and she doubted Mother would be able to do much to help.

"Let's get her boyfriend down first." He spoke softly, but his voice had the same sharp edge as the blade. "Come on," he coaxed. He moved his leg slightly, widening his stance. A life spent around fighting men, Elen knew he was taking a position to better defend himself.

"It's all right," Elen said. "There is no trouble here."

He smiled but didn't take his eyes from Eugenius' hiding place. *Like a frightened wild animal*, Elen thought. She'd reacted just the same when she'd heard his voice. Maybe it was the usual reaction to someone afraid for their life.

Tunic roughly wrapped around him, thickly muscled thigh bared as he felt for the top step, Eugenius backed into view...and with a slap of his sword slipping home, the Scotti chuckled. "Her father tells her she must marry and so the first thing she does is lay with another. I like her spirit! Seems mother and daughter both have some secrets to keep!"

"This is the girl that the survival of your tribe depends on," Gula said sharply. Her tone was a clear warning, but the words made no sense. The Scotti's smile was gone in an instant though, and to see her mother have the same authority over a tough fighting man as her father did of the soldiers, was a real shock.

In a protective gesture, Eugenius slipped his arm around her waist and his big hand squeezed her hip. "Don't hurt her," he said. "What we did was my idea, not hers. Blame me."

"No one is going to get hurt," her mother said.

"Well, that might depend on what you heard," the Scotti said.

"Nothing, I swear," Eugenius said.

"He was sleeping," Elen protested. "We both were."

"You swear to silence about everything that happened here?" the Scotti asked, then added. "On your lives?"

"Corath," Gula said, another warning.

"If they're found rolling in the hay together, it's some shame for them and it will soon wear off. Maybe a flogging, if that husband of yours is as strict as you say. But for me, it will be my *life*, so I apologise for being a little cautious."

"I swear!" Eugenius said.

"Go!" her mother said and there was a sliver of light in the dimness of the barn as she tried to press a gold coin into Eugenius' hand. "For your silence."

"You don't need to pay me!"

"Take it!" Gula insisted. "Elen has got something very important to listen to. She'll come and find you later."

"I'll be all right," Elen said, forcing a smile.

"She will be safe?" Eugenius asked Gula.

"She is my daughter."

He nodded his agreement, refused the coin again, cast a last warning look at the Scotti and peeked through a crack in the door to make sure the alley outside was clear.

Elen breathed with relief, but as he slipped away she felt sick. The day before she'd thought he'd been executed and that she was the reason for it. Now she'd just brought him into the company of a Scotti. She wondered how many more times she'd put his life in danger just for the crime of being with her.

Gula took a deep breath. "Daughter of mine, this is far from how I intended to broach the subject with you. And a lot of what you're about to hear will be confusing, shocking even, I'm sure. But I need you to stay calm and listen."

Elen wanted to protest, but supposed what Mother was about to say couldn't be any worse than what Father had.

"This is Corath Mac Eochaid."

"He's a Scotti," she said.

The man dipped his head in deference. "You noticed!" As he smiled, a long white scar from the corner of his mouth to a deformed ear, pulled at one side of his face. "I am here risking my skin for a simple reason, and that is I want to settle my people on your land." He grinned as though what he was saying was the greatest joke.

"*My* lands?" Elen asked. She spoke slowly, so he could understand, as obviously there had been some misunderstanding somewhere. "You must be mistaken. That has nothing to do with me. Such a thing is for my father to deal with..."

"Ah, no. There's no point for a man like me trying to talk to the Governor. Not after the battle of Adrianople. With the Goth army running around Macedonia like a fox among the hens, there'll not be any more of us barbarians setting foot on Roman territory for a generation, at least. Your father would probably have my head off and my body dumped in a ditch before I even opened my mouth."

Gula sighed again. "I think we've skipped a few important steps here." She rested a hand on Elen's shoulder and squeezed a little. The touch was meant to be reassuring, but was far from it. "Your father sent out some letters. Has he explained what he expects of you?"

Elen felt her face flush. Discussing which man she'd have to allow into her bed in front of a stranger felt unseemly. "To marry whatever man he chooses," she forced herself to say. "He even started writing them right in front of me."

"I am sorry. That was cruelly insensitive of him. But in his own way he has the best intentions to find you the best husband to marry. One of power and influence."

Elen had to force herself not to scream. "So what," she seethed.

"You father is getting old, ageing and ailing a little more with every passing season. Some people think it an opportune moment to prepare the next generation for what…will soon come."

Elen could tell she was trying to wheedle around something she was hesitant to say, but had absolutely no idea what that could be. "If you wish to discuss matters of lands, why aren't you talking to Kenon? It will be him who inherits everything from Father, not me." She noticed a look of sadness fall across her mother's face like clouds passing before the sun.

"He has been sent away," she said.

"Only for a while," Elen snapped. "Father said so. A year at most."

"A little longer than that," she sighed.

"Why? What?"

"He's gone," she said, a little more forcefully. "For the task ahead it's not him we need, It's you. You are your father's heir now." She stared deeply into Elen's eyes. "And mine."

Task ahead? It felt like a few more blocks of stone had been pulled away from what, just yesterday, Elen had thought was the solid foundation of her life. "Where's he gone?"

"To another fort. One far from here," she said wearily. "Many days ride. He'll be a soldier, he'll get to fight, maybe one day lead men, so he will be happy."

"What task?" Elen asked, barely able to keep her voice calm.

"We will find you a strong husband, one with a noble connection."

"*Mother*!"

"I know…that's the last thing you want to hear, but you'll marry who I find for you. That's not negotiable. Just as it isn't for any girl. You know that's the world we live in."

"And my *task*?"

By the way Mother took a deep breath Elen was sure she didn't want to hear what was coming.

"You will convince him to settle the Deisi on the land."

"What?" Elen gasped. It was such an impossible thing for Mother to say she wondered if she was still in the hay next to Eugenius having a very vivid, but rather unrealistic dream. If a boatload of Scotti set foot on the empire's land, the whole garrison of Segontium would be sent out to cut them down. Protecting the coast against raiders is the reason the garrison had been stationed there for three hundred years.

"And in return, should you need us, you will have the sword of every fighting man at the ready for the defence of the land," the Scotti added, which sounded just as absurd.

Elen was close to crying with frustration. "Swords…then that's for Kenon…"

"No," her mother said. The weight in her words made Elen uneasy. "He's not what the land needs…"

"And what does the land need?" Elen asked nervously.

The softness of her demeanour gone, her mother looked her straight in the eye. "A bridge." It was as though Elen had been doused with a bucket of freezing water. She'd been called that before and in a secret place Father would have skinned her alive for going to. How could Mother have possibly known about the visit to the old augur?

On her mother's face, the look of love came back, but at the same time, it was tinged with an apologetic sadness. "A bridge of blood. This land will soon need someone with a foot in both of our worlds. Both Roman and Briton in one person."

Elen had absolutely no idea what she meant. She'd been utterly appalled to listen to her father speaking casually about a man she'd be expected to bear the children of, but hearing this from Mother, it was much harder to listen to.

"Maybe I could speak?" Coranth said.

Gula nodded her consent.

"Your father is in this part of the world to look at building a series of defences like the Saxon shore to protect from raids by the Scotti sailing over from Hibernia, yes?

"When the money comes from Rome," Elen nodded.

Gula scoffed at that.

"All over the empire there are tribes friendly to Rome, and those that are not. It's the way it has always been, since the days of Caesar. It's the same with us Scotti. Niall Noigiallach raids our lands, kills the men and takes all the women and cattle. He has become too strong to fight against, and so we are helpless. These days our people don't think of themselves as parents, only slave breeders waiting for Naill to come and take the children. It is no way to live. With Niall as our neighbour, sooner or later, we'll all be slaves. Or dead."

"The Deisi hate Niall almost as much as we do," her mother interjected. "And so, although these are rather inauspicious surroundings for such an arrangement, we are brokering a deal. By giving land to the Deisi and in return they will defend our coast against their enemies and ours."

"That's *Father's* job!" Elen said, nearly in tears of frustration. "Why aren't you talking to *him*?"

"Because he doesn't believe that Rome will fall," Mother said, and Elen froze.

The same words could have expressed the sentiment when the world comes to an end. Hearing Mother say such a thing was as though she'd been punched in the belly. "Fall..."

"If Rome falls and the legions leave Britannia, we'll be able to defend ourselves about as well as a foal in the forest with a broken leg."

"If Rome falls?" Elen only just managed to get the words out. "Why would Rome fall? How..." It was easier to believe that one day there would be no more water in the sea, or the sun would fail to rise. Despairing of getting through to Mother, she dared address the Scotti and doing her best to sound polite and respectful, said, "I am sorry for the misunderstanding, but you will have to go back to your leader and tell him that we are unable to help you."

"My leader?" he asked, a cheeky gleam in his eye.

"He's not just a messenger," Gula said.

"Who is he then?" Elen asked defiantly, feeling as though she was coming to the end of her tether.

"He is the *king* of the Deisi."

At that, almost quicker than she could blink, his sword was free, the polished steel flashing before her like a bolt of lightning. He didn't need to cut her throat with it, as with the shock of having it brandished in front of her, the sharp edges about to cut through her defenceless skin, it seemed that all the blood had drained out of her body. Legs as weak as a foal's, she was about to slump to the floor...but it was the king who went down on a knee. So dizzy at the shock of thinking he was about to kill her, she watched dumbfounded as he rested the blade across his open palms, proffering it to her.

"I come in supplication," he said, although his Latin wasn't at the level to pronounce such a word properly. "My people are in desperate danger. I come here, to you, to put their lives in your hands."

A man twice her size and twice her age, offering himself to her in such a way was all wrong and made her panic. But as much as she wanted him to get off his knees, she wouldn't dare speak a command to a man as her mother had done.

Father wanted her to marry a stranger, mother wanted her to grant the impossible wish of an enemy king... and believed the world was coming to an end. It was far too much and the only thing Elen could do was run. Before Mother could stop her, she bolted towards the door.

"Elen," her mother hissed. "You're not dressed!"

She didn't care, and out in the street, she headed away from the barn as fast as she could without bringing too much attention to herself, although surely gossip of the Governor's daughter running through the vicus streets looking flustered would spread like fire, but a whipping would be no worse than staying any longer with Mother and her guest.

As she got to the fort gate, trying to brush her hair with her fingers, one of the guards laughed.

"That's the Governor's daughter, fool!" his colleague spat and the amused one snapped straight back to attention.

Elen nodded as she passed, but was aware of how their eyes followed her. Once inside the praetorium she noticed the long piece of straw stuck in her hair. It might as well have been a red flag of the legion's standard proclaiming her dalliance in the hayloft. If word of such a thing was to get around the fort, everyone would be whispering about who she'd lain with, laying wagers on a list of names. And if the rumour got back to Father through his men that she'd been with Eugenius again after he'd expressly forbidden it, perhaps she should be more concerned for herself than Eugenius.

She got to her room, closed the door behind her and stood with her back to it. Only then did she realise how much she was shaking. Then something from the conversation with the king came back to her: Mother had said *she* would choose a husband for her!

As she tried to pour herself some wine, spilling some over the table, she remembered the most shocking thing of the encounter: Mother had said that the empire would fall!

V

Kenon hadn't had a moment of sleep all night. Too worried that any noise he heard from the others was one of them creeping out of his bed to come and stab him, he'd lain like a mouse knowing a cat was right outside its nest. He'd grasped his sword so tightly for so long that his fingers still ached. The weak, watery soldiers' porridge for breakfast had done nothing to nourish him, and as soon as he'd started riding, the movements of the horse exacerbated all the pains from the previous evening's brawl.

The six of them rode for a way through the densely wooded hills in silence, the crisp air of the morning doing nothing to clear the blinding incandescent rage which he aimed at his father like a wave of Greek fire for forcing him through such a painfully pointless escapade. Although they'd only done a mile or two, Kenon was ready to pitch up, make camp and drink enough wine that by the time he woke up again the stupid nightmare would be over.

He noticed how the Areani paused to listen to the songs of some birds, and raised his head like a dog to test the air. It was the smell of wine and the perfume of a lithe woman Kenon wanted to fill his nostrils with, not the damp stink of the wilderness. Fresh air is what the barbarians breathed.

At the thought of the Areani being so sensitive to the smells of nature, he chuckled to himself at what must he make of the miasma of foul odours in the fort? Or in the vicus?

The four young riders rode in frint in pairs, their horse's hooves clattering on the muddy flagstones in a cacophony that did nothing for his throbbing head. Since leaving Canovium no one had said a word to each other, friendly or otherwise, so when Kenon heard a heated, yet hissed, argument spring up, he strained to listen. So too did the Areani. He recalled again the words he'd heard someone say just before the fight. 'Kill him tomorrow' He felt stupid for not mentioning it when he'd had the chance.

"*Now*," one of them seethed, and the fine hairs at the back of Kenon's neck rose in warning. Instinctively, he tested the handle of his gladius.

The one he'd fought with the evening before noticed the movement. "Worried about something, bastard?" he called back.

The others turned in their saddles to see what was going on. Their nervous demeanour was very different from their enthusiasm for riding the day before.

"Not yet!" one snarled, and with that Kenon knew he hadn't misunderstood the words of the previous night. Five against one were helpless odds, although maybe it would be four against two...he didn't know. The Areani was much older and had said he didn't trust them, but that was no indication they would be fighting on the same side if it came to it. He was about to find out though, as the fighter drew his sword and turned his horse to the side.

"Don't do it," the one who seemed to be in charge snapped. Again, Kenon wondered just how far Father had gone in arranging this little scare. Sending him on a ride for a couple of days, pretending to be going all the way to Rutupiae and now staging a pre-arranged fight with swords. It had to be a game. It couldn't really be happening.

He decided to play along and was ready with the suggestion that they raise the ransom they'd pretend to ask Father for...and when he got back to Segontium, he'd have a story to tell like Caesar himself. But the Areani bumped his horse into his and knocked his hand away from the sword. "Don't!" he spat. "They'll hack you to pieces!"

In a flurry of hoof falls the four soldiers pulled their horses around into an agitated semi-circle, each with his hand on his sword hilt.

"Hold. Hold!" the leader shouted as the Areani forced his horse between Kenon's and the others.

"Kill him," the lad who'd caused the bruises on Kenon's face snarled.

"He will be spared," the Areani said.

"He's *Octavius'* son!"

"Aye, and I'm sworn to protect him, so whatever you've got planned, you'll have to kill me first to get to him. But only two of you will be on your way to the Wall, or wherever it is you think you're going. Maybe even only one of you, if I am still as fast as I was."

"Aye, let him go," one said.

"Whose side are you on now?" the fighting lad exclaimed.

"My own, for fucking once. These next days we'll need Fortuna on our side, so let's not scorn her favour by killing someone who doesn't need to die."

"Fortuna!" the fighter laughed, as though he'd just had a great idea. "He never gave the other dice back. He's still got it. Let's decide his fate with that. Evens he lives, odds..."

Kill him tomorrow. Only one sword was drawn, but with a smile of cruel intent on the fighter's face, Kenon started worrying that things were becoming a little too real.

He took the dice from his pouch and shook it in a clammy hand.

"Boy!' the Areani hissed. "You're rolling for your life!"

If they'd been instructed to give him a bit of a scare, they were doing a very good job, but he was the Governor's son, and he needed to show them that he wasn't frightened by a few auxiliary soldiers, ones his father executed at the click of his fingers. He flicked the battered little cube into the air. As it sailed over his horse's neck, the Areani reached out to try and catch it. He missed, but before the others could see what number it was showing on the ground, he shifted his weight in the saddle slightly and leaned over to make sure the horse trod it into the mud.

"You fight *fate*," the fighter cried.

"Aye, I do," the Areani shouted back. "Some say that fate is a man's own thing to master."

"They live!" the leader announced in no uncertain terms. The other two, probably used to unthinkingly obeying barked orders, stayed still, but looked like the taut coils of rope of a loaded ballista, ready to snap at any moment. The leader nudged his horse closer and said, "Drop your swords and get off your horses. Slowly."

Numbly, feeling that everything was happening too fast for him to understand, Kenon drew his sword. There was an image in his mind of a swing of his arm, a couple of deft strokes of the blade and four heads would be rolling across the ground. But the rational part of his mind knew he'd stand no chance against just one of the hardened fighters, never mind four of them together. He dropped it so it landed point down to stick in the soft earth. The pugio he'd handed back to Father was more of a symbolic implement than a real weapon, but letting his sword slip out of his grasp in such a situation made him feel terribly vulnerable. Naked. Helpless.

Two of the lads dismounted and cut some lengths of rope from a coil on one of their saddles. Enough to bind wrists and ankles.

Wanting to slap himself for not realising sooner, it finally clicked what was happening. "Deserters?" he spat as they helped him down from the saddle. He'd been so angry at Father, he'd thought everything had been his doing!

"Quick aren't you, Bastard!" the fighter mocked as one of his friends lashed Kenon's hands behind his back. The rope was pulled so tight it shot so much panic into him that he wished he was back at the latrine in Canovium.

"But you're Roman soldiers!" he protested.

"We're *not* Roman though, are we? Just auxiliaries," he said as though it was a bad word.

"You *will* be!"

"Yeah, after fifteen, twenty more years of this bullshit to be a Roman. That's what they tell us when they sell food fit for pigs at prices fit for a feast, but Rome is as rotten as a ten-day dead dog. Everyone knows it. Fucking Gratian with his Alan guards!"

Kenon was pushed to his knees in the wet mud, then knocked forwards so he fell on his already bruised face. "You'll be *crucified*!" he cried as his feet were bound.

"Starved, frozen, or nailed? Or beaten to death for no fucking reason. From where I stand it's not so much of a difference, is it? Fuck Valens getting fucked by the fucking Goths, and your cunt of a father for killing Lucius. For fucking *what*? For his bastard of a centurion putting him on double shift. *His* fault, but he didn't get his head caved in, did he? No. Why punish a precious centurion when he can smash an auxiliary to shit to scare the others into having some more discipline? Discipline! Fuck, if I hear that fucking word where we're going, I'll rip out the fucker's tongue. So fuck your father and fuck Rome. From today, we're done with both!"

"I still say he should come with us," the youngest looking one said.

"Have you gone mad?" the fighter spat.

"He's being sent away, isn't he? It'd be good for those in charge to see the son of the Governor standing against them. Good for others thinking of leaving too."

Horrified and enthralled in equal measure, from his prone position on the ground, Kenon asked, "You're going to the Wall?"

The lads laughed. "*Beyond* the Wall."

"What? Why? To join the Picts? You're mad!" But even though he was trussed like a pig about to be spit roasted, the thought of joining a band of outlaws flashed through his mind. That would make Father properly mad. But before opening his mouth he realised that if he intended to get his father's lands back for himself, it might be best not to raid them and torch the farms and villas. Staring at a pair of boots, he was aware of not speaking from a position of authority, but what he thought was a brilliant idea occurred to him. "If you kill my father, I'll make you rich."

The leader side-stepped his horse so its hooves stomped in the mud frighteningly close to Kenon's head. He squirmed to look up, but didn't like the look he gave him. It was similar to that of a man who'd just realised he'd just stepped in a pile dog's mess.

"Men of our people don't kill their fathers," he growled and hacked a ball of spittle in Kenon's direction.

"Let's take him as a hostage then. There'll be less chance of arrows flying at us if they know we have the son of the Governor with us," one suggested, but was thankfully ignored.

Three of the deserters rode off, but the fighter lingered for a moment. "If I ever see you again, Bastard, I will *fuck* you!" With that, he charged off after his friends. To what kind of lives they hoped to lead, Kenon couldn't imagine.

He tried to twist into a more comfortable position, worried that it could be a while before a trader or patrol came along and found them.

"Roll over to my feet," the Areani said. "I have a knife there. Hurry before they change their minds!"

With the cold mud seeping through his tunic, Kenon rolled over and fumbled for the small blade at the Areani's ankle. They lay writhing and grunting for a painfully long time trying to slice through the rope and by the time they got themselves free were thoroughly soaked.

"Come," the Areani said and pulled Kenon up with a strong arm.

Kenon shook as much muddy water from his cloak as he could, but knew it was ruined as it would need to be washed so thoroughly that half the dye would come out. He watched bemused as the Areani strode off as though nothing untoward had just happened...but in the same direction as the deserters had just ridden away.

"Home is the other way," Kenon called.

"We'll make a report in Deva about what just happened, get new horses, and carry on from there."

"But...To where?"

The Areani looked, confused. "I told you where we are going last night."

"Rutupiae?" Kenon laughed.

"Aye."

"But..."

The Areani's stance softened a little. "You really thought all of this was a performance to get you to fear your father? Even now?"

Kenon shrugged.

"You told them you want to protect me. Father will want to know I was attacked and..."

"Didn't say anything about swearing to your *father*, though, did I?"

"What?" Kenon asked. "Who else would you swear to? Mother?"

"No, lad...Your *grand*mother."

Absolutely nothing made sense. "And who the fuck is my grandmother?"

"You don't know her?"

"No! I don't!"

"Well, you just offered coin for deserters to kill your father, so perhaps family connections don't mean all that much to you."

Suddenly, Kenon felt dizzy, and while the trees spun around he had no idea which way was home. He was completely lost. "I demand that you explain everything! I order you!"

"Aye? On whose authority? Yours?" the Areani replied, amused. He pretended to look for something hiding behind some of the trees. "And whose army? Your father has sent you to Rutupiae, your grandmother tasked me to escort you there, that's all you need to know. But if we're to have a hope of sleeping with tiles above our heads tonight instead of stars, we need to start walking."

"But..."

"In social standing, you're now just one step higher up the ladder than those who just rode off. Your father took your dagger back, remember?"

Kenon did remember. To give it to another man, he'd said...Maybe the one who would marry his sister, and with that thought, the reality of the situation hit him harder than any punch the deserters could have given. Without his Father's name, Kenon was nothing. Elen would inherit everything. The lands would be her dowry and they'd go to her husband. Kenon had just lost everything. Usurped by his sister.

Disinherited, sent to the furthest fort without the name he'd worn like an insignia all of his life. Rejected, banished. Maybe he should have gone with the others to the Wall as a deserter. But the Areani had protected him, and was talking to him as an equal, so he didn't have *nothing*. At that moment, the company of a man apparently sworn to protect him was the most precious thing. But still, to turn and walk the opposite way from home was the hardest thing in the world to do.

Then he caught sight of something at the side of the road. He bent down, wincing at the pain in his face that it caused, and picked up the dice tower. It must have fallen out of a saddle bag while the deserters were packing the stolen swords. As he wiped the worst of the mud off it, the beautiful pattern was revealed. Now with only a filthy cloak and his boots to his name, the tower was instantly his most prized possession.

As they began walking his mind raced with the shock of what had just happened, but after a while, he began to wonder about why a grandmother he'd never heard about had arranged an Areani to escort him to Rutupiae. And whether even that was also some kind of joke.

On foot, the milestones seemed to be placed much too far apart, and noting where the sun was in the sky, his biggest disappointment was that he wouldn't get to Deva in time to find a good brothel.

VI

Rome

"Keep your eyes closed. Both of you." Theodosius said. He spoke in a stern tone, but Magnus and Marcellinius both knew it was part of the play. With a big hand on his shoulder, the young Magnus bumped into his uncle's hip as he walked, but despite hearing people talking, the clipping of horse's hooves frighteningly close, he obeyed his uncle and kept his eyes tightly shut. He hoped his brother was doing the same, but didn't dare peak.

That big hand, guiding, protecting, pulled him to a stop. "All right. You can open them now."

In front of Magnus was a wall, but it was the size of a mountain. He looked up and up and still couldn't see the top. Marcellinius, struck with equal awe, lost his balance and fell to his backside. Theodosius gave a hearty laugh as he picked him up. "This is the Colosseum," he said. "Anything you want to know about the empire, you can find here. It's power, its conquests, and..."

"Who are *they*?" Marcellinius asked, pointing up at the giant statues.

"They are our heroes and gods."

"Heroes and gods," Magnus repeated, and imagined Theodosius standing up there with them one day.

The day he'd first seen the Colosseum was many long years ago now, but the curved wall still towered above them to what still seemed an impossible height and the memory of standing in slack-jawed stupefaction at the sheer size of it, had never left him.

In tandem with the nausea welling up, the panic tightened around his chest again. He tried to tell himself it was just some lingering after-effect of whatever the slave had given him still in his blood. Or maybe he was wrong about that and it was some illness. Sweat beaded on his forehead, but the terror didn't feel as strong as it had before. He could sense the presence of Theodosius near him though, towering over his shoulder, as real as though he could reach out and touch his beloved uncle. He was sure it was the poison, yet it still took a lot to stop himself from turning around to look for the man who'd brought him up and taught him everything he knew. Made him everything he was.

Ignoring the vendors near the entrance selling olives, walnuts and berries, both he and Marcellinus looked up at the big golden letters proclaiming Vespasian as the man who had funded the building. Not for the three hundred years since had any other man put his name to any structure close to anything like it, so it was no wonder Vespasian's name was still spoken with such reverence. But the empire was far away reclaiming such grandeur and he was sure that there would be nothing like this to carry Gratian's name through history, much less Valentinian's. The only thing built by the boy were his toy blocks on his nursery floor.

Such thoughts caused a hollow sense of despair. No man wanted to admit that he was living in a time of decline. After the disaster Valens had caused at Adrianople, he wondered just how far that would go.

It was his own decline rather than that of the empire he wanted to speak to his brother about though. "Do you remember being brought here for the first time?" he asked.

"Not really. I was too young," Marcellinus replied, his neck straining as he looked up at the rows of twice-life-size statues and the huge bronze shields mounted around the exterior. Most gleamed as they caught the late afternoon sun.

"I couldn't believe it was built by men," Magnus added. "So for a long time, I thought it was some house for giants. People who were as big as the statues."

It felt strange to talk about such things. They were both hard men, Magnus a former general and Marcellinus, newly elected to the senate, and childhood memories from a long forgotten age of innocent wonder weren't the easiest subject to put words to. As Magnus was leading up to ask such a favour, he judged it a good idea to remind him how close they'd been as children.

"That one is Diocles the Charioteer," Marcellinius mused. "Then Apollo, then Flamma the Gladiator. Two of them will stay up there forever, but lately, I fear for Apollo and the other gods."

Magnus' laugh sounded bitter to his own ears. With how weak the armies were after Valen's poor judgement at Adrianople it wasn't uncommon to hear such words spoken by those who understood the empire's true vulnerability. "The Edict of Thessalonica?" he asked.

"Our cousin Theo, emperor of the east," he continued, "a Nicean Christian like us, has basically just outlawed the religious practices of the Arian...whose faction happens to include the Empress Justina. With a stroke of a quill, he has made the empress not just an enemy, but a criminal! Practising her faith in the way she's always done before, could soon be punishable by death. Heretics, they are now, and foolish madmen."

Magnus couldn't help a chuckle at the woman he thought was trying to kill him being called such a thing.

With the Goths, Huns and Sassanids pressing against the barely manned borders in numbers that could now easily overwhelm what was left of the empire's fighting forces if they chose to, any internal conflict had to be avoided at all costs. The three emperors engaging themselves in a civil war was unthinkable...but men with vast wealth and power were renowned for fretting over anything and everything that could make them a tiny bit poorer or less influential. "It's not as serious as that, surely?" Magnus said.

Lowering his voice a little as they passed the guards at the entrance to the lower tiers, Marcellinus said in a half whisper, Marcellinius said, "You are a martial man, trained only in the use of steel weapons and battlefield formations. You don't see the subtleties of such a thing. It is the most serious thing the empire faces. It could lead to another civil war! Not against Goths, Huns or Sassanids, but Christian against Christian. After Valens, how will we survive that?"

"Then our cousin is playing with fire," Magnus said. He was about to say more, but felt the tremors in his hands begin again. Maybe it was just hearing Marcellinius' dire thoughts, but his legs went weak, and with it came the sensation of falling, the same as Icarus must have felt when, too close to the sun, his wings melted and he pitched towards the earth. The last place he wanted to be was in the tunnel under the rows of seating, the darkness pressing in from all sides. It felt like how he'd imagined the moment of death would be, and he realised he was clinging pathetically to his brother's arm.

"What is it?" Marcellinius asked, but Magnus couldn't even tell where his voice came from. He was desperate to get out into the sun, so shuffled for all he was worth towards the blinding light at the far end of the tunnel as though he was fighting death itself.

"What's wrong, brother?" Marcellinius asked again. "Tell me!"

"I will," Magnus replied as he fought against the nausea that washed through his body as though he was on a boat at sea. With a weak arm over his brother's shoulder to stop himself from slumping to the floor, they worked their way along the row of scandalised-looking men, who probably assumed that Magnus had disgraced himself by getting blind drunk before coming to the Colosseum. They could mumble all they wanted, without Marcellinius' help he wouldn't have made it to his seat.

He sat down heavily and heard more disparaging remarks aimed at him from behind. He said nothing to them, but if they knew the number of men who'd died at his hand or command, they'd surely be a little circumspect in their insults.

"I tried to question the slave who was serving me food," he whispered. "But was so angry I killed her before I got anything out of her.

I felt better for a few days, my thoughts were clearer, but now I am afflicted once more."

"Afflicted with what?" Marcellinus handed him a flask and the sensation of clean water he knew wasn't tainted passing over his tongue was a deeply relieving one.

If he was ill again, it meant the attack was a sustained one and that someone seriously intended that he should die. Or maybe he was completely wrong about his slaves slipping something into his wine and it was something he should send for a doctor for. The confusing possibilities, all without proof, rolled around in his head.

With the fear of not knowing what was wrong, that he might be about to slip away from the mortal realm without knowing who had killed him, another flush of sweat washed over him. Usually, the warmth of the late August sun on his face was a welcome sensation, but now it burned as hot as though he was in the depths of Africa. Under the folds of his toga, he was drenched as though he was in a bathhouse's steam room.

On the sand in front of them, the day's entertainments had begun. It wasn't much of a relief, but at least he wasn't down there, the last moments of his great life nothing but entertainment for the braying throng of plebs and women in the upper rows.

The first breath of the dust the pair of gladiators kicked up in their scuffle took him back to his days in the endless desert. Lips cracked, skin on his face and ears peeling from being exposed too long in the harsh sun, he listened to breathlessly recounted reports from the scouts. He was commanding detachments to head out and encircle the swarthy-skinned local men who'd set up an attempt at ambush in the rocky crags. He was counting the bodies into a proud tally for General Theodosius' report. Dozens of Berbers loyal to the usurper Firmas, who'd chosen to charge to their deaths rather than surrender to the punishment of having their hands cut off. He was laughing with his cousin Theo, now emperor of the east, arms around each other's shoulders as they regaled each other with their blood-soaked feats. Theo, named after his father, was a cousin, but taken in by Theodosius when Magnus' father died, the three of them had been brought up as brothers. Magnus and Theo had trained, fought and killed side by side over so many years, that their bond was even stronger than that of blood.

They stood together at the top of a dune casting their gaze over the vast empty landscape, wondering what cultures, what wealth waiting to be reaped, lay beyond.

He was there. It felt so real, yet every part of him knew it was a dream. From the Colosseum a decade in the future from their days in the desert, Magnus was impatient to tell Theo that he would rise to the purple. But then remembered that it would only be over his father's body...and the pain and rage snapped Magnus back to spectating the gladiators sparring.

"The cowards butchered him because they *feared* him," he said without thinking as he wiped away some of the sweat pouring off his forehead.

"Theodosius?" Marcellinus hissed and looked around fearfully at those sitting nearby, shocked that Magnus could speak such words where others could hear.

Despite being addled by whatever it was, Magnus was still aware that if such words were overheard, his life would be at even more risk than it already was. The anger continued to rise, and was so raw and untamed that the words seemed to speak themselves. "One of the greatest generals to ever grace the empire with his command since Caesar. For most of my life I wished he'd been my father so that I could hear him call me his son. And they put him to death like a common criminal. Have I told you that as soon as I heard, I made a vow to avenge him?"

"Shh. Not here," Marcellinus warned.

"My vow is stronger to me than any blood oath any barbarian had ever made. God was my witness."

"It could have been any one of a dozen people," Marcellinus said. "But *here,* let us not talk of such things!"

Magnus pressed his mouth close to his brother's ear. "But I know now who killed him. I am sure of it."

He felt Marcellinus stiffen and his angry whisper was a growl in Magnus' ear. "We sit in a nest of vipers! Hold your tongue!"

"And she intends that I am her next victim."

"*She?*" Marcellinus gasped. "Oh, no, no, no. You don't mean..."

Carefully, so as not to make the swirling in his head any worse, he turned to look at the prime seats between the golden standards of the Valentinian family... which was not even a shadow of what it was since Valentinian had died. In pride of place, the Empress Justina sat so still and bolt upright, as though someone had carved a statue of her right in the moment she'd had something shoved up her bony arse. Beside her sat her son, the boy emperor Valentinian the Second, the young son of the man Magnus had long served under, who was no more than the bitch's ticket to power and influence.

Magnus' hate for her didn't stem from the usual complaint that she'd managed to rise to such a position due to no other merit than spreading her legs for two former emperors and now paraded her ten-year-old son around before her like a standard bearer on a battlefield. Not even because she was Arian. It was because he was convinced she was trying to kill him.

Magnus looked at the boy emperor. There was nothing in him that even hinted at his great and strong father. He'd bet that the lad couldn't even spell half of the titles bestowed on him. It was said that he and his mother didn't often travel from Milan for fear that the people would see just how young the boy actually was, but the show was too important to miss. Magnus wondered how many silk cushions he was sitting on to make him look taller and older. And stronger. They'd probably been the first to arrive and would be the last to leave, whisked away in a covered litter so no one could see how pathetically small and weak one of the most powerful people in the empire was.

"She won't risk having me stabbed in the forum, as she can't have rumours of dark deceit staining her son's good Christian reputation. Poisoning me slowly is a death that takes some weeks and will look like an illness, leaving her free of all suspicion. You know the saying; strong generals breed fear into weak emperors. How long have I been ill? How long has she been in Rome?"

"Brother! Seriously! If you don't hold your tongue, I will rip a length of your toga off and stuff it in your mouth!" Marcellinus leaned in close. "That's all you have to accuse the *empress*? Even if you had the most unquestionable proof, you'd do better to fall on your sword than to speak such words openly. And even if you are right…what can you do? Nothing!"

Sadly, Magnus had to admit he was right. "The accusation is unfounded, I grant you. But who else? After all, poison is a woman's weapon!" He leaned even closer so he was speaking in a ragged whisper into Magnus' ear. "Theodosius was one of the best generals the empire has ever known. If he'd wanted, he could have clicked his fingers and half the legions would have roared with the proclamation of him as Augustus. With her infant son still suckling at her teat, Justina would have offered no competition. And now she sees me as a threat, as she did Theodosius. I languish without a command, despite being as qualified and as capable as our cousin, the Emperor of the East."

"Brother, I *beg* you. Hold your tongue!" Marcellinus pleaded. "Not *here!*"

Magnus pushed his brother's hand from his mouth. "One thing. One thing and I will still my tongue," he seethed. A little nod and Marcellinus acquiesced. "Promise me this, brother. If I am to die soon, you will avenge my death as well as Theodosius' "

Marcellinus groaned and turned away. Assuming he was deep in thought, Magnus let him mull his words and tried to focus his attention on the fight, along with the tens of thousands of others in the amphitheatre. The gladiators, one with a gleaming gladius and well-battered shield, the other armed with a trident and net, alternatively struck at each other, but Magnus almost spat at them in disgust. Experienced in the ways of combat, he was appalled at how there was nothing natural in the way they fought. One lunge, then two steps to the side. Trident clashes off shield, two steps. Sword thrust thwarted by the net, two steps. It helped them move around the arena so every section got a view of the clash of weapons, but it was nothing more than aggressive sparring, the form of which had been discussed and agreed beforehand.

There had been a time when countless wild animals, jaw-dropping beasts like elephants and lions had been fought and cut down on the same sands. Somehow, although these days it seemed impossible, the whole floor had been flooded and actual naval battles had been staged, with vessels sunk and hundreds of prisoners drowned along with them. Not only could Gratian and the younger Valentinian between them never hope to build something as grand as the Colosseum, they couldn't even host such a spectacle in it. Such things were just stories now, memories of a former, grander age. One he wasn't sure the empire would ever get to see again.

The shield-wielding fighter slammed into the net fighting one, knocking him to the ground, and as he rolled, apparently miraculously, away from the sweeping slash of the sword, the roaring of the crowd was a travesty. What they were watching was nothing more than a spectacle, entertainment for the masses. If only they knew the levels of brutality, the horrors, the massacres, and mass executions that it took to keep the borders secure, then surely they wouldn't cheer at such stupidity.

Magnus looked at the boy emperor again. He was engrossed with the gladiators, lost in the fight. Only ten. He was so young the fighters couldn't be much more than animated life-size versions of the toys he played with. He couldn't have anything more than the most basic understanding of the political intricacies of the entertainments in the Colosseum, of keeping the populace enthralled so that their minds wouldn't wander to other, more important, things, such as whether they wanted their lives and destinies to be held in the hands of a child. And his scheming whore mother.

But Marcellinus' question refused to leave his mind. What could he do?

Magnus tried to focus on the fighters below again, but the sweat from his fever, or whatever it was, was running into his eyes, blurring his vision. The one with the net had a bad gash on his upper arm and with so much blood running down he could barely hold onto his trident. It seemed a wound too serious for an exhibition fight. Perhaps there was some bitter rivalry spilling over and it was a real fight after all...

For a reason Magnus had missed, the crowd seemed to have taken the side of the one who was about to be victorious and were crying out for more of his opponent's blood. He cursed their simplicity for being so enthusiastic about something so obviously not real, but then that was what the Colosseum had always been for. The set fights stopped the populace realising that the true battles, the ones the fate of the empire arrested on, weren't taking place on the sand, but in the first row seats.

He drank some more water and felt a bit better. What could he do? There was no answer, and so the question made him feel helpless. Legions at his back while he roamed the land hunting down two child emperors, seemed a bit too much to pray for, especially as for some reason the preachers told that it was the meek and humble who were rewarded in heaven. Those with the ambition to clash armies into each other were often used as an example of how a Christian should not be.

What could he do?

It seemed the only prospect of staying alive was to quietly take himself off to Thangugadi, the veteran city in Africa. He'd helped install Gildo as Rome's client over the body of his hated brother Firmus, so he'd be welcomed there, could have a comfortable life, one possibly free of the threat of the Empress' reach. But for the rest of his days he'd be throwing rocks at lizards, trying to ignore reports of Theodosius' killers promoting themselves up through the ranks until they assumed the powerful and important roles they could have only hoped for after his death. Running away was the coward's plan though and Theodosius himself would berate him remorselessly for having such thoughts. No, he had to fight. How, he didn't yet know. As the sword thrust was knocked harmlessly away by the trident, he wondered if that would be a more suitable question to form into a prayer.

The entertainments lasted well into the evening. All Magnus wanted was to leave so he could sleep and let the dreams take him back to the girl in the distant land. That would have been an open snub to the Emperor though, so Marcellinus forced him to stay in his seat.

All the way back to the family home up in the Fields of Mars, the litter pitched and rolled so much Magnus was sick from that more than whatever Justina was getting a slave to put in his food. He took his mind away from throwing up by trying to decide what to do with his remaining slaves. Whether just keeping them in close chains for a few days while he ate nothing but street food would make any difference, or if he should heat the brassiere up, get the pokers ready, and spend an evening questioning them properly. Methodically.

The litter was set down with such a jarring thud that he bit his tongue. As he got out, Magnus glared reproachfully at the carriers, but had no strength to reprimand them, or to bother getting a message to their owners to have them flogged.

One of the two surviving slaves opened the thick gate to his old family house. For a moment he thought she was the girl from his dreams and the familiar welling of longing swelled up in his heart. She was here! She'd travelled up rivers, across mountains and was waiting for him in his house! He didn't have to search the length of the empire to find her after all...but the hope deflated into disgust as he realised it was just a slave. Pretty enough to fetch a half-decent price if he was to take her back to the market, but nowhere close to the beauty of the maiden he dreamed of.

"What did you say?" he asked her as Marcellinus' litter was set down.

"An imperial messenger, Dominus," she said breathlessly and wild-eyed.

Magnus' heart skipped a beat. It was obvious that the bitch empress had heard he'd killed the other slave so was worried he knew of her plan...and had decided to be more forward. A denunciation perhaps, or a charge of treason, just as she'd done with Theodosius. A written command for him to kill himself to negate the hassle of a trial and execution.

Not many houses in Rome had stables but Magnus' family had been horse breeders for generations and so the messenger's exhausted beast had been brought inside rather than left on the street. It was filthy and was panting hard, so the message had come much further than Rome. The chances that any news, or command, from Gratian's court at Mediolanum could be good were slim to none.

Leaving his mount to take an interest in the ornamental olive trees, the messenger strode purposely across the yard, a folded piece of parchment held in front of him. From the effect it created in Magnus' chest, it might as well have been a knife. With as much reluctance as though he was guiding a blade to his own heart, Magnus took it, but handed it straight to Marcellinus.

"From the emperor Gratian," the messenger announced, causing Magnus' heart to skip a beat.

Gratian, and Valentinian together. If two of the three emperors were against him, he wondered if Theo would defend him against the charges, or if his cousin was also in on the plan to get rid of him.

In that case, he would have no hope and it would be best to just fall on his sword and be done with it.

He wondered if it was already too late to escape Rome, or if guards on the city gates had been ordered to hold him if they saw him.

Once he and Marcellinus were in, the slave closed the gate behind them and with a heavy thud locking all the threats of the outside world out, he felt a little more secure.

Beside him, his brother was ashen-faced. Marcellinus had immediately grasped the severity of the situation. There could be no good news from an emperor a man considered an enemy.

"Care for the horse," Magnus snapped at the slave boy and told the girl to lead the messenger to a side room to await his response. He led his brother to the dining room and flopped down on his side on the couch, feeling the last of his strength and hope seep out of his poisoned body.

Her task with the messenger done, the girl skipped back and asked if she should pour wine. He really wanted some, but couldn't trust that for some coins, or perhaps the hope of freedom, some grubby fingers hadn't tipped some of Justina's powder into it.

He wondered what story she would tell if he was to hold the glowing tip of a poker close enough to her skin that it caused agony before even touching her. He didn't really have enough income to kill any more of them, so decided it would be best if he just sold both and bought others that he wouldn't let out of his sight.

But soon he'd have much more to worry about than the sale of slaves. "Let me save my last moments as a free man before you read to me that I am condemned," he said as Marcellinus made himself comfortable.

The slave acted as though she was absolutely terrified of him. Maybe it wasn't guilt. Maybe she'd done nothing and it was just because she'd had to dispose of her friend's brutalised body and feared the same gruesome fate awaited her. She knelt at his feet and with shaking hands, began unlacing his sandals.

Magnus looked at Marcellinus. If his brother believed there was any hope the note could contain good news, now would have been the time to say it. The girl pulled his sandals off in silence.

"Surely some wine," Marcellinus said at last.

"I will take a glass." Magnus sighed. If Gratian had condemned him, poisoned wine wouldn't be the worst way to go. "But I warn you against drinking any. If the empress has any of my slaves in my employ…"

Marcellinus smiled. "If I have some visions afterwards, either you're right about her, or I will have been visited by the saints."

Magnus smiled. The wine was Falernian. It tasted as though the vines grew on a south-facing slope in heaven, its leaves basking in the light of the Lord himself. If it was poisoned, dying with the taste of it on his lips would be an acceptable way to leave the world.

In a wave of sorrow, and the aching gulf of knowing that with his demise Theodosius' death would remain unavenged, Magnus said, "Read me the verdict and sentence." He wondered if this was in any way like how his uncle had learned of his impending death.

"A summons to Mediolanum." Marcellinus said.

Magnus scoffed. "And what does that mean?"

"It could be anything," Marcellinus said. "A promotion, or a new posting?"

Magnus couldn't believe for a moment that there would be anything positive waiting for him in Gratian's palace. "Or an execution," he mused.

"Well…" His brother couldn't deny it though. "A berth will be made available on the imperial ship," he added as he read further.

The idea of being trapped on a boat, even one of such luxury to sail an empress, was far from appealing. "On the open water with Justina?" he scoffed. "I wouldn't last a day. No. I am a horseman. I shall ride."

"That could be seen as an insult."

"How much would you care that you offend a man who wishes you dead?" Magnus asked. "Besides, does it say anything about urgency?"

Marcellinus scanned through the text again. "No, but...You could just ride off. On your horse, no one would catch you. Maybe get to Africa? You would find welcome there."

"And where is the honour in that?" Magnus asked. "Living as fugitives, counting what is left of my coin every month. Not to mention the risk it would be to our friends. No. I don't want to die, but even less, I don't want to die a coward."

"So what then?"

"I will face my fate like a general. But I will go slowly and enjoy the journey. The country will be beautiful this time of year."

Out of ideas, his brother shrugged.

"Settled then. We leave in a few days. I have some friends to say my goodbyes to. And some slaves to sell."

VII

Segontium, Britannia Secunda

Gula led Elen urgently along the narrow warren of winding lanes of the vicus. The air was so rank with the putrid smells of both man and animals, that Elen had to put a hand over her mouth and be careful with her steps so as not to slip on the slops and slime.

For over three hundred years, by the soldier's sword and the administrator's quill, Rome had tried to force civilisation onto these lands. But while the hypocaust, bathhouses and latrines worked for the men in the fort, the rude shacks pressed together, some built with whatever materials their builders had been able to find, seemed a different world. A dangerous one. One where people lived by different rules than those of Rome.

Elen wondered at how confidently her mother walked in such a place. A woman alone with a young girl without a guard could easily catch the attention of the wrong type of person. As Gula, with a strong grip on her elbow, steered her between another couple of rough buildings, Elen also wondered how her mother knew where they were going.

A fat bureaucrat reclining on a litter, probably on his way to inspect goods in the harbour, tottered along, the feet of his slaves splashing in the muddy road. His opulent robes, gleaming bright white in the sun, were the opposite of all the slaves who strained under the effort of his transportation.

"And that is the problem right there," Gula muttered, but didn't elaborate.

Across the main thoroughfare, pressing between tables piled with baskets of sad looking wares, limp vegetables and fly-covered cuts of meat, Elen cried out how much mother hurt her as she pulled her arm. "Hurry!" she snapped, then half way down the next alley, pushed her into the lee of a doorway. "Wait!"

It took a moment for her to realise Gula was making sure they weren't being followed. By some thief or men from the fort, she didn't know, nor did she want to ask. Eventually, satisfied they were alone, Gula led on, Elen slipping on the mud still slick from the last rain, wincing from Mother's vice-like grip.

A little further into the labyrinth of shacks of the native-born, Gula parted a sheet from an opening, the tattered old blanket making do for a door, and ushered her in. Still overwhelmed by what had happened in the last days, Elen didn't protest. But she knew where she was. In the two and a half years she'd been in Segontium, she'd only ever been in one house in the vicus. This one. "The old augur?"

"She'll most likely not appreciate you calling her old. And careful with the word augur as well. It's not a safe word to speak these days."

As her eyes adjusted to the darkness, her nose protested at the musty smell. Cloves, and strange perfumes from far distant lands. The petals, leaves and roots of what plants had been distilled though, she couldn't imagine. And the lamp was burning cheap fish oil!

A large shape moved against the far wall and Elen's heart leapt in fear.

"A woman now," the bounds of dark cloth said. It was a soft voice though, almost familiar, and it put Elen at ease. "Let's get a look at you, shall we?" Shadows flashed around the strange room as she struck a strip of iron against a shard of flint. After a few attempts, the lamp wick caught and the soft light revealed a rotund woman. Everything about her was round, from her kindly yet piercing eyes, smiling face with its several chins, and her body, almost bovine in its girth. If she made money telling fortunes, it looked like she feasted on a good deal of the profit.

"Come to glimpse a future you can scarcely imagine, have you?" she asked as she moved the light around in an arc in front of Elen's face.

"I err..." Elen stammered, her mind recoiling with all the possible reasons Mother had brought her to such a place. Probably to find which husband she would soon be married to. More revelations about what tribulations awaited in the coming days and months didn't seem very appealing.

"Come closer to the light. Closer. Let me see you," the woman said but she didn't wait for a response and Elen felt the woman's hands on her shawl, pulling her so near to the flame she could feel its heat.

"Ah, yes, you have your mother's eyes. What a delight that is to see. And do you know what they say about her eyes?"

"What?" Elen asked nervously.

"That they look like *her* mother's!"

Elen saw it then, and even though it made no sense, blurted out, "Grandmother!" Through the surprise, she couldn't help returning the smile as the old woman's face lit up in a beaming grin.

"Pleased to meet you, properly, at long last."

"But why are you..."

"Secret?"

"It's not safe," Gula said from near the door. She had a hand in a fold of the sheet so she could keep an eye on the activity in the street.

"Such is the world we live in,'the old woman added. "Your father wouldn't have wanted you around someone like me, and so I had to content myself with admiring you from afar. Until today."

"But why?" Elen asked.

She laughed. "Keepers of the old gods, followers of the old ways, people like your father consider us barbarians, you see. Can't have Romans of good families found in the company of an augur, can we?" She pointed to a chair and as Elen sat in the place where hundreds of people had learned their futures, the old lady said, "I am indeed your grandmother, and that is what you can call me for now, until you're ready, as my name is rather dangerous, I'm afraid. Some have had to die because they knew it, and I don't want that for you." As she shuffled the roll of flesh over one hip on her chair, it creaked in protest. "Quite a couple of days you've had, haven't you?" she said. "Your father tries to marry you off and then a king takes a knee at your feet. I say that we'll call yesterday the last day of your childhood, and today we will make you something else."

Something else?" Elen asked nervously. "What?"

"What indeed?" she smiled. As she leaned forwards across the table, the small flame of the lamp flickered across her face and made the wrinkles dance. Elen gazed at the slightly otherworldly visage of someone in contact with a world forbidden to normal people. As kind as she was making an effort to appear to be, Elen could sense the hardness in the woman and wondered if she really had ordered men to their deaths just for knowing her name. As she looked into her grandmother's eyes, she was sure what she was about to hear was going to be just as bad as Father arranging her marriage and a king pledging his people to her in a barn.

"Long ago, when you were here last, with questions about kittens and when you could go back to live in Deva, I told you that you were something. Do you remember what that was?"

It was a couple of years ago now, but Elen remembered how she'd lain awake for a few nights trying to figure out what the words she'd heard could have meant. She couldn't ask anyone for fear of them finding out where she'd been, and had eventually forgotten about it. Until yesterday. "A bridge," she said, a heaviness starting to settle on her chest.

"Good girl. A foot in both worlds is perhaps a better way of describing it."

That smile again. The sparkling in the round eyes. Elen couldn't imagine how such a kindly seeming woman could hurt her...but knew she was teetering right on the edge of something awful. "I think Father will soon have me firmly planted in his world," she said with a sigh.

"Why not?" Elen asked. She was sure she'd be worrying about

them until the day there was a strange man waiting in the courtyard to claim her.

Grandmother smiled again. It was like the sun coming out from behind the clouds. "You might have seen him writing them, but I can assure you none will reach their intended destinations."

"How do you know..." Elen started, unsure what powers the woman wielded. Unsure if she wanted to know.

Grandmother reached to the side. The hefty rolls of fat made the movement hard, but she dropped a bundle of rolled up parchments onto the table. "Because they are right here. Do you recognise them?"

"No," Elen shrugged.

"Are you sure? They are the ones your father was writing. Addressed to powerful men across Britannia. Men he would marry you to." She held one up to the lamp flame and Elen saw her Father's seal.

"How?" she gasped. It must be some magic the woman possessed.

"I often wish I had some of the powers of the druids, but the answer is simply because I control some of the messengers."

For an old woman in a rude shack at the edge of the vicus to claim she had power over state communications seemed incredulous. And then Grandmother broke the clay seal! Breaking the Governor's seal on an official document would get a man executed, but she watched aghast as her grandmother unfolded one as though it was addressed to her.

"If you don't think them real, you wouldn't be so concerned about me breaking them open would you?"

She angled the parchment to the light. "Marcus Valentius. A lot of land in the north. Lots of sheep. Hmm. I thought your father had enough sheep. Joining both the lands together and he will be able to set a better price for wool. A monopoly."

She tossed it casually to the side and unrolled the next one. "Cousin's family in Dummonia. Involved in the tin trade. A kind man, as I understand, so that's nice." She tossed it aside as well. "Business deals, expanding his holdings, discussing trade. All fine, I suppose. But he thinks far too small for you. He has no idea of your true worth. You're 'just'a woman, so he overlooks you."

"But I am just his daughter, though," Elen said, confused.

"But are you not also someone else's daughter?"

"I...err. I don't understand," she stammered.

"Your *mother*!" the old woman huffed, but Elen still had no idea what she meant.

She sighed and shook her head. "Such a world we live in when it's dangerous for a daughter to know who her mother really is. I suppose you have lots of questions about me and how I come to find myself here saying the things I am. First, I am going to tell you a story about someone else. Someone far more important than me."

"Who?"

"You!"

Again, Elen was at a loss for words.

"Many, many years ago Queen Heulwen and Prince Arwel had a daughter."

Elen had heard the story before, but wasn't in the mood for tales Mother had whispered to get her to sleep when she was a little girl. "That's just a story. A legend," she said dismissively.

"To us, yes, stories and legends are all they are. But to the people who lived on this land three hundred years ago, they were very real. Just as real as you or me. Now, this daughter they had was a very important woman. Her grandfather on her mother's side was Gwain the Great, a man who fought in battles with a hammer so big no other man could fight with it. Did you hear that story?"

Elen nodded, silently willing the woman to get to the point.

"Ordovices, they were called, which means People of the Hammer. And Gwain was the greatest fighter of them all. No one could match him in a fight, never mind beat him. On her father's side, through Arwel, she was granddaughter to Cadwal the Great, the last hero of the Ordovices."

Elen knew this story as well. "He died. Agricola killed him."

"Ah, good. The girl knows her history. That's important."

"History?" Elen asked. "They are just bedtime stories."

A huge grin spread over Grandmother's wide face again. "Bedtime is the best time to tell stories! But did Agricola really kill Cadwal? Yes and no. In body, yes, he did. But in doing that, he gave birth to the hero. A generation or two later and no one remembers the person, but they will never forget the legend."

"How does this mean anything?" Elen asked, getting frustrated. "They are just *stories*!"

As the old lady grinned, the wrinkles at the sides of her eyes deepened. "Don't underestimate the power of a story, my dear. Stories are just like the foundation stones of giant temples that have stood for a thousand years. Stories are what civilisations are based on. Romulus and Remus, Jesus…"

Elen was about to shout out at such outrage, but the woman held up a finger. If it had the power to break the Governor's seal, it had the power to still a girl's tongue.

"Yes, even your precious Jesus. Just a story made up for powerful men to control the weak. But your Jesus is no different to many other gods in that regard."

Hearing such a blasphemy against her beloved Lord, meant the woman was a heretic. And that made Elen angry.

"But one day, my precious child, *you* will just be a story as well. One day, all that will remain of you will be a name from the far distant past. You as a person will be forgotten, corroded away by time itself like flesh off a bone. But in stories, your name can live forever, like letters chiselled into stone. Bodies will turn to dust, but names can be immortal."

"Immortal? How?"

"If people remember them and keep speaking them."

"I still don't understand why you are telling me this."

"Because the daughter of Hewlyn and Arwel came in time to have a child herself, and that girl some years later, also had a girl.

And so did the next. For generation after generation, daughter after daughter. There were boys born of course, but in every generation a girl survived to pass on the blood through a daughter. But I won't bore you with all of their names..."

"You know them all?"

"Of course. Druids are long gone from this land, but the lineage was kept safe from the men of Rome. And I know the last one as well."

"The last?"

"The one *before* the last is called Gula."

"That's the same as Mother's."

As Grandmother laughed, her jowls wobbled, and as she leaned closer her chair creaked. "That *is* your mother," she said quietly. "*You* are the last."

"Me?" Elen gasped and in the jolt of such a shock the cough turned into a choke. Yesterday she'd wanted to run from the king of the Deisi, and the day before burn Father's letters, but listening to the old woman's words, now she wanted to rip her own skin off and crawl into someone else's body. Someone whose life involved only *her* own responsibilities, not other people's.

Mother hadn't moved from the door and Elen realised that as much as making sure no one was coming, she was guarding against Elen leaving before they'd told her all they wanted her to hear. The old woman continued, the words thrumming into Elen's head like the blades of a whip against the backs of her legs.

"You, through the blood of your mother, through me, my mother, through an unbroken female line all the way back to the last heroes of the Ordovices who lived in these lands free of the yoke of Rome. And the most important of them all sits here in front of me."

"The bridge," Gula added softly from the side.

"They're just stories," Elen said again, a little louder this time.

"Show her," her mother said.

Grandmother's eyes gleamed in the light of the lamp. "If it's all just stories, then what is this?" She beckoned Elen to see something at the side of the table where she carefully, almost referentially, unfolded a bundle of cloth. On the outside the material was dusty black, but inside it was crimson red. Gula left her post guarding the door and came to hold the lamp so Elen could see it properly. It was a large rectangular lump of iron. Ancient knotwork patterns were etched into the faces and the sides were dented with impact marks. A piece of splintered wood stuck up from the middle.

"Try and lift it," the old woman smiled.

Elen could just about tip it to the side, but there was no way she could get it off the floor. The size of the man who could actually fight with it, she couldn't imagine. "This is the hammer you used to tell me stories about when I was a girl."

"The very same."

"Gordd-ap-Guwia. The hammer of the Ordovices," Elen breathed, in awe at seeing something she used to imagine as she fell asleep.

"Agricola killed so many of us that day, and since then the yoke of Rome has sat so heavy around people's necks for so long we don't call ourselves Ordovices any more, just Britons. But if I wasn't who I said I was, you wouldn't be looking at this, would you?"

"And one day," Gula added, "the hammer will be your secret to keep,"

"I told you though, Father..." Elen started to say, but when the realisation came, she felt one of the foundation stones Grandmother had just mentioned, one she'd thought her life was built on, shift under her feet. "You? You're the leader of the tribe?"

"Shh," Grandmother smiled, her eyes radiant with mirth. "That's a *real* secret and I beg you, for the love of all the gods, or God, if you prefer, hold your tongue. I do not lie when I say that men have had to die to keep my name from the ears of the wrong people."

"But Father sends men riding out to look for him."

"Completely blind to what is right in front of them, under their noses, such is the way of Rome. And they probably wouldn't even imagine looking for a woman, let alone one who shares his bed and bears his children."

"Mother!" Elen gasped. Struggling to keep up with what they were saying, she had to steady herself from the strange dizzying sensation that came with such a revelation. "But how?"

"After the death of his last wife," Grandmother continued, "your father was old and wealthy enough that he didn't need to marry into a prestigious family. And so, heroically, for the good of Rome, he sacrificed himself and married Gula, hoping the locals would then look to him as their lord. Turning the lands into the biggest wool industry in the whole of Britannia Secunda was just an afterthought, I'm sure. But, then who do you think truly commands the loyalty of most of the men in this land?"

"Mother," she whispered. Such a secret. Gula's appearance hadn't changed but it seemed to Elen that suddenly she was looking at a completely different person. One she knew nothing about. One who thought of Father as an enemy. Realising that she'd not known who her mother really was for all of these years, she was aware of the yawning gulf that had opened between them.

"And that makes you a very special person, doesn't it? Daughter of the Governor, heir to lands it would take half a moon to ride around the borders of, and the daughter of Gula of the Ordovices. A foot in both worlds."

"You never told me," she said to Mother.

"I couldn't. We couldn't risk you repeating anything to your father. We had to wait until you were old enough."

"Such is the world we live in," Grandmother shrugged. "Your father is far beyond the age of retirement for normal men, and is richer than almost anyone else in the land. He has just lost his son and that is a grievous wound for a man of his standing, not least because the men will think less of him now. For how can he lead them if he can't lead his own boy? One way or another, I believe the post he occupies will soon become vacant."

"And then what?" Elen asked.

"And then it will be a new time for our land and its people. A dangerous and uncertain one. One where we face a threat not seen for three hundred years."

Sitting before the grandmother she'd never known, with the mother she'd just found out she knew nothing about, Elen realised that whatever they were hoping for and were planning, they were depending on her. She waited tensely for what they would say next.

"He married Gula for business, and he'll marry you off to a man for business as well. But that is not what we need for you."

"I thought you said I didn't need a husband!"

"As horrible as it may seem to every girl in your position, you do need to marry. But at least he won't be a man of your father's choosing."

"*Whose* choosing?" Elen asked.

A little impatiently the old woman rolled her eyes. "Mine."

"And who will it be?" Elen asked, her voice rising in pitch, heart beating faster.

Elen didn't like how Grandmother sat back and took a long, deep breath, ready to pay attention to her reaction. "If all goes to plan and the gods are willing, your husband will be the next Dux Britanniarum."

Elen's head swirled with the implications. But worse was that the man expected to be the father of her children now had a name rather than being just a human-shaped shadow looming ominously over her future.

But Grandmother wasn't finished.

"And your task, as the king of the Deisi already asked you, will be to agree to get him to let the Deisi settle on our land."

Elen laughed so loudly, Gula hushed her and pulled the blanket a little aside to check outside.

The most powerful man in the whole land in her bed. And they expected her to get him to settle the Scotti. When Valens had tried to do that with the Goths, it led to Adrianople. They wanted her to act against an edict of Rome. It all seemed like a bad dream. "Who is he?" she managed to ask, her mouth dry.

"Oh, I have no idea."

"Are you toying with me?" Elen asked, close to tears. "You know my husband-to-be's title but not his name?"

"We don't know *yet,*" Gula said calmly. "There are candidates."

"Candidates?" Elen shouted, "Do you understand how mad you two are sounding? Controlling a powerful man of Rome from this little shack?"

"Shh," Grandmother cooed. "It's a lot to take in, I know. Let me explain a little. It is known that the men who hold power around the boy emperor Gratian have three men in consideration for the position of Dux Britanniarum. From the contacts I have spent a lifetime cultivating, I have arranged a little influence with people in the circles of each of them. It is my hope that when the man arrives on the shores of Britannia, he will be desperate to marry the daughter of Octavius. Infatuated with her, even."

"How?!" Elen gasped. "How can you possibly do that? With what magics?"

The old woman chuckled. "One day the knowledge to do these things will be yours, I assure you. The lessons will begin soon."

The weight of expectation, the incomprehension of what Grandmother had just told her, all seemed to crush down on her like a bug under a rock. "I can't do this," she said. "I want to go home!"

"Then home you will go!"

"Not to the praetorium. Home! To the villa on the plain. Out of the mountains and away from the army!"

Grandmother nodded, and said, "Very well. We'll talk again soon. Whenever you are ready."

"I won't be!" Elen snapped. "Never!"

"Oh, you are a bit stronger than you think, my girl. Just as strong as any man from Rome."

"I am just a girl!" Elen cried.

"Oh, you are much more than that!"

"How can you think so? You don't even know me!"

"Because you *have* to be," she said, her expression suddenly turning hard.

At that, Elen stood up, ready to bolt for the door, but Gula blocked her way. Gone instantly was any motherly softness, and she held onto her arm in a vice-like grip. "Not like yesterday," Gula warned. Her voice had such a warning edge to it that it sounded strange. "No running blindly down the streets." Elen tried to pull her arm free. "No!" Gula snapped. "We walk as though we're out for some shopping. It's important. Understand?"

Elen harrumphed.

"It's *vital*!" Gula snapped, hand still grabbing her arm. "Do you understand?"

"Yes! You're hurting me!"

"Not as much as your father will if he finds out where we've been!"

At that, Elen stopped fighting and turned back to look at Grandmother. The flame of the lamp flickered wildly in the disturbed air, casting odd shadows over her deeply wrinkled face. "We'll meet again soon," she said sternly.

Elen didn't know how she felt about that.

On the way to the augur, Gula had half-dragged her, but going home, it was Elen pulling Mother, despite the warning she'd given.

"Calm down!" Gula said under her breath, almost in a growl. Elen didn't care though. She wanted no part of their plans. A family with Eugenius on a small farm somewhere was all she dreamed about. A simple life of love, watching the seasons turn and their children grow. Now, in the space of just a couple of days, father wanted to marry her to some sheep farmer and mother expected her to make illicit deals with Rome's enemies. All she wanted was to curl up under the blanket and cry herself to sleep. Maybe if she had some space and peace to think, she could think of where she and Eugenius could run away to so that neither Mother or Father could ever find them.

Gula cursed and Elen looked ahead to see a crowd of people pressed around the main gate to the fort. As soon as she saw why, bile surged up in the back of her throat. Thick nails through his forearms and ankles, the man was pinned to a cross in a twisted, crouched position. Some poor soul had been found guilty of a capital offence and was slowly paying the ultimate price.

The only indication he was still alive was a slight movement of his head.

Mother's fingers gripped the flesh of her arm just above her elbow like an eagle clutching its prey. "Not a word," she hissed. It wasn't Mother's voice, it was the leader of the tribe Elen heard and obeying the command, she clamped her jaw tight shut.

As the curious people parted to make way for the wife and daughter of the Governor, Elen saw that the man's crucifixion was only the end of his torments, as he must have suffered unimaginably before they'd nailed him up. Every lash of Father's flail she'd ever suffered wasn't worth one stroke of the scourger, a whip tipped with stones or shards of glass, that could strip a man's flesh from his bones.

His face was so beaten and bloody that it was only from the long scar on his cheek that she recognised him.

He wouldn't recognise her though. His eyes had been gouged out.

"A Scotti," someone said with disgust. "Caught prowling around the vicus like a rat."

It took a moment to realise it was Father speaking. Her mother's grip on her arm tightened even more.

"It's funny sometimes what comes out of the mouth of a tortured man," he mused.

"Is that right?" Gula said with forced politeness.

"He said he was here to speak to the two of you."

Elen's heart felt as though it was impaled by a pilum.

"Hilarious, isn't it? You should have heard how desperately he begged us to believe him."

"He's a Scotti, you said?" Gula asked. How she could keep her voice so calm, Elen couldn't imagine. She was as close to screaming as much as Corath must have done. "You know they speak with forked tongues at the best of times."

Octavius nodded thoughtfully, but his eyes were full of the cruelty of a man who could give the command for another to be tortured to death. "And he claimed to be a king, no less. The burning of his flesh must have broken his mind."

Elen wanted to speak, to tell him that the king had come in peace for the good of his people. Anything to get him down from the cross, even if only for a merciful death. Like an eagle with a mouse in its talons, the pain of her mother's nails digging into her skin was so intense that she could think of nothing else.

"Come across the sea to speak with my wife," Father said. He turned to Elen, eyes boring into her like red hot irons pressed against her skin. "And to my daughter!"

Suddenly, from Gula's grip biting into her flesh to warn her to silence, Elen's legs went so weak Mother had to support her.

"Is everything all right?" Father asked.

Gula sighed dejectedly. "I'm afraid we've done something you will not approve of. I feel I should confess it."

"Really? Meeting with Scotti kings were you?" he scoffed.

"Oh, much worse," she said, at which Elen was ready to slump to Father's feet to plead for mercy. "This sweet, beloved daughter of ours begged and begged, and I gave in and took her to the old augur in the vicus."

Father's eyes turned from predatory to confused, then back to cold and distrustful. "Did you now?"

"The poor thing was fretting herself silly about the husband you're choosing for her. You know how girls get about such things."

Elen was about to cry out in protest at Mother for admitting such a thing so easily, but saw how anger bloomed across Father's face. With a flash of understanding, she realised Gula knew how guilty they looked and was trying to deflect his suspicion onto a lesser crime. Admitting seeing the augur might get them both lashed, but that would be nothing compared to what would happen if they were charged of conspiring with a Scotti.

"I see," he mused. "Did she name anyone in particular?"

"Oh, only the Dux Britanniarum himself," Gula replied with a beaming fake smile, and again Elen was shocked that Mother could tell him such a thing. But all he did was snigger at the thought of someone with such a powerful rank marrying his daughter. The Dux would outrank even the Governor, and he obviously didn't think his daughter was worth that.

"So you were nowhere near a barn?"

"A barn?" Gula asked, still somehow composed. "I admit…It smelled a bit like one in the augur's house." The mask of confused innocence would have impressed the greatest actors. Elen begged the good lord above to help make the performance convincing enough.

"I see," Father said and for a moment Elen allowed herself to believe she was the recipient of some divine intervention and she and Mother were going to be allowed back to the praetorium without harm. But he reached out to hook a finger under Elen's chin and lifted her face up.

The king of the Deisi groaned from the side and it was as though his agony was her own.

"No barns?" he asked,

She shook her head, his finger holding her as helplessly as a fish on a line.

"No? Then perhaps you can explain why yesterday the gate guards saw you with straw in your hair? When I expressly forbade it!"

It wasn't the prospect of a lashing that terrified her now, she honestly thought he was going to scourge her back and nail her up next to the tortured king. But even worse was the thought of Father doing the same to Eugenius. For him, she had to be strong.

The absolute last thing she should have done was to antagonise Father but desperate to be free of his scrutiny, she knocked his hand away. He was so surprised that she managed to step out of his reach, then, despite his shouts, ran as fast as her bandy legs would carry her to the fort. The confused looking guards didn't stop her from running inside. The walls would offer her no protection from him as any father in the empire had the power of life or death over his children. It would be even less of an issue for him to kill her than the Deisi king.

She barely made it to her room as her limbs had turned into those of a drunk man's and with the fear of expecting Father to burst in and grab her by the back of the neck, flail in hand, she threw up over the mosaic. With the image of the nailed king flashing in front of her eyes, she wondered if the acrid taste in her mouth was that of a child's love for her father turning to hatred.

She knelt against the bed and tried to calm her breathing, stomach and bladder all at once, just as she'd done dozens of times before when she knew a punishment was coming. This was a lot worse though.

No one came to drag her away…nor to offer any comfort, and wondering if something awful was happening to Mother, she retched. After what she'd learned in the visit to the auger though, Elen was quite sure that Mother had ways of defending herself that Father didn't know about. At least, she hoped so.

She wanted Eugenius to be standing guard, sword drawn against anyone who would do her harm. She ordered a slave to bring a jug of water and reassurance that Mother was all right. When the boy came back, eyes full of worry that whatever was going on in the house would impact him, he told her that Mother was in her room. Elen took the cup of water, but her hands were shaking so much she spilled half of it.

If Mother wasn't here with her, it meant she was confined, and that was far from good. They were both now helpless, and she knew that at the mere sight of a strange man walking towards her, manacles in hand, she'd scream out the truth about everything before he'd even set foot in the room.

When the cup was empty she thought about smashing it so she'd have a rudimentary weapon to defend herself with. But with the thought that she'd need something to stab her father with, the disgust she felt for him turned into a perfectly clear hatred. Almost as much as she hated herself for causing the king's execution. If she hadn't have run straight back to the fort yesterday so carelessly that there was straw in her hair, maybe no one would have been suspicious, and the king could have sailed back to his family.

She ordered more water, took a long swig and splashed the rest of it over her face. In the refreshing shock she had a flash of an idea. If she was married to the Dux Britanniarum, the man of the highest rank in all of Britannia, higher even than the Governor, then Father wouldn't be able to touch her. She wouldn't be helpless any more. And maybe she could even find a way to protect Eugenius.

And as she paced back and forth, eyes constantly on the door, the idea that she could, for the very first time, control something of her own destiny, gave her a sense of strength.

She realised that she was ready to learn some of her grandmother's magics.

VIII

Mediolanum, Italy

With the late autumn sun casting its golden glow over the fields of almost ripe wheat, Magnus decided that riding at such a sedate pace through the countryside along the Via Cassia, rather than the forced marches he was used to, was a nice way to travel. No logistics for thousands, sometimes tens of thousands of soldiers to worry about, no intelligence from scouts to consider, no reports of enemy movements that needed to be planned for. Only twenty miles a day, sometimes just twelve. Sometimes, none at all.

Marcellinius had insisted on coming with him and Magnus hadn't protested, as sharing the journey with his brother would be a wonderful way to spend what could well be his last days. Riding, stopping at some places for days, enjoying the clean air, Magnus had spent more time with his younger brother than he'd had since they were boys. And he'd cherished every moment.

The message he'd given to the rider to return to Gratian was a politely written missive explaining that he was a man of horses and so would be riding. And if he needed to hurry, a messenger should be sent to find him and he'd push the horses. What he didn't write was that if he was being summoned to his execution, he intended to damn well take his time and so if the weather was bad, he'd lounge all day in the steam rooms of the baths in whatever town they found themselves at, without concern.

Marcellinius never spoke it, but he surely shared the same fear of Gratian's intent. Maybe because of that, they talked freely, and laughed as they rode, recalling memories of their childhoods. Those days weren't distant just in years, as both of them were so far from the boys they'd been on the hacienda in Hispania it was amusing to remember some things, as it seemed it had been completely different people who'd done them. Marcellinius only had a few memories of their father, so as he'd done a few times over the years, Magnus talked to him about his earliest recollections. It didn't matter that Marcellinius had heard them all dozens of times before, Magnus was his only connection to their father and the stories were a way of keeping his name alive. He had much more to say about Theodosius, their uncle who'd taken them in when Magnus was six, the same age as their cousin Theo, now Emperor of the East, and Marcellinus was four.

Occasionally the two of them raced, pushing the family thoroughbreds to the limit of their speed, and almost endurance, then lay dozing under a tree while Marcellinius' slave with the pack horses caught up. If there was a new church in a town, they went in to visit, dropping to a knee at the entrance and leaving a few coins on the alms box, and more in the grubby palms of any beggars they found outside. Every night they went to wash off the day's road dirt in the local bathhouse, and, if the stable master gave one a good recommendation, visited a brothel. Endless wine they drowned. Not falernian, but the best they could find in the provinces was plenty good enough. And going to bed blind drunk was the best way to get some sleep.

Strangely, in the early mornings, when the dawn mist still lingered in the trees, the birds sang and the deer were close to the road, something in his heart blossomed. No killing to consider, felt good for a man's soul, but the constant underlying thought that these were his last days alive gave an added beauty to everything, as bittersweet as it was,.

They were close to Mediolanum now, but in all the hundreds of miles they'd ridden, neither of them had come up with any reason to be optimistic about the coming meeting, and the closer they got to the imperial court, the slower they began to ride. Marcellinius was still worried about keeping the emperor waiting, convinced the delay would make any proclamation even worse. Magnus was less concerned about delaying his death for as long as possible.

Nearly two weeks it took. On one of the last nights, a roadside inn had a map of the empire painted on the wall. Someone had rubbed away some of the provinces in the east, possibly marking the redrawing of the borders after the Battle of Samara against the Sassanids. That was in the time of Julian, in the same year as Magnus had gone with Theodosius to Britannia to quell the Conspiracy, but what caught his attention looked like a cross of smeared blood a little above Constantinople: Adrianople.

As he stared at it, he fumed again at what losing that battle had cost the empire. Magnus downed the last of his third cup of wine: Maybe the fourth. Blood was the perfect substance to mark it with. For the whole journey from Rome he'd been resigned to his fate, but the more he looked at the map, the closer he was to erupting in anger. He only just managed to restrain himself from throwing his cup at it.

A weak, vain idiot like Valens, more interested in personal glory than the well-being of the empire, had squandered some fifteen thousand men in a battle, just because he hadn't wanted to share the victory with a teenage emperor. His misplaced confidence had almost cost the entire empire. Two years later and cousin Theo still hadn't managed to expel the Goths from Macedonia, and so they remained free, roaming the country at will.

And the empire hadn't yet raised an army capable of facing them.

If the boy Gratian, or those around him who held the real power, judged the interests of the empire higher than their own, they would promote Magnus, a strong and experienced general with a proven record of reinforcing weakened borders. Instead, because they feared him in a position of power where he might have the possibility of threatening their interests, they were going to get rid of him. Just like they'd done with Theodosius.

Only Marcellinius' hand on his shoulder stopped him from spitting the last mouthful of wine over the map, aimed right at Mediolanum. As his brother sat him back at the table with soft words, he felt calmer, yet more inclined to listen to the sceptics and doom-mongers who believed they'd see the end of the empire in their lifetimes; hat the children of senators would become slaves to the Barbarians. Or even worse, the Huns.

A serving girl brought more wine. Magnus looked twice at her, but it wasn't the one he was looking for...and then he had something else to think about. Although he thought he saw her sometimes, selling snacks on a busy town street, or with a strigil scraping the skin of a man in the baths, he never mentioned the dreams to his brother. Whether it was the shame, or fear that there really was something seriously wrong with him, he didn't want to think too deeply about it. When Marcellinius asked him why he woke up screaming and drenched in sweat, he didn't explain it was because he was pushing desperately through thick foliage following her trail as though he was a wolf chasing a young roe. Or running desperately through the market of a busy town, grabbing any girl he could reach and turning them around to see if it was her. Putting words to girls from dreams was for poets, not fighting men.

He'd sold his slaves and so considered himself far from the reach of Justina and her poisons, and yet the girl still stalked him. Looking back, he wished he'd questioned the slaves rather than just selling them to get rid of them. There would, of course, have been several intermediaries between them and whoever had given them the poison that made him dream, but at least he'd have confirmed there was actually a plot.

But then again, Justina didn't matter any more. Her subtle ways hadn't worked and so it seemed she and Gratian had conspired together to adopt a more direct approach. Any charge at all could be levied against him. Outrageous, or rooted in a kernel of truth, it didn't matter as emperors didn't need boring, inconvenient things like evidence or proof to pass judgement on lesser men. Theodosius' fate was testament to that.

If he wasn't to be banished to Africa, he hoped that at least the end would be quick. Sitting for days in a pitch dark, foetid prison pit had, in his darker moods, worked itself into his worst fear.

For the last day, they rode almost in silence, and then, still far too quickly for Magnus' liking, Mediolanum lay on the wide plain before them. The bitter taste of knowing he was almost at the feet of the emperor, his fate in the hands of a boy, almost made him want to spit.

The way the sun caught the marble that most of the central part of the city seemed to be built with, made it look like it was a reflection on a pond of the snow-capped mountains beyond. With a grinding sense of unease, he wondered if they could be the ones of his dreams.

Through the huge sturdy gates, rivals in stature and sturdiness of those of Rome, Marcellinius griped at the stench of human occupation which assailed their senses as soon as they were inside. "Maybe we could stay in the country for a few more days?" he laughed.

Magnus wanted nothing more than that. But he didn't have a few more days.

The air was admittedly rank, but the hive of activity felt welcoming. The shared focus of thousands of men all striving for one purpose, to dig a defensive ditch, set up a palisade, march to a battle, or to make roads through the mountains, invigorated him. He was sure that life exiled in a village, with every day being the same as the next, would drive him even madder than he already was.

A call of warning, and amid a loud crash and plume of dust, a beam of wood in a construction site fell. At the clatter and the cries, Magnus ducked down as shields were raised over his head to form a tight testudo, the sling-shot fired stones and spears of their foes shuddering off them. The shrill shriek of a whistle was the signal for those in the second row to step forward and it was Magnus' turn to hold his shield in a death grip in his left hand and stab guts out with the sword in his right...

"Brother!" Marcellinus said concerned, his hand on Magnus' arm and Magnus was surprised to find himself back in the town, the sudden silence shocking...yet the echoes of a barbarian horde bearing down on them still reverberated off the building walls. It had been so real that his heart pounded and he had to wipe sweat from his brow. Slowly, so his brother couldn't see, he had to release his fingers from the reins one by one.

Maybe Gratian didn't have to kill him. Maybe he was dying anyway.

He had to force his fist to open to hand the reins to the young stable lad. Before his mount was led away to be fed and groomed, he ran his hand down the side of its neck. The feeling of the lithe power under the skin had always fascinated him, but the thought that he could have just had his last ride tore at his heart. As he patted the rump affectionately, he had a lump in his throat.

They got cleaned up in the grand bathhouse, its arched ceiling towering far above them, scraped with a strigil and dabbed dry, and then it was time for the attendant to wrap Magnus in his toga. He hadn't worn the cumbersome robe since... well, he couldn't remember. But now was not the time to work himself into a rage about the injustice of Theodosius' murder. It had been in a bag on the horse for weeks so smelled a bit musty. Some of the thin golden band was beginning to fray and he knew such a detail wouldn't pass the emperor's notice.

He wondered if it was a mark of civilisation that a man facing his execution cared about how he was dressed.

He stood still as the attendant expertly bundled up the folds of cloth into the nook of his left arm. He hated the constricting feeling of it, like Vercengetorix's throat at Caesar's parade. The weight of it too. He reasoned that if things you wore had to be heavy, they should at least offer some protection in a fight.

Once he was dressed and on his way to the palace, he wondered if he would ever see his brother again. As they grasped wrists, tears were in his eyes: for just himself or the empire in general, he wasn't too sure.

Those who knew him, knew not to mention it. Those who didn't, soon learned, but the morning before any fight, Magnus' body had its own peculiar pre-battle ritual, one he was helpless to control. In a flush of sweat, a wave of pathetic weakness washing over him, he doubled over and spilled his lunch over the flagstones of the imperial city. A few slow breaths and the nausea passed. He wished he could blame Justina for the ailment, but it had plagued him since he was a boy, from the very first time he'd held a steel sword in a small hand.

The men at the palace gates took his mind off the complaint though. From the Senate to the street cleaners, Gratian's personal guards had been the talk of Rome for some time, and seeing the brace of Alan guards for himself, Magnus understood why. With their swarthy skin and strangely colourful tunics. Some were even wearing trousers. They were so worryingly out of place at the entrance to the palace that, as he approached, Magnus couldn't help wondering if he was looking some years into the future to a time when the borders had finally fallen.

However, their smell out him at an even deeper unease. To his nose, their perfume was part horse, part woman and he cringed as one slid his small hands down into the folds of his toga. They checked for any concealed weapon he might harm the emperor with, untucking it, making him look unkempt and making it pointless to have paid the attendant to dress him.

The one with his hand on Magnus had an oddly intensive stare, as though he was barely able to control his bloodlust. It seemed there was some madness there. Or maybe Magnus was misreading it, and it was just pure, confrontational arrogance, as though the man wanted him to know how proud he was that he, a barbarian in dress and style of hair, stood between toga-adorned men and their emperor.

Neither their presence nor their demeanour, give Magnus any confidence that what awaited him inside the palace was going to be in any way a positive experience.

"Take no offence, friend," a gruff but high-pitched voice said. "It is an ignominy visited on everyone who steps inside, I'm afraid. Necessity. These days you can't be too careful." It was Ausonius, Gratian's tutor, advisor and, most famously, traitor.

Magnus had heard many things about the old man. How he was still alive had been the topic of many conversations back in the capital. Openly defying the Imperial command to march every last available soldier from the Rhine frontier to support Valens at Adrianople was outright treason. But if Ausonius had followed Gratian's orders, the whole of Gaul would have been lost to the Alemanni army who'd seen an opportunity to invade too great to resist. Ausonius' retained force had cut down some thirty thousand of them, so for such a victory, Gratian could have perhaps pardoned him, even if the battle was won despite him, rather than because of him.

But eclipsing even that, in an act that still seemed unbelievable, a few years earlier the old man had managed to make Gratian's then four-year-old half-brother Valentinian co-emperor. For a serving emperor to just find out that someone had arranged it so that he now shared his portion of the empire, was unimaginable.

And yet, Ausonius still lived.

He led the way down a marbled corridor, acting as a host, but it wasn't the boy in the purple who had power in these walls. Magnus knew he was in the company of one of the most powerful men in the empire. A power to make even the emperor jealous.

Magnus had no knife hidden in the folds of his toga, but one look at the Gratian's neck as the lad lounged on a gold-covered couch, and he didn't think it would stand much chance if he could get a grip around it. Long before he was at the age Gratian was now, Theodosius had taught him tens of different ways to kill a man with his bare hands, whereas he was sure Gratian had never even held a sword in anger. The staged matches when he pretended to be Commodus in front of bored onlookers, against men probably threatened with execution if they dared to fight properly, didn't count.

Twenty-one was an obscenely young age for a man to wield such power. With no life experience of his own to draw from, all of his decisions had to be made on the words of his advisors. But his easy life in the sumptuous luxuries of the imperial court had been kind to his skin and he looked noticeably younger than any similarly aged army recruit Magnus had ever met.

But it wasn't the effeminately smooth skin that was the most shocking thing about the emperor; it was what he was wearing. Like most men in Rome, Magnus had heard the rumours that Gratian had taken to dressing in the foreign fashions of his Alan guards, but seeing him reclining on the throne in a pair of sky-blue trousers was still a disappointing shock. Magnus had long mused on the decline of the empire, and now he was looking upon it. Gratian dressed like their enemies. Sharing power with his ten-year-old half-brother and his scheming mother, Theo locked into a desperate struggle with the Goths with no certainty of victory… it wasn't just in decline, Magnus judged the empire was hanging by a thread.

Ausonius handed him a glass of wine. Dark red, and if it was fit for an emperor, it was obviously the best there was. Magnus stayed standing to take a sip, as was befitting in front of an emperor. It tasted divine. The glass too, was another exquisite piece of art.

Gratian reached slowly behind his shoulder, and in a display he'd obviously planned beforehand, slowly drew his purple toga over him, a little tug here, a pull there, until he'd practically covered himself in it.

The display, if that was what it was, didn't work on Magnus though. He felt no sense of awe to be in the presence of someone with such power. Far from it. Life had been trudging along endless roads to fight endless wars and defeat endless enemies, and to think that all of the blood that had been spilled so a soft child could spend his days lounging on a throne in a marble palace, clothed in the garb of those who would sack Rome if they had half a chance, seemed a terrible affront.

The toga was ill-suited to someone so young, especially since the last time he'd seen it, it had been over the broad shoulders of Gratian's father, but the colour of the Tyrian purple was astounding. It would have been made by only the very best artisans and materials in the whole of the empire. The wool from the best bred sheep, to the most skilled weavers, dye makers and gold thread embroiderers. He didn't doubt that anyone involved in its creation would consider it one of the highest honours of their lives to have their part in making such a garment.

Only three men in the empire could wear one like it. Well, two men and a child, although that was perhaps giving undue credit to the one lounging before him.

"I trust your journey was a pleasant one?" Gratian said, beaming with a facetious smile.

Magnus would have been less sure of his impending death had he been thrown into a nest of vipers or an arena full of starved lions. "Yes, thank you," he said, a little unsure of how to speak informally to an emperor.

"I suppose me elevating your cousin to the exalted position of Emperor of the East left you a little...aggrieved. A totally understandable reaction, though."

"I am sure that you and your advisers are best suited to decide who to put in which position," Magnus said. Hearing himself talk like a diplomat, speaking as softly as though he was treading on a freshly laid mosaic, seemed strange.

"Anyway, I have reports, quite disturbing ones," Gratian said, and even though Magnus had been expecting to hear such a sentence for weeks, his heart turned to stone. *Come on, then,* he thought. *Let's get it over with.*

"It appears that a man close to me has taken advantage of his situation. To a point that vexes me seriously."

Keen to avoid Theodosius' fate, Magnus had spent the last couple of years being careful that his words and actions did not invoke the ire of the imperial court, as he was very aware his life depended on it, so of course the charge would have to be something invented. He wondered just how spurious the one that would see him erased from history would be.

"To all intents and purposes, he's taken retirement in a fort near the coast. He's moved his family into the praetorium with him, can you imagine! Children, right among the soldiers!"

Trying to follow the meaning of Gratian's words, Magnus' mind fluttered about as erratically as a butterfly, but when he realised it wasn't him being talked about, one of the hardest things Magnus had ever had to do in his life was not to shout out his relief. Interrupting the emperor in mid-sentence to praise the Lord for his life would be very poor etiquette.

"But most worrying is that he has been buying up the land he is supposed to be governing. Vast tracts of it, and in the process he has made himself exceedingly wealthy, yet very unpopular at the same time. Do you understand?"

The rich enriching themselves further at the expense of those under them was the usual way of breeding contempt and fomenting unrest. As sure as the sun would come up in the east, this man wasn't the first and he wouldn't be the last. Maybe he was accumulating power enough to make those in Mediolanum nervous. "You want me to go to Britannia and assassinate him?" Magnus asked.

Gratian recoiled, piggish eyes wide, clearly alarmed at such a suggestion. "Oh, no, no. Nothing so vulgar as that. How could you misunderstand me so completely? The island has been noticeably, and pleasingly, free from issues since you and...your uncle's work there. What is it now, some fifteen years past? Quite remarkable."

Magnus fought those battles in a distant land while Gratian was still learning how to walk. But the successes he spoke of, were not Magnus'. He felt his face flush at how close Gratian had come to saying Theodosius' name. He couldn't, and was it guilt that stayed his tongue? With a real bitterness, Magnus wondered if the command to execute his uncle had been voiced in the same room in which he now stood.

"I fear a man who busies himself with such business can't have his full attention on the protection of the empire, so your remit from me is to simply...*complement* him. These days, the empire's borders always seem to be under threat at one point or another, it's a constant fight to keep them impermeable, and those who populate the wilds outside the borders of Britannia are particularly vicious creatures. The successes you had there after the Conspiracy, then in Africa, and on the Danube, are often talked about in high circles. It seems such a waste having a man of your capabilities sitting idle in Rome with no commission to polish your armour and sharpen your sword for. You will make the borders of Britannia secure so that I can concentrate on the Goths and Alemanni without having to worry about a hostile army crossing the sea to the north."

Being sent far away to the land of Britannia was a kind of banishment, but he would live. And exile in green forests was infinitely preferable to spending his days in the sand and rocks of Africa. And he'd have men to command. At the thought of that, he realised just how much he'd missed the life of the army.

"Do you accept the posting?"

"I err...In which position?" Magnus asked.

Ausonius stepped forward. "As Dux Britanniarum," he said, filling in the vital piece of information Gratian didn't seem too concerned with. "You'll have command of the northern frontier guards along the Wall, but you will also take command of the defences to the west of Britannia Secunda, those that Octavius should be overseeing. You will have your pick of the men of the Twentieth from Deva, the Sixth from Eboracum and the Second from the Saxon Shore."

"Do you accept?" Gratian asked, his tone suggesting that he didn't much appreciate asking the same question twice.

"I do, of course," Magnus said, surprised almost to the point of confusion at how quickly everything had seemed to have turned around.

"Of course you do," Gratian scoffed. "You wouldn't have said no to me! Ausonius will arrange the papers and seals and the other paraphernalia of your office. You are now an important man. Thanks to me."

The threat in the compliment that without Gratian's good grace, Magnus would be nothing, was easy to hear.

Official business done, Gratian relaxed and a look of cloying smugness settled on his face. "I have a question for you, a Nicean Christian, as am I. Tell me, what would you think if I took the Altar of Victory from the Senate, like Constantinius did? Would that teach the old-fashioned pagans in the Senate that Christianity is not only in its ascendancy, but is now dominant?"

"Inspired," Magnus heard himself say, but hoped the disdain he felt wouldn't show on his face, as he knew with absolute clarity that losing the Emperor's favour would seal his fate as that of Theodosius; that of the Elder, not the Younger.

As he fought to maintain a respectful composure, he wondered how many other men of power had acquiesced to an emperor's unwise requests just to maintain or improve their own status, the good of the empire be damned.

The Altar of Victory had stood proud in the Senate as the very symbol of Rome for hundreds of years, but if Gratian wanted to make himself deeply unpopular with the richest and most powerful men in Rome by insulting the gods they believed in and worshipped as devoutly as any Christian did the Father, Son and the Holy Ghost, then who was Magnus to stop him? Although the more the boy talked in a self-congratulatory tone, now saying something about Adrianople, a thought crept into Magnus' mind. One that if it was to find its way to his tongue, would have him executed on the spot. He knew he would make a far more competent emperor than Gratian could ever hope to be.

Such a wildly inappropriate idea popping into his head while he was standing right in front of the Emperor seemed so shockingly out of place it made him wonder if Justina was in the palace and had sprinkled something into his wine. In an unthinking response, his stomach clenched in an attempt to purge itself. He only just managed to prevent the hues of the wine he'd drunk from mixing with those of the purple cloak.

But with him ruling in the west with Theo in the east, son and nephew of Theodosius working in unison to bring stability and secure borders...together, the two strong, proven military men, who would have the respect of the soldiery from the legions to the auxiliaries, and to the foederati, could work to stem the decline. One day in the not so distant future, perhaps they could construct edifices as grand as the Colosseum again. He could almost feel the sensation of slipping that gorgeous cloak around his shoulders. He was so close to it, could almost feel it, and for a heartbeat wondered if he could simply dive at Gratian and snap the boy's neck before the Alan guards at the door could reach him. Stratagems played out in his mind, about how much time he'd then have to convince Ausonius to call the Alans off and declare Magnus as emperor, as the old man had done with Valentinian some five years before.

"Are you all right?" Gratian asked, looking more amused than concerned. "Your face has gone from pale to rouged. Should I send for somebody?"

"No, no," Magnus said. "You're right. There's just something here I'm not used to."

"Yes, you might find the wine here a little richer than the posca in the barracks. It often happens with...men with...less sophisticated tastes. You can winter in Treverorum while you assemble your commanders and entourage. I'm sure being close to the border will be more suitable for you than remaining any longer than necessary in Mediolanum."

Magnus cast a glance at Ausonius. The old man was considered one of the most revered tutors and advisors in the empire, but Magnus thought he'd failed dismally at teaching Gratian some basic manners about not insulting those he wanted to be loyal to him. The boy obviously had no idea how to foster a sense of loyalty in his men, which was absolutely vital in a good leader. As he took his leave, Ausonius walking beside him, Magnus knew exactly how to get men to follow him to the end of the empire. And the boy had just given him access to three legions.

Footfalls echoing off the shining marble walls, his legs felt oddly weak at the thought of how close he'd come to attacking Gratian with his bare hands. He wondered which of the techniques Theodosius had taught him, he'd have killed the emperor with.

As his heart started to calm down, he wondered if he had gone mad. He also wondered if Ausonius, the man who spent his life among the most powerful men in the empire, knew just what thoughts had gone through Magnus' head.

He was sure that he wasn't wrong. The empire would be in a much better state if he was in charge of it along with Theo.

Before they got through the grand doors back into the daylight, the question if Ausonius would prefer Magnus as emperor was on his tongue, but he couldn't be sure if speaking it would cost him his head, but when Ausonius said, "Come to me in a week and I will have everything prepared," the moment to proclaim himself as Augustus was lost.

He wondered if there would be another.

IX

Segontium, Britannia Secunda

"Magnus Maximus? The Greatest Great? What kind of name is that?" Elen asked, half expecting Grandmother to be joking as she couldn't imagine a man choosing such a name for himself. "It sounds like a little boy dressing up in his father's clothes and pretending to be the emperor."

"Exactly!" Grandmother beamed.

Elen was sure that there was some real magic in that smile of hers. Every time it appeared, like the sun rising above the horizon in the morning, a flood of the warmest love and happiness poured through her heart.

From her position by the old sheet of hide that did for the door, Gula harrumphed her agreement. If anyone was too close with the intent to disturb them, she would give enough warning for Elen to escape out the back door. Grandmother wouldn't be running anywhere though, she was too big and old to move at a normal pace, never mind getting anywhere quickly. Over the winter Elen had barely seen her move from her chair at the table at all. On the other hand though, she had no need to run from soldiers. It seemed Grandmother wasn't afraid of anyone, and that was exactly how Elen wanted to be one day. Not living in fear of any man was the most perfect luxury she could imagine. Today though, back in Grandmother's rough little house for the first time since the king's execution, she was just happy to be away from Father's control. It was the first time she'd felt safe for days.

"You're right about the name," Grandmother said. "But as much as it makes us laugh, it does give us a valuable hint of his personality."

"How?" Elen asked, painfully aware that there was a lifetime of learning between the two of them. And before she was thrust face-first into the murky midsts of political intrigue with one of the most powerful men in the empire, it seemed there was almost no time at all.

"I would assume that a man so vain that he calls himself by such a name will be much easier to manipulate than a man of modesty and humility."

It felt so easy to understand when Grandmother explained it in such a way, but the thought of her, a young girl with almost no experience of the world, trying to guide the plans and decisions of the Dux Britanniarum, a man even more powerful than her father, still filled her with absolute dread...and she noticed the trembling in her hands had started again.

In the terrible days after the crucifixion she could think of nothing else than how Father had stood next to the cross, while the king's tortured body twisted in agony, fresh blood glistening in the evening sun, as though nothing untoward was taking place. When she'd managed to banish that awful image, the one that sprung up in its stead was of him beating the boy who'd been caught asleep on duty until he was dead, and the sickening fear she'd felt from thinking the blood spattered over his cloak was Eugenius'.

Locked to stew in her room, all the love she'd felt for Father had turned to nothing but bile and in her disgust and hatred, she realised that she now saw him as Mother did; as an enemy. She was resolved to stab him with his own pugio before he married her off to any man he chose. She wanted to tell Grandmother this, but had a suspicion that she already knew.

Now, able to breathe again without the crushing pain in her chest, all she wanted was to be in Eugenius' strong arms, and although she wasn't sure she wanted to know the answer, she had a question she'd been waiting for days to ask. The king, Mother and Grandmother had all said the same thing, but the idea that the biggest empire the world has ever seen could just one day cease to exist seemed utterly inconceivable. "How will Rome fall?" she blurted out.

Grandmother's eyes gleamed. "Like the end of any empire, my dear. From hubris, greed, corruption and a stroke or two of bad fortune. But it's a very good question for one tasked with such an undertaking. In the natural turning of the world, as even the most powerful of men will age and die, so too will the empire itself. Rome is like an old tree, one rotten to the core, and that means the next gust of wind will bring the whole thing crashing to the ground."

The answer was so simple, so matter of fact, it caused another twist of something deep in her belly, something that had become a familiar sensation over the last few days. "Then what?" she asked, holding her hands together to try and stop them shaking so much.

"And then new light will reach the ground," Gula said.

"Then new weeds will grow," Grandmother added quickly. "The crisis we face is..." she said, shuffling her considerable bulk in her creaking chair, "Once, a long time ago, the Ordovices were great fighters. Like Rome has her legions, they had a caste of warriors, the fiercest and bravest men you could ever imagine. They were glad to die in battle as they believed it would make their gods proud. But in one last battle, Rome killed them all."

"Cadwal the Great?" Elen asked.

"Yes. He was the last of the warriors. But for all of the three hundred years since, Rome has not allowed anyone of this land to hold a weapon, unless he was a first son being trained to fight for a legion stationed in a distant land. Too many generations of subjugation, we are not fighters any more. Maybe it won't happen tomorrow, maybe not even in your lifetime, but fall, Rome will. And the day after the red banners no longer flies from the walls of their forts, the Picts will flood from the north, the Scotti will sail west from Hibernia and the Saxons will come from the south. Just as they did a few years ago."

"In the Conspiracy?" Elen asked.

From behind, Gula scoffed. "Conspiracy is far from what it was."

"Just an understandable reaction of people from whom Rome takes far more than it gives," Grandmother added. "Nothing has changed since then, so the same thing can happen again any day. And we will find ourselves in the same helpless position. Again."

"So you need me to marry this Magnus and convince him to settle the Deisi on our land to protect us when the empire falls? That's all?"

"That's all," Grandmother nodded, eyes sparkling.

"It sounds so easy, but how will you arrange the marriage? If he's so powerful, he can choose any girl he wants. Men from all over the empire will be lining up to marry their daughters to him."

"Hopefully he'll be so besotted with you from the first moment he lays eyes on you, he'll do anything you ask of him." It wasn't the first time Grandmother had said something far beyond Elen's understanding, but she wanted to believe her. "Will I have to love him, though?"

"Ha!" As Grandmother chuckled, her belly and bosom wobbled.

It was Gula who answered. "Real love is a precious thing and must be protected wherever it is found. You might not find love in your husband, especially one who named himself in such a way, but I promise that you will find it in the children he will give you."

At the thought of bearing a strange man's children came another stab of terror, but marrying was a duty expected of every girl and she managed to temper the dread with the knowledge that Mother had done the same thing, and probably Grandmother before her. Yet the expectation of being able to influence Magnus as Grandmother hoped was overwhelming, almost unbearable, and she yearned for some familiar comfort and to be in the place she felt safest. "I need to go and find Eugenius," she said.

"No, you don't!" Grandmother snapped and in an instant, the sweet understanding tone she normally spoke with was gone. Elen heard it as an order. "That door is now closed to you, I'm afraid."

"But..." Elen began to protest, the feeling of being trapped in someone else's plan tugging tight around her heart.

"No. There cannot be even the slightest *hint* of suspicion that you are anything other than a perfect and diligent wife. If Magnus ever has half a thought that his sons might not be his, everything we've been working for will be lost."

"But..."

"No. The role you will have to play in what may unfold is far too important. I forbid it."

"But I love him!" she cried. "He makes me..."

"No!" Grandmother almost shouted like she was addressing a soldier, and the loving twinkle in her eyes was extinguished. "I didn't want to have to say this to you, and had half hoped you'd work it out yourself, but my dear, you *cannot* be with him."

"No!" Elen cried.

"It has to be this way," she said a little softer, yet the words still fell over her as harshly as the blades of Father's whip.

It felt like everything was being forced from her grasp, as though she was a chicken being dragged out of the coup, her neck laid on the chopping block under the uncaring blade of fate.

She stood up so quickly the chair fell back behind her. She heard Gula begging her to stay and listen, but stormed out the back way as quickly as though soldiers were chasing her. She was aware enough to take a few false turns and slipped to the side in a doorway or two to make sure no one was following her. Mother or anyone else.

The sight of the barn usually filled her with an all-consuming joy, but she knew it would be awfully lonely to be in there by herself and to see the nest she and Eugenius had made for themselves up in the loft empty. It was still the place she felt safest though.

Halfway up the old ladder she heard a rustle of straw and stopped, frozen. Someone was up there, and with a coldness in her heart, she wondered if it was one of Father's men waiting to catch her in a compromising tryst.

She made her way up the last few rungs, determined to confront whoever it was. After what Grandmother had just told her, the last person she expected to find there was Eugenius. Relief and passion both erupted and she couldn't throw herself into his arms quickly enough…but stopped when she realised it wasn't a coincidence he was waiting for her. "What are you doing here?" she asked.

"I got a message to be ready for you," he shrugged.

"From who? Grandmother?"

He nodded.

"When?"

"Ages ago. I was getting cold and starting to think you weren't coming."

Ages ago…Before she'd even got to Grandmother's house.

She crawled next to him, into his embrace with the relief and need of holding the man she'd feared she'd never see again. She was bemused as to why Grandmother would arrange for him to be here when she'd said she was forbidden to see him, but wasn't about to question it. "Are you all right?" she asked. "Did my father do anything to you?"

She recalled the look on Grandmother's face as she stormed out. Had it actually been a satisfied smirk? Had Elen done exactly what she'd wanted her to? As his thick arms held her tight, she realised that the infuriating old woman had made her fight for him. Had she been trying to teach her how to stand up for what she wanted? Whatever the test was, Elen knew exactly what she wanted and pressed herself against Eugenius' muscled body, ready to take it, but suddenly had a much better idea. It was crazy, and was wrong for many reasons, but was right in the only one that mattered…that she and Eugenius would be together.

Mother had said she wanted her to have a foot in both worlds, for her to make sure the needs of the local people were considered by those of Rome. Her idea would certainly accomplish that. Yet, on the other hand, it went against so many precepts of Christianity she was sure she'd burn forever for it.

She concentrated on the feeling of Eugenius' arms around her. It must be the same sensation a soldier has knowing he is surrounded by the impenetrable walls of his fort. No one could do any harm to her while he was beside her.

"We need to go back to Grandmother's house," she said.

"Now?" he asked as she pulled away from him.

He looked dismayed from having his passion interrupted, but Elen knew he wouldn't think of trying to force himself on her. He wasn't that type of man.

"Come on," she said. "Hurry."

Eugenius obeyed, rolled the blanket up and hid it under some hay, then made his way down the ladder after her.

A wish of Elen's was that one day the two of them could walk through the vicus streets together with no concern about what anyone who saw them thought or said. No vicious punishments looming over them if the wrong person was to see them. Today though, they needed to be careful and took separate routes from the barn back to Grandmother's shack.

"That was quick," Grandmother said with a knowing, almost cheeky, smile on her face. Elen wasn't too surprised that her mother was also still there as they'd been waiting for her to come back to continue the discussion. Neither were they expecting Eugenius to follow her in a few moments later, though.

"Careful when you play with the flames, my dear," Grandmother said, suddenly cold.

"You had him waiting for me because you wanted me to fight for what I want," Elen said.

"Did I," Grandmother sighed as she shook her head slowly. "Or maybe he was there one last time so you could say your last goodbyes."

Elen stood with her mouth open, shocked and disappointed at herself for so completely misunderstanding Grandmother's intention.

She felt her cheeks flush, but didn't forget the feeling of imperviousness of being in Eugenius' arms. "Well, *this* is what I want!" she said, reaching out to hold his hand.

"Is it now?" Grandmother asked cautiously.

"Marry us!"

"Elen!" Gula gasped and Grandmother chuckled, but not in a particularly nice way. "And how exactly will you be able to marry the Dux next spring if you're already the wife of one of his soldiers?" she pressed.

"You want me to have a foot in both worlds, remember?"

"Not like this!" Mother snapped.

"I will marry Eugenius in the old ways, *your* ways, and when he gets here, I will be a Christian wife to this Magnus."

"By the gods," Gula sighed. "You can't!"

"Now, let's wait a moment," Grandmother said. "A foot in both worlds? She's quite right about that, isn't she?"

"You can't seriously consider such madness!" Gula spat.

Grandmother tapped her finger on the table thoughtfully. "Let us not act in such haste."

"Mother!" Gula protested.

"To go against her life-long, deeply-held beliefs, to put a man she wants before her God…this is no small thing. It shows real strength and determination, and that is exactly what I wish for her. While I think it could be a dangerous idea, one of the lessons I wish to teach her as she comes into her power, is that if she is clever enough to work out how it is possible, then she can have anything she wants." She turned to Elen. "I will agree to your demand, my dear, but with one very serious caveat. You must keep your relationship with this man as secret as your mother kept me from you. The consequences of being found out are dire. For all of us. Any scenario where a man of Magnus' power finds himself a humiliated husband cannot end well. And perhaps more pressing for you, it could mean your lover here ends his days in the same place as our unfortunate Scotti king."

"I agree," Elen said, even against such a warning.

"And what about you, young man?" she asked Eugenius. "Did she bother to consult you on this plan?"

"No, but…"

"Good. That's exactly how I wanted her to treat the men in her life! Do you agree to be wed?"

"I err," he stammered, looking nervously at the three women in the room.

"It seems a perfectly simple question," she prompted.

"I do," he said.

"Well then." She beckoned him forward and asked for his hand. Elen thought she was about to cut his palm to initiate him into her mysterious world or something, but all she did was hand him a small gold coin. "Take this to Iacomus and tell him to take you across the straits to the old island."

Once Eugenius had left, Grandmother turned to Elen, her expression stern. "This *must* be a secret that is kept from your father to the dirtiest boy of the streets and all between. Even a baseless rumour easily has the power to be the death of a man. And if your Eugenius does anything to interfere with our arrangement with the Dux, I might give the order for his blood myself."

"He won't," Elen said defiantly.

"We'll see."

The next hours were both the longest and quickest of Elen's life at the same time.

Humming a happy tune, Gula plaited her hair, twisting and winding it into an intricate style no Roman woman would ever dream of wearing. Barbarian. Elen wondered if she would need to cover it under a shawl while they made their way through the vicus.

Apparently, a secret pagan wedding didn't take too long to organise as once one of Gula's servants had arrived back from the fort with one of Elen's nicest tunics they were ready to go.

As she always did before leaving, Gula slipped a finger down the side of the sheet covering the door and checked the alley for anyone acting suspiciously. "Come," she said, finally.

The litter waited for them in the side street, Grandmother already inside, but it was the compartment under the open seat that she pointed at for Elen to get in. "Quickly!" she snapped at Elen's reluctance.

She was too confused to protest, so stepped in, crouched down and curled up.

"If the guards check us, I don't want your father wondering what you and I are up to together," Gula said as she closed the seat, trapping Elen in the darkness.

As they swayed along through the vicus, she could hear the feet of the slaves carrying them splashing on wet ground, but as the sounds of life got louder the closer they got to the fort, she couldn't help chuckling to herself at the absurdity of being carried around so secretly. It wasn't long before doubts about what she was doing began to creep in, though. One was that she was being selfish to put Eugenius in such danger. His life would be terribly at risk if anyone close to Magnus was to somehow find out they were married. Of roughly equal dread was that she was committing a terrible sin. There had been no time to find anyone qualified enough to ask about it. Besides, the bishop in Deva was one of Father's closest friends, so even if he was visiting Segontium, she couldn't have trusted her secret with him.

Mother had said that no true love could be a sin though, and in His essential element, God was love and forgiveness, so she reasoned that she had less to fear from His wrath than Father's. In ant case, it was only in the old ways, the native customs, that could she call Eugenius husband, so it was perhaps somewhat out of the Lord's jurisdiction.

She also knew that a life following Grandmother's old ways would be far more rewarding in every way than Father's.

With a thump that made her squeal, the litter was set down and as Gula let her out she squinted at the bright light. From being curled up in the dark to emerging into the light, it felt like some rebirth. And like a newborn, she had no idea where she was. They were somewhere in the country and for some reason Grandmother was swapping her shawl with a portly woman Elen had never seen before. Then, as the large woman got into the litter, Gula helped Grandmother over to a rough farmer's wagon. Elen didn't think they needed to bother with the subterfuge. If Father had sent someone out to watch them, by the time it took to bunk Grandmother up into the back, his men would have had plenty of time to catch up.

With comfy seats exchanged for sacks of grain, they bumped along a track next to the coast for a couple of miles, then helped a now grumbling Grandmother into a small boat and were rowed across the choppy straits. Elen could barely contain her excitement. Being out on the water gave her a wonderful feeling of freedom, of escape, of leaving a life she didn't want behind. On the far shore, she knew the small figure was Eugenius waiting for them, and her heart leapt with joy.

She was a little disappointed that they docked a little way down the beach from him, especially as they could have used his help with getting Grandmother out of the boat. Eventually, the three of them got out to stand on the sodden, muddy sand and seaweed-covered rocks looking back at the mainland.

"Well then," Grandmother shrugged, doubled over as she supported herself on her stick, wisps of unkempt grey hair waving about in the breeze like the flames of the fire. "This is a special place we've come to," she said, trying to catch her breath. "Where we stand is where Suetonius landed the Twentieth Legion and swam his soldier's horses across. The Black Year, they called it. And back over there was a sacred grove of oaks."

Elen looked beyond the small island to the bank of trees on the low hill behind. She'd heard the stories of the massacre from Mother, but couldn't imagine what it must have been like for those who'd witnessed a whole culture being destroyed in front of them.

"One day, I don't doubt, the Christians will come here, know this is our sacred place, and will build a church on it," Grandmother said, full of disdain. "But not today. Today we are here to do honour to our ancestors, by remembering them, and by carrying on the traditions. Another reason we are here, my dearest girl, is that, young as you are, you are a girl with power enough to get anything she wants. If you decide to have two husbands, then two husbands is what you shall have. And much more besides."

Down at the water's edge, Eugenius and one of the soldiers from the fort Grandmother controlled crouched around a little pile of stones stacking twigs to build a small fire. For what reason, Elen had no idea.

"I am a servant of the old gods," Grandmother said. "But I know you adore the new one, the usurper god, and perhaps you worry that the life you will lead with two husbands is punishable by eternal damnation. I can't tell you how much I despise the idiots who preach such inhumane fears into men's ears, but I want you to remember this; true love, whatever form it takes, is sacred and can never be a sin. And besides, your Christian god is not welcome here today."

"I am a *Christian*," Elen reminded her. Many things Grandmother said shocked Elen, but nothing more than when she spoke disrespectful words about the Good Lord and the One True Faith. Every time she did, Elen froze with a terror that they were about to be incinerated in a bolt of lightning or turned into a pillar of salt. The usurper god, indeed! She would ask for Grandmother's soul to be spared in her prayers. And when the time was right, she would have to explain that although she was determined to learn Grandmother's ways, keeping her faith wasn't going to be negotiable.

"Here?" Grandmother asked, still dismissive. At first it seemed that she wasn't too impressed with Elen's statement, but that special smile crept back across the broad face. "Take a look at us. Maiden, mother and crone. How can you get any more of the old ways than that? I feel the great wheel turning in my bones, and it is a thing of the deepest beauty. Soon, my dear, you will have your own daughter, and I ask that at least once in her life you will bring her here to lay a stone on my cairn and tell her who I was."

"Grandmother!" Elen protested. "You talk of things that will come to pass only many years from now!"

"I wish that was so," she sighed. "Not even your first-born son will I see, I fear. Something else I feel in my bones. But that is the way of the world. One other thing I wish to do for you, my dear, a wedding gift, if you like. The wife of the Dux will need security, so I have a hope to arrange for young Eugenius to be the head of your personal guard. That might keep him close enough to you that you shouldn't pine too much to see him."

The thought of that hadn't even crossed Elen's mind, but she immediately knew that was what she wanted. In a voice so calm and confident that she shocked herself, she said, "I will get Magnus to appoint him. And he will know nothing about us."

Eyes wide in delight, Grandmother clapped her hands in joy. "Oh Gula, she's everything I dreamed she would be."

Elen meant it though. If her fate and duty were to couple her with a man she neither desired nor wanted, she would do her best to influence things to her advantage. And another thought popped into her head, one she'd never even had an inkling of before. *And my people's.*

She shivered at the thought that the ancestors were watching…communicating…in the place her god wasn't welcome.

They stepped carefully over the slippery rocks, steadying Grandmother because her legs were barely strong enough to support her weight, she saw that Eugenius had got the fire going on a little pile of pebbles that was turning into a tiny island as the tide made its way in. Grandmother shuffled Elen to the side, so that one foot was in the cold water and the other was on land, and Eugenius did the same too.

"Water, earth, fire and air," Grandmother said as she pulled a small knife out of her clothes. "And blood!" A priest would have intoned the words solemnly, but Grandmother spoke jovially through her smile and that in turn caused everyone else to grin.

"Keep in mind, every moment, that what we do here today is a mortal secret you keep between yourselves," Grandmother said, bringing Elen back to reality. "If it gets to the wrong ears, your lives will be in danger. Especially yours, young man," she said to Eugenius.

His nod was for his understanding and acceptance of the risk.

"Elen has a difficult and dangerous road to follow. She will be dancing next to an unpredictable fire, with many people depending on her for their lives. I don't exaggerate. You'll often have to love her from afar for long periods, but..."

"Such as the world we live in," Eugenius finished.

"Good lad" Grandmother smiled.

"In the sight of the old gods who choose to bear witness, do you agree to be bound together?"

Elen smiled at how Eugenius' eyes gleamed. "Yes!" he almost laughed. "Of course!"

"Good. Eugenius, you are now in both my employ and my protection." She tilted her head in the direction of the lonely looking soldier out of earshot down the beach. "He can explain the ins and outs of what that means. In return, I require that on your life, you swear to love, cherish, honour and protect this sweet girl of mine."

"I will."

"And the children she will have with another man."

With a gasp, Elen had to bite her tongue not to snap at Grandmother to not ruin the special moment.

"I do," Eugenius said again, but the edge to his voice was unmistakable.

"Well then," she said and nodded.

But Grandmother's last words had the effect of opening a wound in Elen's heart. She'd been worrying about it ever since Grandmother had told her Magnus' name that morning but hadn't had the chance to put words to it. Having to bed another man was a duty forced upon her for a greater cause and was beyond her power to do anything about. But if the situation had been reversed and she knew that Eugenius was somewhere pleasuring another girl, a duty foisted upon him or not, she couldn't imagine how she'd cope. Terrified of what the answer might be, she forced the words off her tongue. "Will you still love me..." she started. "When..."

"When you'll be the wife of the Dux Britanniarum?"

She nodded.

"Of course, I will," he sighed. "It will be hard, I know. But if I can't have you how I want, I'll have you as I can."

They were words that Elen desperately needed to hear and she almost sobbed with relief as she held her palm out for Grandmother to nick a little cut into it. She did the same to Eugenius and as they held hands, mixing their blood, Gula wrapped a sprig of mistletoe around them to symbolise their eternal joining.

As Eugenius squeezed her hand it was quite possibly the happiest moment of Elen's life. All the torment of being confined to her room, not knowing if Father would send someone to interrogate her about the Deisi king, or whip her for visiting the augur, was released like a bird from a cage and her heart soared with joy.

She was also aware that in the last few days she'd been forged fully into her mother's daughter. And she was determined to learn everything that she and Grandmother had to teach her.

About the old ways. And the new.

X

Spring AD 381

Rutupiae, Britannia Prima

In a wild, uncontrolled swing, Kenon smashed the heavy wooden sword into the post, not caring how much the shock of the contact ran up through his arm and shoulder. After the forced twenty mile march, carrying weapons and equipment that weighed almost half as much as he did, and the twenty miles the day before, everything from the neck down ached so much it was impossible to work out what hurt the most.

Barely able to hold the thick wicker shield up off the ground, he struck again. As a focus for his raging anger, the post alternated between being an effigy of his father and the weapons instructor whose chosen purpose in life was to make Kenon's every waking moment an utter misery. Half-starved from reduced rations, back still burning from the most recent flogging, blisters on his feet burst into open sores, he struck the post unmindful of any technique that had been drummed into him over the past awful winter.

He'd failed pathetically again at the hand-to-hand combat lesson, in the instructor's eyes at least, and as though the bruises on his arms and ribs from his opponent's sword weren't enough, his punishment had been demotion back to stabbing at the post. Again.

Some splinters showered across his face and, although he knew it was meaningless, doing some damage felt good. His deepest wish was that it was a fountain of his father's blood and viscera. It was his fault he was trapped in this festering pit. For the thousandth time, he imagined how different his life would be now if the deserters had taken him up on his offer to kill the Governor. Instead of being worked to death in the training yard, he'd be lounging in a huge villa, mosaic floors warmed by the hypocaust, the most attractive slaves attending his every whim.

The heavy training sword was close to slipping out of his sweaty grip and with another hard thrust into the post, it was almost shocked free of his grip. He heard a man shouting, but he seemed far enough away that he didn't pay any attention.

He thought bitterly of the estates, the vast lands he should be the absolute master of. The crops that somehow just grew themselves right out of the ground with nothing but sun, rain and cow shit, and the sheep that made their own babies. It was a magically self-generating profit that he would have to do nothing at all for. It had all been rightfully his, and all had been ripped out of his hands.

All the letters he'd sent to Segontium, each one unanswered only increased the already crushing sense of abandonment. The jarring injustice of it all riled him. All because of the harbourmaster's daughter. He aimed the sword lower and slashed instead of jabbed. How could messing around with that meaningless bitch have cost him so much? He was half dead in half a year and knew he couldn't go on like this, life nothing more than endless marches, parades and drills.

There was only one thing that sustained him through the hunger, the long sleepless nights on duty and the frost forming on the shoulders of his cloak as he stood on watch duty at night, and that was hatred. It was the fire he huddled around that kept him alive. At the pre-dawn musters in the frost and snow, thoughts of revenge were the only thing that gave him the strength to stay standing. If he could survive another day at Rutupiae, he would still be alive to exact his vengeance in the future. One day.

The low early spring sun wasn't strong enough to offer any comforting warmth to his aching bones, and his breath steamed in the cold air, but at least it should be the last of the snow...although, he thought ruefully, the spring wasn't exactly welcome either. The two dozen or so nearly fully trained recruits were almost ready to be sent off across the empire to join the army somewhere, to replace the ranks of those retired or killed on campaign. The decree that no man should stand guard over his own people was hundreds of years old, and the rumour was that he'd go to the Third Legion Augusta in Africa. Plenty of times over the winter Kenon's bones had ached so much from the constant cold that he'd dreamed of the heat of the baking desert, but there was almost no legion in the empire further away from the lands that should be his. Every now and then that thought had been comforting, but trampling down goat-fucking Berbers in the sand would not help him reclaim his birthright. And the army was for twenty five years. Such an unbelievable number filled him with a feeling of dread and helplessness.

He struck the post again, the bitterness in his blood as tangible as the sheen of sweat that covered his body in the cool April air under the layers of heavy armour. Most was for Father, but a part of the hate, he reserved for himself. For nearly six months the only possibility of escaping his suffering that he'd managed to come up with, was joining the others who'd left his escort after Canovium. Deserting. As he drilled, marched and scoffed down weak porridge, he often imagined the freedom they must be enjoying. Waking up whenever they wanted, feasting on fresh meat they'd caught, roasted over an open fire. Whatever the punishment for desertion was, it couldn't be worse than what his life was every day.

His thoughts flitted away from the post as he wondered with a little more attention about how he could join them. There was no way to get from one end of Britannia to the other by himself, even if he somehow managed to steal a horse. If he could find a way of getting it arranged, the last line of the empire in the north was supposed to be a place for the dregs of the army, the most undesirable auxiliaries and those lacking in their training were constantly being threatened with being sent there as a punishment.

The Wall.

Up there, far away from the bastard instructor, he'd wait until no one was looking and simply jump over and run north into the wilderness. Or if he was out on patrol, he could slip silently away into the thick forest and disappear. No Romans would bother to come looking for him, but son of the Governor of Britannia, the barbarians who lived beyond would hail him as their leader on the spot. And he could bring an army of painted men and savages south. Maybe, with all the disgruntled soldiers freezing on the Wall joining him, he could even stir up another Conspiracy to back him.

He wondered about the look of Father's face when he turned up ready to swarm the walls of Segontium.

Banished to the far reaches of Africa, beyond the central sea for a quarter of a century, or a leader of the barbarians. If they were the only options he had to choose from, the decision wouldn't be too hard to make.

Air driven from his chest, head spinning in shock, he found himself sprawling in the freezing mud with no idea what had just happened.

"Where are you?" the instructor spat, a look of absolute vehemence on his face.

In desperate defence, Kenon, still wrapped up in the thought of being hailed as the king of the savages, slashed up at him with the wooden sword.

As unconcerned about such an attack as a father over his toddler's tantrum, the instructor gave Kenon a boot to the back of the leg. Intended more as a warning than to incapacitate, it caught a nerve in the wrong place and snapped into an agonising cramp. As he rolled around in the mud trying to alleviate the pain, the instructor kicked him in the same spot again.

Kenon screamed, but instead of anyone coming to offer him any sympathy or concern, all he heard was laughter.

"Get him up!" the instructor commanded.

Strong hands grabbed his arms and he was hauled to his feet. With the weight of his armour, he wouldn't have made it up by himself. His wooden sword was thrust back at him, but instead of holding it as a soldier, he used it to help him stand.

Bassus was a veteran, with more time served in the army than twice Kenon's lifetime. Weathered and white haired, he wasn't the biggest man in Rutupiae but he had the strength of a horse. One swing of his arm and out of nowhere Kenon would find himself on his back gasping for breath. He'd grown up with beatings from Father, but while the marks from his whip had hurt for days afterwards, it was always for a well explained reason. Bassus beat him close to senseless and punished him purely from a brutal cruelty. Kenon hated his father, but feared Bassus much more. A couple of days before he'd punched him out cold for being too out of breath after a long march. And now Kenon had just tried to hit him with a sword. He didn't imagine Bassus would see much of a distinction in the fact that it was a wooden one, not steel.

"You did not wish me harm, did you?" he spat.

Huddled over like an old beggar, agonising twinges of sharp agony flashing down his leg, Kenon was in no position to defend himself, nor to come up with an acceptable excuse, so just cowered, waiting for the inevitable fist.

Bassus didn't shout at the others to continue their practising, so it was probably going to be a beating they would learn from too.

Kenon looked nervously around. Every man in the whole yard had stopped what they were doing to stare at the spectacle. Even the idiot prefect, the dullard in charge of the whole garrison, was watching,

"Swinging a weapon at your superior. Do you know what the punishment for that is?"

No one had ever been stupid enough to ever do such a thing, so Kenon had no idea. He'd been here long enough to guess it was worse than just a flogging or a kicking, though.

"Which is why I can only assume you were dreaming. Some far away land where you have nothing to do all day but eat grapes and choose which slave girl you'd like to have warm your bed. Am I right?"

"Yes, sir," Kenon stammered. It wasn't actually too far from the truth.

"What?"

"Yes, *sir*!" Kenon shouted.

The instructor ran a hand over the notches on the post. "This was me, was it?"

Without thinking, Kenon called out, "Yes, sir!"

"So, you imagining killing me? That's good. Killing is what you're supposed to do. But actually *trying* to kill me…I could nail you up and leave you for the crows to feast on your eyes for that. You are not in any legion, you don't have any home to go to, so what would be if I simply kicked you out? A beggar? Someone's slave? Although I pity anyone foolish enough to pay a good coin for a useless whelp like you. Huh? What would you be without this?" He swept his arm around to indicate the training yard and the hulking north wall of the fort a short walk away.

Free, Kenon thought. "Nothing, sir," he said.

He didn't even see the slap coming so was surprised to find himself staring up at the pale blue sky with yet some more pain to dedicate to his father.

He was hauled back to his feet again.

"Latrine duty?" the instructor suggested.

"He's already on that," one of the men behind him said helpfully. Kenon could hear the mirth in the man's voice. He had no friends to defend him here.

"Reduced rations?"

"Already on it, sir."

"A flogging then?" the bastard mused.

Kenon's own ambivalence about being bound to a post and lashed, again, surprised him. He wondered if dying felt similar, when a wounded man actually welcomes his enemy freeing him of his suffering.

"Maybe I'll do us both a favour and cut your balls off and you can go and worship Galli as a eunuch!"

Being a priest would be a much easier life than that of a soldier. Spending the days on his knees praying seemed infinitely preferable to marching, but the cult of Galli wouldn't be his first choice. He didn't think there would be any benefit in pointing out that her adherents cut off their own balls.

Bassus had his mouth open, ready to pronounce some sentence to make Kenon's life even worse, but the trumpets started blowing and a pair of horses charged up to them. Kenon held his breath, anticipating another kick or slap, but the instructor seemed more concerned with the riders than the skin on Kenon's back.

"What is it?" the prefect snapped.

"Invasion force docking, sir!" the clearly frightened rider said.

Kenon's wooden sword fell to the floor.

"How many of our men are out on march?" the prefect asked Bassus.

"All of them."

"When are they due back?"

"Any moment."

"Send out riders. Go out and get the garrison back here as fast as they can run!"

Before he knew what was happening, Kenon was being manhandled across the training yard to the fort, feet trailing in the mud, wooden sword forgotten.

"This is not a drill," someone shouted urgently over and over. Horns and whistles were blown from the gate towers and frantic shouts came from inside.

"Still think all this training is a waste of your precious time, do you?" Bassus snapped. "I'll do better than giving you another beating. I'll show you what it's like to be in a fight! Bring him to the fort!" he shouted at those around them, his voice stern with urgency.

Someone splashed some cold water in Kenon's face and suddenly a little more alert, he was curious about what was going on. He wasn't alarmed for his safety, as there was no one in the land who would dare attack a fort with eight metre high walls. But if some locals had a grudge strong enough to pick up arms, instead of cutting them down with swords and spears, he wanted to join them. But then, who would come in ships?

He was already wearing full armour, but exchanging the training sword for a real one felt good. There was something almost magical about a length of sharpened steel at a man's hip. A power that imbued the man who held it with a strength far beyond anything of muscle and bone…even if that man had no real idea how to wield it properly.

The chin strap of his helmet done up tightly, he limped out to the parade ground and lined up unthinkingly in the same position with the others as he'd done a hundred times over the winter and noticed with concern at how quickly the prefect mounted his horse. He was in a real rush, as though his life depended on it, worry written clearly over his face. The five thousand men of the Second Legion were spread out along the coast in the dozen forts that made up the Saxon Shore, so the legion prefect was in charge of those stationed at Rutupiae. Some five hundred men. If Kenon had any authority, he wouldn't leave the idiot in charge of a clutch of chickens.

With most of the men out marching, the sensible thing would be to bolt shut the fort gates and get the ballistas wound up and loaded…and so Kenon wasn't all that surprised when the prefect did the opposite and led the hundred or so left in the fort out of the gate. Once the noise of their clattering armour had died down, only the frightened looking recruits were left. Young men who'd been training for less time than Kenon.

"You! With me!" Bassus snapped, waving a finger at Kenon. Confused, he stepped away from the others and followed the bastard instructor on a fast march out of the fort and down the hill and around to the docks. He was out of breath in just a few moments. It was almost as if the months of training had weakened him rather than made him ready to be a soldier. He scuffed the shield on the ground and stumbled so much that Bassus bumped into him. Kenon would have expected such curses from a savage enemy. Hearing them from someone he was supposed to learn how to fight from was more than a little disconcerting. Hopefully, whatever nonsense they were heading to would occupy Bassus' attention long enough that he would forget about where he threatened to shove the end of his spear.

The chafing on open sores, the weight of the armour pressing on his knees, the back of his leg aching like he'd been kicked by a horse, all of it was forgotten when Kenon saw the army ahead. No ragtag band of locals coming for a skirmish to prove their manhoods; it was a force of a thousand or more, complete with a flank of cavalry and heralds. An invasion force. And Roman! With a flush of panic, he realised it was the garrison of Rutupiae who were the underprepared fighters, and without having completed his training, he knew he shouldn't be anywhere near them.

The colourful curses that spread through the men echoed Kenon's thoughts.

"What are you going to do now?" Bassus sneered.

As he watched soldiers and cavalry file off the ships, his answer didn't come from any weapons or tactics training, but from the men Father sometimes let him listen to. "Stop it," he said, but the sounds of the armour and weapons of hundreds of men back from their drill running towards them drowned him out. They looked tired but alert, and like any soldier worth their salt, they were ready to fight... but were going to do nothing to diffuse the situation.

The prefect called out orders, which were repeated by the decanus' down to the optios, and just as they'd done countless times in training, everyone around him got their spears ready to hurl. All of the exhaustive drilling had been so they could cut down half-naked barbarians by forming a testudo and stabbing them to death from behind the safety of the wall of shields. What they were lining up in front of was another testudo about to be bristling with spears and swords. No one had ever mentioned anything like that, never mind prepared them for it.

Despite being terrified, he could still see an opportunity in such a situation. A little happy that his superiors hadn't completely broken him, he wondered that if the coming fight was vicious enough, maybe he could find a way to escape. If he could grab a riderless horse, he'd be away back north. Hopefully Bassus and the prefect would be far too concerned with losing the battle than chasing him.

"Do anything stupid and *I'll* be the one who cuts you down!" the weapons instructor growled, disavowing Kenon of any thoughts of imminent freedom, so how to just stay alive for the next few moments became his main concern.

Over the shoulders of those in front, he watched the approaching army fan out. A detachment of cavalry rode off to cover the flank, and a thick-necked man in front waved his arm, giving orders. They had obviously arrived unannounced, which was strange, but they were no band of deserters. They looked like men Father dealt with at Deva and Segontium. Roman soldiers, imperial insignia...maybe someone had claimed themselves emperor without anyone at the fort knowing about it and had come to install themselves in the power structure of Britannia?

Whatever their intention was, the detachment of Rutupiae certainly wasn't going to stop them.

The cavalry taking position clearly spooked the prefect as he started shouting his own orders. "Ready spears," he called and all of those around him followed the order. The idiot was about to clash two armies together without even trying to find out what was going on.

"Send a man out to negotiate!" Kenon called out.

Bassus turned around, face aflame with anger. "You're *dead*!" he spat. There was no mockery in his voice. It wasn't a threat either, just a statement.

Unperturbed, Kenon shouted out again. "Send someone to *talk*!"

The opposing fighters had drawn up, all battle ready, waiting to see what the first move would be. Whoever they were, Kenon reasoned that they would listen to the son of the Governor of Britannia, perhaps long enough to stop the fighting. Before he knew what he was doing, Kenon had dropped his spear and was pushing through the men ahead, and once in open ground started to run. Not as fast as he would have liked, as Bassus' treatment had taken its toll, and he jinked to the side just in case someone had ordered weapons thrown.

"I am the son of the Governor!" he shouted out ahead of him. "I am the son of Octavius!"

A few moments before, he would have spat a curse if anyone had reminded him of that. Now it was going to save his life.

XI

Andragathius leaned over the side of his horse and retched again, trying his best not to get anything on his leg. He hoped to make his name, and possibly his fortune, in this land so he could spend his last years in the comfort of a large farm with plenty of servants and the hypocaust system he'd always dreamed of. Spitting bile and strings of thick saliva at the new province wasn't the most auspicious welcome to offer it.

To ease the burning in his throat, he took a sip of water from his leather flask. It was a green and pleasant looking place. The sun was out, which was a lot different from the constant driving rain the men had been moaning about for the last few weeks on their way here. The mystical druids had all been wiped out hundreds of years ago, so there were no wielders of strange magics to be afraid of. It didn't look or feel any different from the part of northern Gaul they'd spent the last weeks travelling through and so he allowed himself to relax a little.

As well-trained for battle as his horse was, it was unaccustomed to the noises and movements its rider was making and its sideways movement felt a little like being back on the damned ship. With another curse, the little water he'd just drank came back up again.

He'd forgotten what he'd threatened to do to the next man who laughed at him, but from spending the whole crossing heaving, his fingers and face were tingling and he felt light-headed, so was in no fit state to mete out any punishment.

"You think you will live?" Magnus asked, if not openly mocking, still amused at his struggles.

If there was one man in the world who he'd allow to find mirth in his situation, it was Magnus. The man he owed everything to. "I will live," he croaked, but was interrupted by his spasming stomach. He spat at the grass and struggled to pull himself up straight again. If he were to die in this strange land of Britannia, at least it would mean he'd never have to set foot on a boat again. Staying for the rest of his days on an unmoving and solid place that didn't bob up and down and sway beneath his feet would be very welcome indeed.

They crested a rise, and the shouts of alarm from the men in front turned the queasy feeling into a burning fear. He wiped the tears out of his eyes again, but didn't believe what he saw. Instead of casting his eyes over a sweeping vista of well-kept farmlands, he saw an army of soldiers hurriedly lining themselves up in battle formation. He rubbed his eyes again, but they were still there. "Gratian?" he asked.

Magnus' face had set into that of a well-trained soldier about to fight for his life and those of his men. Andragathius had seen the strange change many times before, when from one moment to the next, all of the jovial banter is gone and a man is suddenly more of an extension of his sword and pilum than he is of flesh and blood.

He could guess what the new Dux was thinking and he also wouldn't put it past those mewling for power around Gratian to drop Magnus' contingent off, turn the ships around as soon as they disembarked, then attack them as invaders with one of the local legions. It was an elaborate plan, but Britannia was a strange place where strange things happened, and with some careful control of the tongues of any who might survive, the boy emperor could spin the death of Magnus and all those who were loyal to him as just a tragedy.

Andragathius was pleased to see no panic or despair on Magnus' face. Any who faced Magnus' entourage would need to be the empire's best commanders, or to have them heavily outnumbered to have any chance. Magnus, famously, had never lost a single fight in his life, so had well earned his rather arrogant name.

In a clear voice Magnus ordered the lines of infantry to drop their packs and line up. At first they looked like ants outside a disturbed nest, but almost quicker than he could watch, they coalesced into neat, ordered rows. Such a movement never failed to impress him.

"Scouts!" Andragathius called out to his mounted men and pointed up the hill to the side. That's all it took for the whole detachment of cavalry to charge off to cover the flank up the lower hill. A few others tore off around a stand of trees to see how bad the trap they'd ridden straight into was.

As the last of the foot soldiers hastened into their neatly ordered ranks, the cavalry scouts wheeled back. The action told Andragathius that there was no surprise attack planned from the flank. Their opponents hadn't prepared themselves too well.

When Magnus looked his way, he gave a nod to indicate all was clear, but with no further command from the Dux, he looked again at the enemy, trying to judge what advantage they might have and what weaknesses could be taken advantage of. It didn't seem that there was much more than a fort's garrison of men. Three of four cohorts. And for that he could offer no explanation. Maybe Gratian had underestimated how fiercely mounted Batavi could fight. Maybe Britannia was as strange a place as people had said. There were so few men he worried that he was missing something.

A few moments later, there was some disturbance in the ranks ahead and he watched rather bemused as a scrawny boy with a pronounced limp bounded towards them. With no standard with him, he wasn't an emissary or a negotiator, just a terrified looking lad waving his arms as though he'd just disturbed a wasp's nest. It made Andragathius nervous, not because he saw any threat in the boy, but because it was so unusual. He wasn't a man who appreciated surprises.

A nod from Magnus and he nudged his horse forward. The well-trained roan knew exactly what he wanted and trotted off to intercept the boy. Despite it being a contravention of any negotiation process, he drew his sword and made sure the boy could see it.

When they got a little closer together Andragathius could see it was clearly a look of terror on the lad's face. How he threw his hands up defensively as though he was protecting himself from a hail of arrows that Andragathius couldn't see was so odd the fine hairs on the back of his neck rose in warning.

He angled his horse a little to the left so if the lad was going to do something stupid, one flick of Andragathius' arm he'd have a clear swing at him.

"Governor Octavius…" the boy shouted and suddenly Andragathius was listening. He and Magnus had spent most of the winter learning all they could about the men who held power and influence in Britannia, and the one at the top of the list had been Octavius.

"I am the son of Octavius, Governor of Britannia," he wailed.

Andragathius had no idea why a boy of such standing would be crying like a slave trying to run away from a whipping, but it didn't make him any less nervous. "If that is so, what, by the Lord above, are you doing running between two armies?" he called out.

"The prefect is a fool. He thinks you are invaders. You need to stand down so no one gets killed."

"See that man on the horse at the front of the line? That's the new Dux Britanniarum," Andragathius said.

The boy looked so relieved it seemed he was about to swoon. "If I am not who I say I am, you can take that sword and cut my head off. I beg you for protection. If you force me to return, they will kill me. Protect me and I will see to it that you are rewarded!"

After breaking formation and running to the enemy, any man would need protecting, Governor's son or not and he certainly spoke like one used to authority making bargains with a man who clearly held a high rank. Andragathius had known enough of them in his time to recognise an entitled sense of superiority when he saw it. "If you take me for a fool, or are setting up some trick, I'll do much worse than cut your head off." From the boy's reaction, he could tell the fear was genuine. He wouldn't envy him if he was about to lie to

Magnus about his name, so he let him run off, giving the signal to Magnus that there was no threat.

Making a show of it, Andragathius slid his sword back into the scabbard and rode towards the opposing line with his hands outstretched, indicating that he came in peace. At last, someone with some authority rode out, a pair of blood-red standards topped by golden disks and the imperial eagle held up by bearers behind him. The man began to speak, but the high-pitched indignant voice annoyed Andragathius, so he held up his hand to cut him off. He'd held significant power over his own Batavian cavalry unit for many years, but the man in front was a true-blooded Roman, someone with hopes of a high office one day. As Magister Equitum, Andragathius now far outranked the little shit, by more degrees than he could work out, and decided to enjoy his new position. "Are you the prefect of Rutupiae?"

"I am," he replied, proud but outraged.

"Get off your horse and tell your men to stand down," Magnus said calmly.

The prefect, pretty obviously the one the boy had called an idiot, looked as though he was about to scream. "There are protocols. You don't just ride through the land unannounced..."

"Aye, we do." He cocked his thumb over his shoulder and said, "That is the new Dux Britanniarum. You are about to *walk* over to him and you will tell him, very politely, how sorry you are for this misunderstanding. And if his mood is anywhere near as sour as mine is right now, I would advise that you also beg his forgiveness."

The excitement had calmed him, but his stomach chose that moment to erupt in a belch as loud as Vesuvius.

The prefect didn't seem to take offence. "And what about the boy?" he asked.

Andragathius sighed. The lad had just shown up his superiors in front of the entire garrison, so was right to fear for his life rather than just a beating. He'd averted an embarrassing fight though, and probably saved a few lives, so was maybe due some reward instead of having his head mounted on a spike. Perhaps being allowed to live would be good enough. "He is under my protection."

"You have no right…"

"Have you dismounted yet?" The idiot was about to speak again. Andragathius guessed it would be something about rank and protocols, so preempted him. "I am the Master Equine of Britannia, and *you* are in charge of a little fort in the ass end of nowhere, who can't tell his commander from a raider. Now get off your horse, or I'll have you demoted so far that the lad will be giving *you* orders!"

The look of fire from the prefect as he slipped out of his saddle made Andragathius chuckle. Some prickish administrator's prickish son who knew exactly what he could do with the ranks of men below him, but with Magnus' arrival wasn't too sure about the degree of his authority. Shoulders slumped, he began walking towards Magnus, but Andragathius decided a show of authority would do well to dispel the tension. He clicked his fingers and held his hand out for the man's reins. Handing them over wasn't just a gesture of obedience, it was one of surrender.

He'd only been in Britannia for a few moments and had already made a mortal enemy. As he rode on towards the nervous looking men arranged in formation before him, he realised he hadn't even asked the man's name. It didn't matter.

Before he got to the line of shields of the opposing soldiers, he wiped some sick out of his beard. It was important to look the part. "That man you see on the big horse over there is the Dux Britanniarum," he shouted. "I've never set foot on your island before, and maybe you do things differently here, but on the mainland raising swords and shields is not how we greet our commanders."

A lone rider in front of a whole garrison of men who still weren't entirely sure if he was a superior officer or an enemy, watched with amusement as confusion rippled through them. Some shields were lowered as a few were still confused about whether they should take commands from the newcomer or their centurions. He laughed, but the movement reminded his body that it hadn't quite recovered from the crossing yet. The belch would have been impressive in the roughest inn. Before five hundred soldiers who didn't know if they were about to cut him down or obey his orders, it worked very well as a gesture of disdain.

"About turn. March!" he yelled and laughed again as less than half the men moved.

Eventually, the calls of the centurions were repeated by the optios and the whole garrison marched back into the fort, filing through the gate in the impressively high flint and mortar walls. Andragathius assumed he'd be riding to the central principia to further remonstrate with the prefect, but was a little confused at the open space where it should have been. Every fort across the empire was built on a strictly uniform design, so it was strange to see an open space in the middle. He rode to the odd cross shape of stones on the ground that looked like they'd been the foundation for something and waited for Magnus.

"It used to be a huge archway," the Dux said as he rode unhurriedly in. "A rival to the triumph in Rome, apparently. They called it the Gateway to Britannia."

"What happened to it?"

"I heard that the fort walls weren't always so high."

Pulling important monuments down to reinforce the defences was something Andragathius hadn't heard of before. "Things have changed," he mused.

Magnus nodded, and with a rueful smile, added, "And we'll be changing them even more!"

XII

Durovernum Cantiacorum, Britannia Prima

Magnus reclined on his side on the couch at the back of the inn. After the day's ride from Rutupiae he was famished and scoffed down the stew. As he wiped the last of it up with a thick piece of bread, he was struck by the smooth, light-brown plate it was served on. Despite how unbelievably vast the empire was, it seemed incredible that so many things were the same from one end of it to the other, no matter if you were in Mauretania or Anatolia. The villa he'd grown up on in Hispania had been full of the very same type of pottery, he'd supped wine from a similar cup while hunting down Firmus in the deserts of Africa, and had toasted the death of an Alemanni chieftain from another on the banks of the Rhine. It was an odd thought that no ordinary man tied to his land, his employer, or his master, could possibly understand the real scale of the empire he was a citizen, or slave, of. It was hard enough for Magnus to contemplate, and he'd spent most of his life travelling and fighting across it.

Here he was, back at the northern edge of the empire, another province he'd fought, commanded and killed in...and was possibly only a few steps away from ruling it all. Those steps would be perilous though, as at one slight mistake, one slight miscalculation, then his death awaited. As did the empire's final destruction if he managed to get as far as facing Gratian's army with his and it went wrong. His head staying on his shoulders was a great concern, but he couldn't allow any situation where he'd be remembered in history as the man who brought the final collapse to the greatest empire the world had ever seen.

The path to the purple was open to him though, as clearly as following the Appian Way. All his lifetime of experience of command

and being commanded told him that in his hands the empire would be much better off than it was in Gratian's. Apart from the inevitable trauma of the transition, there was no disadvantage he could think of with him elevated to the western equal to Theo. The cousins in power together in the triumvirate could only be a good thing…and surely Valentinian and Justina wouldn't last too long.

The previous night the men had camped outside the fort of Rutupiae. Coming a little too close to a pitched battle for comfort, he'd ordered his whole entourage to be ready to muster and therefore they'd had to stay strictly sober. Maybe he'd been overcautious, but meeting an army as soon as he'd got off the ship had deeply unnerved him and so he'd ordered full guard duty, and for everyone to sleep in in their armour with weapons at hand. Not many had got a good sleep. But tonight, on the outskirts of Durovernum Cantiacorum, twelve miles away, with no hostile army blocking their way, those inside the inn were in a jovial mood and the wine was flowing freely. Magnus grinned to himself at the thought that probably none of the men in his inner circle had ever taken up a position in a new province that they didn't have to conquer first.

The well-fed innkeeper dripped with sweat as he directed the handing out of food. Quite rightly, he'd secreted away the young girls who'd welcomed them in, but Magnus didn't think the boys pouring out posca and surreptitiously trying to lay fresh straw a handful at a time hoping no one noticed, would be too safe with some of the men. A few were Batavi, so perhaps neither would the horses.

Every now and then a glance was cast Magnus' way and smile frozen, the man's thoughts flashed across his eyes, like the mysterious finger language of the Berbers. It was a language Magnus couldn't read though. He was a soldier, brought up in the army where, if ever he didn't like someone, a punch in the face and that would be that. Soldiers could bicker among themselves, but if an infantryman insulted an optio, the lowest man of the five thousand against the second lowest, then may God have mercy on the skin of his back.

Suddenly he found himself nostalgic for the harshly enforced stratification of rank of the army.

He took a mouthful of wine, watered down and a little sour, and cast a look around the room looking for someone he trusted. The thirty or so inside were the top officers of his new administration. All commanded either men or coffers. Many of the younger ones were dependent on him for the careers they hoped to advance, but while a logical minded, and naive, man might expect that helping with a successful governance would be in their best interests, Magnus was sure he was not surrounded by such men. Far from supporting him at every turn, he expected most would be seeking to use him every way they could to aid their own rise. He couldn't really judge them too harshly for that though. There weren't too many among them he wouldn't sacrifice if it would get him any closer to the purple. He'd probably climb over their dead bodies without a second thought. Such had always been the way of ambitious men with the right blood.

Apart from Andragathius. The Batavi was as close to his heart as even Marcellinus. They'd fought together and he'd never been let down by the loyal horseman, so Magnus could sleep easy knowing the big, hairy bastard was on guard. While most men were in animated conversation, downing wine in a carefree manner, no one deigned to speak a word to the Master of Horse. Standing a head above most of them, and with an unfashionably long and thick beard, perhaps he was too close to the wild men beyond the borders for them to be comfortable talking with. Too beneath them, perhaps?

And yet he was by far the best amongst them.

Magnus had chosen a good few of his entourage, with Gratian's consent, men who'd served under him over the years, over the empire, but a few too many had been foistered onto his entourage by the emperor's inner circle for him to be happy. Mixed with those who might prove to be worth their weight in gold would be ones tasked to make sure that every success he had in the province was attributed solely to Gratian. And if he was to deviate too much from his strict remit, or was suspected of working too much in his own interests, one would be ready to find a way to slip a knife between his ribs. It was a strange sensation to be sitting in a room full of men, knowing one, or more, had orders that if certain criteria were met, he would be dead.

He looked through them again, trying to note who was talking to who, which ones seemed the most facetious and therefore least trustworthy and who might be watching his habits and movements to deduce what would be the best way to kill him, but quickly gave it up as a hopeless task. He knew that men gifted with both power and the intelligence to go with it, as rare as they were, must have ways of sorting the grain from the chaff, of knowing which men could be set on guard and which had to be guarded against. He imagined that the suspicion and distrust that flared up from every sour grin, or look in the eye that didn't quite match the other gestures he was making, could easily drive a soft man mad.

Developing the complicated and confusing symbiotic relationships with such self-centred bastards would be key to his success. If he wasn't just going to survive, but prosper in his new posting, he was going to have to very quickly master the insidious intricacies of having to second guess every man's meanings and motives. And not for the first time, he lamented that there was no one to ask for advice, no one to teach him how to navigate the treacherous way to the purple. Then he was thinking of Theodosius again; the one man who could help him now. His fist clenched tight around his cup at the thought of what the cowardly bastards had done to him.

As his knuckles turned white and his teeth ground, he caught the furtive eye of the scrawny lad who'd been brave, or dumb, enough to run from his assembled ranks to Magnus' side across the field that had been close to becoming a battleground.

For averting a fight that had threatened Magnus' tenure before it had even begun, the boy had more than earned Magnus's favour, so when he'd begged to be taken north, Magnus couldn't refuse.

Rescuing the governor's son was at least something slightly positive to come out of the sorry situation. The gratitude of a man with such overbearing and long-embedded power in the land was definitely nothing to scoff at.

A little reluctantly, Magnus waved him over, but was immediately disappointed at how, with a pathetic, pleading expression, Kenon leapt up like a starving puppy thrown a bone. He skipped to the side of the couch and dropped to his knees in utter supplication, like a man lost at sea grasping at a plank of driftwood. What a lad like this had been doing anywhere near real soldiers, Magnus had no idea.

"Thank you, sir. Thank you!" he cried. "Bringing me with you...you've saved my life!"

Running out through the formation was so outrageously insubordinate his commander would have had every right to beat him to death in front of the other men as a lesson, so maybe he wasn't exaggerating. For running from his ranks and interfering in the life and death affairs of his superiors, Magnus wouldn't have hesitated to do the same thing to a man. Although, seeing who the boy's father was, perhaps that was not the fate which would have awaited him.

Besides, although he would curse anyone for saying it out loud, Magnus had a soft spot for anyone without a father.

"So tell me about this father of yours. Octavius. Is he a good man?"

Magnus noticed how at the mention of the name, the boy's relief at being allowed to approach soured. "His men love him."

Magnus understood the unspoken meaning. "But why don't you?"

Deep with melancholy, Kenon sighed. "He cast me away."

Magnus couldn't imagine what would drive a man to disavow his flesh and blood. Children might be impudent sometimes, but in them, especially a son, his entire legacy was invested. "Yesterday, his name saved your life. What did you do to make him choose to do such a thing?"

"Nothing!"

"Don't lie to me," Magnus said and almost laughed at how the boy's face paled, even at such a slight raising of his voice. To be so afraid of authority, he must have had a really hard time at Rutupiae.

"I messed around with the harbourmaster's girl."

Magnus gave him a stare hard enough to make the boy feel the need to protest his innocence again. "I don't think I will like a man who chooses politics over his children. Does he have other sons?"

"No. Just a daughter."

Jokingly, Magnus asked, "Is she fair?"

"I don't think so. But others do."

Without knowing why he asked, without expecting any answer, he said, "This sister of yours, does she have green eyes?"

"Erm, grey-green, I would say."

It was as though he heard the horn blown for battle and he sat up straight. "Segontium? It's near the mountains, and a river?"

"Yes."

It was stupid to ask, and if anyone overheard it would be a question ridiculous enough for men to question his sanity. But the urge to make something unreal real, to take something out of his dream and put on a map, a place he could ride to...or to prove to himself once and for all he was a complete fool, he asked, "Does your father play ludus?"

How the boy laughed stabbed at Magnus' heart. "He's obsessed with the bloody thing. He makes the counters for it himself. Sits in his chair for hours whittling them away."

The familiar sinking feeling assailed him more powerfully than it had ever done and the nightmare crept back to life around him, like impossibly fast growing vines wrapping around his arms and legs, working themselves into his mouth and down his throat, choking him. Suddenly the air in the inn was far too hot and cloying.

For some reason the boy was mocking him in the worst possible way and the anger surged like a pot over boiling and hissing on the fire. He stood up, grabbed the boy's tunic and pressed him up against the wall as though he was a child's toy, his feet dangling helplessly in the air. "Do you jest with me, boy?" he spat close to his face.

"No!" he wailed.

"Swear it on your father's life!"

"I'll swear it on my *own*!"

Magnus let him go and Kenon, close to pissing himself with terror, slumped to the floor. Magnus' head went so light, he almost joined him. All the mad thoughts crashed back about how eerily similar to his dream the journey from Rome to Britannia had been. About the rivers and mountains, how, embarking on the large vessels for the crossing from Gaul, he'd thought of the whale bone walkway and had half expected the gangplank to raise itself behind him. As sweat beaded on his forehead and something in his bowels knotted tightly, he was aware that such musings must be the fevered thoughts of a very ill man. Perhaps even one close to death.

The dozens of excited voices in the room seemed far too loud and every muscle in his body trembled as though he was in a wagon speeding down a rocky road. "How many days ride to Segontium?" he asked.

Kenon stared up at him, eyes wide, mouth moving but no words came out. Magnus wanted an answer and he didn't care what anyone who could see thought of him.

From the kick, Kenon screamed like a beaten child, a cry that almost sounded otherworldly, and suddenly the room was deathly quiet as everyone turned to watch what was going on. In a measured, but no less threatening tone, he asked again "How many days?"

"T... Twelve!"

Magnus tried to work out the distance in his head. If they pushed the horses from dawn to dusk, changing them at every mancio, he and a handful of Andragathius' best riders could get to Segontium in four, maybe even three days.

Andragathius was at the far side of the inn, cup paused halfway to his lips. "First light," Magnus called out to him. "Four men with us. And a horse for the boy."

Without understanding, but without questioning, the big man nodded his head.

Decision made, order given, the silence began to drag on and the pressure it caused in Magnus' head quickly became unbearable. On uncertain legs he headed to the door, aware of all the eyes boring into him as men tried to discern the reason for such a drastic and unexpected change of plan.

The air outside was cooler than a winter evening in Hispania, and it helped a little to clear his mind. The courtyard was full of men and although none had heard what he'd just announced, when they realised the Dux, the man on whom their immediate futures depended, was among them, they either cowered out of the way or stopped what they were doing to stand to attention.

Out of the gates, the road was crowded with people, each one here in a strange land to serve Magnus.

The air was thick with the smoke from dozens of small cooking fires for those unable to be accommodated inside. Over a thousand had crossed with his on the flotilla, all ostensibly to serve or support him in one capacity or another, to make his posting as Dux Britanniarum as successful as it could be. A thousand he could direct at will to almost anything he wanted. A thousand he could use in one way or another to get him that much closer to standing over Gratian's dead body. And tomorrow he would leave them all behind. Almost every moment of every day over the winter he'd spent thinking about how he could wrest power from the emperor and those around him. He'd lain awake most nights worrying about it, weighing the direst risks against the ultimate reward, but all of a sudden none of it seemed important any more. Only a girl in a dream he'd had a few months before.

He realised his hand was tight around the pommel of his sword, but he had no one to swing it at...only the madness swirling around in his own head.

The bed in the inn's best room could have been the most comfortable in the whole of Britannia, but Magnus didn't sleep for a moment. Lying there watching the shadows from the little lamp dance over the undersides of the roofing beams, his mind raced with the implications of what he'd decided. Part of him screamed at the stupidity of it, but in the perfect stillness before dawn he got dressed, pulled the three layers of armour on and fixed his gladius to his hip and went outside. His horse had been prepared, so all he had to do was strap a bag to the saddle and he was ready.

He'd explain to those who needed a reason that he had to meet with the governor urgently. Octavius was stationed in Segontium, so if Gratian got a report about Magnus' strange behaviour, the story was at least plausible.

The stable hand placed the stool next to his horse but before he mounted he looked at how the smoke from the cooking fires lingered in the trees. It was his last chance to change his mind. In a well practised movement, he sprang off the stool into the saddle ready to ride straight to Segontium.

Andragathius nudged his horse over and making sure no one was close enough to overhear, he asked, "What is this about?"

Magnus was keenly aware of how his Master of Horse asked as a friend not as a subordinate to superior, and welcomed it. "There is something I have to do first. I will do my duties as Dux afterwards, but I can't before."

Andragathius shrugged his wide shoulders.

Magnus was keenly grateful for the Batavi's friendship and loyalty, but men like them didn't speak of such things and so he just nodded.

As Marcellinus, now in charge of the welfare of the entourage, and more importantly, the bullion wagon with the wages for three legions, waved him off, Magnus noted the look of sorrow on his brother's face. He knew why. Making their plans over the long winter months, slaves kept under the strictest segregation and frequently exchanged, Magnus' strange spells had completely stopped, apart from some particularly vivid dreams. But they weren't like the unbelievably realistic apparitions he'd had in Rome. Now his brother was watching him slip away again. It must be like seeing a friend drown, hand up above the waves one last time before disappearing forever.

Despite their destination not being a real place, they pushed the horses as hard as they could along the paved roads, dodging slow going oxen-pulled wagons and poor travellers on foot. Every twelve miles they rode their panting horses into a mancio and every twelve miles Magnus had to explain, shout, then threaten the horse master to exchange six fresh mounts for their half-dead ones.

Late that evening, they rode across the wooden bridge to Londonium, the longest one Magnus had ever seen. In another time he might have looked upon it with wonder, but he was too far wrapped up in his thoughts to pay anything but the most cursory attention.

Once they were settled in as guests of the confused Praetor of Londinium, a crowd of curious officials gathered around, all with varying degrees of complaints and grievances they wanted to burden Magnus with. Octavius was apparently too busy with his estates on the other side of the province to worry about them. It would have been a perfect opportunity to impress some of the most important men of Britannia with his diligence and consideration. Instead, by dismissing every one of them in a single gesture, he didn't just disappoint them all, he made them feel insignificant. The worst insult came from instructing his Batavi guards to use force to keep men from pounding on his door demanding an audience. Treating them as annoying commoners was the most efficient and effective way of getting them to hate him before he'd even spoken a word to them. In a few days, when the entourage pulled in, there would be many among them to sympathise with the aggrieved officials, so he knew that from the very first days in Britannia his reputation would be marred. All for a girl in a dream.

That night again, sleep refused to come and instead of dreams, he imagined what he'd do to the pathetic whelp of Kenon if he was to find out the boy had an ulterior motive for making him rush like a madman to Segontium.

The next day the six of them rode on into the heart of Britannia in silence. The first time he opened his mouth was in the evening when he had to threaten the mansio owner to go and find two more suitable horses for the two half-lame ones he wanted to foist on them for the next twelve miles.

The road was dead straight and every rolling hill, wheat field and stand of trees looked much the same as the next, and so after a few days of changing horses, Magnus had the impression they weren't moving at all, just stuck in the same horrible dream where he had left his army far behind, but also couldn't reach the girl.

That night he realised part of the reason he couldn't sleep was because he was afraid to. All of the men he'd killed by his own sword, the ones he'd pulled apart under interrogation in order to extract information, the row of Berber captives stubbornly loyal to Firmas he'd lopped the heads off, none of them had ever come back to him when he closed his eyes. Every now and then he thought about their bloodied and brutalised bodies, but none had ever come to stand before him in his dreams to haunt him. That only a girl he'd never met could do that was another terror.

As the birds began to announce the coming dawn, he almost sobbed at what his madness was costing him. How men talked of Nero and Caligula, spitting at the mention of their cursed names, dragged him down into a deep misery. Two days of riding face first into the unrelenting rain didn't help with that. Yet still he rode on.

Andragathius had to stick a leg out and kick him to get his attention. The sun was out, but he was still uncomfortably drenched from the most recent heavy shower. The sun would have to be as hot as the one of Hispania in August to dry him out properly.

"We're being followed."

At the thought of ambush, a horde of Alemanni about to surround them, his sword was out in his hand, reflecting in the sun, before he even realised he'd drawn it.

"Just one man," Andragathius said, trying to calm him.

A spy was more of an annoyance than a threat and he slid his sword home. Someone passing messages back from each mansio to Gratian's agents was easy to understand and they'd done nothing to deviate from their tale that they were rushing to have an audience with the governor. How someone had managed to keep up with them when half the mancios hadn't had enough fresh horses was quite impressive.

It wouldn't be hard to find out who he was and who he worked for though. And the distraction would actually be a welcome way of having his mind on something else for a few moments.

At the next mansio Magnus pressed two boys to don the armour of two of the Batavi and rode off while Andragathius' men stayed behind to catch the spy. When Magnus was a few miles up the road, they led him to Magnus with hands bound behind his back.

"Who are you and who do you work for?" Magnus asked as the pair of stable boys tore back off to their mansio.

There was a flash of insolence in the man's eyes, but it was Kenon who answered. "He is here for me."

"Is this true?" Magnus asked the man.

He gave the boy a look of disappointment and shrugged.

"He works for my grandmother and was charged to protect me, but that was months ago. And he left me in that place...while they..."

"To protect your *life*," the man interrupted. "And it seems to me you are still living."

Magnus noticed the dignified and confident way he held himself, despite sitting with his hands bound behind him.

"Who is your grandmother?" Magnus asked Kenon.

"I don't know," Kenon said. As the others scoffed, he must have realised how stupid that sounded and he blushed. Magnus didn't see it as a joke though and was instantly alert. He might have been a novice at the subtleties of having to work with and appease his enemies, but he was sharp enough not to miss the implication of an old woman who had power enough to have a man follow him from halfway across Britannia and be a secret to her own grandson. He was equally sure the man wouldn't easily divulge all he knew. "We ride to Segontium. Is this where we will find this woman?"

"It is," the man said reluctantly.

How the spy smiled as he shook his head, told Magnus she was someone he needed to talk to. Politely or otherwise.

He wondered if she had power enough to reach into a man's dreams. It was something he burned to know, but didn't dare ask in front of the men. "Untie him. He rides with us," Magnus commanded.

As Andragathius patted his clothing for concealed weapons, the man said, "I know you Magnus Maximus. I was Areani for the Sixth in Eboracum when you were here last."

"Areani? You helped the conspiracy?"

"Many did," he said as he rubbed his wrists where the rope had cut into them. "But I was loyal to Rome, and if it's worth anything, I'm sorry about what they did to Theodosius. He was a good general, and a good man."

The last time Magnus had been in Britannia, rounding up roving bands of barbarians and defectors, the many different units sweeping up valleys would meet, camp, eat and share stories together, then head off in their separate directions the following dawn. He couldn't know if they'd ever shared a campfire, but with those words Magnus wondered if he had a new ally. Maybe even someone he could trust?

Andragathius called out for them to push the tired horses, but by the next time they let them slow down to catch their breath, Magnus had decided to ask the Areani another question. "What do you know of this woman's granddaughter?"

The Areani shrugged, doing well, but not perfectly, to hide his surprise at such a question. "Nothing. Daughter of the Governor and the daughter of a local chieftain. She's just a girl. Younger than the lad. I know no more than that, but if the boy is truly banished, then her husband will be a very wealthy man."

Magnus didn't care what lands she stood to inherit. He wanted to know if it was possible for this mysterious woman to cast spells half way across the empire. He mused that it was much easier to get a man to talk when he was bound next to a glowing brazier watching the irons heat up, but found that he didn't distrust the man. At least not as much as some in his entourage.

At Viriconium Cornoviorum Magnus watched the sun set behind the brooding mountains of Britannia Secunda, the ones they were about to ride into.

At the auxiliary fort of Canovium, one of the most isolated outposts Magnus had ever been to, there was a little commotion when Kenon was recognised. So close to Segontium, it would have been a good idea to learn more about the obviously strained relationship between the boy and his father. But before he could form the question, he realised that he wasn't that bothered. All he cared about was the lad's sister...and the Grandmother who had kept herself secret all of his life.

They were close now. Up a steep road, up into proper mountains where the cold wind whipped at his clothes and hair, constantly threatening rain Magnus kept an eye out for a stream, one like the one he followed in his dreams with the expectation that he would soon have a face to put to his fears. The woman would have some serious questions to answer. And it was her he was thinking about when Andragathius called out a warning of riders approaching.

A few miles out from Segontium and the nervous scouts pulled their horses up, demanding to know names and purposes. It didn't escape Magnus' notice that the Areani was known to the riders and as they tore off to put the fort on alert his heart was racing. He was more nervous than watching a horde of Berbers or Alemanni charge towards him, but the fort, when he first laid eyes on it, seemed a real disappointment. Square, white-washed walls, red banners draped over the gates, it looked just the same as any other in the empire. The smoke from dozens of little cooking fires in the barracks was the same as he'd smelled a thousand times before, the stench from the vicus just as bad as any he'd waded through a hundred times before.

A pair of guards stood stoically on picket duty, but walking out of the gates to greet them was a white haired man. Magnus' bowels turned to water and his voice sounded higher pitched than the boy's as he called out, "Salva."

He wanted to present himself as a strong man, a ruler to be respected and feared but after six days of hard riding, he could barely walk, and with strained tendons and a few blisters in uncomfortable places, he limped from his horse like a beggar alongside the governor. The familiar sounds and smells of hundreds of tough but bored men forced together into a confined space assailed him. In a way, it was calming, something familiar, grounding, *real*. He felt a desperate need for a latrine, and despite it being cold and gusty, he broke out into a sweat.

A slave rather than a soldier opened the principia doors. As he stepped into the relative calmness inside, more slaves made themselves known, should they want anything, and in the stillness Magnus caught a whiff of himself after the day of galloping over the mountains and wished he'd taken the time to go to the bathhouse first instead of entering the governor's home stinking of the road.

Octavius' slave offered him a damp cloth to wipe his hands and face and another a glass of wine, which he sniffed and wetted his lips with suspiciously. It didn't smell strange.

But then he noticed the black and white squares of the ludus board. Of course it had to be there, set out ready to play. Octavius was asking him something but Magnus could see nothing but that bloody board. He limped over to it, picked up a counter and looked at the marks on it made by the careful and skilled cuts of the craftsman's knife. "You..." he started, but nothing else would come out.

And there she was.

It wasn't like the dream. No whalebone gangplanks raising themselves, no vividly coloured banners fluttering from towers. His heart pounded and his rolling stomach told him he was in the world of flesh and men. Everything was perfectly real. But there *she* was, and she was real. The counter fell out of his useless hand, bounced off his boot and rolled to her feet. She was pretty, but not mind-numbingly beautiful as he'd dreamed. Not a match for some of the girls in Rome's pleasure houses, but before her, he still felt like an absolute brute.

It was far from love in his heart. As she stood back up, counter held in a delicate hand, he looked at her with a total gut-wrenching fear.

She placed the counter back on his open palm and felt the delicate touch of her fingertips. It was like being struck by lightning.

His mind reeled as he tried to work out what was real and how he could find himself fighting not to throw up in a dream.

XIII

Segontium, Britannia Secunda

The messenger was still huffing from his sprint from the main gates as Father dismissed him. Although Elen hadn't heard what he'd run so quickly to announce, from the way Mother urgently ushered her away, she knew something was seriously amiss.

"He comes quickly," she mused, clearly agitated.

"Who does?" Elen asked.

"Quick. Too quick. But I suppose at least it means the plan has worked. Maybe too well!"

Over the winter, Elen had spent a lot of time in Mother's and Grandmother's company, more often than not discussing things she scarcely dared believe. They'd always been serious, sometimes concerned, but in all those weeks of her new life, she'd never seen either of them worried. How Gula's complexion had paled made Elen very nervous.

"What plan? Who is coming?" she demanded as Mother led her into her room at the back of the building.

"Your husband."

"Eugenius?" she asked, feeling her belly sink with panic.

"No. Your *other* husband."

The difference from one moment to the next was like when Kenon had dared her to

jump from a bridge and she'd hit the freezing waters below. "When?" she heard herself ask. "How many days do we have to prepare?" And to say goodbye to Eugenius after their glorious, but bittersweet, winter together.

Gula knelt at the side of her bed and opened a large wooden chest.

"Days? We have no days."

"What do you mean? I thought you said we'd have a week's warning at least before he arrived?"

"I thought so too. Maybe the magic was too powerful." She laughed, but it sounded pained as she fumbled frantically at the bottom of the chest.

"*When?*" Elen asked.

"*Now!* He's here! He will arrive within the hour," Gula said

Drugging a powerful man in Rome and getting his slaves to whisper a story about a green-eyed girl in a far away fort had seemed so fanciful she was never convinced it would come to pass. Magnus magicking himself to Segontium had just turned the distant dream into a horrible reality. Despite long months listening to Grandmother, she knew she was nowhere near ready to face him, and even worse, everything she had with Eugenius was suddenly over. She felt herself flail helplessly around in the dark river, not knowing which way was up. Drowning.

Gula held a small pouch triumphantly. Pressing it into Elen's hand, she said, "Go and pour this in your father's wine. Quickly."

"What is it?"

"Something to make him a little slow. Confused."

"Why would you want to do that?"

Gula rolled her eyes impatiently. "How many times have we discussed this? *You* have to lead the conversation with this Magnus, not your father."

Elen started to say something, but Gula cut her off with her hand held up between them. "This is it. This is what we have been preparing for. The stage is set, now it's time for you to go out and dance." She ushered her out. "Now *go*! Oh, and you must arrange a ludus set. Put it somewhere in plain sight. That's important!" Then she scuttled off to do something else.

Although Mother had spoken kindly so Elen wouldn't fret too much, she knew how much depended on them getting what they needed from the new Dux. But a few months of keeping her liaisons with Eugenius secret and practising how to hold her hand to receive little scrunched up messages from people on the street had done woefully little to prepare her for what was coming.

Father was hurrying with his formal clothes and as a slave helped him with the folds of his toga he grumbled about the lack of protocol the new Dux had for turning up unannounced. As she tipped the powder into his wine glass, she almost burst out laughing at the thought of how much protocol was about to be broken. She made some arrangements to the folds of the cloth over his shoulder. Unnecessary, but it gave the impression of a diligent daughter. "Here," she said, offering him the wine. He took a quick sip but cursed at the strange taste.

"It's just been sitting a while," she said, urging him to finish it. "Best to have a fortified heart to deal with a man who cares so little about the right way of doing things."

As he downed the rest of it, her first task was complete. The easiest one.

Once Father had left and the praetorium gates had thudded shut behind him, a heavy silence settled on the courtyard. Her fingers were shaking so much it took ages to set the black and white counters in their opening positions on the ludus board. Finally done, she had nothing to do apart from pace along the rows of ornamental juniper bushes, imagining what fates and futures were about to clash and be entwined in the next few moments. It all seemed too much and was happening far too quickly.

After a while, Gula re-emerged and looked a little calmer. "Grandmother is informed," she nodded. When she noticed Elen's damp eyes, she wiped the tears away. "Don't worry. If it doesn't work, it won't be the end of the world. We'll make a new plan with another man, so don't cause your heart to stop beating with fright."

The tears weren't from her fear though, but from not having a chance to say any goodbye to Eugenius.

The lock of the large doors being pulled back was like a ballista bolt to the heart and both of them gasped out loud.

"You'll do fine," Gula said as she hurried off to her room like a good wife.

Elen cowered behind a colonnade, holding onto it in case her trembling legs gave way. The ludus board was half in the light and half in the shade. She supposed Grandmother would have something to say about the meaningfulness of that, but it was lost on her.

Father came in, but it was the hulking brute of the man who strode beside him that her attention was drawn to. He was grubby and although his scaled armour gleamed in the light it needed a good polishing and his crimson cloak wasn't on straight, but the feeling he created in her was that of prey being stalked by a wild animal. As she tried to control her breathing, she wondered if that actually wasn't too far from the truth.

With her special herbs and contacts, Grandmother had made him dream of a ludus maker and while instructing her on her actions and behaviour for this moment, she'd said he'd be surprised to see the board. When he laid his eyes on it, just as she'd said, she saw one of the most powerful men in the empire reduced to a lost little boy, close to tears. All the tumultuous doubts she'd had about the things Grandmother had taught her over the last few months all burned away with the surety she now felt. Every secret Grandmother had told her, everything that had seemed too far-fetched and fanciful to believe, it was all happening right in front of her, and not only was such power all real…it could be *hers*.

He picked a ludus counter up, mesmerised and gasped as it fell out of his trembling hand and rolled right to her feet. Fate itself seemed to be leading her by the hand. On that wave of fortune, she stepped out of the shadow, knelt gracefully down to sweep it up, and offered it back to him.

With the way he looked at her, as dumb as though he'd been struck in the head with a spear shaft, she now believed every word Grandmother had said about being able to mould him to her wishes; as easy as pressing soft clay in her fingers.

His face was hard, square, with a strong jaw, but his sky blue eyes had something in them that she wasn't expecting. Helplessness. Like a little boy who'd got lost.

She couldn't believe she'd been so afraid of this for so long. "Have you travelled far?" she asked, tilting her head slightly in a seductive way that Eugenius had taught her. She wondered if there was any kindness in him, whether one day they'd actually come to like each other. Be friends.

"Across the empire," Magnus sighed. If she didn't know any better, she'd have thought it was him who'd drunk the laced wine.

Father began to say something, but seemed to forget what it was before he'd finished the sentence. The powder was working and as Mother had said, it was Elen's chance to lead the conversation. So much rested on her shoulders, she was surprised she could still stand. She took a deep breath and feeling as though a beam of light from the heavens was illuminating her for the whole world to see, she said, "Father, you may leave us now."

If Father had been annoyed at some protocol being broken by Magnus' unannounced arrival, now he would be livid. If he could speak. She wondered if this would teach him to write letters to strange men offering her for marriage. Watching him struggle to focus his eyes felt even more satisfying than burning those letters. She almost laughed at how both men looked as shocked and confused as each other.

"You may go now, thank you," she said again.

Father stood with a vacant dumbfounded expression on his face and when Gula came to lead him away, like a man whose wits had left him, he didn't protest. Elen hoped the effects wouldn't wear off too quickly. Every time she'd looked at him since that awful day in the autumn, she couldn't help seeing an image of the tortured king. She wouldn't be all that bothered if whatever the powder was turned out to be long lasting.

But Father wasn't her concern now. It was Magnus she had to deal with, her task to blur the edges between the girl from his dreams and the real one he needed to be convinced to marry.

"You look somewhat...familiar. Have we met somewhere before?" she asked in a soft voice. "Do you recognise me?"

"You have no idea..." he began.

He was very wrong about that, but she carried on with her ploy, more confident than she'd imagined she could be. "You are the man of my dreams," she breathed. "How can you be standing before me, my imagination made flesh!"

"You too?" he gasped and she struggled not to laugh as his expression turned once again to sheer stupefaction. A dream he'd had all the way away in Rome becoming real at the far end of the empire would surely be enough to challenge the sanity of any man. She thought she could push him a little more though. "I dreamed of the fairest man in the world, who will come to me from a land far away to bestow upon me the most handsome sons."

"It can't be real," he gasped, running a hand over his face and blinking slowly. "It can't..."

"I am real," she breathed and reached out to delicately touch his hand, but recoiled from it as feeling his clammy skin seemed like such an awful betrayal of Eugenius.

"Yes," he added, slowly reaching up to her face. "It's real."

The power and control she had over the Dux Britanniarum made her a little light-headed, but she fully believed she could do anything she wanted with him. It was absolutely invigorating, and she felt daft for all the long nights worrying about this moment. Surely it would be the simplest thing in the world to get him to settle the Deisi on Roman land. He would do absolutely anything for her. But as Magnus took a deep breath and stood up straight, she wavered like a flame in a draft. The sheer size of him was intimidating, and she knew what the flared nostrils and slightly open mouth meant as she'd experienced it almost every day over the winter with Eugenius. She was far from prepared for what he wanted to do with her though, and realised the advice she needed about that should come not from Grandmother, but a girl who worked in a brothel.

She felt even less sure of herself when he said, "Your father seems a little...muddled. Perhaps something in his drink didn't quite agree with him?" His eyes too, focused, the way a cat looks at a mouse just before it pounces.

Something deep in her belly began to clench tight.

"Real," he muttered. "What is real is that I am the Dux Britanniarum. And tell me, how real is your grandmother?"

He might have well as slapped her in the face with his huge hand and smashed her head open against the wall. She was back in the freezing river, fighting for breath, completely at Magnus' mercy. She'd been so foolish to believe she had any power at all. She was just a stupid little girl who'd been playing with the flame and was about to get herself properly burned.

"I think we should go and see her now so I can introduce myself. I think she's been expecting me. What do you say?"

Elen could feel her mouth moving, but couldn't get any words out. Desperately, she looked around for Mother, but she was away tending Father.

Magnus' hand clamped around her upper arm, the callouses rough against her soft skin. She tried to protest but swallowed the wrong way and started to cough. Before she knew it, with as much control over her own destiny as one of the slaves watching them openmouthed, she was being led out. As she was being pulled away, her thoughts were of Eugenius and if it was to come to it, no matter how much this brute wanted to know who he was, she was sure his name would never leave her tongue.

"You and you," Magnus snapped at the guards on the praetorium gates. Terror and confusion in their eyes, they only needed a moment to decide that Magnus had the authority to command them, so obeyed and followed.

The Dux pulled her again. It was the same feeling as Father dragging her for a whipping. On the other side of the gate tower, she saw the open post hole where the king's cross had been set and almost in tears of despair, wondered if he'd felt the same desperation when they'd dragged him out to it.

"Which way?" Magnus asked.

He didn't seem angry, but his cold determination didn't suggest there was any prospect of disobeying, and of its own accord, her finger pointed in the direction of Grandmother's house.

Down the narrow alley, she went in front, Magnus' large hand in the small of her back forcing her forwards. She saw some of the grubby-faced young boys who took grandmother's coins for errands stare at her, frozen with indecision at the sight of Magnus looming behind her and the pair of soldiers behind. There was no time for them to do anything to help. A couple of the men stood alert, but she shook her head as only Grandmother could confront the Dux, not one of her guards.

Despite the feeling in her legs gone from the thought of Magnus doing to Grandmother what Father had done to the Deisi king, Elen didn't fight against the hand in her back forcing her forwards. The only thing she could think of doing was to try and lead Magnus out into the fields so Grandmother might have a few moments to organise men to come and confront him, or to protect her. But with such power radiating from the man, she didn't dare. He would find Grandmother one way or the other, so perhaps it was best not to antagonise him.

She stopped at the inconspicuous sheet over the door.

"Here?" Magnus asked suspiciously.

All she could do was nod meekly, but when he drew his sword, she wanted to scream a warning...even if it was to cost her life. She knew well that such an action from a soldier meant he was prepared to kill with it. Grabbing her arm again, he forced her in front, using her as a shield, the flat of his sword pressing against her hip.

* * *

Kenon had held back from entering the fort, thinking it best to wait for Father's summons rather than simply strolling in. He wasn't sure that Father's reaction at seeing him again wouldn't be to just ship him straight back off to Rutupiae again. And with a more trusted escort this time.

Left to look after the horses while the others went as escorts with Magnus, he was getting bored, and began imagining that he'd been forgotten, but then Magnus strode purposely out of the fort gates, forcing a girl in front of him. His first thought was that the Dux needed the relief found in a brothel before seeing his father, which he could well understand. But, although she had changed a lot in the last few months, he recognised his sister...and suddenly he understood that Magnus would marry her and inherit everything of his father's. The full scale of the deceit hit him harder than any weapon instructor's fist.

It looked like they were in a hurry. They probably couldn't wait to sign some official papers to snatch away what was rightfully his, so they could have everything for themselves. As soon as the documents were signed and sealed, with Father's blessing, he would be sent back to Rutupiae to be beaten and starved half-senseless before being shipped off for a quarter of a century in Africa. Discarded.

If he hadn't forgotten his dice tower in his haste to leave Rutupiae he could have seen what the numbers said, but he didn't need Fortuna to tell him what he had to do. He looked through the horses, judging which was best. He chose the one with the fullest saddlebags and fastened the least tired looking of the horses to its saddle. He pulled himself up, kicked the reluctant horse into a run and with a cry, tore off back the way they'd come. The thudding of its hooves on the ground was reassuring. But he knew he'd have to be careful with it as he wouldn't be able to change it for a fresher one at Canovium or Deva. If it went lame he'd have no other way of getting to the Wall. He didn't dare let it gallop any slower though. If anyone from the fort was to catch up with him, he'd be dragged off to a fate he feared more than death.

The curses he screamed at the top of his voice encouraged it on. With gritted teeth, he made a promise to any god that cared to listen that he would get the lands and women he deserved, would see his traitorous sister tremble and Magnus would take a knee before him. And one day people would call him Lord.

XIV

Magnus had spent his whole life in the army. One of his earliest memories was holding a toy sword pretending to stand at the foot of an Alpine pass warding off Hannibal's elephants, or protecting Caesar from the traitors. His new station gave him command of the whole detachment of men in the fort and so with a word he could simply have had this old woman dragged to him in chains. But such was his indignation, he barged blindly into the dark room alone where he expected one of the most powerful people he'd ever met was waiting for him. Holding the small girl in front like a shield of flesh would offer no protection at all.

With the blade ready to jab or slash, he held his breath as his eyes adjusted to the dim interior.

The only person he could see was a fat old woman, and from the way she was looking at him, it was immediately clear that she was the one he'd come to see. A soldier with a sword in his hand should have been a gut-wrenching terror for most people, especially unarmed ones, but not only did she not seem afraid, she actually appeared pleased to see him.

"An augur," Magnus scoffed. "That explains much."

"Does it?" she smiled. "Very good. In that case, perhaps I will have less to explain. Please, won't you join me?" She indicated the rickety chair at his side of the table as though he was a young girl come to hear what her future held.

"Do your ungodly spells say anything about why I shouldn't kill you right here where you sit?" Magnus imagined an old woman should have cowered in the corner at a threat from such a man, but the infuriating smile didn't leave her face. Instead, with all the confidence of someone who knew themselves to be his equal, perhaps even his superior, she looked him straight in the eye and said, "I am far more valuable to you alive than dumped in a ditch for the crows and rats. And if you can take a moment to see through your anger, as understandable as it may be, I am sure you will agree."

"Will I?"

"Indeed. And you can put that sword away too. It's far too big and sharp to swing around in here. You could hurt someone with it, if you're not careful. All we're doing is having a polite discussion. No one needs to get stabbed, or slashed, or whatever it is you do with it."

"I wouldn't be too sure about that!" he said.

"Really?" she beamed. "I give you my word that I will not harm you. Does that make you feel better?"

The cheek of the fat old hag was shocking. Even the girl he was still holding gasped at the sheer brazenness.

"Do you know who I am?" he asked, wondering if she'd got him confused with some common fool.

"I do," she nodded slowly and with a knowing smile, added, "I know exactly who you are. But even more importantly, I know who you wish to become."

Instinctively, he knew what she meant and his mind reeled with how she could know such a secret. Andragathius and Marcellinius were the only ones he'd told. He instantly dismissed the thought that the Batavi or his brother could be selling his words to her. "Do not push me, woman," he warned. But again his words had no effect on the incessant grin. It was like trying to frighten a statue.

"Do not underestimate me, boy," she replied. "Try to think clearly for a moment. When you were halfway across the empire from me, I had the power to not only get into your villa, your room, but your *dreams*. Doesn't a power like that make you shudder in awe? It certainly made you run all over this land quicker than an imperial messenger. But now where are you?"

She admitted it so freely, which made him feel equally as nervous. It was as though a ludus opponent had been sacrificing pieces to make it look like an easy game, only to discover he'd been led into an inescapable trap. He was silent.

"Exactly. You are in *my* place now, and as my guest, I don't consider it particularly appropriate for you to be threatening me, especially my granddaughter, with a drawn weapon. I think you've made your point with it, so please put it away now and let us discuss what we can achieve together."

"Together?" he asked. The word suggested equality, mutual respect, not things he thought this woman deserved.

"My dear, I would have expected a man of your reputation to be able to see passed these outward accoutrements of mine and realise who you are talking to."

She looked like a vendor at a street store, a fixed smile to attract customers and trick them into thinking she was an honest trader, completely harmless. Yet the words she spoke could have been uttered by Shapur the Great as he used Emperor Valerian as a horse stool.

Magnus was about to speak, but she held up a hand and he found himself letting her continue. "I am sure your expensive and exquisitely crafted armour would do wonders to protect you from a stroke of a sword, but your skin will offer no such protection from a poisoned barb. You see these sheets on the walls? Pretty decorations at first sight, although, I have to admit, rather shabby and tattered these days. But tell me, which one has a boy behind it with a poisoned dart aimed right at your neck? Perhaps there's more than one. Now then..." and instantly, as though it was a feat of magic, her face turned from stern back to disarmingly friendly. "But silly me. Of course, you wouldn't want to harm your future wife, would you?"

It seemed that with each new thing she said, his thoughts were slammed in another direction. "Wife?" he scoffed. "I think we've jumped a few steps ahead."

The girl, so full of confidence when he'd first seen her, had now drawn in on herself in fear and seemed much smaller. Just a child. From the awe that had surged through him as she'd stepped out in front of him, now he thought about crushing her throat with his hands. He pushed her away, partly from disgust, partly because if he was going to decapitate the old woman, she'd be in the way.

"Well yes. You are already in love with her enough to leave your entourage behind and tear across half the length of Britannia like a madman to get to her." The old woman's eyes flashed cold again, as quickly as blowing on a lamp. "But let me say this to you. Harm a hair on the head of this dear girl and you will be dead before you take half a dozen breaths." Again, she did the trick of snapping from threatening his life to smiling sweetly as though she'd just found a bird on the windowsill.

"I think she might have more to worry about from her father than me. I don't think he'll be too impressed when he comes round from whatever was in his wine."

How the girl tensed up at such a thought was pleasing, but he was here for more important things than putting little girls in their place.

"Please, I implore you," she said. "Sit down, as we have a lot to discuss, I believe. We have a lot to offer each other."

Magnus wasn't sure he'd heard her right. "Offer me? What could you possibly have to offer me?"

There was something in that damn smile of hers that made him want to kneel at her feet so she could stroke him to sleep. As he debated with himself whether or not to sheath his sword, he realised she'd brought back a long-forgotten affection for his mother, some forty years past when she'd dab his cuts and bruises with healing ointments and praise him for some childish feat. No other woman had treated him that way since. The hilt clicking against the bronze neck of the scabbard snapped him back. He hadn't even noticed he'd slipped it back in, and with another flash of fear, he wondered if she'd got back into his head again. But he'd come so far, and to do what she'd done, she obviously wielded some real power, so he reasoned it would cost nothing to listen. He could kill her when he got bored.

As he set his weight on the creaking chair, he reasoned that she could have probably done the same to him whenever she'd wanted on his journey between Rome and Segontium, so perhaps a man versed in politics would consider it to be more advantageous to have her as an ally than an enemy.

"I would offer you wine," the old woman said with a wicked grin. "But I can imagine how uncomfortable that would make you feel."

Fresh from a daughter lacing her father's drink, she was absolutely right about that. As he shifted his weight on the chair it creaked and he could feel its loose joints move under him. "Speak woman. What do you have to offer?"

"Oh, not so much. Only everything you have ever dreamed of."

He hadn't expected a straight answer, but that was enough to make him even more annoyed. "And what is that?" he sighed, gritting his teeth.

"Obviously you want to make your term as Dux Britanniarum as successful as possible. To do that you will need the men of the three legions stationed here to be loyal to you. To you, over the emperor. Do such words have a ring of truth to them?"

That she seemed to know his heart just as well as he did was a very unnerving sensation, but such treachery was not something he could openly admit. With a curt nod, not admitting anything, he let her carry on.

"I would suggest the best way to make that happen is not to appear as some foreign commander come to rule over them from a distance, but to be one of them."

"And how do you propose to do that?"

"Like many of the best ideas and plans, the plan is beautiful in its simplicity. You marry the daughter of one of the most powerful men in Britannia and the sons she will give you will tie you to the land."

As Magnus turned to look at the young girl, the chair creaked again, threatening to collapse under him. She'd tried to play him for a fool in the worst way imaginable and for months he'd been truly under her spell, like in a story a mother told her children when they were in bed. If her brother hadn't blurted out about his grandmother when they'd caught the Areani, he wondered if he would still be held by her magic. The boy, as weaselly and pathetic as he was, had saved him twice now. He would have to think of how to suitably reward him.

"Perhaps it would be fitting for my treasured granddaughter here to explain." She ushered the girl to the table. "Don't be worried," she said to her. "He can't harm you, and there will be others if he is not...suitable."

Yet another insult. "Expendable, am I?" he asked. Had anyone else said such a thing to him, they'd have found themselves at the end of his blade, begging for their lives.

"I mean you no offence," she said, which was a blatant lie. "But you did ride off from your entourage to where only your God knows. As I said, you are in my realm now, so if you are not the man we need, this can be where you command a few legions and have a few skirmishes with some barbarians and disappear from history. Or..."

"Or?" he prompted impatiently.

"Or perhaps when you look back on this moment many years from now, you can recall it as the point your bid to have your likeness stamped on gold coins begins."

It was as though her herbs were flowing through his blood again. She spoke such simple words, but they were like sparks and he was an oil-soaked candle wick. "I am listening," he said, now fully aware that she was no ordinary woman.

The young girl cleared her throat and it was she who spoke. "I am the daughter of the Governor Octavius. Not only does he have the highest rank in Britannia, he owns lands from here all the way to the other side of Deva in the province of Flavia Caesariensis. You must have ridden through them on your way here, probably for a day or two at least. As my...husband, these would, of course, be in your name. My father came into much of the lands *west* of Deva through marrying my mother, who is a native."

Magnus noticed how she spoke in a stilted voice, nervous to the point of trembling, but it seemed she'd practised her words well.

"What about your brother? The son of the Governor, surely it is he who..."

"The boy is inconsequential," the old woman snapped.

With that, whatever had caused Octavius to banish his own son, Magnus was sure that the old woman had been behind it. "You got the boy's own father to disown him, just for your plans?" Magnus asked.

"Just? I didn't remove the boy from his birthright lightly. But my greater concern is with the land and its people. You've brought him back with you from the south, and have therefore made him your responsibility, so let me warn you about him. Throughout history, some men and power go together like a fine marriage and manage to make the world a better place, be that their intention or not. Others though, unfortunately much more often, will use any and every power they possess for their own gain and advantage, over everything else. When he was a boy, I loved him as I do Elen here, but that was as a grandmother. As he became a man, I feared I saw another Nero in the making. In my other role, I judge that he is wholly unsuitable for assuming any measure of authority. Besides, the fact that he holds no claim to his father's lands is the very reason you are here sitting with us having this conversation."

How she could make such an awful, unforgivable thing sound almost reasonable, seemed to Magnus to be another magic. But about Magnus coming into vast lands only because the boy was disinherited, she was right. Perhaps it was best that he remain inconsequential. "Carry on," he said.

The old woman nodded back at the girl, who took a long breath before she spoke. "We have been here in Segontium for two years waiting for funds to come from Rome to build the forts of a line of strong defences similar to the Saxon shore to the south to protect us from the Scotti. But we are sure the gold won't come as this far from Rome, the empire's ability to properly secure its borders is... stretched. And so we have another solution to propose. One that should suit your purpose as much as ours. And one that your reputation says that you're the best man to oversee it."

Magnus was amused at how she'd changed from a vixen sinking her claws into him to a kitten terrified even of how he looked at her. If they were really to marry, he decided that he would prefer this second version. "Really? And what is that?"

"We wish to settle a friendly tribe from Hibernia on our land, which they will farm in times of peace, and protect with the sword in times of need."

"And what would you want to do that for?" Magnus asked, confused.

"Security."

"Security? For what?"

"Us," Grandmother said. "Imagine, for example, if one day, a man with such hate in his heart for the emperors was popular enough with the soldiers of three legions that he could convince enough of them to board ships and sail to Gaul in an attempt to take the purple. What would happen to us here at the far end of the empire? How would we defend ourselves from Scotti raiders, or the Picts who have ships enough to sail raiders down from above the Wall."

Having his secret desires spoken out loud chilled him to the bone. Not least because if word got back to Gratian he'd be assassinated on the spot.

Standing in front of the emperor in Mediolanum, he'd felt nothing but contempt. Sitting in front of this woman, he had to admit that he was in awe. "How do you have such power?" he asked.

"Recognise it now, do you? Very good. In this part of the world, we are Romanised, but not Roman. For some three hundred years, when the interests of Rome were not aligned with ours, we've had to look after ourselves, however we can. We can't fight with swords and spears, of course, so a more subtle way to wield an influence for our benefit was needed. The network of spies, informers and helpers is hundreds of years old. I didn't build it, only inherited it, and have, for a time, been its custodian. Soon, I will pass it on. It's nothing unusual, as you doubtless have your network of spies, as do all of the tribes that crowd your borders. Lives depend on knowing soldier movements and planned incursions. We are probably a little more creative in our methods, that's all."

Magnus looked at the girl next to him. She seemed timid, but he wouldn't put it past her that it was just another act. Although absolutely everything seemed a great shock, and standing over their bodies as they bled out from stab wounds would also be a satisfactory scenario, he was still coherent enough to know that having a wife with such power working for him could be invaluable. "What do you think Gratian would say to inviting the empire's enemies onto Rome's land? Surely even here you have heard about Adrianople? There are some that say the chaos of the Goths in Illyria even threaten the whole of the empire."

"Really?" the woman asked and Magnus knew another challenge or insult was about to come. "A strong man like you caring so much about the demands of a mere child. How old is Gratian? Is he still in his teenage years? Adrianople came about purely, and predictably, as a result of mismanagement. The greed of your people trying to take advantage of others' suffering. Starving the poor Gothic refugees, trying to get them to sell their children into slavery. Disgusting. Of course they rose up. They were fighting for their lives, they were given no choice, so what do you really expect they would do? Adrianople, that torpid idiot Valens created that outcome by a succession of poor decisions, all of which stemmed from his flawed character." She paused to look at him. "Do I say anything you disagree with?"

Magnus shook his head. It was outrageous to hear her speak in such a way about an emperor of Rome, but she wasn't wrong.

"I believe I have made known my thoughts about keeping power out of the reach of those who are unsuited to it. We will handle the situation much differently than your Valens, of course. Good farming land is already allocated, a winter's worth of grain is procured for them. And if it helps, you may call them foederati. Decreeing such a thing would greatly benefit you as well, as would serve as a direct challenge to Gratian's authority. Yet, it is not something he can do anything about, and so it will demonstrate that you have complete command over Britannia. And by settling the Deisi, you will have more control over your domain than your cousin Theodosius does over his."

Hearing words of such grandiose and wide-reaching plans from a woman, especially one who seemed to know him better than he knew himself, made him feel strangely helpless, as though she'd turned him inside out and was poking things that should never see the light of day with a stick. He'd never been faced with such a situation, so was ill-equipped to deal with it properly.

"And..." the old woman said, her large, beguiling smile back again.

"And? There's more to your plan?" Magnus asked, incredulous.

"I will allow you to inform Gratian that it is all your idea."

An incandescent rage almost erupted in him with the power of Vesuvius. Such words were tantamount to slapping him in the face. But apart from whatever scowl was on his face, only the creaking of the old chair betrayed his displeasure. She had gone too far though. In a low voice, he said, "*Allow* me? Old woman, those who dance too close to the fire are in danger of getting burned."

Out of the corner of his eye, he caught the movement of one of the musty old drapes. Maybe it was just a draught from outside...he wasn't sure if he saw a small foot at the bottom.

Completely undeterred by such a threat, she looked him straight in the eye and held his gaze, just as someone of equal standing would. "Sometimes those you think are too close to the fire...are those who control the flames." She let the words settle between them, knowing that in the heavy silence where he could think of no quick retort, they could take their full effect. Magnus realised that she did have as much power in this dynamic as she believed.

"Do this for us and I have something else for you. Something your heart yearns for, possibly as much as the purple."

What could be more than that, Magnus couldn't guess.

"Apart from presenting the girl of your dreams to you, two names."

"Whose names?" He was beginning to get impatient now.

"You can do better than that," she smirked. Surely she could see his temperament beginning to sour, yet incredibly, she was still playing with him, daring to tease the Dux Britanniarum. Just when Magnus was about to slap his hand on the table, or his blade through her throat, she said, "One. The man who killed your precious uncle. And two. The man who ordered it."

The effect was startling. The chair creaked beneath him as he recoiled and his whole body felt suddenly weak, as though an opponent had come close to bettering him on the battlefield. "I," he stammered, struggling to compose himself. "How could you know this?"

"Oh, you mistake me," she smiled with feigned innocence.

"Then you joke with me!" Magnus boomed, right at the edge of his tolerance.

"Oh no," Grandmother replied, pretending to be shocked. "If I have the power to put a dream into a man's head, does it not seem unreasonable to imagine that I can get a truth out of one?"

It didn't seem unreasonable at all.

"Do we have an agreement?"

"We do."

"You will marry Elen and settle the Deisi?"

"I will."

If Magnus could look beyond the feeling that he'd just agreed to the rump end of a bargain with some Berber merchant, he knew that what the old woman had offered was more than he could have hoped for. Being beholden to an old woman with such power and temperament wasn't the most appealing prospect, and he could taste the sourness of it in his mouth, but bedding a girl he didn't legally own and confirming the names of those he suspected were responsible for killing Theodosius wasn't the worst possible outcome.

"You should get the agreement about the marriage done with her father as soon as you can. Immediately, I would suggest."

"Before the effects of what was in his wine wear off?" he sighed.

"It seems we understand each other very well. Thank you for your time and I am sure that we will talk again soon."

Just as Gratian had done, she decided that the conversation had concluded and dismissed him.

XV

Elen tried to swallow. One day, when she was young, Kenon had found some cloth belt from their mother's clothing to play with. At first, as he chased her around the garden with it, pretending it was a snake, they were whooping with laughter. But somehow it got looped around her neck...and although she stopped laughing, Kenon didn't. She remembered how, as he pulled it tighter, the vision at the sides of her eyes darkened and the burning in her chest was as though she'd breathed in the flames of a fire. It had taken long moments sprawled on the floor as Father beat Kenon as though he'd captured a raiding barbarian, to drag enough breath back into her lungs to beg for mercy for her brother.

The feeling was much the same as Magnus left, and the power he radiated like the sun itself trailed behind in his majestic wake. Her throat had clenched tight and she felt light-headed from trying not to gasp for air too loudly.

"That went well, don't you think?" Grandmother beamed. Somehow she looked as though she'd just enjoyed some wine with a good friend.

"Are you mad?" Elen seethed. "Why did you keep taunting him like that? He's the most powerful man in Britannia! He could set the whole legion from Deva against you. *Us!*"

Grandmother seemed wholly unperturbed. "How many times did you obey your father without question, even though you thought him wrong?"

Over the winter Grandmother's infallible calmness often amazed Elen, but now it was infuriating. Struggling to bring her mind back from images of the Twentieth Legion laying waste to the vicus to concentrate on Grandmother's question, she thought for a moment, but the answer was simple. "Always."

"Because you fear the consequences."

"Of course." Bad dreams recalling the worst episodes of father's displeasure sometimes woke her up at night in a sweat.

"Fear is a very valuable form of control, one the Romans have absolutely mastered. But I simply chose not to let our Magnus wield that particular weapon over our heads." She tapped a yellowing fingernail on the table. "A slight change of plan is in order, I believe."

All Elen cared about was getting Eugenius set up as her personal guard, and had pretty much come to terms with everything else, so changing what she'd spent the winter preparing herself for didn't sit too well.

"We spent the last year making plans to have you wed to the Dux, but it seems that after all of that, we were selling ourselves a little short."

Something painful seemed to blossom in Elen's chest. She knew she wasn't going to like what Grandmother was about to say. "What do you mean?" As quite often happened when talking to Grandmother, she wasn't too sure she wanted to know the answer.

"My dear, how about we have you married to the emperor himself?"

"Gratian?" Elen gasped.

Grandmother shook her head.

"Valentinian? But he is only *ten*!" The thought of being married to a little child filled her with a new kind of terror.

"To Magnus Maximus," she smiled calmly. "Emperor of the West."

Of everything Grandmother had ever said, these were the most shocking words, and she imagined she could feel Kenon pulling the cord around her throat again.

"I can see straight through our Dux, like the wing of a dragonfly," Grandmother mused. "His hatred of the young emperors, disdain for the political and military prowess of those who run the empire... I am convinced he wants the purple for himself and he is only using the rank of Dux to prepare for taking an invasion force to Gaul. In which scenario, of course, all of our worst nightmares would come true."

"How could you know that?" Elen gasped. "How do you know anything he told you was true?"

"Be in my position for long enough and you will get to know when a man speaks the truth, or not. You'll get an ear for it, like a lyre player can tell when a string is out of tune. He came here, angry, livid, everything raw, open and on view, so showed us who he really is. A proud man, but one who will stop and consider the position of someone he believes is an enemy if he thinks it could benefit his situation."

Elen's head seemed to swirl. She'd spent the winter listening to Grandmother tell her about history, politics and the art of subtle persuasion with words, gold or steel, but she'd never mentioned influencing the emperor. The only reaction, apart from a burning need to be held by Eugenius, was a strong desire to cry.

Still tapping her nail on the table, Grandmother mused, "If we act against him, then if either he wins or loses on his little quest, we stand to lose everything. Now then... if we were to support him and he wins, what, my dear, would we have to gain?"

"Grandmother!"

"Gratian is deeply, deeply unpopular all across the empire and what strength is there in an empire whose people, politicians and army, don't love its emperor?"

"Grandmother, please stop it!"

"Oh no, my sweet child. We're going to *start* it!"

The nail tapped slower, but louder. "Gratian himself has no military judgement, which is a serious issue in the times we live in.

Our Magnus, on the other hand, has an empire-wide renown for shoring up and securing its borders. The Senate will surely see merit in that, and for making their lives more secure, the people will come to appreciate him too. If he can usurp Gratian cleanly, without too much of a messy fight, I think Magnus in Gratian's position would actually be of great benefit to the empire. And therefore, and possibly more importantly, to us."

"By 'messy fight' you mean civil war?" Elen gasped. It had been incredible enough to listen to Grandmother talk about putting the dream into Magnus' head, now she was talking about crashing opposing armies into each other and putting the man of her choice into the purple. Elen wondered if someone was putting a strange dream into her head as Grandmother had done to Magnus.

"What we need to do is to get the fighting men behind him. The legions first, then the rest will follow."

"How, by the good Lord above, do you think you can achieve that?"

"I have a man here, a man there. A word in an ear, a shout in a crowd..."

"And that's it?" Elen asked, incredulous. "A few whispers is all it will take to make a man an emperor?"

"The greatest building was built only after the very first stone had been laid. Let's let Magnus make his grand plans, and we'll help him with the foundations. If it's done properly, it can be done well. And if it is done well, we will have a lot to gain."

Elen gave up. It was useless to try and argue.

"Go now. I have some letters to write," she said, ushering Elen away with a wave of a fat hand.

* * *

After having to breathe the cloying fragrances that the old woman used to mask the foul smells in her airless hovel, Magnus found the air of the vicus very welcome, even if it was a long way from being fresh.

The two guards he'd left outside the old woman's door had spent years of their life training to fight against hordes of barbarians, smashing skulls with shields and stabbing guts out at close quarters. In the lands above the Wall, a group of such men would be impervious. But the alleyway full of dirty children was a threat they were ill-prepared for, which was maybe why they looked completely lost trying to half-heartedly shoo them away. Seeing Magnus step back out, they looked as terrified as the girl had been. She'd had Magnus to deal with, so her fears had been well-founded. The guards didn't have such an excuse.

Magnus roared a good impression of the lions he'd seen tormented in the Colosseum and laughed at how the soldiers jumped as much as the boys did. In no mood to deal politely with so many snotty noses, he tossed a few coins over their heads and while they scurried about fighting among themselves like starving rats, the way to the fort was clear in the heartbeat.

The impressed men followed him out of the vicus with much more confidence than they'd had on the way in, and that was exactly what Magnus needed. Just multiplied by several thousand. There were two ways that could happen. One was to wait patiently until a situation presented itself to him which he could use to demonstrate his leadership qualities and compassion. Or he could make something happen himself.

Playing with fire, indeed.

At the main thoroughfare before the fort gates Andragathius and his men were waiting. A man was on his knees before them. They'd probably beat him to try and find out which way Magnus had gone. As he approached, the man scrambled to his feet and scurried off, clutching his bloodied nose. Back in the company of elite men he trusted with his life, Magnus' temper calmed a little.

"Everything all right?" the big Batavi asked.

Magnus hadn't been blind to Andragathius' unspoken concern on their long and frantic ride across Britannia. A good enough friend to care about what might be wrong, a good enough soldier not to dare question the actions of a superior, was a rare man. And one Magnus depended on more than he cared to admit. After being spoken to in such a way by women, he was in a cruel mood though. "I just got betrothed and now find myself one of the wealthiest men in Britannia," he smiled and had to fight not to burst out laughing as the relief on the Batavi's face to see him safe, clouded back to a clear struggle to keep his teeth firmly clamped on his tongue.

He was just about to give up and say something, but the soldier in him managed to win again. "What is to be done?"

Magnus noted to never forget what an invaluable man the Batavi was. "I am not sure yet."

Through the fort, between the rows of barracks and granaries, he led the men back to the praetorium. It was a little sanctum walled off from the rest of the fort so the man responsible for the welfare and discipline of the thousand men in the barracks could stay separate from them. The thick wooden doors closed behind them, it offered some relative tranquillity.

Magnus snapped his fingers for the slaves to work out among them which should run off to find Octavius.

A few moments later, as if the old man was nursing the hangover of his life, Octavius staggered out to offer a more formal greeting than he'd had before. Whatever he'd been plied with was beginning to wear off, but his nervous looking wife clutched his arm.

"Magnus Maximus," he said formally. "This is my wife Gula."

Magnus dipped his head in greeting, but outrageously, it was her who spoke first. "My husband welcomes you, but he is feeling a little unwell. Perhaps you could…"

"I understand," Magnus said as he tried to control the irritation of dealing with three generations of women who had no idea of their place in a single afternoon.

"Thank you," she smiled.

"No. I understand," he said a little sterner, no longer too concerned with the pretence of etiquette. "I've just had a most enlightening conversation with your daughter, and an old woman who, I assume, is your mother."

He was glad to see the woman's smile wiped clean off her face as though she was a cocky teenage sparring partner who'd thought himself a match for a seasoned soldier. Without taking his eyes from her, he raised a hand and ordered the two gate guards to fetch a chair. He hoped that how they ran like slaves to obey wasn't lost on Octavius. Or perhaps more importantly, his wife. The old man sank into it gratefully, and with a hand on his temple, tried to soothe what looked like a splitting headache.

Magnus stayed standing and looked down on him with pity, amazed almost to the point of disbelief that the man could have no idea what schemes his wife was a part of. And who his daughter was about to let herself become involved with. Then again, without the revelation from the boy on the way here, maybe Magnus would still be just as ignorant, and so helplessly besotted with a girl he'd seen in his dreams that some half-barbarian woman could control him as she saw fit. But although he was aware of their plans and could now defend himself against them, he still had to calm an involuntary shiver at the power they wielded to have brought him to them in the way they had.

As the old woman had said, he'd be a fool to discount such a partnership. Still, this Gula was out of place like a thimble on a ludus board...and that gave him an idea. He cast a glance at the ornate board with its delicate patterns inlaid around the edges and was glad that the sight of it no longer made him feel as though the ground was opening up under his feet. He motioned the guards to bring it over and had them set it in front of Octavius. Magnus tried not to break the appearance of stoic authority by laughing at how Gula looked like a startled deer torn between standing stock still or bolting to where she thought safety lay.

"Is your head clear enough to play?" he asked the old man.

Octavius leaned forward, the stiff movement showing his years.

"Of course. Some strange turn, that's all. Something I ate, perhaps." He laid a slightly shaking finger on a black counter and slid it to the side.

"Or drank," Magnus added as he bent down to counter with a white piece. Out of the corner of his eye, he saw Gula flinch as though she'd been slapped.

"I must apologise for my daughter's behaviour earlier," Octavius said. "Speaking out of turn like that, it was most inappropriate."

"Not to worry," Magnus said as he watched the old man move his second counter. He could have used the move to set up an attack, but instead chose to place it to defend the exposed first one. Magnus wondered if that showed the mind of the man, or just his mood.

"I am sure you know how to teach her her place," Magnus said as he slid his second counter. Ocatvius' first piece was now doubly threatened. "Or maybe I could help you somewhat with that."

The woman's hands balled slowly into fists. Magnus was pleased to see that she understood. Octavius was a bit slower though. "As Dux Britanniarum, I wish to make this province as secure and wealthy as I can. With the hand of the Governor's daughter in marriage, those who consider themselves natives of this land will come to view me as one of their own, and those who think to threaten these lands will have the full force and fury of the Dux Britanniarum to contend with."

Octavius' third move wasn't very well considered and for the next half a dozen turns at least he would be playing defensively.

"Perhaps the custom up here is that you need to discuss it with your wife?" Magnus spoke the insult softly, trying to make it sound like an innocent question.

"Of course not!" Octavius scoffed but looked as bewildered as when the powder in his wine had taken its full effect.

Magnus jumped the first black counter taking it out of play, and landed in the position that the second would be lost at the next move. The son and his inheritance out of the picture and the daughter in

Magnus' hand, it was as if fate was spelled out on the ludus board in front of him. With a shiver down his back, he wondered if the Lord above was watching the game.

Octavius looked up, noticing some movement behind Magnus' shoulder. Before Magnus turned around to see who would interrupt a meeting between two of the most important men in the whole of Britannia, the flick of the woman's fingers caught his attention. It could have just been a nervous twitch, and itch, or her trying to brush away a fly. If Magnus hadn't spent long months in the deserts, trying to do deals with honourless and deceitful Berbers, maybe he wouldn't have noticed. The men of the sand had a way of communicating rudimentary messages in hand and finger movements that enabled them to speak with a friendly smile to your face while simultaneously plotting your murder. And while he hadn't learnt more than a basic few, he could recognise when they were using it. Gula's gesture certainly wasn't as subtle, but its meaning seemed clear. Not now. Go away.

Before whoever the message was intended for could leave, Magnus raised his hand and called out, "Halt." Hand still raised, he waved his finger to beckon whoever was there to approach. He wasn't surprised to find out it was the Areani.

"Urgent news?" Magnus asked, pointedly ignoring the flash of indignation on Gula's face. He'd made some tentative deal with the old woman, could marry the young girl if he wanted, but in the mother he knew he had a real enemy.

The Areani looked between Octavius, Gula and Magnus, humorously unsure about where his loyalty now lay.

"You can go and ask this mysterious Grandmother you serve for permission to speak with me, if you like. Second alley on the left, seventh...*shack* down on the right. I advise care about making any sudden movements, so as not to frighten the boys behind the drapes."

Still, it was only with a barely noticeable blink from Gula that the Areani spoke. Magnus noted the power this woman also held.

"Kenon has ridden back east."

"Kenon?" Octavius asked. Looking up quickly must have hurt his head as he winced with the discomfort. "He's here?"

Magnus couldn't tell if surprise or disappointment was the old man's strongest reaction.

"He should be back before dinner," the boy's mother said, once again completely out of place in the discussion of men. While the arrangements for the marriage were being made, Magnus decided he had a lot to teach Octavius about setting women in their correct places. And keeping them there.

"I fear not," the Areani added.

"Why not?" Octavius asked. "Where else would the lad go?"

The Areani was certainly nervous about passing on his thoughts. Magnus was sure he'd be speaking much more freely if he was alone with Gula.

"North."

"North?" Octavius coughed. "He will go straight back to Deva to be with his friends before he has to go back to his training in Rutupiae."

"I fear not," he said again, a little firmer.

"He's going to the Wall, is he?" Octavius mocked.

The Areani sighed. "Beyond."

The game of ludus abandoned, Octavius tried to get to his feet, but sank weakly back into his chair. Gula steadied him and all attempts at playing with power unobserved from the shadows discarded, she demanded, "Why? What does he plan there? Speak!"

"Last autumn, the men of his escort all deserted and planned to go North."

"And why would *he*?" Gula snapped.

The Areani straightened his back and assumed the role of a soldier relaying bad news to a superior. Eyes on the wall behind, he said, "They invited him. As the Governor's son, if he was to join the cause..."

"What!" she gasped. "Why?"

"He was disinherited and hated his time in military training, as he must have written in his letters."

Octavius looked confused, but the woman seemed to know her son better. "The fool! Chase after him and bring him back before he gets himself killed! Leave now."

Before the Areani could agree, Magnus said, "No."

"No?" Gula spat in amusing outrage.

Octavius stared up at his wife, eyes wide, too shocked to stop her.

"It's my son we're talking about," she continued. "Not a cursed ludus counter!"

Magnus took a long breath, trying to pull together all the loose strands of ideas and possibilities that were flailing about in his mind like a madman's hair in a stiff breeze and weave them into an actionable plan. He put a hand on the Areani's shoulder and he turned him away from Gula. She stayed open-mouthed as they walked to the other side of the praetorium. With slaves and guards milling around he wasn't convinced he could speak without being overheard. What he was going to say needed to be a secret guarded with lives. He waved Andragathius to him, and they walked together along the rows of barracks, but it wasn't until they were in the clear space in front of the fort gates that he felt he could speak freely.

"You really think the boy will lead an army from the north against me in the hopes of getting his lands back?" he asked the Areani.

"No," he said with a rye smile. "That's what I believe he *thinks* he can do. More likely, if he can even get over the Wall by himself, as soon as they find out who he is, they'll try to get a ransom for him, and pull him apart piece by piece until the gold arrives."

"How easy is it to get over?"

"If you know the right people, fairly easy."

"And if you don't?"

"Then you'll be going in the ground, not over the Wall."

"Do the tribes on the other side still want to raid?"

"Any chance they can get. It's in their blood. They're born with a longing for the bounty of the South. But since Theodosius the Elder put down the Conspiracy, they've been too afraid."

"You plan a trap?" Andragathius scoffed, disapprovingly.

Magnus shrugged and wondered if the big Batavi speaking out of turn was trying to protect him from doing something stupid. His friend was far from a subordinate though and Magnus would always welcome the cautious counterbalance he offered. Just a few moments before, as he'd walked away from the old woman's house, he'd wondered about waiting for an opportunity to present itself, or make one of his own. And now he had the possibility of some barbarian raiders coming south, led by his brother-in-law, with an Areani sworn to protect him, just couldn't be something that had happened by chance. Maybe he could make this opportunity work for him...

The Areani was the old woman's man, though, so as Magnus could be sure that every word he spoke would be relayed straight back to her, he'd have to be extremely careful with his tongue. He needed to create a situation where it would be irresistible for the barbarians to come south that at the same time wouldn't make him 'replaceable' in the eyes of the old woman. Even better, to be beneficial to her. "Gratian did not give me a full entourage," he said, listening to himself as he spoke. "The last thirteen years in Britannia have seen a rare stability, so he didn't see the need to allocate all I asked for. So, what if I actually wanted a northern army to come south, but in a controlled manner? An incursion curtailed before it can cause any real damage, but be enough to get Gratian alarmed about the threat of weakening borders, so I can get more resources sent here to better protect them?"

"It sounds reasonable," the Areani nodded, but spoke in a tone that told Magnus he was not convinced. "What part would you have me play in such a plan?"

"Instead of stopping the boy and bringing him home to his

mother, you help him over the Wall and convince an army to come south. A small one. An incursion, not an invasion."

As the Areani laughed heartily, Andragathius cleared his throat loudly.

"I think you will have to think of a better idea than that to get the old woman to allow a raid in her lands."

"What if she wasn't to know?"

"I thought you've just met her?"

If all she'd said about the power she held in the land was true...and she'd put the dream in his head, so he had no reason to doubt her, he could be sure that not much would get past her. "What if I could offer you something that she can't?"

"And what might that be?"

"You tell me."

Every man had something he wanted. Every man had his price. The Areani almost named it, but before he said anything, stopped himself. "Anyway, I can catch him for you, but going to the other side of the Wall...for that, you'd better send someone else. I have some...history with the Votadini tribe up there. They'd likely kill me as soon as they see me."

"It has to be you. Not only are you an Areani, you are oath-bound to the boy, so no one else would protect him as well. Name your price."

The Areani laughed, but seeing the seriousness of Magnus' expression, thought for a moment. "I doubt even a man as powerful as you could pay what I would ask."

"Try me!"

The Areani scoffed. "My price is to have my wife and daughter brought back to me."

Magnus was surprised at such a simple request. "Where are they?" he asked.

"Taken by the Scotti of Hibernia."

"The Scotti!" Magnus laughed.

The fact that just a few moments earlier the old woman had told him she wanted him to deal with the Deisi made it feel as if the whole situation he found himself in was divinely ordained.

A king and a slave. The highest and the lowest people in the land. The balance seemed meaningful in some important way.

Magnus knew a man's pull for his family was one of the most powerful forces in the world. He was a little shocked at how jealous of the Areani he was for only having his wife and daughters missing as he had the hope of rescue and reunification to keep him warm at night. For Theodosius, all Magnus had was the deathly cold need for revenge. It wasn't the same. One was hoping for life and love, the other was repaying death with more death.

"I would have expected you to say no straight away," the Areani asked. "May I ask what you are thinking?"

"I did just meet the old woman. It was a very…interesting conversation. She asked me to settle the Deisi tribe here on Roman land. So, if you do as I ask, and speak to no one about it, I will allow them to settle here on the condition that the king himself brings your wife and daughter back. Will that be good enough?"

The Areani looked shocked. "Even if I don't make it back from the Wall?"

Magnus had him. "My word is my honour. I will write the letter to the king of the Deisi tonight."

"Do you know what happened to the last king of theirs who came here?"

"Do I want to?"

"They nailed him up right where we are standing."

"On Octavius' order?"

The Areani nodded.

"And so the new king will be wanting revenge against the Governor of Britannia?" he mused. It was all getting very complicated, like a ludus game with a worthy opponent. A single counter slid to a different position could easily tip the result one way or another. But in the great game, northern raiders and Hibernian kings were just counters he knew he could move to strengthen his own position for the ultimate prize.

As outrageous as it was to think it, even getting rid of Octavius would work in Magnus' interest, as married to his daughter, all his lands would be in Magnus's name with such wealth at his control. Then he would have no trouble paying anyone who couldn't be convinced to follow willingly.

"And you won't execute the boy for treason?" the Areani asked.

"Your oath to his grandmother will not be threatened. In fact, if it goes to plan, I intend to reward him. But how long will it take him to get to the Wall?"

The Areani smiled. "You mean, how many days do you have to come up with your plan?"

The man was fast. Magnus was impressed. "Careful," he smiled. "You sound like the old woman."

"A few days won't be a problem. A week maybe. I know where he is going so it won't be hard to find him. I will wait for him in a brothel in Eboracum."

"Done then," Magnus agreed.

All he needed now was to come up with a suitable trap for the raiders…And to trust that the wet whelp who would soon be his brother-in-law, could lead the Votadini south.

As they walked back to the fort, Andragathius mumbled, "Nothing you are saying makes any sense." He'd finally decided that things had gone so far beyond his liking that speaking out could be no worse than breaking his silence.

"What I want is so extraordinary, it seems that no ordinary measure will help achieve it," Magnus said.

"All to make yourself a hero?"

"For men to believe I am a worthy leader, yes."

"Haven't they heard the stories?"

"It would be best to give them their own."

"If Gratian finds out you're playing ludus with some of his provinces, he'll send men to act against you. An army, I can stand against. An assassin in the night..." A little quieter, and close to a growl, he added, "You're playing with fire."

Magnus smiled. "My friend, I treasure your concern, but some men control the flames."

XVI

The smell of the fresh straw made Elen's nose tingle, but there were many more pleasant and powerful sensations surging through her body to enjoy.

With his body weight, Eugenius had her pinned to the blanket, almost crushing her into the barn floorboards with every thrust. With his hands pushing down on hers she was absolutely helpless... but she wasn't afraid of a thing. As the wave of ecstasy began to grow, she looked into his eyes. From the way they were rolled up, and the dumb smile she loved, she knew he was feeling much the same thing.

She'd always known they only had the winter to be together, but despite Magnus seeing straight through Grandmother's plan, and her deeming him to be even more important than a 'mere' Dux Britanniarum, she couldn't allow her time with Eugenius to end, even though the cost of them being caught together could be his life.

She knew that if he was to suffer the same fate as the Deisi king, she would just curl up at his feet and die on the spot.

"Don't stop," she gasped.

At the same time, to have a secret lover behind the back of the man she despised was an exhilarating thrill and helped her believe that one day she'd have the power to speak to the Dux as Grandmother had done.

Then she was there...in that incredible place where everything seemed perfect and possible. To stop herself from screaming she bit into his shoulder.

Eugenius, spent at the same moment, lay on top of her, breathing deeply for what felt like a long while, before one last lingering and sweaty kiss and he rolled off, flopped onto his back and sighed loudly, satisfied. His big hand found hers and squeezed gently.

She turned to her side, still wanting to be close to him. The flickering light from the oil lamps glowed over his glistening skin. She ran her hand over his clammy chest, feeling a thrill at how hard his heart was beating. She marvelled at his size. With all the training he did in the army, his muscles made him look like a Greek statue. So perfect.

Yet they were about to be forced apart.

The world felt so cruel. Being with the man she loved didn't seem too much to ask, but slowly, insidiously, like how the coming autumn bleeds away the days of summer, what Grandmother had asked her to think about forced its way back to her mind. How to help Magnus become emperor. Daughter of the Governor, she may be, but a girl thinking about how to help a man ascend to the purple seemed more incredulous than when Grandmother had told her she'd made a man in Rome dream about her.

"We have to go out and march at dawn tomorrow," Eugenius sighed. "So fucking pointless. Walking miles just because your father wants to impress the Dux with how hard he trains his men."

"It's what all soldiers have to do, isn't it?" Elen asked. Almost every day that she'd been in a fort, be it Segontium or Deva, long lines of men had filed noisily out of the gates at dawn for a hard day trudging around the hills, the sounds of their heavy equipment clattering off into the distance.

"It's just so pointless, though. We could be doing something constructive at least," he mused. He ran a big and heavy hand along her still sweaty side, pulling away a few pieces of straw that had stuck to her skin. She arched her back so he could touch all of her.

"Constructive? Like what?" she asked.

"I don't know. Anything."

"Like roads?" she asked.

He shrugged. "I suppose."

She pushed herself up and rested on an elbow. "All men really hate marching that much?" she asked.

"Every single one. If any soldier thinks about giving up with the army and heading to the Wall, it will be while he's out on a march."

"And if your commander didn't make you do it, you'd be grateful to him?"

"Grateful?" Eugenius laughed. "We'd hail him as emperor!"

A chill cold enough to wash away the last glow of her orgasm ran through Elen, but replaced it with something even more powerful. The answer was roads, but her first thought was to dismiss the idea, because how could a girl think of something that would involve the five thousand men of the Twentieth Legion and help make a man an emperor? The next was that it had come too easily. She'd thought about a problem that no other girl in the whole of Britannia had ever had to consider, and it had popped into her head from nothing but a flippant remark from Eugenius.

The more she considered it, though, the more it made sense.

"You've got goosebumps," Eugenius said, gently touching her forearm. "What's wrong?"

"I have to go and see Grandmother," she said.

"Now? Can't it wait until the morning?"

She didn't think it could.

"At least let me take you to her," he said as he watched her pull her tunic on with a look of disappointment.

"I'll be safer in the vicus than you will," she smiled.

She leaned over to kiss him, but before their lips touched, she stopped, suddenly convinced she'd had a flash of the intuition Grandmother had long been telling her to pay attention to. At that moment, leaving Eugenius here was the absolute last thing in the world she wanted to do. It would be the first time for perhaps the rest of their days that she would have to leave Eugenius for Magnus, and now it had come to her, she couldn't do it.

"What's the matter?" he whispered softly.

She had an idea that could affect the future of the whole empire, yet was ready to stay right where she was while the whole thing crumbled and fell around them because she couldn't let her short few months of real happiness be over, and despite being sure what his reaction would be, she had to tell him Grandmother's new plan. "I won't be just the wife of the Dux Britanniarum."

Slowly, he pulled himself up into a sitting position. "Is two husbands not enough for you?"

Despite herself, she laughed.

"Grandmother plans on helping Magnus become emperor."

"What!?" Eugenius gasped, blinking quickly as he tried to understand just what she'd said.

"She believes he will try it himself anyway, so it will be in our best interests for us to help him."

"Help him?" he gasped, incredulous. "You're talking about a civil war! She should be doing everything she can to *stop* him, not support him!"

"Having him rule with his cousin in the east, don't you think that would be better than an unpopular boy like Gratian?" she said slowly, aware of how much she sounded like her mother.

"If you compare them like for like, then in *theory* yes, of course it'd be better to have an experienced fighter and leader like Magnus in charge. But you can't just swap them over peacefully and hope that no one notices. And that is even before he somehow convinces a few thousand men like me stationed in Britannia to desert their posts and follow him. That's not an easy decision for a soldier to make. As soon as he leaves for Gaul there'll be Picts, Scotti and Saxons pouring all over Britannia, just like what happened in the Conspiracy. If the borders aren't properly secured here before he takes any men to Gaul, you'll be…"

"Britannia Secunda will be overrun by barbarian raiders," she finished for him…and everything Grandmother had worked for would be lost. So might be the whole empire.

"You are absolutely serious about Magnus as emperor?" he asked.

"Grandmother is."

"Well... the first thing you will have to do is to get enough men in every fortress, every auxiliary fort and lookout, to believe that he is someone special, not just another commander giving slightly better orders than the legate or the tribunes, not just someone who makes sure that they get paid on time...he needs to make the men feel like he's the man they *need*."

"Like building roads?" Elen suggested.

"What?"

"No marching. Something constructive."

His eyes went wide again. "Sometimes I forget that you are much more than just my wife! You really are the girl that your Grandmother hopes you'll be, aren't you."

"Maybe. One day," she said.

And as they planned how to make her second husband the most powerful man in the empire, she wondered where the limit of love was.

It seemed impossible...but at the same time, Eugenius knew exactly what needed to be done to make it possible. Someone who cares about them.

"And food is well-priced..." he added.

It was easy to move unnoticed, through the narrow, muddy vicus streets at night. Just another girl sneaking home after a midnight tryst. Until she got close to Grandmother's house. The men didn't look like guards, not Roman ones, at least, more like they'd drunk so much they'd forgotten where they lived. Or had no home to go to. It would be a deadly mistake for a Roman to assume that, though. If one thought someone was heading to Grandmother with ill intent, they'd strike quicker, and probably deadlier, than a snake.

From the doorway he'd been lurking in, the first one moved to block her, but as soon as he saw it was her, the challenge changed to a welcome. "Trouble?" he asked in a gruff voice that didn't sound as though it often spoke softly.

"No. I just need to speak to Grandmother."

"Now? She'll be sleeping," he exclaimed, accentuating the words as though she was doing something so important she couldn't be disturbed, like performing some sacred rites.

"It's important."

"Well, as long as you'll be the one waking her," he whispered a little sheepishly. "She got a little grumpy at me last time I did it."

Grumpy was probably his polite way of saying that she'd threatened to kill him in an imaginative way.

So she wouldn't bump into or trip over something unseen in the darkness, she took the big hand he offered. How many faces it had punched, how many necks it had snapped, she didn't want to know.

It was simply unbelievable to think that Grandmother expected her to command men such as this one day.

"Thank you," Elen said at the door to Grandmother's house. "What is your name?"

"No need for that," he chuckled nervously. "Just think of me as some loyal street dog."

"I would like to know. Really," she said and for the briefest moment saw his expression change. For a heartbeat he looked as happy as a puppy before the hard look fell back across his face.

"It's Maglorius," he said proudly and gave a little bow.

The house didn't have windows and with no lamp burning it was pitch dark. If she wasn't sure which room was Grandmother's, the porcine snoring guided her like a beacon.

At first, she tried gently ruffling her big body, then shook her shoulder a little harder. Only by using two hands did the snoring turn into a snort and then a fat fist was grabbing at the front of her tunic.

"It's *me*!" Elen gasped.

"By the gods! I'll be gone soon enough, but you almost ended me right now." She tried to catch her breath, and slipped a hand between the folds of her billowing breasts to press against her heart. "What is it?" she gasped. "Is Gula all right?"

"Mother is fine, but I think I have an idea that will help Magnus with his plan."

"Really?" she asked and Elen glowed with pride at the thought of how proud Grandmother would be of her for coming up with such a good idea so quickly. "That's what you almost stilled my heart for in the middle of the night?"

"Let me tell it to you!" Elen said, excitedly.

"No," she snapped. "I don't want to hear it."

Elen was instantly crushed. Whatever her idea was, as soon as Grandmother woke up she knew it was going to be worthless, so couldn't even be bothered to listen.

She was glad of the darkness as Grandmother wouldn't be able to see her tears.

"It's your idea, my precious little girl. If you believe it warrants shocking me from my sleep, then whatever it is, you go to Magnus and tell him. It's your time now, not mine. It's all up to you now. Trust yourself."

Elen kicked herself at how she had misunderstood, and at the level of trust that Grandmother was bestowing on her, she was speechless.

"Empress Elen," Grandmother chuckled as she rolled over. "It has a nice ring to it. If only I could live to see the day. Go now, child. Knock on his door in the middle of the night, shock him awake as you just did me, and your words will carry more weight. Now leave me. I need to get back to my dreams. I was young... I was running..."

On her way out, the waiting guard whispered, "All well? She didn't bite you for waking her?"

Elen laughed as she put her small hand back in his and followed as he led her quickly through a series of lefts and rights until they got to the main street.

"The gods be with you," he said as he slunk back into the dark alleyway.

I only need one, she thought as she walked confidently into the light from the torches on the fort wall flickering in the breeze. The picket guards tensed up, spears scuffing on the ground as they stood ready for a confrontation. The difference between the caring man of the alley and these was a world apart. Elen knew which one she preferred.

"It's the Governor's girl," one hissed urgently and a few moments later, with a couple of calls of 'clear' the gate cracked open and pressing against the thick wood, she slipped inside. Such a thing was strictly against protocol, and for a soldier, there could be serious consequences, but being the Governor's daughter did bring a few privileges. She slipped a couple of coins into the nearest man's hand.

Another pair of guards were on the praetorium. A couple of soft knocks and the guard inside opened it.

With a tense arrangement, Magnus had taken a room in the praetorium and the guard at the gate watched her suspiciously as it was Magnus's door she went to, not hers.

As she stood before it, she realised, with surprise, that her hand wasn't shaking.

* * *

Magnus was a light sleeper. It was a good trait to have for a man who often found himself not too far from danger. It was a light tap, so definitely wasn't a Batavi, but even though it had brought him back from a dream about the sands of Mauretania, hunting down Firmas, he was instantly awake and alert. It was still pitch dark, so it had to be a message of the utmost urgency, and for that a soldier would be hammering. Such a knock meant whoever it was didn't want to disturb anyone else in the praetorium. He got up, slid the wooden catch back and with a smile wasn't surprised to see his bride-to-be there.

"Can we talk?" she whispered.

As she slipped inside, he sparked an oil lamp to light.

"Oh my..." she gasped and quickly turned her back to him, hand over her mouth.

He hadn't realised he was naked, but was nevertheless quite disappointed at her reaction. Perhaps she hadn't come to seal their deal in a physical way. Still, the time for that would soon come, and he wouldn't be bothered if the sight of him disturbed her.

He pulled his tunic over his head and, so as to appear a little less threatening, sat down on the end of the bed. "What is it that can't wait until dawn?" he asked

"I think I know how to get the men of the army to be loyal to you. Well, I mean. Err...the Twentieth, at least."

Magnus wondered if she'd rehearsed her little speech in her head on her way to see him. If she had, he supposed it would have sounded a bit better than it had done to his face.

"What I mean is..." she stammered. "Grandmother and I wish to support you becoming Emperor of the West."

Before he realised it, he was up off the bed and his hand was around her throat, but hearing her pathetic croak, he quickly let her go. He didn't need an explicit warning from the old woman to know that harming her granddaughter would not be in his best interests.

"We want the same thing," she replied, rearranging her tunic and coughing to clear the throat he'd almost crushed. In the soft light of the lamp he could see the start of a tear forming. She was very brave to carry on so quickly after what he'd just done.

"Everyone in the empire knows you would be a much better emperor than Gratian. We just need to get the soldiers to see you as someone... special. Not just capable of ruling well, but also capable of *becoming* emperor."

Hearing such words coming from a young girl, ones that not even Andragathius dared to speak to him, felt like a new madness.

"And you know how to do that?" he asked cautiously, his paranoid mind imagining dozens of Gratian's agents with their ears pressed up against the other sides of the walls listening to the treachery being discussed.

She nodded. "A system of roads."

"Roads?" he asked, disappointed. "Why would I want to build roads?"

"With no wood, mortar or dressed stone needed, roads will cost the state much less than the series of forts that have been planned for so long, but never started, but more importantly, they will need no manning. That is the *real* cost of them. If metalled roads were to be made for defence purposes, soldiers could be moved quickly to counter any threat. Also, the budget would come from the state. Once we are married, these will be *your* lands, so with roads for soldiers to travel quickly on, you would be better able to defend them without it costing you, personally, a single denarius."

Magnus was quick enough to realise that there was more than just a kernel of merit in such an idea, but much more than that, it could even be the answer for the raid he'd been waiting for…and hadn't thought of himself. If he could get most of the soldiers out of Deva into the mountains to build military roads, the fort would be undefended. It would be the perfect way to lay a trap for some northern raiders to fall into. Let them attack Deva, or at least the lands around it, and he could simply quick march the men back to cut them off and be celebrated for a great victory in his first month in Britannia.

"Secondly," she continued. "It is known that all soldiers absolutely loathe the long marches they have to do. Out working in the fresh air, undertaking a real project instead of pointless drilling and marching in circles, the soldiers will be very grateful to you for it."

The lamplight illuminated the face of a girl not much older than a child, and he chuckled, despite the flush of cold sweat down his back that the scene was becoming a little too close to the drugged dream. Despite a young girl saying it, she was right, such a project would be a perfect way for him to endear himself to the men he'd need to follow him to Gaul, and at the same time, four of the five thousand of the Twentieth Legion would be out of the fortress, leaving it manned only by a minimum crew...

It could work.

His heart pounded with the gravity of the idea, but it still felt absolute lunacy that he was talking about killing the emperor with a child.

XVII

Coria, Maxima Caesariensis

"No. A pussy is a pussy. The act of castration just takes away your balls. It doesn't give you a pussy!"

Kenon looked back from his place among the bundles and boxes on the back of the wagon and was glad the two hired guards riding behind couldn't hear.

"Right at the moment of orgasm, the very last orgasm of our lives, that's when we do it."

"Do what?" He knew what members of the Cult of Galli did to themselves. It was a threat the weapons instructor had often used to get him to march faster or strike the training post with the sword harder, but from some sickened curiosity, he wanted the strange man to keep talking.

"The act that separates the maleness from the body is how we become devoted servants of Cybele. It's how Attis punished himself for his unfaithfulness to the Goddess, and so to try and be as close to her as he was, we do the same. It's very simple." With one hand, he pretended to close the clamp around his groin and with the other motioned a cutting movement.

"You cut your balls off? Your own balls. Yourself?" Kenon asked, intrigued and repulsed in equal measure.

"Clamp them first, to stem the loss of blood, then the knife. A very sharp one," he said with a dreamy look. "Forget these soulless new churches and listening to a boring sermon, self-castration is the most powerful religious experience a man can imagine."

Kenon had experienced ecstasy enough times to know how much he liked it, but the idea of such pain certainly didn't have the same appeal. "Didn't it...hurt?"

"Wrapped up in ecstasy, the pain is the sacrifice, but it's not something I can explain with just words. You need to experience it yourself to truly understand."

The sun was getting low on the horizon and as the Galli struggled to put a woman's shawl around his shoulders, the movement of the cart clattering over the rough flagstones knocked them into each other. Kenon had run out of money from selling the things that had been in the saddle bags long before he'd satiated his urges in the brothels of Eboracum, and the sight of the Galli's effeminate body rocking under the figure-hugging dress was making him very confused.

The wagon driver decided that the evening was cool enough to stop and get a fire going. The two other carts in the little convoy pulled off the road into a circular glade in the woods. Judging from the old fire pits dotted around, it was a regular place to stop for those who couldn't afford a bed at a mancio. Kenon went straight off to scout for kindling. It was a slave's job, but the ones being transported for sale at the Wall were kept securely chained to the wagons. Besides, it gave him some welcome moments away from the constant crashing of the wagon's wheels on the stones of the road, although if any quiet time drew on too long, the sheer stupidity of his plan came surging back to him. Gathering up an armful of dry sticks, he knew he was fast running out of miles and days to think of anything less idiotic.

This far north, the land was already so uncivilised that even wagons carrying junk for soldiers needed an armed escort. He couldn't imagine what it would be like in the wilderness beyond the Wall. Seeking some comfort in it, he mulled his current plan again. Sell the horse and he'd have more than enough coin to pay someone to find him a way over and out of the empire. That part seemed simple. It was the bit about convincing a horde of barbarians to raid his father's lands that was troubling him.

Another shiver of dread ran out to the tips of his fingers.

With Magnus and his sister fawning over each other, and all that should be his now in Magnus' name, he was certain there was nothing left for him in the south, nothing he could obtain in any legal way.

Whatever was to happen in the next few days, it would be better than spending years of his life alone and forgotten in a dusty sun-baked fort in Africa. Endless years of being screamed at and beaten for not being a good enough soldier. And that was if they didn't just beat him to death for desertion as soon as he was dragged back to Rutupiae.

When he got back to the camp with the twigs and sticks, the slaves were hurriedly arranging the cooking utensils. It was with a familiar longing he watched the chained girl do her work. The wagon master was adamant she wouldn't be touched as there'd be a better price for her at one of the towns at the Wall if she wasn't marked. Kenon supposed it was a fair point. If he managed to get his way with her, her bruises would quite probably last a few days.

As she bent over, her short tunic rode up her legs. The urge was strong enough he found himself looking at the Galli again. Although the self-made eunuch looked just about the strangest sight Kenon had ever seen, and must have been raving mad to have done what he did to himself, he was the first person in months who'd spoken to him as though he was a normal person. Not a useless recruit, or an unwanted son, or a despised brother. For that, his company was something precious. Even if he did half suspect that the Galli was trying to convince him to cut off his own nuts.

The fire was dying. Starved of new wood, the last of the flames licked up in what seemed like some pathetic desperation. The wagon master was already asleep, snoring loudly. The food the slaves had made had been passible, warm and filling at least, and they were bound securely under the wagon, arms behind them so they had no hope of escape. Kenon wondered if they were grateful for the wagon driver's protection...even if they knew it was only to save them for whatever fate awaited in a few days in a market at the Wall. Even if they managed to free themselves from their ropes, he had no idea where they could run to. It was hard enough to travel around as the son of the Governor, never mind for someone with the status of property.

"So," one of the rough-looking escorts grunted as he aggressively poked what was left of the fire. "What's your story, boy? The *real* story!"

The agitated flames flickered across the man's rough face, deep scars marking the hard fights he'd been in, and just about survived.

Kenon shrugged.

"C'mon! We know your fancy friend is going to the Wall to try and get some of the toughest bastards in the empire to cut their own balls off, even though he'll probably get his *head* cut off instead for his troubles. But what's *your* story?"

"Yeah," the other agreed, "Such a nice horse, and so young. Just a whelp, aren't you? Your girlfriend's cut her balls off, but yours haven't dropped yet." They both laughed so raucously at their own joke, one of the wagon drivers shouted at them to be quiet.

"A very nice horse. Fit for the imperial messaging service, I would say."

With a sinking feeling, Kenon was sure that they weren't about to make an offer to buy it.

"Leave him alone," the Galli chimed. "Such brutes you are. No wonder he doesn't want to talk to you."

"Shut it, you!" the first snapped, pointing the glowing end of his fire poking stick threateningly.

Kenon heard the threat in the voice. The pair hadn't been friendly since Kenon had paid the wagon driver to let him ride with them from Eboracum, but they hadn't been openly hostile. Until now. The clear change made him nervous and he wondered what had caused them to act so differently. Maybe it was because they were nearly at the end of the road and they wanted to rob him before they were too close to Vindolanda and the thousands of soldiers along the Wall.

Hoping they wouldn't notice, he slid his hand to the hilt of his sword, wondering if he could get it free of the scabbard before they realised what was happening. It was probably an even worse idea than going over the Wall. Six months of jabbing at a post and marching laden with equipment had made him stronger, but had done absolutely nothing to prepare him for a one-on-one fight with a professional guard.

"Still saying you're going to find that long-lost father of yours?"

That was what he'd blurted out when he found himself on the spot when they'd asked a few days earlier. It wasn't a story that fitted well with the fine horse and gladius at his hip, but that's what he'd come up with, and rather than admit the lie, he decided it would be best to stick with the story.

The Galli leaned in close and put a hand with painted nails over Kenon's ear. "Best not to sleep too deeply tonight."

"What's that, bitch?" the more grizzled of the two asked. "Got some secrets over there? Something to share?"

Kenon knew it was coming, but was also well aware he was no match for just one of them, never mind both. And the Galli would be as useful in a fight as a little girl.

The loud cracking of a stick nearby snapped them all to attention. Well polished steel flashed in the firelight and the guards were on their feet in a heartbeat. Kenon had his blade out almost as quickly, but was ready to defend against the guards more than who or what was prowling around in the darkness. The two big men hunched down, but after staring into the fire all evening, they moved as though they were blind.

A whistling sound, a thud and the bigger man crumpled down without a word. The Galli knocked into Kenon as he tried to run. There was a flash of steel as the other guard slashed wildly at him and then he too fell to his knees groaning as the crashing through the undergrowth got louder. Kenon was the only one still standing and instinctively took a defensive pose with his sword, although he'd never got the knack of attacking the training post, so didn't expect to last too long against whatever was coming at them.

"Put it down!" the Areani said impatiently as he calmly wound the slingshot cord back around his wrist.

They were on the far side of Britannia from where they'd last seen each other, so Kenon couldn't imagine how the Areani could just casually stride out of the forest as though he was back after popping over for a piss. It was said that the trackers and scouts really were a breed apart from normal men, and now he believed it.

His legs about to buckle under him, instead of fighting with the sword, he used it to stop himself from slumping to the floor. He was about to utter some words of gratitude for being saved from whatever the guards had planned, but the existence he was about to be dragged back south to didn't seem any better than being stabbed to death in a dark forest. Not much different from a slave huddled under the wagon. A slave's existence was nothing to envy, but at least they didn't have to march twenty miles a day with all the equipment on their backs.

"What's going on?" one of the drivers called out nervously.

"Maybe a bear," the Areani called back with the same effortless authority of Magnus and Andragathius. It was a power Kenon longed for but knew he'd never be able to muster. "Think we frightened it off."

"Bear..." Kenon heard the driver moan and curse, then the clinking of chains as he pulled the slaves from under the wagon to haul them up with him where they'd be slightly better protected. Kenon didn't think they'd be too much safer with a man who hadn't even noticed his guards were dead.

It wasn't only the guards lying lifeless on the mulch though. The dress pulled up over hairless thighs, the Galli lay sprawled next to the guard who killed him, huge stab wound in the middle of his chest. It surprised him, but Kenon almost wept at the loss.

He was allowed no time to mourn though as the Areani got him to help drag the guard's bodies away from the light of the fire, then stripped them of anything useful. Swords and cheap knives he tossed to the side, but the coin pouches he dropped next to the Galli.

Kenon wanted them, as from their size there would be coin enough for a fine night in the nearest brothel, but he didn't want to ask.

The Areani was about to drag the Galli away, but Kenon stopped him.

"A friend?" the Areani asked, a little surprised.

Kenon wasn't sure.

"Tomorrow we'll pass through the town of Coria. We can find a cemetery and bury him properly, if you like."

"Coria? Kenon asked, surprised, as he'd assumed the Areani had come to take him back to Rutupiae. "Why would you want to take me north?"

"Because your father has been deposed by the new Dux Britanniarum. He's forced your sister to be his wife, and claimed your father's lands for his own."

The rage in Kenon burned as hot as the sun, but only half at Magnus. An equal amount was for himself. He'd seen them together the day they'd arrived back at Segontium, but instead of rushing to Elen's rescue, he'd assumed she was betraying him, and so he'd ridden off the other way. The idea that he had a chance to be a hero in his father's eyes, instead of such a disappointment he'd had to be banished, flushed him with so much pride and excitement he was almost embarrassed. But the euphoria lasted only until the realisation hit him that it was the Dux Britanniarum he faced. A boy who couldn't even swing a sword properly against the man who commanded any soldier in the land he wanted. Fighting his father seemed an order of magnitude easier than setting himself against Magnus Maximus.

He slumped back down and in the weak light of the campfire slid his gladius back into its scabbard. He'd been heading north for the past two weeks with a half-cocked plan of glory in his head, but now all the effort of the journey, and being constantly afraid of what was awaiting in the north, seemed a complete waste. "What can we do?" he asked, not expecting a real answer.

"Get them back," the Areani smiled.

Kenon scoffed. "How?"

"Your father has sent me with a message. You are to get any fighting men you can to go and stand against Magnus."

Father asking for Kenon's help! It was a feeling sweeter than anything he'd ever experienced, even in the most expensive brothel. "But how?" he asked. The Areani shrugged, as though he was waiting for Kenon to explain the plan. "We'll take men from the Wall?"

It was the Areani's turn to scoff. "The Dux Britanniarum commands them."

"So how?"

"Not from the Wall. From *beyond*. You were brave enough to get here with the idea of bringing a barbarian army against your father to get your lands back. It's an insane plan, but an inspired one. And right now it's our only option. We'll do exactly what you planned, but instead of getting them to fight against your father, they will fight *for* him."

It all seemed so perfect, a dream come true, and the fact that he'd had the same plan as his father had come up with swelled Kenon's chest with self-worth. Perhaps he actually had a better military mind than anyone had given him credit for. In the long winter of loneliness, he'd imagined many ways of hurting and killing his father, but he'd never once considered how he could make him proud. It was a wonderful thought, and instantly, he'd never wanted anything so badly.

But there was one thing he didn't understand. "You could have taken a fresh horse from Segontium and caught me before I'd even got to Canovium that first night. You could have told me this weeks ago, instead of jumping out of the bushes right at the perfect moment like someone out of a children's story!"

"I could have, but I needed to see if you were strong enough to go through with your plan to cross the Wall. I figured it would be an easy test to see if you had the strength and fortitude to actually do it. The Votadini would never follow a man they think weak. I doubt you'd have survived a fight with these guards, with only a Galli to defend you…so I…" He looked at the dead bodies. "Let my presence be known."

Kenon would thank him for saving his life later.

"One question though," the Areani asked. "What are you going to offer the Votadini in exchange for them fighting a battle for you?"

"I…err," Kenon stammered and felt his face flush with the shame of having no answer. "What do you suggest?"

"A share. Your father has enough gold to make them happy to stay north for a whole generation. But one more suggestion…"

"What?"

"When we get there, *I* do all of the talking."

Neither of them slept for the rest of the night. The Areani because he was on watch, Kenon because he was terrified of what would happen when the drivers found out that their guards had been slain and the man who'd done it was sitting in the camp waiting to have breakfast with them. Kenon was dozing as he heard the footsteps of a couple of drivers coming to revive the fire so they could cook their oats into porridge. "Some bear, that," one remarked as he looked down at the Galli's blood-soaked body. "Didn't know a bear could stab a man with a sword."

The Areani stood, arms crossed and legs apart, stern expression on his face. While the guards were intimidating brutes, the Areani had the steel poise of a camp prefect and his demeanour put an appropriate amount of respect and fear into the terrified drivers.

"I suppose it dragged the others away, did it?" one asked.

"It did."

"And I don't want to go into them trees for a look?"

"You don't."

"Well, I'm still alive, my load is still secure in the wagon, so I suppose I don't need to be asking too many questions."

The Areani nodded. "The Galli's bag might have a purse or two in it. Maybe it will buy you a few meals in Vindolanda. Maybe even a night in a soft bed somewhere. And you've just acquired yourself a new pair of horses."

"Well then, seems the day started well after all."

As they set the Galli's body on the wagon, Kenon fought the temptation to take a look up under the dress.

A short ride and they got to the town of Coria where the Areani bribed a nervous churchman to bury the Galli in the same cemetery as the locals, despite his obvious...differences.

The drivers were anxious about wanting to put a few miles on before lunch, but Kenon wanted the ceremony done properly. "Why don't we just ride on ahead of them?" He asked as a pair of young boys worked silently but quickly to wrap the body in linen. "We'll get there much quicker."

"Because right now we need them much more than they need us. It'll be very hard for us to get into Vindolanda without them. Two riders without insignia, documents or goods won't get anywhere near."

"So why don't they start and we'll ride on later and catch them up?"

"Because we need to keep an eye on them so they don't go blabbing to anyone with a sword about what happened last night."

When they'd lowered the body into the hole Kenon could think of no words to say, so let the priest chant some pointless and boring liturgy and then turned his back on the only friend he'd never known.

"There it is," the Areani said.

It was just a line on a distant hill but when he worked out they were still a day's ride away from it, the full scale of it became bewilderingly apparent. Apart from its massive size, it had another energy, as its stones defined the absolute limit of the empire. Beyond was a truly wild place where no laws existed. At least not Roman ones.

The drivers were openly distrustful of the Areani all day, and Kenon wondered if they were half expecting him to rob them. Understandably not too keen on spending another night in a camp, they were a bit more relaxed as they pulled into a large mansio that evening. The Galli's purse had been fuller than anyone had expected and they were all smiling as they headed off to the nearby bathhouse to get cleaned, and maybe a whore, on a dead man's coin.

"Why don't they just call a guard and tell them what happened?" Kenon asked.

"You are going over the Wall and yet you know so little of the men on *this* side of it," the Areani huffed. "So close to the Wall the road here is pretty safe. Those guards did the hard work and got them through the dangerous places, and now they don't have to pay them. In fact, they profited a lot, so we did them a real favour."

The next day there had been soldiers on the road a few miles from the fort who'd rifled through the sacks and boxes of stuff on the back of the wagons and tapped the amphora. Others did the same thing before they got to the first buildings of the vicus. None seemed too concerned about the searches and looked so bored as they read through the documents Kenon thought their eyeballs would roll back in their heads.

None had given the slightest attention to Kenon or the Areani, who the soldiers unthinkingly assumed were just a pair of guards, and Kenon realised how right the Areani had been about needing to be seen as part of the convoy. And, as the Areani had also said, none of the drivers saw fit to report the murder of a couple of men two days slow ride to the south. He was deeply relieved to have the Areani with him. He would never have gotten so far without him.

For Kenon, a vicus was nothing more than a stinky and often dangerous place he had to ride through to get away from the fort. If you held your nose and had an armed guard with you, the settlement around Deva was actually rather fascinating, if you were at all interested in how lower people lived. He didn't think the one outside the walls of Segontium, populated by men descended from those who lived in the mountains, was a place fit even for animals, but somehow, despite the stiff breeze, Vindolanda seemed much worse. Maybe burying the Galli had affected him more than he'd thought, but the whole place had the sombre feel of an auxiliary fort after the garrison had just come back from a long forced march.

The cloying smoke from dozens of fires was usual but as they walked past a butcher's shop someone dumped a bucket of entrails into the gutter. The flies that had been feasting on the previous offering made the air hum and the stench was so bad he had to concentrate on not heaving his guts up.

They turned off to find somewhere to stable the horses before they sold them and the drivers even waved a farewell at them. Something else the Areani had been right about was that they would be grateful he'd killed the guards. Kenon didn't think he'd ever understand the ways of these strange Northerners.

It was generally customary for people, soldiers and farmers alike, to be excited about new faces, as it meant news. A stranger was often invited into a taverna to be fed and plied with drinks while he regaled stories of distant battles or some recent scandals involving the emperor, or those in his close circle. Here, the few men he dared look at stared back as though they were crows circling a fresh corpse. Obviously hungry, but not quite ready to settle and start pecking at the eyeballs.

The empire ended at the Wall, but it seemed like proper civilisation had petered out quite some way south.

The smoke from the burning of strange things made him cough and the sight of a runny-nosed street kid turned his stomach, almost as much as the offal and he watched in disgust as the Areani bent down to talk to him. "Netacius? Do you know him?"

The boy nodded, but his expression was vacant, but at the sight of a shiny coin in the Areani's palm, he suddenly snapped to attention.

"Bring him to the inn."

The boy scampered off.

"Keep your mouth shut here. If there's anything that will get us killed, it will be your pretty southern accent."

The large inn near the fort wall was no place to relax and to slew the dirt off after a long day on the road. As they entered, men who made the Areani look like a perfumed diplomat stared at them. A couple sat with their heads tilted back trying to stem the flow of blood from their noses as though they'd been fighting just a few moments before.

A slave, her face covered in bruises and walking with a limp, set two tankards of ale in front of them. It wasn't just bubbles floating on top. "Drink up," the Areani said. "This will be the last of civilisation we'll be seeing for a while."

The ale was warm and to Kenon's taste, appeared to have been brewed for the specific intention of attracting flies. The Areani drowned his almost in one go, but Kenon couldn't imagine how he managed to keep it down. When the girl came back with two bowls of stew, they looked just as revolting.

"Soon you'll be having fond memories of this," the Areani said as he dumped his spoon in so quickly that some splashed on the table.

As Kenon watched the not too unattractive shape of the slave walk away, he noticed the fire and understood why the whole place smelled so strange. They were burning what looked like dried mud.

A little while later, as Kenon pushed a few things around at the bottom of the bowl trying to determine what they might be, the man at the counter caught the Areani's eye for a moment, and gave the barest of nods towards the back door. The last of the bread stuffed in his mouth, the Areani pulled Kenon out into the yard. Even in the fresh air, it somehow managed to smell worse than the inside. He was sure some of the puddles hadn't formed after the last rain shower. He supposed he'd be wanting to do something similar soon when that foul beer had passed through him.

Waiting for them was a man who looked even rougher than those inside. "When?" he snapped with a slight lisp as so many of his front teeth were missing.

"Can you arrange it for tonight?"

"In a rush, are you?"

Perhaps the man had meant it as a joke but the Areani didn't reply and the stony silence meant that he'd overstepped the mark by asking about someone's business. Friendly smile gone and eyes harder, "What have you got?" he asked.

"Two horses."

"Lame?"

"No," the Areani scoffed, offended. "One is from the imperial messaging service."

"Done! Eleventh bell," he said.

Knowing that they really were about to go over the Wall, Kenon's stomach lurched.

"There'll be a rope fifty paces west of the first tower you get to from here. You won't be getting back the same way though. Got a new commander, and he's a strict bastard."

The Areani nodded.

"You taking the lad out with you?"

The Areani nodded again.

"You know they'll have him for breakfast."

Kenon noted nervously that the Areani didn't refute that.

"How can you sell a horse to a man who hasn't even seen it?" he asked as he followed the Areani out into the main road.

"Men live by different rules up here, lad, I told you. He knows me and if I swindled him for a few extra coins, I'd be dead next time I set foot in the vicus."

As the Areani was too nervous to go back to the inn, explaining that it wouldn't be a good thing to have untrustworthy men interested in the dealings of two strangers, they hunkered down in the stables next to the horses they'd just sold. The Areani packed some handfuls of straw together so he could lie in a more upright position and settled down with his sword drawn.

Kenon hadn't imagined there could be such danger on this side of the Wall, but with just a few hours to go after so many days riding to get here, the madness of his plan broke like rocks rolling down a mountain. On the other side, being the Governor's son wouldn't save him if something was to go wrong, like it had any other day of his life, and that made him feel worse than naked. He knew he couldn't simply turn around and go back south, though. Being forced to spend the next quarter of a century at a fort in the sand until he was an old man, and Elen's grandchildren had inherited Father's riches, seemed worse than anything waiting over the Wall.

And if the plan worked, he would get to hear his father call him a hero. In some grand ceremony, with the whole fort of Segontium watching, Father would hand back the pugio with words of gratitude. For that, any risk seemed worth it.

The wind was so strong a couple of times Kenon reached out to grab the Areani's shoulder so he wouldn't get blown away. He pulled himself out of the deep ditch, trying not to gag at the thought of what he'd trodden in at the bottom of it, but all thoughts of traipsing through a midden were forgotten as in the deep dark of the night the mass of the Wall loomed up near them. Kenon couldn't see it, but he was sure he could sense it. He could just about work out its hulking, oppressive size by the stars it blocked out in the lower sky.

It was as high as the walls of Rutupiae, but knowing that they didn't just encompass a fort, but stretched off for some forty miles in either direction was almost impossible to believe.

The Areani gave a warning hush but the wind was blowing so hard that Kenon could have screamed at the top of his voice and no one on duty would have heard.

They crept slowly towards it, careful with every step. A few torches burned in the distance. From the dots of lights Kenon could make out the line of the wall as it rose up the crest of a nearby hill but they were too small and too far away to reveal anything around them.

Kenon was at it, touching it, feeling the territorial limit of everything he had ever known. The stones felt rough. Cold. As unforgiving as the men who guarded it. His breath came in quick gaps. All it would take would be for a guard with a torch to peer over above them and they'd be as good as dead.

"Wait here," the Areani said, but standing in silence in the dark was the worst feeling. Hunched up against the buffeting gusts that felt like the wind was trying to tug his clothes off, he wanted to run as fast as he could back south. When something flapped close to his head, with the sound of a large bird landing on its prey, he almost screamed.

"Go on! *Up*!" the Areani hissed. It took a moment to realise it was a rope he had to climb. He did as he was told and grabbed onto it for all he was worth. He began shimming up, but couldn't see where the top was. He knew he was far enough above the ground and that if he was to fall, his body would be broken beyond any hope of recovery. When he finally made it, he flopped onto the worn stones of the walkway and lay panting and shaking. A few moments later, the Areani sprang up behind, quite effortlessly, and with a few short whispered greetings, or instructions, the rope was flung off the other side. Kenon's hands were weak and his palms sweaty and he wasn't sure if he'd be able to lower himself down the other side... but paying no heed to his hesitation, the Areani bundled him over. Scuffling his way down the rough blocks in the pitch dark, Kenon dropped down onto the short grass below and no sooner had the Areani landed next to him, the rope was yanked back up. "Mad bastards," the now slightly richer guard called down, unconcerned with what two fools wanted in the wilderness on the other side.

The end of the rope whipping against a crenellation as it was pulled back up, was the sound that announced they were beyond the point of turning back.

"Now what?" Kenon asked.

"Now we run for our lives."

The boggy, uneven ground was just waiting to snap an ankle, but when they were a mile or so away from the Wall they came to a track of mostly compacted mud. It was not what Kenon would call a road, but it was much easier going and they settled into a jog. At least the wind was at their backs, strong enough to push them along.

"Did you hate every moment of the marches they forced you to do at Rutupiae?" the Areani asked.

"Yes. Or course," Kenon said as he worked to match his pace.

"Well, now you should love them, because all of that training is about to save your life."

"Why?"

"Because if we're caught out here come daybreak, men from either side of the Wall will kill us."

Splashing through the puddles, soggy mud and occasional stretches of bedrock, Kenon asked, "Didn't *you* hate the marches?"

"Only half of them."

"Which half?"

"The half where we had to turn around and head back to the fort."

Despite the severity of the situation, Kenon laughed. When Caesar had been young, he'd been captured by raiders and every child knew the story of how he made them increase the ransom because he thought he was worth more. Kenon wondered if leaving the empire alone was an even braver thing to do than Caesar's expedition to Britannia. Caesar had the power and might of two legions at his back. Kenon was doing this by himself.

In the gaps of the thin clouds scuttling across the sky, he saw constellations of bright stars and wondered if they were the same ones that sparkled over Britannia and the rest of the empire, but he stumbled over something unseen and fell to his face. As the Areani pulled him up, he asked if he was all right.

"Yes," Kenon said, rubbing the scuffs on his palms and realised it had been a very long time since anyone had been concerned about him enough to ask him that. He'd buried the Galli a couple of days before and wondered if he was saying goodbye to a friend, but as the Areani patted him on the shoulder, now he was sure he was making a new one.

Before he'd been banished to Rutupiae, Kenon knew he'd have died from exhaustion from trying to march so many miles without rest. As the sun began to come up on the strangely barren landscape, he was bone tired, but also exhilarated.

He wasn't quite ready to think any grateful thoughts about Bassus though.

The Areani led him down into a steep little valley with a fast running stream pouring over the rocks. The rivers Kenon had known were wide, muddy, meandering things you could row a boat on. This one was noisy, rocks in it turning the water white as it flowed over them in what seemed like a panic. Beyond the Wall was a different world, one much, much older. And much more dangerous.

Cutting ferns and a few low branches from a stunted tree, the Areani put up a rudimentary shelter against the side of a moss covered rock. "We rest and when it's dark we move again."

"Who will take the first watch?" Kenon asked, but didn't like how the Areani chuckled. "What would you like to watch? If someone finds us here, shall we fight them? Or shall we run back to the Wall? If they find us, boy, we're dead. So best to get some sleep in case we wake up alive."

Kenon lay on the soft, but annoyingly damp moss behind the twigs trying to listen for any sounds that weren't the bubbling stream. Despite fearing for his life, and fretting every time the wind blew through a bush near the ridge, making him think it was a band of men after his blood, he soon fell into a deep sleep and dreamed of a villa with the floors covered in the most exquisite mosaics, and being carried on a litter around his own house.

The sun was still up when he woke. The Areani snored so loudly Kenon appreciated what a good idea it had been to camp next to the noisy stream. Slowly, careful not to make any sudden movements or knock the shelter down, he found some dried meat in his bag, and as he chewed, wondered how much he would laugh at the memory of this day in the future.

The Areani insisted on waiting until full dark before venturing out, then did a full reconnoitre of the area before pulling the shelter down and scattering the tree branches.

They marched all through the night again. As inadvertent as it was, Bassus had prepared him well for this adventure. Kenon wondered if he'd see the bastard again one day, and what would he do if they did.

The Areani ignored the shrill calls of an owl but when he heard a dog bark stopped so suddenly that Kenon bumped into him.

"It's far away," Kenon whispered.

"If it has our scent, it will be close soon. Up here there are many ways of dying. Some are a lot worse than others."

"You've been up here before?"

"I am *from* here! That's why I know how much danger we are in."

Heart pounding, legs not feeling so strong any more, Kenon carried on. To where, or who, he was starting to get more and more nervous about.

The next morning they walked through the dawn, the sun casting the landscape in a soft, golden hue. The beauty of the treeless scrubland was stark, but he'd never imagined that anything beyond the Wall could be pretty. For some reason it gave him some hope for the future as though it was symbolic of things working out well. Hope. It was a feeling he hadn't experienced for so long it seemed unfamiliar.

That unknown future was about to become a little more known as the hillfort they were heading to had smoke rising from half a dozen fires.

Kenon hadn't really known what to expect, but it wasn't the half-ruined settlement perched on top of a barren hill.

"It's just a trading fort, or if things have gone to shit, a lookout station," the Areani said. "If you think Vindolanda was rough…"

It didn't give Kenon much hope that he was about to meet the men who would do his bidding…and he watched as two huge dogs bounded out of the gap that once was the fort's gates.

"Stand still," the Areani ordered. "Very still."

The dogs were huge, mangy, and with lips drawn back threateningly, had the biggest teeth Kenon had ever seen. One barked for all it was worth, but the other prowled around, head down, growling. He wasn't sure which was more frightening.

"Do not move," the Areani said again, quite unnecessarily.

The dog nearest Kenon lunged at him and as he bumped into the Areani, he slipped to his knees. Suddenly, the nearest dog's face was in his, saliva dripping from its bared incisors, breath foul enough to turn his stomach.

A big hand grabbed the back of his tunic and he was pulled to his feet. "Why don't you just roll over? Maybe they'll tickle your tummy!" he mocked.

A couple of men strolled down the low slope, walking far too slowly for Kenon's liking. Nor were they shouting to try and control the dogs. After a few moments, one whistled, but instead of running away, the dogs darted behind them.

"Walk," the Areani said. "Slowly. Maybe concentrate on not falling over."

The growling dog lunged at Kenon's heel and with a yelp, he staggered forward in a flailing gait as he tried to keep his ankles away from the sharp teeth. He saw the men laughing and realised that the dogs had been trained to herd them. The barbarians were treating the son of the Governor like a sheep. He only just managed to stop himself shouting out his outrage.

"Even more important than not getting your face bitten off, when we're inside, only I do the talking. Pretend that you have no tongue. Understood?"

"All right," Kenon said, a little sullenly as he thought his status should mean he was the one dealing with the diplomacy.

"Your life depends on it. Understand? That doesn't bother me too much, but mine does!"

"Who are we meeting?" Kenon asked and was almost knocked off his feet by the slap to the back of his head. "Not even a whimper!" the Areani snapped, his voice no less threatening than the growl of the dogs. "Their leader is Padarn and while having you for breakfast might be a little exaggeration, he might save a little of you for dinner."

When the two approaching men recognised the Areani, they started howling with laughter, but in a way that was far from friendly. Scarred faces, missing teeth, rough, patchy beards and an odour that emanated clearly from ten paces downwind, Kenon quickly reappraised his opinion about the wagon guards or the men in Vindolanda being rough bastards. He wondered if they'd trained the dogs to be so vicious, or they'd just picked up such behaviour from being around them. Then they spoke. He'd heard his mother speak the guttural native tongue to his sister before and had always snapped at her to shut up, but coming out of the mouths of these men it brought the realisation that he was out beyond the reach of the empire crashing down on him. There was no protection out here and suddenly he was sure that his father's name might even be a danger rather than the privilege it had always been. The Areani's command to keep his tongue still seemed like a very good idea.

The two men had their swords drawn. The rusty spots and nicked edges would have earned them a beating from their optio in Rutupiae, but they would still be lethal in the hands of such burly men, and as they trudged up the hill, they didn't resheath them. It was almost as lacking in etiquette as setting dogs out to herd them in.

The fort had once had a perimeter wall, but some raised earth and weathered timbers poking through the brambles were all that was left of it. There were a fair few houses inside, all oddly round and not plotted in any sort of pattern. The ones the locals deemed still habitable had roughly repaired thatch and walls. As they were led among them, the dogs still fixated on the backs of Kenon's legs as though they were fresh steaks, he noted how confusingly unorganised the layout was. There were no straight lines to be seen anywhere, and the well-trodden muddy path wound haphazardly with no sense of direction. The disorientating effect was terrifying, and that was before the smell hit him. Rotting meat, shit, and something else he wasn't sure he wanted to put a name to. It was even worse than the vicus at Segontium on a windless summer's evening.

A hard shove in his back and he stumbled into a muddy clearing. At the centre was a smouldering fire, the bones of the last few feasts scattered around like a battlefield a few months after the fight. His first impression was that leading such men into the empire was not such a good idea after all. The thought of having men like this anywhere near any of his farms and slaves made him so nervous he was almost sick at the thought that these were his mother's people. He was related to them...

One of the men who'd brought them in ducked down under the thatch of one of the houses and a few moments later a huge man stepped out into the light. No optio, centurion or prefect, even one with a whip in his hand, had ever elicited such a feeling of raw terror in Kenon's heart.

He was old. Maybe late fifties, maybe even sixties, but far from having the frailty of a man soon to be ending his days, he had the power of a sturdy oak about him. With his huge, dirty, grey beard and thick bear skin draped over his shoulders, he looked more animal than man. His weathered face, with its leather skin and deep spiderweb lattices around the eyes, wasn't the most notable feature. That was his ice blue eyes. This was Padarn.

"I won't honour you by speaking your mother's tongue," he spat to the Areani. "You chose Rome, so I will speak to you in their cursed tongue."

Rather than being glad that they weren't about to kill each other, Kenon was deeply disturbed that terrifying dogs and drawn swords were the way barbarians greeted their kin. If this was an example of them being friendly, it begged the question of what they did with their enemies. It was far from a friendly smile on Padarn's face though.

He came to stand before them. "Looks like half a life sucking at the teat of the empire was kind to you," he said.

His accent was so thick it sounded as though he was abusing the Latin words by speaking them over his tongue.

"I never imagined I would see your face again," Kenon thought he said.

"Sometimes the world turns strangely," the Areani replied.

"Do you remember my last words to you?" Padarn asked

"I've not thought about them for so long," the Areani replied glibly. "Something about tearing my head off my shoulders if I should ever stand before you again?"

"And here you are," the old beast smiled, holding his wide hands out and looking up at the sky and clouds as if to thank the gods.

Kenon had thought that men like this would hail him as a leader just because he was the Governor's son. The difference between them and him was that of the eagle to the mouse. If he was to survive the coming day, he would really have to reassess how smart he thought he was. Rather than try to persuade Padarn to do anything for him, he'd wondered if it would be better to take his chances with the dogs.

"I always regretted what I had to do," the Areani said.

"What you *had* to do," the big man mused, a hint of a smile just visible through his beard. Then, eyes wide, teeth as striking as the dog's, he yelled, "You left us for the wolves!"

Kenon took a step back. It was as though Padarn's voice, his searing rage, rent a tear the fabric of the world and it was some monster of the natives' underworld who was speaking. It was so powerful, it made Kenon shudder with dread.

Somehow, the Areani had the courage to talk back. "If you'd given me men who could actually fight instead of just plundering and raping and getting blind drunk after every raid, I would have led them. I tried to warn you."

Kenon clicked that they were talking about the Conspiracy. It had happened when he was a boy, but he remembered it as the only time he'd ever seen Father truly frightened. He wondered what the garrisons on the Wall had been thinking when they'd let an army of people like this through. They must have known they were condemning countless people in the south to absolute havoc. The two of them were talking about a grudge that was thirteen years old.

"So we fight?" Padarn said.

"If we must."

"The gods demand it!" Padarn shouted in that gut-churning voice. "I will wear your teeth as a necklace, your head as decoration for my house, and the rest of you I will throw to the dogs."

"Seems fair," the Areani shrugged. "But I will spare your life, as for the plan, I have come to tell you about, I need you alive."

"We can discuss everything over your dead body," Padarn snarled as he tossed his bear skin to the side. One of the men who'd crowded around in a semi-circle to watch, caught it. Then, without any ceremony, any agreement or sizing up his opponent, he charged. His movement was so quick that in an instant Kenon knew all of his months of hard training with wooden swords and wicker shields had been for absolutely nothing. Never in his life would he learn to be fast enough to dodge, or strong enough to defend against, such an attack.

The Areani managed to swing his upper body to twist out of the way though. The movement seemed more of a dance than a fight and swinging his fist harmlessly in the air, Padarn lost his balance and fell face first into the mud. Laughing as he stood to back up, the beast closed in again, slower, more calculated this time. He tried to use his superior height and bulk to bear down on the Areani, but after some punches, knees aimed at groins and chests, the Areani got inside his grip, twisted around and dropping to his knee, rolled the beast over his shoulder. Still grabbing him by the wrist, he could have yanked Padarn's arm out of his socket, but left him sitting in the mud, defeated, and stepped back.

The men shouted encouragement but seeing their leader on the ground, easily bested, dampened their enthusiasm somewhat and the dynamic had changed.

In his previous plan, Kenon wondered if this would have been the moment he'd have stepped up and offered to be their leader. He was quite sure now that Bassus had valid a point about his mental acuities.

"You always were fast," Padarn said as pulled himself up to a knee and flicked the rancid mud off his hands. "Like a weasel." On his feet again, he threw a massive swing with a balled fist that would have knocked a horse down. The Areani ducked under it, and with a shoulder, barrelled into Padarn's ribs. The beast landed flat on his back again, but this time was winded and stayed lying with his arms and long hair splayed out in the mud.

Kenon almost called out for the Areani to stamp on the big man's neck and finish it properly. Instead, panting, he held his hand out. The gesture seemed to offend the big man, and he called out some strange words and a moment later a boy ran out of the house with a sword bigger than Kenon had even seen before. It must have been twice the length of a spatha, something boys told stories about when they were pretending to be brave Roman soldiers standing strong in the face of a brutal barbarian army. The sheer length of it elicited no sense of childhood awe though, just pure dread.

"What could you possibly offer me to earn the forgiveness of your betrayal?" Padarn asked as he held it in two hands. The size of the muscles in his arms would have made the strongest gladiator weak with jealousy.

"Redemption."

That seemed to be the secret word to blow out Padarn's anger like a candle. With a roar, the beast swung the huge sword and rammed it point first into the mud. "If the business you speak of is less than worthy, this is where your head will roll." He motioned for everyone to stay where they were, and pointing an accusatory finger at the Areani, bellowed, "Speak!" And then he was pointing at the house. "At the fire! But you are far from me calling you son again!"

Kenon coughed in disbelief. The fight he'd just witnessed had been between a father and a son! If only he could fight like the Areani against Father, he mused. Padarn was looking at him. "And who is this?"

"The boy is part of the plan," the Areani said.

With a surge of self-importance, Kenon stepped forwards, but when Padarn said, "You haven't forgotten my tastes!" all sorts of alarm bells went off in his head at what that could mean. He was so shocked that the Areani had to shove him to get him to move.

As they walked to the house Padarn tried to sluice some of the mud off his clothes, but realised just how dirty he was and pulled his shirt over his head. Kenon marvelled at the stringy muscles under the loose, leathery skin and the cicatrices of old scars that could have been caused by swords or whips. Whatever had happened to leave him marked in such a way, Kenon was sure that other men wouldn't have survived such an ordeal.

As Padarn ducked down under the mossy thatch to enter his house the Areani quickly touched his finger to his lips. Kenon understood the gesture as a command to be silent. That was fine. He didn't have the nerve to bargain with Padarn to get fighting men south of the Wall to fight for his father.

He bent his head under the maw that was the door to the roundhouse and the sudden darkness inside was overbearing. It seemed more like a mausoleum rather than somewhere people lived. Tutors had told him that the half-wild ancients had worshipped the sun and living in such a dark place he understood why that would be.

He was almost glad that he wasn't allowed to speak as he would have surely muttered a deep insult to the people who somehow called this a house.

The mewling of a baby from somewhere in the darkness was a welcome sign of life.

"Another son?" the Areani asked.

"Aye. Maybe this one will survive Roman steel and will live to be a man to fight the eagle. And won't grow up to betray me!"

Kenon made his way uncertainly to the fire in the middle of the floor. The warmth drew him close but with the thick smoke hanging under the rafters, it seemed as though the idiots were camping in their own house. He imagined the dumbfounded look on the barbarian's faces if they ever saw a hypocaust.

"Some very important news you must have ready on your tongue for you to even *dare* to come back after so many years," Padarn said as he settled himself in the big chair at the head of the fire.

"I do," the Areani said and as he sat down a woman stepped out of the darkness to set the baby in his arms.

"This plan of yours, will it change my circumstances and make me a rich and well-respected man?"

"It will."

"Then maybe it will be worth your journey. And your life. Tell it to me."

"Raiding?"

"Where? South?"

"Yes."

"It gets better. You talk to me like a girl slowly opening her legs."

Kenon turned slowly to see how the mother of Padarn's child would react to such an insult. He wasn't too surprised that she didn't seem to care.

"Thirteen years ago they sent Theodosius against us," the Areani said.

"Theodosius..." Padarn mused and licked his lips as though he was tasting the name. "That is a name I have heard even less than yours over these long years."

"Do you remember the two men with him, sucking his tits like Romulus and Remus."

"Aye. One was his son with the same name. I hear he is now emperor in the east. And the one who called himself Magnus Maximus over the spilled blood of my men."

"And who has just been made Dux Britanniarum?"

The big man leaned over, suddenly more interested. "Magnus Maximus is back in Britannia. And he has been rewarded for what he did to us?"

The Areani nodded. "Richly."

"You didn't come all this way north and bribe yourself across the Wall just to tell me this. What more do you have to say? Tell it to me. Stop teasing me!"

"I have it on trusted authority that Maximus will take almost the whole Twentieth Legion from Deva to Segontium."

The big man's brow creased with a distrustful frown. "And why would he do that?"

"To build roads near the coast instead of the forts that they've been planning for years."

"Roads. They gave up the idea of building their forts? Roads are a good idea. Move men across the land fast. So the whole fortress of Deva will be empty?"

"And the lands around Deva will be undefended."

"You think we could take the fortress?"

"We took the whole Wall once, but I am not thinking about the walls of Deva. The land around it is rich and full of undefended villas bursting with spoils. Gold and women. We can raid them."

"One last time," Padarn mused. "It would be a very good story to be told around the fire by my son when he is older. One last raid so I can give meat and gold to the men for them to remember my name with. I like this idea. But before I agree, I will send some eyes to make sure what you say is true. An insult, for sure, but your betrayal still tastes sour in my mouth after so many long years."

Kenon was confused. Magnus had fought his father and they needed the Northerners to help get his lands back in return for a good payment. This is what they'd come over the Wall to organise. The cold dread began to grow and he hoped desperately that the only reason the Areani had changed the story was because it was a better reason for Padarn to lead his army south. But that still didn't sit right, because how would he get Padarn to agree to such a change of plan when they were already in Britannia?

"And now, tell me, what does this nice looking boy have to do with all of this?"

"A gift."

The terror that something was very wrong exploded in Kenon's gut like a punch.

The Areani was lying to either his father, or to Kenon and he couldn't work out which. He began to panic. He didn't dare to open his mouth, though.

"Really?" Padarn grinned and looked at Kenon again. "Why do I suspect he has some more value, apart from the obvious short-term pleasure?"

Short-term pleasure? Kenon didn't dare imagine the man meant what he thought he did. Only the fear of the dogs outside stopped him from bolting out of the door.

"A little. Do you remember a general named Octavius. Eudaf Hen, we called him."

"I do, of course. Another name I have cursed for years under the full moon. A blood-oath I made for his head."

"He was also rewarded richly for the men of ours he killed."

"The Governor of Britannia. This, I know. And now he spends his time fortifying the coast to protect against my ships. Now building roads."

"I can't offer you his head, but I can give you his son. Octavius will pay very good gold for his return."

Kenon was about to blurt out a protest that being a hostage was not anything like the plan he'd agreed to, but still didn't dare to say anything. He looked at the Areani again, silently imploring him to laugh and say it was all just a joke.

"It might take half a moon at least while we wait for my eyes to return," Padarn said. "Does he know what I expect of him?"

"He made friends with a Galli on the way here."

The big man laughed loudly. "Then he understands everything."

And Kenon realised that he'd been betrayed again. This time though it hurt even more than what Father had done. His head swirled as he tried to work out the Areani's hidden agenda. The ransom for the Governor's son would be very generous indeed, if that son hadn't been disinherited.

Padarn clicked his fingers and pointed into a recess at the back of the house. "My bed is there. Get yourself ready."

His stomach felt as though it was full of lead. His mind reeled, but even worse than what was coming, was knowing the Areani had lied so that Kenon would get himself over the Wall rather than being forced across it…He'd been so naive, so stupid. And now he would never get to hear Father call him a hero.

XVIII

Britannia Secunda

In unison with the three men next to him, Magnus hacked his pick into the ground.

To be back in the easy familiarity of men who trained and lived together felt a great relief, and although making a road through the mountains was hard work, there was something deeply calming in it.

Bare-chested, labouring like a common recruit, sweating with the others, obeying the commands of the over-seeing engineers, he chuckled at the thought of what Theodosius would say if he could see him now. Demoted out of the rank of officer on the spot would be the least of Magnus' worries.

They were digging out the foundation for the road and as he paused to stand up and look back at what they'd done over the last week or so, he saw how it cut dead straight through the valley in a long open wound. It wasn't just an enjoyable way to spend the day in the sun, not just a nostalgic throwback to the days of his youth when he'd first been signed up to the army and made his first friends. All he'd done for the past half a month was to get himself endeared with the men of the Twentieth.

Hard as a hobnail boot, most of them. As he'd marched some four thousand of them west from Deva to the mountains at the empire's edge, he'd felt their scorn and mistrust. But a few days working with one crew opening a quarry, others temping the compacted gravel for the upper layers, as well as eating with them in their mess tents, the change had been remarkable.

Staked out along the side of the trench, spears had been thrust into the soft earth, armour and helmets draped on them like drying washing, and shields leant against them. Scouts roamed the hills and lookouts had whistles to alert them to any threat, so they would have ample time to armour up and get into formation if anything was to happen, so they all worked with bare backs.

The shields all had their owner's names written on the insides. The one nearest had Vectovecius COH II THR LEG XX. That was the guy with the dark curly hair with the spade behind the man to Magnus' right. Once again, he almost laughed out loud at the idea of making such an effort to learn the names of individual soldiers…such a strange thing for a commander to do.

He'd noticed that in general, it was the older men who were the least enthusiastic about him. They were close to retirement age and were looking forward to the pension and parcel of land they'd be given to till, sow and harvest. So at this time of their lives, with more than twenty years done, that was a lot more appealing than being on the field between a clash of emperors. It would be these he left behind to man the forts and the Wall.

For the rest, young men, those for whom twenty-five years service seemed an unfathomably long time, two weeks in and he was sure that if he announced he was going to sail to Gaul to oust Gratian, most of them would follow.

As he began digging again, matching his rhythm to the men on either side of him, he laughed at the sheer absurdity of the situation. Toiling away with a road crew covered in dirt and sweat was a strange enough experience for all the men, never mind himself. But unbelievably the Dux Britanniarum, commander of three legions, was doing it at the suggestion of a young girl. He remembered the night she'd woken him to creep into his room under her father's nose and had told him her idea, and how it had kept him awake for the rest of the night wondering if it had actually been a dream or not.

The alternative would have been pacing along the walls of Segontium waiting in the cold wind for news of raiding ships heading their way, which had seemed less than appealing, so he'd done what she'd suggested and moved almost an entire legion. And not only had she got him to bring some four thousand men to the far side of Britannia Secunda, she'd also convinced him to work with the men as though he was their equal.

The mystery of how a girl only just past her first flowering had got such an understanding of the hearts of soldiers had started to vex him. He hadn't slept well since ridding himself of the old woman's herbs, and now he had something else to keep him awake. She'd sworn that no one had put words in her mouth, but he wasn't fool enough to trust the answers of anyone related to the old woman. His suspicion of how a young girl could have such insights of hardened soldiers was tending towards the idea that one of them was whispering things into her ear. One from the Segontium garrison, more than likely one of the four she'd made him post as her personal guard. It would be a shockingly brazen thing for her to do, but he'd met the girl's grandmother, so wouldn't put it past her.

The constant wind was enough to keep the sweat from beading on his brow, but he was still thirsty. Without breaking rhythm, he looked up, and right on cue, saw the water cart inching up the line, the slim figure of his wife-to-be passing out cups into the hands of grateful labourers. The scene seemed so like Jesus with the loaves and fish it was a little unnerving.

When he'd first arrived in Segontium, half-mad, and discovered the shocking depths of her deceit, he'd wanted to rip her head off and smash it against the wall. Now, he was wondering just how far he could go with her at his side. Mysterious ways, indeed.

She wore a finely embroidered tunic, its lines concealing some of her feminine curves, accentuating others. At a feast she would have been the talk of the evening, but out on an exposed mountain among the burly men of the road crew, she looked absolutely divine. Such attire was ill-suited to her task, but was obviously a carefully considered choice. Hers or her grandmother's, he wasn't sure, but definitely not her father's. What he was sure of was that at night, more than a few of the men would be worshipping her in their own, private, ways. Marrying such a girl could do nothing but enhance his standing among them.

In a fluid, circular motion Magnus swung the pick up over his shoulder and slammed it into the earth again. Behind him, another row of men shovelled what he'd loosened to the side. Revelling in the feeling of his muscles flexing, his mind settled on the simple task of digging. Such thoughtless, menial work was a very welcome relief from the weight of his plan and the consequences that would come with it. Stripping the fortress of Deva of her soldiers so the surrounding lands would be irresistibly ripe for barbarians to raid would cost Roman lives. Ever since he'd set the Areani off to entice the fighters of the Votadini tribe south, he'd lain awake until the light of the dawn crept over the horizon. If he ever did manage to drift off, he'd wake in a sweat. No matter how much he told himself it was a step towards being able to usher in a new age for the empire with secured borders, and an emperor the soldiers of the empire respected, rather than reviled, he knew it was for his glory they would be sacrificed.

He wondered again how much their spilled blood would weigh on his heart in the coming months and years. And on his soul.

Mostly, though, he worried about Octavius finding out that some of his villas and workers

had been wilfully sacrificed for no other reason than Magnus wanted to be held in high enough regard by the soldiers. If the truth of the situation was ever to crawl out from the lies that buried it, not only would his downfall be assured, the truth would be his death. Whether it would be an order from Gratian, or a command from the old woman, would have little difference. He'd tried to steel himself with the fact that every other emperor who'd ever lived had spent their days dealing with such a conscience, and many had done much worse things to their people.

"You're building this road so fast, we have to ride much further every time we come back," Elen cooed in that quite attractively sweet voice of hers.

She handed him the big clay cup, but he remembered how she'd told him to not be the first to take the water. How such a simple, meaningless gesture as letting others drink first could have such import for such hardened men was something in all his years in command he'd never once considered. He did so now, passing the cup to one of the men. 'A superior putting a lesser man before him makes a man feel valued and respected' she'd said. Soldiers being grateful for such a small thing was almost as surprising as much as it being something the girl could have known.

The four men in her personal guard, all in perfectly polished armour, stood to attention and Magnus wondered which one was whispering things into her ear for her to pass on to him.

If he found out that one was any closer than his station dictated, that man had better hope it was only advice about the behaviours of soldiers he was putting into her.

Then again, he wondered if it would be more advantageous to reward him, as his suggestions, as daft as they'd seemed coming from the lips of a girl, were laying the foundations for his bid for the purple.

He just wished the Votadini would attack soon, as rounding up raiders was much easier than weaselling his way through all the intrigue. Staking all he had, or hoped to one day have, on untrusted alliances, felt as precarious as playing ludus on a three legged table. Again, he wished that there was someone he could ask for advice or guidance. Theo might have some insight from his palace in Constantinople, but writing a letter that would have to travel almost the whole width of the empire about how best to gather men for a civil war would be tantamount to penning his own execution order.

He laughed again at the madness of it all. His fellow labourers looked at him quizzically, but he thought it best not to tell them he was thinking of asking the old woman for advice on how to best usurp the Western Emperor.

Elen dunked the cup into the barrel on the back of the cart and, squatting down, held the dripping cup out for him in a delicate hand. As he took it, their fingers touched, but far from being a sweet caress with the woman he was about to be married to, he still had such a shock of her being in his dreams that he pulled back quick enough to spill some of the water. Before he took a sip, recalled the state of her father from whatever she'd put in his wine the first time they'd met.

He took a long swig, reasoning that if she'd put something in the barrel, then all the hundred and sixty men in the section's crew would be having strangely vivid dreams together. Whatever could be said of the climate and customs of this strange part of the world, at least the water tasted as though it came from heaven itself. There could be no herbs in it, as it was as fresh as the stream that ran through the Garden of Eden.

Thirst slaked, he said, "Thank you," as he handed it back.

She gave him a sweet smile and seeing how beautiful she looked, a base longing welled up. She'd been reluctant to agree to a date for them to be married, but Magnus knew when the ceremony would be; the day after he'd led the men to destroy the raiders. A capable commander who'd just won a crushing victory, marrying the daughter of the Governor of Britannia and a woman of a local chieftain, would be a perfect scene. As long as he could keep smiling through the guilt of the farmers about to be slain. Once the Twentieth were behind him, then he could go north to Eboracum and do the same there with the Sixth Legion, and then onto the Wall. When the time was right, he would enact the next part of the plan, the one that would take him back to Augusta Treverorum in a much different status than the one he'd left with.

He tried to focus on the rhythmic work again.

Annoyingly though, everything now depended on Elen's brother, and he was the weakest link in everything. Kenon was a sad disappointment to his father, a Nero in the making according to the grandmother the boy had never met…Magnus winced as the pick found a stone sending a shock up his arm...and everything he hoped for was balanced on the knife point of the pathetic little bastard managing to bring a band of Votadini into the trap. It had been weeks since the Areani had ridden off after him. They should have come by now. Not only was he impatient, he was beginning to worry.

Only stunted hawthorn bushes grew in the poor soil of the windswept landscape and he wondered where he would get the wood he needed for all the crosses he was going to nail the raiders to. He was looking forward to christening his new roads with the prolonged suffering of the Barbarians as Crassus had done with Spartacus' slaves along the Appian Way. He was sure the Twentieth would enjoy the spectacle. Maybe he would let them all take turns with the hammers.

A horse pulled up to a halt on the other side of the pile of rubble they'd dug out of the long trench. It was a fine animal, rich brown, the colour of the mud Magnus was digging, tall and strong.

Andragathius looked down with a surly scowl, not quite managing to mask the look of disgust that Magnus would lower himself to the level of dirt-covered men. The natural order was that rule came from the top down, so the commander should not be shovelling road gravel with the common soldiers.

"A word," he said tersely.

Magnus shrugged. "Speak." At Andragathius's reluctance, he added, "I have no secrets from my men." But before the Batavi took that as permission to reveal something about the Votadini, which needed to be kept a secret on his life, he pretended to give up. "Empire business," he shrugged before clambering out of the hip-height trench.

The centurion standing guard, spared the labour thanks to his rank, would have had an ordinary soldier whipped dropping tools and walking away from his task without permission. He looked confused as Magnus wiped his brow with a cloth, but stared at the others in case anyone had the same idea and needed reminding of their status.

In a smooth, effortless movement, a demonstration that he'd been brought up on saddleback, Andragathius dismounted in a way so graceful it belied the man's size.

A cluster of tents stood nearby, shields, swords, armour and spears stacked up at the ready in case they were needed in a hurry, as even with a shovel in his hand, a soldier of Rome never stopped being a soldier. Andragathius shook his head so they carried on beyond the tents, only stopping near a little bridge they'd finished a few days ago. It only spanned a little stream a good horse could leap across. Compared to the incredible feats of engineering that were the aqueducts in Hispalis or Rome it was absolutely inconsequential, but it was Magnus' first arch. Seeing the amount of work it had taken the engineers to make the wooden supports and seating the precisely cut stones, he now had a real appreciation of the skills and effort that must have gone into the monumental constructions around the empire. Watching it get built, he couldn't help but wonder what buildings would be erected in his name one day.

"Unusual activity sighted off the west coast of the Wall," Andragathius said gruffly.

Magnus' heart leapt. "How many?"

The Batavi was a staunch traditionalist so was uncomfortable out of the rigid structures of command he was used to. The thought that Magnus wasn't just allowing an incursion by the Votadini, but actively arranging it, disturbed him deeply. Magnus' reaction to the news was the opposite, and he was greatly relieved and only just stopped himself thanking the Lord. Inviting raiders to the land was far from the actions of a good Christian.

"Enough to worry about," Andragathius said as he handed over the scrap of parchment. The scribble was barely legible, as though whoever had written it had done so with such haste he didn't think there was a single moment to spare.

A flutter of nerves washed through Magnus and with a churning of his stomach, his mouth was suddenly full of saliva. The soldier in him itched to blow the horn and quick march the whole legion back to Deva to confront the bastards before they could even get out of their boats. It was such an unfamiliar feeling to stand there knowing a threat was coming but not rousing the army to action. The same message would have already been seen by the legate of Deva and Octavius, but they had dozens of such reports every week.

As he crunched the note in his fist, he knew that the most important thing was that he couldn't allow even the merest hint of suspicion that he knew about the raids and did nothing. The sighting of boats off the Wall was nothing on its own, as the barbarians traded and raided each other, so if anyone were to ask, he had a reasonable explanation as to why he dismissed the note.

"Can I speak freely?" Andragathius asked.

"Of course. Always. And as a friend."

Even with such permission the Batavi still looked uncomfortable. "Now, with this news in your hand, perhaps it would be a good moment to lead the men back to Deva and set blockades at the estuary mouths. It could be that you read the note and decided to act straight away to *prevent* the raids. It could be that they will call you a hero for that."

The courage of the Batavi to say such a thing was impressive and on one hand, Magnus was touched at his friend's concern. On the other though, it meant he didn't have full faith in Magnus' plan. The suggestion did have merit, and perhaps an honest man would have agreed, but for the reaction Magnus needed from the men of the Twentieth, it wouldn't be enough. "If I lead them back to the fortress now, there will be no battle."

Andragathius took a moment to formulate his response. "Exactly."

Magnus sighed. "Preventing a battle is not the same as winning one."

Changing tack, Andragathius added, "For the Dux Britanniarum, perhaps foresight is also an important quality."

Having a lower ranked soldier question him would have resulted in discipline and as the Batavi's superior Magnus could just snap an order at him to obey and that would be the end of it. In Andragathius though, he didn't want a subordinate unthinkingly carrying out his orders, he wanted a friend fighting with him, and having a friend concerned about him was touching. He wished he could explain this to the big Batavi, but it was easier to say he was going to kill the Emperor than how much he cherished his friendship. "Can you name one battle, one skirmish, one fight that I lost?"

"No," Andragathius said tersely.

"I wouldn't risk any man," Magnus added.

"Only yourself," Andragathius said.

Magnus huffed. There was no way around that.

They walked back to the nervous centurion. "This note comes from the Wall," Magnus said to him. "Probably nothing, but I am a cautious man with a sworn duty to protect this province, so get it to Octavius and the harbourmaster. Order him to get two ships ready to sail to Deva, fully manned and supplied and kept on standby, but he is to pull anchor only on my express command."

"Yes, sir," he snapped and jogged off to find a horse. Magnus jumped back into the trench and grabbed his pick. "Up," he said. "And...down!"

With the three others, all desperate to know what was transpiring, but nowhere near confident enough to ask, he began digging out the soil.

XIX

Territory of the Votadini

With what little strength left to him, Kenon tried to count how many days he'd endured the pain and humiliation meted out by the Votadini warriors. His best guess, for the long days that had merged into one endless nightmare, was that more than a week had passed since the Areani had 'gifted' him to the leader of the tribe. Perhaps two. It was hard to tell. From his place at the back of what they called a house, some moments he'd noticed light spilling in from the door, others just the dark of night that matched what was left of his spirit. Padarn was the worst, but being passed to his men as a gift or reward was a horror he didn't think he'd ever recover from.

Every now and then he'd catch the Areani looking at him, but with the shame burning in his chest hotter than the eternally lit hearth fire, he couldn't look him in the eye, never mind ask him why he'd betrayed him so deeply.

There was no door to the house, just some wooden thing to block the gap, nothing with hinges and a lock, so he could simply have sneaked out any night while the others slept. No gate blocked the way out through the perimeter ditches either... but there were the dogs, and the thought of being ripped apart by those dripping teeth was a worse prospect than what Padarn did to him. Almost. He'd begun to have thoughts about just kneeling down and offering his throat to the beasts.

For some reason, he thought about the slaves who had been kept under the wagon he'd travelled with south of the Wall. With bitter tears he wondered if they were living easier, less painful lives than him.

He still tried to count the days though, to hold onto some measurement of the passage of time. He was frightened that if he lost that last little thing, he'd lose everything. Some more nights to endure, to survive, and something would change. It had to. They'd find that the Areani was telling the truth about the Twentieth Legion leaving Deva, and then they'd go south. Not to fight for his father, but to raid.

Dreams of living a life of luxury in his villas all gone, if he slept at all it was nothing but a restless doze, and he always awoke back in the living nightmare.

A big hand grabbed the scruff of the neck. He didn't resist being hauled out into the mud in the circle of huts. Any form of protest, even just reluctance, more often than not earned him a slap or a punch, or a twisting of an arm or finger until the joint was close to snapping. He'd learned not to show any reluctance.

Left on his knees, he tried to look around without anyone noticing to gauge what kinds of threats he was about to face. He saw that the camp was full of activity as men with packed bags and weapons looked like they were making ready to leave. Then, without anyone explaining anything, they walked. Padarn hadn't thought to give him his shoes so he trod barefoot in the mud after the men. With the dogs loping along, there was no hope of making a run for it...not that there was anywhere safe he had the strength to run to. Still, he couldn't help looking longingly at the treeless landscape for a way to escape, a narrow valley he could make a shelter from some branches, where he could lay until the world stopped hurting. It was so overcast that he couldn't even tell which way was south. He knew there was some way of telling, from noting which side of a tree trunk moss grew on it, but civilised people who lived in cities or villas didn't need to know things that concerned farmers. And there weren't even any trees...

The cold drizzle did nothing to lighten his mood and it got heavier and heavier until by the time they got to the river, it was pouring with rain. Some men cowered under oilskins to keep the worst of it off them, but others danced like they were blind drunk, grinning maniacally as though they actually enjoyed being drenched and cold. The rags that were all that were left of his tunic did nothing to keep him dry and while the others called out in joy, he shivered uncontrollably.

There were some women with them too, but not the type he was used to. These looked like they would treat him like Padarn and his men did, rather than pleasure him and he was too afraid to look at them.

In his barbarous tongue, Padarn shouted to the assembled crowd. Whatever he said, those listening loved it and for a moment the cheer that rose up drowned out the sound of the rain falling in the mud. He shouted out again and with all eyes on him, Kenon assumed he was being introduced as the son of the Governor of Britannia with the explanation that he was worth a good ransom. He didn't dare open his mouth to suggest that they raise it. Somehow he didn't think Caesar was as terrified of his pirate captors as Kenon was of the Votadini.

The massive hand clamped around the back of his neck and again he froze. The strength of the push was like getting kicked in the head by a horse, and, gasping as he fell face first into the sloppy mud, he got a mouth full of it. He didn't have the strength to push himself up.

He watched as someone came to stand over him, fiddling with his crotch. To the sounds of encouragement the man relieved himself over Kenon. Far beyond shame, his only thought was that the stream was warmer than the rain; at least it couldn't get any worse than this, but then, "Bastard?" someone called out. "It's *him*! It's Bastard!"

Kenon recognised the voices of the deserters who should have been his escort from Segontium.

"All yours," Padarn laughed.

It could get worse. Much worse! Like a fly stuck in a web, Kenon looked up at the cruel smiles on the sallow face of one of the former soldiers as though he was an approaching spider.

He was saved by hands on him forcing him to his feet and was shoved over to help drag the boats into the water. They were tiny, flimsy little things, but for someone who could barely get to his knees, they might have well have been a full-sized Roman transport ship they wanted him to pull.

"Come on!" the worst of the deserters yelled. "Push, Bastard!" A stick wasn't as sophisticated an implement of coercion as a whip, but being hit with it across the shoulder blades, the effect was much the same. He put all of his effort into dragging the little boat down the muddy slope, but was as weak as an old man. As soon as it was at the river, he sank to his knees again. He really didn't want to get in, but neither did he want to feel the end of the stick again…and so with as much reluctance as he got into Padarn's bed at night, he slithered in.

It was made with a thin wooden frame, but instead of a wooden hull, it was skinned in what appeared to be animal hide, and as it moved under his feet in the water, he couldn't imagine how such a vessel could float, never mind bear two big men out in open water. A hulking man got in behind and although it rocked alarmingly, it just about didn't sink. Trying not to scream, or jump back out, he watched in horror as the flow pulled them away from the bank.

Young children ran along the bank crying out their goodbyes, perhaps dreaming of one day going on such an adventure themselves. Kenon hoped the little bastards would drown on their maiden voyage. With their mothers watching.

"What's the matter?" someone shouted at him from a nearby boat. "Expecting to go sailing on a trireme?"

A paddle was thrust into his hands and as the rain still poured down, after a few moments he was glad of the effort as it warmed him up slightly, but the further downstream they paddled, the more nervous he got. The boat rocked and pitched over the swells, the whole thing twisting and creaking under him as though it was some kind of living thing with joints and sinews. The hide got so soft under his feet that he feared it was dissolving.

He counted more than thirty boats in the sad little fleet. Most had two men in each, so more than fifty barbarians would be raiding his lands, burning his barns and villas, taking his slaves. How he could possibly have thought going over the Wall to lead a band of bastards against his father could have been a good idea...He heard Bassus' words drifting over the waters. 'Stupid, useless, pathetic'...While he'd been at Rutupiae, he'd disagreed vehemently with the assessment, but not any more.

"No Roman would think we'd be out in weather like this. They'd think we were fools!" one of the deserters shouted and Padarn cried out with laughter as he paddled. The man behind used his rusty helmet to scoop out the rainwater that was sloshing around their feet. Kenon found a little relief in the fact that he didn't seem to be worried they were sinking.

The thought of them facing a Roman naval fleet in these little things was absolutely farcical. They wouldn't stand a chance. Roman ships would tear through them like a knife through cloth.

He was expecting that they'd paddle the stupid things all the way to the coast of Britannia Secunda, so was a little surprised when after about half a day they all pulled into a little beach on the bend of the river, and was even more surprised when the boat was picked up, turned over and set on his shoulder. The man in front started walking and so Kenon was forced along behind him. For how long they trudged through the mud, squelching and slipping, Kenon didn't know, but over the first hill they didn't stop, nor the next one. When he stumbled, he was helped up by a big boot kicking his backside, or by the stick across his shoulders. For a long time he walked wondering if a beating could be any worse than taking another step. Nearly every part of his body hurt so much he had begun to think that he'd prefer to be in Padarn's bed.

It was almost fully dark when he was allowed to drop to his knees on the sodden earth. There was no relief to be had though. Wiping the rain out of his eyes with a madly shaking hand, he saw that they were at the foot of another fort perched on a hill. He watched as another band of rough looking men came out to greet Padarn. The one Kenon assumed was their leader embraced him and a few of the men who seemed to know each other tried to crush one another in bear hugs. Kenon knew that several different tribes held territory north of the Wall, but couldn't recall their names as they'd never interested him. None he could see had painted or tattooed faces, so probably none were Picts. Thankfully. The men who painted themselves blue had been feared since the time of Agricola.

There was no feasting though, and despite it being quite dark, they all headed off to a kind of a harbour, one of muddy banks rather than proper walls, cranes and jetties. In fact, the only similarity it had to a Roman one was that there were dozens of boats docked there. Most were much bigger than the ones they'd come down river on. They were still made of animal hides instead of planks, but most had masts and were big enough for several men.

When he realised they were sea-going vessels, Kenon's heart sank even further.

"Beautiful, aren't they?" one of the deserters said.

Kenon had seen prettier things floating out of the latrine.

Padarn's men tethered the now empty smaller boats behind the larger craft and began casting off.

There was a remnant of daylight left on the horizon, so they weren't completely blind leaving the harbour. With what he was sure was the last of his strength, Kenon paddled silently into the full night. Although he couldn't see, after a while the rougher waves told him that they were now out at sea.

They paddled through the whole night. Even with the sail down so the wind helped them along, Kenon wasn't spared for any moment. From a winter of sword and shield practice, he'd developed some thick calluses on his palms, but by the time it was light enough to see again, a whole set of blisters had formed and popped. Drenched with constant splashes of salt water, every stroke of the paddle hurt. He was sure he only lived because a water flask was passed to him every now and again.

He almost didn't notice the dawn. He'd long forgotten that the sun still arched across the sky and that other people in the world still went along with their daily lives. About mid-morning, a cry from one man spread through the flotilla. Kenon looked up but saw only the formless water and clouds so heavy with rain that he couldn't make out where the sea met the sky. A little while later he made out the mountainous island ahead that everyone was excited about. He didn't share their enthusiasm though. Heading towards an unknown land so far off the edge of the empire, filled him with a terror he'd yet to experience, as though he'd been taken to some mythical realm, one told about in fireside stories. One that would be even harder to get home from than climbing a fucking massive wall manned with the roughest soldiers in the empire.

At the beach, the men jumped out of the boats whooping with joy. Kenon tentatively put his foot over the side, and feeling the solid ground had never been happier about anything else in his life before. But just as any spark of hope over the past weeks, it didn't last long before being snuffed out by a new horror. There were more boats here. Some were much bigger. The raiders were joining up and using the island as a staging post.

Kenon didn't make it fully out of the water before collapsing, and he lay with small waves lapping over his legs as one of the deserters waded over to him. He looked far from friendly. His face was sunken, but thinner, he looked an even harder bastard than he had as a soldier. "You didn't just decide to come up and join us did you?" he spat. "You don't have courage like that. You're just a sad little piece of shit!"

Kenon almost piped up that he'd got almost as far as Coria on his own with exactly that plan, but decided against it. Also, he hadn't been given permission to speak. The water was freezing and the cold seeped straight into his bones. With the deserter looming over him, the shivering quickly turned to shaking.

"And does Padarn know why we call you Bastard? That you were disinherited? You even asked us to kill him for you. If he thinks he's going to get a ransom for you, I think he's going to be a bit disappointed. I bet he doesn't know!" An awful smile spread across his face. "With no ransom, do you know how useless you are, Bastard?"

Kenon watched helplessly as the man stepped through the shallow surf and stood near Padarn waiting patiently, respectfully, for a chance to speak. He tried desperately to think of what he could say to save himself. Caesar would have been able to turn this around to his advantage, but Kenon's pathetic mind was completely blank and all he did was wait for the slaughter like a sheep in a pen.

Like he was in a bad dream, he watched helplessly as the former soldier got Padarn's ear. Padarn shouted angrily for the Areani and as they all splashed purposely towards him, he almost pissed himself in fear. If he was about to be worthless to Padarn, he was sure that the big Votadini would just cut him up into pieces to feed to the fish.

"This man is from the south," Padarn said to the Areani. "But I forgive him for that, as he has wintered with me. Proved himself. He says the boy is disinherited, yet you promise me his ransom. Explain this to me. Or die!"

"Disinherited is a strong word," the Areani said.

"So is execution," Padarn replied.

All Kenon had to do was speak the truth about what his father had done and he'd get the Areani killed, which seemed a fair payback for how cruelly he'd betrayed him. No matter how cold or hungry he was, a clever man could have come up with a plan to save himself, but to his bitter disappointment, all Kenon could do was to try and keep his head above the occasional bigger wave and hope the coming beating wouldn't be so bad.

Somehow, despite clearly being in danger, the Areani laughed dismissively. "His father wanted to beat some discipline into him and thought enlistment was a good idea. He just made the boy think he was disinherited, but it was just so he would think it was real."

Kenon was so confused that he thought he'd misheard. Not *really* sent away? Hope flared in his heart again, but not for long, as with a real bitterness he remembered that nothing the Areani had ever told him was true.

"I smell treachery," Padarn said quietly. "Yet your words about the fortress of Deva being empty are true. This confuses me. Such a world we have made for ourselves. South of the Wall a father betrays a son. On our side, a son betrays a father. I don't know which is worse."

Over the next couple of days, more and more boats turned up until there were upwards of two hundred of the dirty, fur-wearing, tattooed bastards dancing and drinking all day and night around the huge fire...The thought of them loose in the rich lands of Britannia Secunda, raiding his farms made him feel sick. Two hundred men were nowhere near enough to pitch against a Roman army, but as a fast-moving band rampaging around the countryside, attacking helplessly undefended villas, they'd be like foxes in a chicken coop. They would cause devastation.

On the afternoon of the third day, the festivities ended and they all made their way to the boats again, singing songs as though they were celebrating some festival, not planning death and destruction.

Through the darkness of the dead of night, the edges of the old sails flapped in the wind as the ragged flotilla sped over the swells towards his lands. The sea was rough and every time the small boat pitched, the mast above him waved violently. He feared he'd be tossed into the waves and lost in the dark depths. He paddled hard, or at least he tried to. Those in his boat didn't seem to think he was putting enough effort in and slapped him on the head so many times to do it faster that his ears were ringing.

"There it is," one of the deserters said quietly and hopeful that the sea-faring nightmare would soon be over, he squinted through the sea spray to see a single point of light on the horizon. A lighthouse, maybe, but if it was a beacon, it wasn't one of hope. It didn't seem to get any closer, but eventually commands were ordered in rough whispers and as soon as dozens of shallow hulls were scraped on the sand of the beach, Kenon was pulled out of the large boat and bundled unceremoniously back into one of the smaller ones that had been towed behind. This time he wasn't given a paddle though as he was pushed over and had his hands and feet tied. The ropes around his wrists were knotted so tight it felt as though they were being crushed. The pain was so intense that all other thoughts, apart from the devastating need to get them undone, were burned out of his head. Before he could cry out for mercy, a gag of dirty cloth was wedged into his mouth. Desperately, he tried to speak through it, but felt cold sharp steel press against his neck. "Make any noise, and it'll be the last sound you ever make," one of the deserters seethed.

It took everything he had not to scream into the gag, and the pain in his hands was so bad that time lost its meaning. All he could do, as the sharp frame of the boat he was lying on cut into his shoulder and ribs, was to whimper. At least it was still before dawn so it was dark enough no one could see him cry. It was the smallest mercy though.

The small boat was pushed into the water again and the deserter in front paddled for all he was worth. A little while later Kenon noticed that the swells which had never ceased to frighten him, had calmed. At the edge of his awareness, he supposed they must already be in the much calmer waters of the estuary. It had to be the river to the east of Deva, as even though his captors were just barbarians, they couldn't be stupid enough to row right past the fortress. Even if it was true that most of the army were in the mountains making roads, there would still be enough soldiers manning the walls to throw spears and shoot arrows to sink every boat.

The deserter paddled as quietly as possible, taking care on every stroke to set the paddle down gently in the water to avoid splashing, then with a few warning hisses, the men hushed to a dead quiet. The deserter turned to hold the knife against Kenon's neck again. A little trickle of something ran across his throat and he desperately hoped it was sweat, not blood. Instead of warning the man that with just one little movement his vein would be opened and he'd be dead like an animal at market, Kenon froze. Just as he'd done when Padarn's men were hurting him in other ways.

It was deathly quiet on the water. Not a single sound. Only the maddening pain in his hands, and it was only the slight movement on the currents of the dawn tide told Kenon that the knife hadn't slipped and drained his life away

What seemed like an age later, the silence was broken by a deserter asking, "Did we do it? Are we through? We made it under the bridge and no one noticed?"

Mention of the bridge could only mean one thing; they were riding the tide up the Dee, straight into the heart of his father's lands.

XX

Britannia Secunda

The thunder of hooves as the Batavi horsemen tore past reverberated through the ground into Magnus' chest and he gasped in awe of the collective power of such beautiful beasts.

It had only been a matter of moments since the lookouts had seen the smoke of the signal post on the distant hill and the detachment of cavalry were already heading off to face the threat. It would be a few days at least before he saw them again and much counted on Andragathius as he ran around the countryside hunting the raiders. In all that time, Magnus knew he wouldn't have to spend a single moment worrying about him.

For a man in Magnus' position, trust in a good man was worth more than gold.

His horse wanted to go with them and pulled at the reins and tossed its mane impatiently. As he watched the Batavi charge off into the distance, he thought that they would be a good test for the surface of the new road.

If everything was to go to plan, they would change their horses, reluctantly of course, at Canovium and would be with the barbarians by evening of the next day. The day Magnus' future would be decided. His heart leapt, the day the *empire's* future would be decided.

He'd faced enemies far more dangerous than a band of raiders, but he'd never been more nervous about a battle in his life.

The sixth and seventh cohorts of the Twentieth that Magnus had spent his time with for the last few days on this section of road, had almost finished striking down the tents and stuffing their packs full of equipment. They'd be ready to march soon, and he hoped they could get to Canovium before dark, as having all the other cohorts at the fort as one unit from the break of dawn would save precious hours. He wanted the raiders to cause alarm, maybe some panic, but it was his lands they were going to be running around in looting and burning so he didn't want to leave them free reign for too long.

The two centurions had positioned themselves a few paces apart ready for the men to form up in front of them. There was an air of quiet panic in the assembled soldiers. Magnus supposed many of the hundred and sixty of them who'd been working on this section of road would have wives and children in the vicus outside Deva's walls. They had no way of knowing what was happening, or how great the threat was, so for them, the coming fight would be as much for the lives of their families as much as the glory of the empire. Magnus wondered if some would be blaming him for taking so many soldiers out of the fortress, therefore inviting the calamity himself. They weren't wrong, of course.

Ordered chaos is how Theodosius had called moments like this and Magnus stood patiently as the men slung shields over their backs. With helmets hanging down in front of their chests and bags dangling from spears over their shoulders, soon they were soon lined up in perfect rows in front of their centurions and ready to march.

The First Spear, his face burning with anger, or barely restrained blood-lust, rode up to Magnus. "On your command, sir," he shouted. His helmet gleamed so brightly Magnus had to squint and wondered if the man had found some special compound that he rubbed on it to make it reflect the sun so intensely.

Magnus nodded and the First Spear bellowed, "Ready! March!" in a voice so loud, even Magnus' horse tried to shy away. To Magnus, he said, "I'll see you in Canovium, sir. I'll have your accommodations readied." With that, he raced off to catch up with the next detachment some miles ahead of them up the fresh new road, leaving little dots floating in front of Magnus' eyes.

As the ranks filed past, he stood to the side, returning the nods some of the soldiers gave him. If they were meant to convey a message, like the Berber's finger language, Magnus took it to mean, 'I will serve you well'

Once the last of them were away, the din of the equipment of a hundred and sixty men jangling together dying down, Magnus headed over to the few men left who would guard the road building equipment, and the one who'd broken his wrist the day before. He handed his reins to his good hand.

"Sir?" he asked confused.

"It will be more comfortable than walking or banging about in the back of a wagon," he said to the bewildered lad. "And besides, I haven't had a good forced march in many moons!"

None of the men had. They were deeply grateful to him for it. Despite it being a little hard to believe, Elen's suggestion had pretty much handed him the hearts of the whole Twentieth Legion. When he found out which soldier had been telling her what to say, Magnus still wasn't sure if he'd promote him to an advising role or hang him up by his balls. With the reaction of the soldiers, he was leaning slightly more towards the former.

The lines of the cohorts were already far ahead and as he jogged to catch them up, he looked down at the surface of the road with a sense of pride. He wondered what Vespasian must have experienced on the inauguration day of the Coliseum as he walked into the adulation of the fifty thousand people packed in.

* * *

Eventually, someone judged that the flotilla of little boats had sailed far enough upstream that they cut the ropes around Kenon's wrists. He couldn't get up though as his hands were numb and useless and in the weak light of dawn, he was horrified to see that they were swollen and discoloured. It was terrifying that his captors would hurt him so much for something so simple as tying his hands. He couldn't even get the gag out of his mouth.

The first gesture of kindness he'd been shown since he'd crossed the Wall, one of the Votadini pulled it out for him and while he spat and tried not to throw up, the man hauled him up into a sitting position. Kenon was about to offer some words of gratitude, but the man thrust a paddle at him. From the angry grunt, Kenon understood that he should start paddling. He held up his swollen fingers and pointed at the ugly purple bands in his wrists the ropes had made as he'd struggled against them. The backhanded slap to the side of his head convinced him to at least try, so he tried to clamp the oar between his forearms. That only awarded him another whack on the ear with rock hard knuckles. He took the handle in both hands, but the pain of all the blood rushing back made it feel like he'd stuck his hands into a wasp's nest and he cried out in agony. Instead of warning him to be quiet, everyone who could hear laughed.

In the early morning light, Kenon could see that they'd left the larger boats with the masts and sails behind and were in a fleet of the small ones. Paddling with the tide, they sped up the river much faster than he would have thought possible.

There were a few tricky bends to negotiate, and they were going so fast that some boats couldn't turn in time and bumped into the bank. Kenon noticed that most of them had an empty one lashed behind the manned ones. He supposed those were the ones they'd fill with loot and plunder, but if they thought they could just float back by the fortress on the outgoing tide that coming evening, they must be raving mad.

He looked at the murky brown waters and the trees on the banks all swathed in a thick mist. Birds sang and one darted across the river in a flash of bright iridescent blue. It must have been a kingfisher, and in that moment he understood how simple people found pleasure in such things...As they rounded a bend, one of those simple people was washing clothes on the bank. With her back to them, she was totally unaware of what horror was approaching her village, that everything she'd ever known in her whole life was about to come to an end in a shocking moment of terror and blood.

The barbarians, as usually told in stories, were famous for flailing around a battlefield in disarray, only concerned with their individual glory, obviously had a plan, as at Padarn's command all of the boats were brought closer together, two to a side. Slowly and silently, the oars were exchanged for spears and arrows were notched in bows. Men about to kill their mortal enemies grinned at each other with smiles full of missing teeth. They hushed each other to silence, as some were barely able to contain their excitement.

Kenon thought about shouting a warning, even if it meant his own life, but before he'd drawn a breath, a loosed arrow hissed at the girl. In a blind panic and utter confusion, she tried to claw at what was in her back and splashed at the water's edge for a few moments. On the verge of a scream, Kenon watched as she slumped lifelessly into the mud. Somehow, in a worryingly impressive display of self-control, the men all managed to remain silent.

The boats at the head of the fleet drifted past her body, but were then angled towards the bank so that as many of them touched the shore at the same moment as possible. The first keels nudging the earth was the signal for every one of the barbarians to burst into an instant frenzy. Kenon's boat tipped and rocked alarmingly as men splashed around it and he watched with nausea as they charged at the village as a wave, as a pack, rather than one by one.

When the boat had settled again, Kenon saw that the young boys had been left behind. Not big or strong enough to fight, their task was to hold on to the mooring ropes so the boats wouldn't drift away upstream with the tide. Others hopped from boat to boat setting the oars so they could get away quicker if they needed to. Three of them, all with knives drawn, guarded Kenon and as he looked nervously at the blades, he listened to the shrieks and cries of the villagers and the crashes as the Votadini smashed down doors.

From behind, a bow twanged and a village boy, no older than the lads who'd shot him, fell to the ground. The arrow had lodged in his leg and as half a dozen barbarian boys pounced on him in a savage stabbing frenzy, he cried out for his mother. Children killing children was another horror Kenon could blame himself for bringing south of the Wall.

The gruesome scene was so shocking that by the time he realised there was a chance to jump in a boat and start paddling for his life, it was already too late. The boys were still wiping their blades clean on the dead boy's tunic when the first of the men came back. They shouted angry orders and the boys fell over themselves to get the boats ready, and with lots of splashing and cursing the raiders tossed in cured hams, cheeses, and a couple of young girls. Before he even realised it, and paddling as hard as he could, they were in the river again and were upstream and around the next bend, before those left alive could raise an alarm. No screams pierced the morning mist though.

They must have killed them all.

Kenon did his best to ignore the pain in his hands and how the men cried with jubilation about the deaths they'd just caused. Once they knew they were safely away, some began singing in joy. It sounded like some coarse seafarer's song, but many had their mouths full of fresh Roman bread as they sang and paddled. No matter how much Kenon wished it, none of them choked on it.

Up the river, the push of the tide was less, and before their jubilation had died down Padarn shouted at his band of bastards to get the boats back into their close formation. Another attack was coming. Kenon caught a glimpse of the Areani, who, pointing ahead of them, dishearteningly, seemed to be giving Padarn advice.

Soon, screams came from ahead and the men again erupted into more shouts of command and cries of pure excitement. As Kenon's boat bumped into the pier, he saw that the next target was a large villa, an orchard stretching almost to the river in front of it. Servants, out of spear or arrow range, were running up the hill crying out warnings and screaming for their lives. Other boats knocked against the pier and it was a mad rush to get out and chase after them. Some men fell into the water, but laughing, dragged themselves out and ran towards death and destruction dripping wet.

Despite how young they were, the young boys were well-drilled for their part and worked quickly to pull the boats out of the water. While guarding Kenon they settled into a nervous silence, eyes darting between the bushes, road and river, in case a threat was coming that they needed to warn the others about. With the sounds of the occasional scream, which got cut off, coming down to them, Kenon began to have hope that a detachment of the Twentieth had caught up with them and were putting all the bastards to the sword.

There were no soldiers coming to the rescue though, and Kenon's attention was taken by the argument between the boys, as a couple of the older ones were a bit more interested in what the captured girls had under their tunics than they should have been.

He had no idea why he did it. Maybe it was just because he felt just as helpless as the girls, but he picked up a fair-sized pebble from the bank and lobbed it at the boy. Probably spear practice was good for rock throwing as well, and despite his bruised wrists and still tingling fingers, it was a good shot. It hit the boy on the arm hard enough to knock him over and make him scream. Furious, he jumped from one boat to the next, and with knife drawn, charged.

Kenon watched him come, and almost wept that all of the grand dreams he had for his life, the power, and wealth and an endless supply of slaves, would all come to an end at the hands of a ten-year-old savage. It was pathetic. A worthless death... but nothing less than he deserved.

Just before the boy got to him, some instinct kicked in and he easily dodged to the side and knocked the knife out of his attacker's hand. And before the boy knew what was happening, in one movement Kenon had swung his leg behind the boy's ankles and rammed his chin up with the heel of his hand. The boy fell against the side of a boat before splashing into the water and was suddenly more concerned about coughing up the dirty river water than fighting.

In a swarm, the others, all screaming incoherently, all waving knives, crowded around him. Outnumbered, it was impossible to defend himself, so he held his hands out in surrender.

"Oi!" came a bellowing voice from behind.

The boys all stopped still, apart from the half-drowned one. Still coughing, he tried to run at Kenon again, but the barbarian man grabbed him, lifted him off his feet with one hand and slammed him so hard to the ground it made Kenon wince. If they treated their children so harshly, no wonder they grew up to be such vicious bastards.

The man shoved Kenon up the path to the villa with such strength, he didn't dare protest. Even when he punched him in the back to get him to move faster.

The range of barns and workshops framed a large courtyard. On a normal day, it would have been a hive of activity. It was busy today, although in a different way. Tomorrow the only sounds would be those of the crows and flies. Sprawled out in twisted positions, the bodies of farm workers and servants were strewn around. Kenon noticed that most were middle-aged, grey hair at the temples. He supposed the raiders had plans for the younger ones that would allow them to live a little longer.

Screams came from inside the main building, and that's where he was pushed towards. his legs didn't want to move though. He'd been here before. It was the villa near the tile kilns, one of the ones he'd spent years looking forward to calling his own. He was walking towards the central range not as its owner, but its destroyer. A few more shoves so hard they jarred his neck, and he was pushed inside. With his bare and filthy feet, it seemed wrong to walk on the mosaic in the corridor, as though he was a barbarian, just as unwelcome as the rest.

With a sinking heart, standing in the middle of shards of smashed vases and imported earthenware scattered all over the dining room floor, he saw Padarn waiting for him. Grey beard bristling with brine, his piercing blue eyes seemed even wilder than normal. He wondered if raiding for a barbarian was as arousing as sex with a nice girl was for civilised men. It wasn't the moment to ask though.

Huddled in the corner near a pile of upended and smashed furniture, was a well-dressed woman, nose bloodied, an eye quickly swelling shut. Padarn beckoned Kenon to him, and as he tip-toed over the broken glass, Padarn asked the shaking woman, "Who owns this place?"

She was trying to push herself deeper into the corner, feet slipping helplessly on the floor. With horror, Kenon saw the bare legs of a little girl she was trying to protect.

"Who?" Padarn bellowed in his special voice that sounded like a creature from a scary children's story, and the woman flinched as though he'd struck her. "Octavius," she shrieked.

"What is the name of his son?" Padarn boomed.

"K...K..."

"Who?!"

"Kenon!" she cried.

Bile rose at the back of Kenon's throat.

"Please spare my girl," she wailed. "She is of no use to you. *Please*!"

Padarn grinned menacingly and shoved Kenon forwards. "Do you know him? Look!"

The woman did as she was bid, and the look of recognition turned into an awful expression of horror, then disgust as she screamed as though Kenon, not Padarn, was the monster from her worst nightmares.

Padarn took Kenon's hand, slapped the handle of a knife into his palm, then pointed at the helpless pair. "Do it!" he snapped as he stepped quickly back out of range.

Kenon turned to see at least two of the raiders in the room had their swords drawn, so he'd be cut down before he'd even raised the knife towards Padarn, never mind burying it in his neck. The only choice he had was between the woman's life or his.

"No! No!" she begged, feet still pounding against the floor as though she was running.

"The girl," Padarn said. "Slowly. I want to know where the gold is buried."

The woman's scream reverberated through his skull, making it feel as though she was tainting his blood with something malevolent, if it wasn't already. To stop it, he seriously considered using the knife to slit his own throat. "I'm sorry," he breathed as he crouched down, but knew such words were worthless.

The woman kicked at him, and in her panic didn't notice that she was cutting herself on the blade.

The knife wasn't long enough to be able to stab from a distance and he could hardly grip it enough to stop from dropping it. It was going to be a mess.

Kenon wondered at what he had become to be doing such a thing. And what he would be after he'd done it. Something in his head screamed at him to at least try and attack Padarn so he could die a hero, but he was too weak for that. He wanted to live... whatever kind of life waited for him.

The girl tried to squirm out of his grip and he had to slash at the woman's hands to stop her clawing at him.

He'd been a bastard all of his life, a piece of shit, he saw that now, using nothing but his father's name to get almost anything he wanted. And the little girl, innocent, pure, deserved to live much more than he did.

The woman's scream tore through his mind like a storm wind through a foundering ship's sails and in a horrible harmony it was joined by his own.

Everything was so intense, all happening too fast, and it felt like he was wrapped in the deepest fever.

And there was an all consuming silence that rang in his head and he saw the little girl's blood-soaked body as the corpse of his own humanity.

He wasn't just a bastard any more. Stripped bare of anything he'd convinced himself he was, he could see the truth now. He was a monster.

XXI

Britannia Secunda

That evening Canovium was a hive of activity. The fort for five hundred men now had more than three thousand in, but mostly around, it. The fields for grazing cattle close to the vicus had been taken over and among the cow pats, the men were busy pitching tents and getting cooking fires going.

Magnus was glad the last part of the long walk had all been downhill, as after the twenty or so miles he'd done on foot, he was absolutely spent. The years were beginning to take their cruel toll on his body. If he'd been in full armour and had had to carry the full set of equipment like the others, he wouldn't have got half way before needing to wait for a lift on one of the wagons following behind. His right ankle was so sore that if Elen had been with them, he'd have asked her to give them a massage.

Several sweaty and red-faced messengers had ridden in with reports from Deva and were ready to speed back through the night with the replies. With the legion legate and camp prefect remaining in the fortress, the most senior officers overseeing the road building were the tribunes. The young, flush-faced broad-band tribune waiting for Magnus outside the fort gates was clutching some scraps of parchment in his hand. He'd obviously already read the reports, but his reluctance to blurt out the main issues like a messenger told Magnus that someone didn't appreciate his authority being impinged upon.

Magnus had learned well over the past few weeks that the way to a normal soldier's heart was to treat them a little less harshly than some dirt under a hobnailed boot. For those higher up in the hierarchy though, another approach would work best. He'd experienced it himself for many years as he rose slowly up through the ranks of the army. Low men appreciated being lifted up a little above what their position usually dictated, but for setting more powerful men in their place, it was best to pull them down a rung or two.

Magnus supposed the tribune had been hoping for a quiet posting in the thoroughly subdued province of Britannia, where he'd never have to put himself anywhere close to real danger. A few years of following the legate around, shouting at subordinates on guard duty and he'd have the qualification he needed for a seat in the senate. The poorly disguised look of fear on his face told Magnus that it would be best to keep him away from the real fighters. Power, prestige and making his mother proud of her little soldier was all he wanted. Battle glory was not something that interested him. Blindly ordering cohorts around without knowing the full nature of the threat was in the best interests of no one.

The tribune was probably well educated in rhetoric so would be a worthy opponent if Magnus chose to confront him with words and so he took his thick, padded shirt, slipped it over his head and laced it up the side without even looking at the toggles. Countless years of practice had made the movements second nature. He doubted the tribune had ever even tied his by himself, never mind without looking.

With a few deft movements, he had his hands in the heavy chain suit and lifting his arms straight up above his head, it slid down to settle perfectly on his shoulders. Without needing to say a word, it was the perfect demonstration that Magnus was a true military man and would be in charge of the coming meeting.

The soldier acting as steward held out the gleaming, scaled suit of lorica squamata, but with a tip of his head, Magnus indicated that he should hand it to the tribune to hold it for him.

His face flushed even redder, but he didn't protest at being treated like a lowly soldier, and held it up for Magnus to slip an arm and his head through. He fastened it at his side himself, still without breaking eye contact with the tribune.

Everything the tribune needed to know about his position suitably communicated, with slightly, but noticeably slumped shoulders, he led the way into the fort.

With his helmet tucked under his arm, Magnus followed to the cramped little principia courtyard which was full of centurions about to receive commands. As Magnus nodded respectfully at them he tried not to walk with such a pronounced limp.

Pacing along the portico in a silent rage was the fort prefect whom the others hadn't deemed important enough to include in the meeting. The indignity of being turfed out of his own office obviously, and understandably, rankled. He hadn't simply relinquished a little authority, he'd had it taken off him in the most public way possible. It wouldn't have been too much effort for Magnus to invite him to stand by the door so he could at least listen, then give a few orders for him to carry out afterwards. But after the long walk, he was too tired for it to seem worth the bother.

Once in the office, the two narrow-band tribunes snapped to attention and in front of them Magnus held his hand out for the reports from the broad-band tribune as though he was no more than a messenger. Treating him in such a way, Magnus didn't need to explain anything about his position to the others.

The two narrow-band tribunes seemed keen for the fight, though. They were at least twenty years older than the colleague they shared an almost equal rank with, but were from the plebeian class rather than the senatorial. Instead of being dropped in a position of command thanks to the names of their fathers, they'd risen up the hard way over the years, one rank at a time, until they were deemed experienced, ruthless and respected enough to be close to the command of the legion. Apart from camp prefect, their rank was as high as men from their class could hope to achieve. And for the many quiet years since the Conspiracy, all they'd done with their days was to train and practise. A never-ending routine of being ready to fight at a moment's notice, but never needing to. The last time their swords and spears had been wetted with blood was just a distant memory, so they were probably salivating at the thought of seeing some real action. And they surely knew Magnus' reputation.

A roughly drawn map had been scratched on parchment and lay open on the table. Magnus set his helmet down next to it and let the three men in the room wait in an uncomfortable silence as he took his time reading through the reports. A fleet of some fifty small boats had made it up the Dee on the tide under cover of darkness. He snorted as he tried to contain his laugh, and pretended that it was a rather effeminate sneeze. Fifty flimsy little coracles carrying maybe two hundred undisciplined barbarians. He hoped that the Batavi hadn't already had them all for breakfast. But knowing it was nothing he wasn't expecting, and nothing he wasn't prepared for, was more of a relief than he'd imagined.

One report stated that those on duty who'd missed them had been detained and awaited punishment. The Votadini's movements were being monitored, but not engaged. That was good. When Magnus had taken men for the roads, he'd ordered that the fortress not be left insufficiently defended for any reason at all.

He looked at the men in the room with him and noticed how they held their impeccably polished helmets under their arms, how the leather of the armour strapping creaked as they stood stiff but not quite still. And how the air in the room was a miasma of sweat beginning to turn sour after their long day's ride, as well as the musk of the horses they'd been on all day. It all seemed beautiful. His moment. One he would no doubt remember for the rest of his, hopefully long and successful, life.

Theodosius would have been outraged and disgusted at the way he was manipulating men for nothing but his own ends, but Magnus knew that the greater the threat the barbarians appeared to pose, the more his victory would be celebrated. For that, he had a show to put on. He cleared his throat. Even though this was a meeting less to arrange a battle plan and more to begin his bid for the purple, he wasn't anywhere near as nervous as he thought he'd be.

They were all probably expecting him to give orders about how to crush the raiders by ordering other men to do the fighting, so he decided to wrong foot them and make them even more nervous. "It seems the Twentieth has a serious problem..." he said and saw all of their eyes widen in surprise. "Can any of you tell me how is it that these bastard barbarians knew so soon that I'd moved most of the legion to the west?" He asked the question in an accusatory tone, intending that each would fear himself under suspicion of leaking information to the enemy. "News of our activities seems to have travelled over the Wall suspiciously quickly."

Expressionless faces stared nervously at the wall behind him and leather creaked as they squirmed uncomfortably at the accusation.

"From this, we must learn two things," Magnus continued. "One, our enemies have very good ears. Too good. The last time I was here, I left the Wall impenetrable, but that seems to have changed. Secondly, it interests me why the Votadini are so desperate to plunder. I would assume it is because every winter they face starvation."

"Good," the young broad band tribune muttered.

"What?!" Magnus snapped at the suddenly nervous man who'd interrupted him.

"I err..." he stammered. "I mean, if they all starve in their own homes, that must be good for us."

"No," Magnus said sternly and saw how the man seemed to shrink. "Maybe your experience in life is different, but in mine, if a man doesn't have enough to eat, he doesn't just keel over and die quietly, trying not to disturb anyone. No, he will do anything he can to survive and feed his children, even to the point of raiding the land under the nose of the Twentieth. For the good of the empire, it is strategically much more important to have a secure tribe on our borders than a desperate one. The Goths crossed the Danube because they were forced to, out of sheer desperation. If Valens had fought *with* them against the Huns instead of trying to exterminate them, we would have allies swelling the ranks of our army instead of militarily superior invaders. And he wouldn't have wasted two entire legions at Adrianople and caused the worst crisis for the empire in a hundred years…which my cousin is now having to deal with."

That was a few of the points he wanted to press home, but as he didn't see any looks of disappointment or discontent, he decided to push a little harder. "I am not Valens. And I say this with as much pride as it is possible for a man to have; I learned all I know under Theodosius. Some of you might remember that name."

Both the battle-hardened narrow-band tribunes nodded, but the other was obviously uncomfortable at hearing an emperor criticised, a disgraced one or not.

"The Votadini's haste to come south and attack our lands tells me that once we've caught up with them, they will be open to offers of better trade in exchange for staying on their side of the Wall."

"You don't wish them all to be exterminated, sir?" the broad band tribune asked, confused.

"How can you make treaties with dead men?" Magnus asked, making it sound as though he was confused by the man's question. "Make it clear to every single soldier that I want as many of them taken alive as possible. The mission is to *capture* prisoners, not to wipe them out."

He moved the oil lamp closer to the map to see it better. Deva was marked with a thick circle and the rectangular peninsula above it to the north had two rivers marked down its sides. On the left, one flowing from the south through the heart of Octavius' productive lands was the one the Votadini had gone up with the tide. The other trailed off to the east. The two straight lines underneath, one almost three times longer than the other, denoted the distances that mounted and foot soldiers could travel in a day.

Magnus made the tribunes lean in closer as he put a grubby finger on Deva. "One detachment goes straight to the fortress in case these bastards are a little cleverer than we give them credit for and have the idea of waiting until we're all engaged before they come in more boats to attack. I want all the men detained in their barracks back out on duty. I want double watch on the walls and scouts out with signal fires."

"But, sir!" the broad band tribune protested. "Shouldn't the men who let the boats pass unnoticed be punished?"

And that is why good men mutiny against their superiors, Magnus thought. "They shall of course be punished," Magnus said. "Perhaps you think a decimation is in order." He looked at the shock and horror on the narrow band tribune's faces. Both men had spent at least half their lives in the barracks, so the idea of beating one of their brothers to death was abhorrent. "Nine soldiers clubbing the tenth, who'd pulled the shortest straw, to death, would definitely instil some much needed discipline, don't you think?"

"Yes, sir," came a few less than enthusiastic replies.

"But if I do that, I must also apportion blame to their commanders for not instilling enough discipline, and so maybe their centurions should be thrown from the walls. Do you think that will be fair and proportionate to the offence committed? And of course, their tribunes must take responsibility for their subordinate's failure as well. When I was in Africa, we found that cutting a man's hands off was good for teaching him a lasting lesson."

The light from the small lamp was still enough to see the blood drain from the young tribune's face.

"And the legate too, he shall not escape recompense. Perhaps a good public flogging? And the prefect? A week of forced marches?"

The broad-band tribune was clearly terrified at the thought of such punitive sanctions about to be meted out, but as the wrinkles began to crease at the sides of his eyes, the sharper of the narrow-band ones understood the joke.

"What do you think?" Magnus asked him.

"I would ask to be whipped by the men who were on duty when the boats passed, sir. They'd probably miss me."

As the laughter, as much from relief as anything else, spread slowly through them, Magnus imagined the confusion of those outside at hearing merriment coming from the war council.

He leaned back over the map and slid his finger across it to indicate the western river. "One detachment is to go to the south. The bullion wagon is down there somewhere. That *cannot* fall into enemy hands. It must be protected at all costs." He didn't mention that the thousand men with the wagon under Marcellinius' command would destroy the Votadini without breaking into a sweat. "The Votadini know they can't simply sail back past Deva, so they must have planned another route back north." He tapped the eastern river. "They came in on boats, so to me it seems likely they'll go out on them as well. Tomorrow, once a detachment has taken over the defence of the fortress, those on duty there now will go east and set up positions on the eastern river. And any tributaries, if the land is not too marshy."

The tribunes nodded between themselves as they silently agreed who should lead which detachment.

"Also, I want as many cavalry from Canovium here as can be safely spared to harry the bastards eastwards so they'll be worrying more about their heads staying on their shoulders than raiding, and will have to think twice about carrying their loot."

He moved his finger to the south. "The Batavi are already riding around here to the east to block off their overland escape route. But, as I said, I want captives, not bodies. That is an express order! Understood?"

"Yes, sir!" came a chorus of consent.

"Anything to add? Any questions?" No one had. "We move at first light!" he said. "Dismissed!"

"Yes, sir," came the reply of confident voices. They turned on their heels and left to go and relay the orders to those they commanded, apart from the brighter of the narrow-band tribunes.

"Everything all right?" Magnus asked him.

"If I may speak, sir?"

"Of course."

"I served putting down the Conspiracy, sir, and I am err…If it's appropriate for me to say such a thing, I'm very sorry about what happened to Theodosius. Tragic. And err…"

"Go on," Magnus prompted.

He looked around the door to make sure they weren't being overheard and a little quieter, added, "Criminal, sir," he said, coldly.

It was an extremely brave gesture to accuse powerful men, ones who had the ear of the emperor, of a crime. Perhaps he was even accusing Gratian himself. It was as much a declaration of fealty to Magnus as if he'd called him Augustus…unless of course, the man was a plant from Gratian hoping to get Magnus to speak out of turn and betray himself. Somehow, he would have to learn how to deal with such distrust. But the unexpected words about his uncle made something catch in his throat. The plan over the last few weeks had been to get the men to see him as more caring, more interested in their needs and welfare than was usual for those at the top of command. Crying like a boy in front of a tribune was not part of that. "Thank you," he said, voice close to cracking. "That means a lot."

Unsure of what to say, the man chimed, "I would like to say that I am glad…honoured, to have you back in Britannia and to be under your command, sir. Anything you need and I shall see to it personally, sir. Your room, I can show you when you are ready."

"We have injured men coming in soon," Magnus said. "Brigio with his wrist, and Ruui probably broke his ankle on the march today. Trying to herd a sheep, of all things. I doubt he'll ever live that down."

Magnus doubted if the tribune knew their names, and the look of stupefaction on his face at the thought Magnus would care so much about men normally considered mere faceless numbers by those so far up the ranks, was exactly what Magnus was hoping for. "See to it that they have the most comfortable beds."

"But...but..."

"I am nostalgic for the last time I was in these lands," Magnus said, which was a half-truth. "Campfires at night, damp tents. Once we have rid ourselves of these rats, I don't intend that there will be any more battles in Britannia while I am Dux Britanniarum. So, if you would, allow me to indulge the memories of my youth one last time."

"Of course, sir," he said with a look that told Magnus he thought he was raving mad.

Before the man left, Magnus said, "Send the camp prefect in."

"Yes, sir!"

The meeting was done, the plans made, and the disappointment that he hadn't been included, Magnus could see it in the man's eyes. Prefect of an isolated auxiliary fort wasn't exactly the highest position of a man to aspire to, but for an ordinary soldier, spending years on drills, it was a promotion to treasure. But being kicked out of his own office so things could be discussed over his head was obviously an affront. Magnus knew how to counter that. "I want you to do something important for me," he said.

The man almost scoffed, assuming Magnus was about to mock him.

"I want you to go out and make sure that every man here knows that the vicus at Deva was not attacked. The boats sailed right passed, so if anyone has a loved one there, they are safe."

"Yes, sir," he snapped, suddenly enthusiastic again. "Thank you, sir!"

And now he'd be the bearer of good news to thousands of relieved men.

Outside, the evening air was thick with smoke from hundreds of small cooking fires. The vicus would have a lot less chickens clucking around it the following day and Magnus decided to leave enough coin with the local farmers so they wouldn't be too upset with the sudden depletion of their stock.

He walked in the direction the wind was coming from, eyes stinging and watering from the fire smoke by the time he got to air fresh enough to breathe properly.

He stopped near a soldier who was wrestling with one of the sheep they'd herded off the moors. As he watched the man standing with his legs clamping its haunches so it couldn't struggle so freely, he wondered at what a strangely pathetic animal it was. No capacity for individual thought, just the instinct to blindly follow others. Not too dissimilar to many plebs, Magnus thought. But then, the army only worked on the principle of men following their leaders without question, so perhaps it was no bad thing.

And Magnus, half-pretending to really care for all the men under his command, was a wolf.

The sheep bleated plaintively, but as the soldier forced its head up, the pitch rose to a kind of shriek, then a gargle as its throat was slit.

The soldier cursed the sheep for making his job of killing it harder and kicked it as it staggered to its knees, when he saw it was Magnus next to him he gasped out in shock and his knife went flying off into the dark. As he stood to attention, his back as straight as a spear shaft, he shouted, "Sir!" and those around him, realising who had wandered into the midst, dropped what they were doing and stood the same way, assuming they were either about to be inspected or reprimanded.

It was at that moment that, just as it had before almost every fight his whole life, Magnus' stomach decided to clench and he retched and suddenly his armour was far too heavy and tight and he pulled at the parts closest to his throat.

"Everything all right, sir?" the butcher asked.

"Would you laugh at your Dux that he got so nervous before a fight he is sick?" he said as he spat.

"No, sir. But if you would wait for the meat to cook, you'd be most welcome to eat with us."

Under normal circumstances, no soldier would have dared ask his centurion such a thing, never mind his commander. Never mind the Dux Britanniarum. Commanders and cohorts were a world apart, and those holding high rank usually took great pains to keep it so. Magnus realised he'd changed that somewhat, and the fact that the soldier thought he could offer such an invitation told him that the weeks of toiling on the road in the windy mountains had been worth it. Getting the Twentieth ready to follow him to Gaul had become a real possibility.

"I would be honoured," he said and although the legate would have believed him possessed by some strange spirit, it was the truth. As the man bent over to start stripping the carcass. He couldn't help the thought that it had all been so easy, though.

Too easy.

Two of his colleagues knelt to help prepare the mutton and from the light of the fire, Magnus could see one lad was struggling to hold back the tears. That was not good for morale.

"It's only some raiders," Magnus said. "Not an army."

"Yes, sir!" the lad snapped and took a deep breath to pull himself together.

"May I speak?" the man with the knife asked.

"No. Don't," the tearful one pleaded.

"Of course," Magnus said.

"He's not upset about fighting, sir. It's his wife. They lost her daughter a few weeks ago and… err… Thing is, she's not taking it so well, sir."

"And you want to be back there with her?"

From glaring murderously at his friend, the lad turned back and nodded.

"So why aren't you?"

"Wasn't allowed leave, sir," the first answered for his friend.

"Why didn't you ask me?" Magnus asked, but realised how stupid such a suggestion was. Trying to go above your decanus, never mind your centurion for something, would result in a real punishment. If a man was in his right mind, he usually tried to avoid things that would result in a flogging.

"You will go back to Deva tomorrow," Magnus said.

"But..." he began to protest.

"You didn't ask. I dragged it out of you. If anyone's nose is out of joint for it, tell them to come and see me before they say anything else."

The tearful lad looked up. "Thank you, sir," he said.

"How old was she?"

"Six, sir."

Just coming into her life, personality beginning to form, dreams for the future coagulating, stories of her father's exploits told by flickering lamplight before sleep. All gone. "I am very sorry to hear that," Magnus said. "The world is brutally cruel sometimes. What is your name?"

"Flavius Claudius Constantinus," he said with a little hint of pride.

As he set more wood on the fire, Magnus was a little confused by his own emotions. He had taken the Twentieth to the mountains for the sole purpose of working them into following his cause, but the more time he spent with them, listening to their stories, the more he'd found out about their needs, hopes and desires. Ones which, apart from scale, weren't too much different from his own.

XXII

Flavia Caesariensis

"We're in the wrong place!" Brocchus called down from the old oak tree he was perched in. "Magnus was wrong. They're heading south. *Away* from us!"

Andragathius waved for him to come down, and while he hung from one hand off a branch and rolled over the one underneath down like a monkey at play, Andragathius took off his cloak and sword belt.

Brocchus dropped graciously to the ground. "I speak the truth," he shrugged as he wiped the green stains of the bark from his palms.

"I trust you," Andragathius said as he stepped on the interlocked hands two of his men had formed. "It's the barbarians I don't trust."

They lifted him up so he could reach the first branch, but his body had changed somewhat since the last time he'd climbed a tree. As he hooked his heels around the branch above and tried to twist himself up, he could imagine the smirks of those below, thinking he looked more like a boar trying to get up a tree than a monkey. He'd do much better without the three layers of armour, but with the enemy so close, there was no way he could risk taking it off. He needed to see the smoke for himself though, so apart from chopping the tree down and making a huge ladder out of it, there was no other way.

"We should start now!" Brocchus called up. "So they don't get such a head start on us."

Not only were the men staring up at him with craned necks getting a good demonstration of how much older than him they were, Brocchus had the gall to openly question him.

"As I understand it," he said as he paused to catch his breath. "I am in command here. Unless something has changed down there since I left the ground."

Suitably threatened, Brocchus dropped his eyes.

One more branch and Andragathius got himself up to the viewpoint. Palms sweaty, legs weak, he tried to resist the urge to look down…but couldn't help it. With the lurching of his stomach, he saw how high he was. Boats, heights and a distrust in the motives of a commander were his only weaknesses, and since leaving Gaul, Magnus had managed to find them all.

Tracking an enemy was one of his strengths though. He'd grown up on the edge of the empire, a Germanic province pressed against the border along the mouth of the Rhine, and for want of anything better to do, with a few friends, he'd spent a couple of character-forming summers on the other side evading detection by the Frisii tribe for fun. If the Areani still had active units, he wouldn't have hesitated to enlist with them. After defecting en-masse and allowing the Conspiracy to happen, they'd been disbanded, and so he'd found himself in a regular unit on the Danube. Everything he'd taught himself in the forests of the Frisii, he used to track and catch those who'd crossed the river and proved himself useful to Magnus and Theodosius. And so had begun his rise through the ranks, as well as the tree he found himself in.

An inexperienced scout could easily assume that the columns of smoke marking the fires of their destruction meant the enemy was heading away from their position and that Magnus had given bad orders. Andragathius knew it made absolutely no sense for the raiders to be heading deeper into Britannia though. The rivers that way would soon become too shallow to be navigable, even for their light, flat-bottomed craft. Unless they intended to carry their craft and spoils over the mountains and get back to the sea in the west. That way, they would completely outflank the Twentieth and humiliate Magnus in the process.

But all of Andragathius' instincts told him that the Scotti were heading towards the Batavi's position so he was sure that the new fires served only as distractions. Farms and lives destroyed only to try and fool their pursuers into heading the wrong way. It seemed a pointless waste, but he'd seen the same thing done many times before. It was an established tactic. The livelihoods of lesser men were inconsequential to those with power and the games they played.

Such a ruse might have worked if someone like Brocchus was in charge, but the Scotti were only roaming freely in Britannia because Magnus wanted them to be. They had no idea how deeply they'd been betrayed by a far superior tactician and a couple of fires would do nothing to save them.

"What do you see?" Brocchus called up.

An inpatient whelp who needs a proper reminder of his status, Andragathius thought. "We wait," he replied.

He was confident that Magnus had the right idea and that their escape route had to be through where the Batavi were guarding. He scratched his chin through his thick beard, mind finally settled on the assumption they were in the right place. The only problem was that his band of Batavi were heavily outnumbered. Probably by something as stupid as about ten to one. Magnus and the foot soldiers were a day away at least, if not two. After three days of hard riding, two on the Roman's horses they'd taken from Canovium, neither the men nor their horses, were in prime condition to fight, and definitely not for a prolonged chase. He needed a way of luring the raiders into a trap. Holding them up until the Twentieth arrived would be sufficient as Andragathius was long past heroics. But coming up with traps was another of his strengths.

A gust of wind hissed through the woods and the sounds of the tree creaking and swaying under him was distinctly unnerving. He really needed a piss but didn't dare loosen his grip on the trunk.

Then he saw movement. A rider pushing his mount at such a speed could only be running for his life. Thoughts about his precarious perch forgotten, Andragathius shouted, "Saddle up!"

From such a distance he couldn't be sure, but thought it was the Areani. As he carefully lowered himself down the tree, he saw how close those chasing him were. "The first man is one of ours!" he called down as he felt for the lower branch with a foot. He was very glad the others were busying themselves with their horses rather than watching him struggle like a fledgling on its first time out of the nest.

The last drop was a little further than he thought, as Brocchus had made it look easy. The carpet of last autumn's leaves weren't as soft as they looked and he landed so awkwardly on his arm that he shouted out a curse. One of his men handed him his sword. There wasn't enough time to mess about with his belt, so he tossed the scabbard away and limped to his horse. From the saddle, he shouted. "And take prisoners!"

The reins in one hand, the sword that felt far too heavy in the other, he kicked his horse into a full gallop, the others doing the same to follow in his wake. As he burst out of the trees and into the open meadow, the Areani instinctively swerved off, thinking he'd been outflanked, but saw Andragathius' raised hand and turned back towards them. "Our man!" he shouted again as the Areani ran past them to safety in the trees. "Half here! Half with me!" he called and let the men work out how to obey his command themselves. To those with him, he pointed ahead to the path the pursuing riders were about to charge along.

He guided his horse in a wide arc and was against the hedgerow, feeling how the horse was so tired its legs weren't so sure under it, and as the sword was about to slip from his grasp, realised now how much he'd hurt his wrist in the fall.

Twenty men were behind him in two rows, as he'd ordered. As the four riders burst into the meadow, Andragathius cut across the back of them, and by the time they saw the other half of the Batavi fan out in front, they realised they were surrounded.

"Surrender!" Andragathius shouted. "Surrender and live!"

Outnumbered and on horses even more exhausted than the Batavi's ones, being left for the crows or led away in ropes were their only options. Andragathius didn't really care which they would choose...he just hoped that they wouldn't all try and fight.

He was on the last man before he'd even managed to draw his sword. He dodged one way then the other, so the rider couldn't know from which side the attack was going to come. Andragathius swung his sword and smacked him hard across the side of the neck with the flat of his blade, hard enough to pitch him head first out of the saddle. And that would have been that...if the recoil hadn't knocked the sword out of his weakened hand. He watched in horror as it slipped out of his grasp and fell to the ground.

Their leader saw it too and in a heartbeat decided that he didn't want to surrender. As he got his horse turned, Andragathius knew the look on his face meant that if he was going to die, he might as well take someone with him. The bastard charged, long sword drawn and teeth bared.

Andragathius went for his pugio, but his belt was lying at the foot of the tree. Cursing, he watched helplessly as the point of the sharp steel came towards him, dead centred at his chest. All he could do was pull back sharply on the horse's reins, and just as the raider was about to impale him, Andragathius' horse reared up and the man got a face full of hooves. The sword passed harmlessly over his shoulder, but the relief of surviving the attack unarmed only lasted a moment as the force of the horses slamming into each other threw Andragathius from his saddle and just as gracefully as he'd got out of the tree, he hit the ground with his shoulders and the back of his head. The thick grass cushioned the fall, but as he struggled to get to his feet, head ringing and the world blanketed in a strange silence, it also hid his sword. By the time he'd managed to push himself up the Scotti had his long blade ready in two hands to swing. At least it would be quick...although without a weapon in his hand, it would be more of an execution than a fight.

A smile spread over the raider's grubby face as he put a leg forwards and swung the sword.

The world went perfectly quiet.

But for the Votadini, it also went dark, as Broccus cracked his skull with the butt of his spear. The long sword fell harmlessly, but the dead man's head, travelling at quite a speed from how hard Broccus had hit him, crunched into Andragathius' face. Cursing as he swallowed blood, he lay flat on his back, he looked up at the clouds as Broccus stood over him. "Will you live?"

The rage at being spoken to in such a way gave him the strength to get to his feet, but instead of challenging him, Broccus put a strong arm around his waist and helped him walk over to the Areani.

"Report!" Andragathius snapped at the Areani, as he wiped away the blood pouring from his probably broken nose.

"A few less than three hundred men, about ten miles from here. Stolen horses. Work ones, not trained. And a couple of carts. There is a river somewhere to the east of here that empties to the north. They plan to come overland, then transfer everything to the boats and sail north. They don't want a confrontation and think they have a day before any soldiers get here. They lit some decoy fires to the south to fool them."

"They didn't fool us," Andragathius said, but cast a glance at Brocchus, who looked suitably sheepish. "Not all of us."

"They should be here by the evening to catch the tide," the Areani said.

"And we will be here for them."

"How many more men do you have?"

"More? We are Batavi," Andragathius laughed.

"We should light a fire. A beacon to lead the Deva cavalry to us," the Areani said.

"No," Andragathius said, and struggling for strength asked Brocchus, "Why would that be a bad idea?"

"Because the Votadini would see it as well and will know they're outflanked. They might split into smaller bands and be harder to catch."

"Exactly," Andragathiu nodded. "A flock of sheep is easier to pen than ones scattered over the mountains."

To the Areani, he said, "Magnus wants as many alive as he can, so best to let them get to that river they think they are escaping along."

"They can move those little boats of theirs quicker than you think," the Areani huffed.

"Oh. I have an idea about that," Andragathius smiled.

XXIII

Britannia Secunda

With its flared nostrils, foam around the bit and wild eyes, the panting horse wasn't going any further that day. Magnus reached forwards and stroked the long neck affectionately, feeling a keen guilt that he'd caused a creature of such lithe beauty to suffer so much.

On its back, he felt its heavy breathing. From awkward newborn staggering around on bandy legs, to cavalry battalion, to meat for soldiers, growing up on the hacienda in Hispania, he'd been involved in every stage of a horse's life. Someone had welcomed this one into the world, made sure it was taking its mother's milk, broke it to the bit and saddle and taught it to respond to the subtle commands of a rider. And they'd done it well. It could almost pass for one raised and trained on his family's estate. And he'd almost killed it.

He nudged it a couple of steps through the last of the trees to the edge of a steeply sloping field. The smoke lingering from the charcoal kilns wasn't so thick here, so maybe the fresher air would help calm it a little.

The rest of his small escort filed out along the edge of the ridge beside him. The lad holding the standard pulled his horse up next to Magnus. He looked up at the open mouth of the bronze creature as it glinted in the sun. One of Magnus' earliest memories was watching a rider tear around in a wide circle, the draco crying out in a high-pitched, spine-tingling wail as the air was forced through it. The horse's ears pinned back in fright as the rider tried to get it accustomed to the strange shrieking noise coming from behind its head. Magnus had been enthralled, and his first dream had been to be a draconarius.

It was his newest dream that occupied his attention now though.

The hill was high enough up that the landscape was arrayed in front of them like a map on a table top at an angle. On the horizon, roughly a day's ride on a good, and well-rested, horse, was a triangle-shaped hill ahead of a line of rolling forested ones. Between them and where Magnus stood was a scene of utter tranquillity. A vista of fields, patches of woods, little dots of whitewashed farmsteads or villas, where people lived their lives with the seasons, growing crops to feed the army.

He wasn't too sure of his orientation though. "What am I looking at here?" he asked.

The young soldier who'd guided him here pointed to the left, north. "Deva is just behind that hill there, sir."

With that, he could work out that pretty much everything he saw on the plain was soon to be his. Octavius was a shrewd and clever man, but also a ruthless one. By fair means, but mostly foul, he'd built himself a miniature empire on the fertile plain south of Deva, as well as in the mountains of the west. It was all soon to be handed over to Magnus. Along with the old man's daughter.

The several plumes of smoke billowing into the evening air could be just ignited charcoal kilns... if someone didn't know that men from the north were down there wreaking havoc. For those on the plain though, the fires would be the backdrop to scenes of utter devastation, pillage, rape and murder. He could almost hear the screams, the wet thuds as unprotected bodies were broken open from the swings of swords and axes.

And knowing he'd arranged such a horror to befall them, his stomach knotted painfully and the reins felt strangely heavy in his hands.

One fire was larger than the others. A full farm ablaze. But curiously, two smaller ones burned a little further south. It was well-known that barbarians found great pleasure in destroying everything they couldn't take with them, but it was puzzling why they would be setting fire to farms so far from what they must be aware was their route of escape, was puzzling. Unless it was a clumsy attempt at a ruse...If his suspicion was correct, he hoped Andragathius was paying attention and wouldn't go chasing false fires.

With a long deep breath, he tried to force himself to relax and told himself that the big Batavi wouldn't be fooled.

He looked at the draco again and indicated to the bearer to pass it to him. The long mouth, the sharp teeth, the intricately engraved scales and its angry eyes, the metal smith had been a master of his craft. Several times over the years he'd had it explained to him how the noise was made by air being forced down its wide mouth and channelled into smaller tubes, something similar to how a trumpet works. But even knowing how the mechanism of its scream worked, whenever he heard one it still held a magical quality that made him feel as excited as a little boy again.

He set the staff at his shoulder, felt the red and orange cloth tails moved by the breeze brush against his shoulder like the nervous touch of his first lover and thought about how the dream he hoped to realise soon, was so much greater than anything he could possibly have imagined as a boy.

And yet he still couldn't do anything about the feeling of deep unease. Something, somewhere was wrong, like a false note played on a lyre, a soldier at muster facing the wrong way. In his heart, he felt the flutter of fear of a man in a busy crowd suddenly feeling an emptiness where his coin pouch had been a moment before. In one moment, he was pretty sure the old woman had something to do with it, the next that it was just the natural reaction of a man putting so much trust into the hands of someone who had the inclination, and the means, to kill him as soon as he wasn't useful to her.

With a rueful chuckle, he realised that whether he liked it or not, he was one of the old woman's ludus counters in her generations-old plan. And he probably would still be even if he made it to the purple.

He went over the plan again, testing for any weaknesses. No matter how fast they moved, how viciously they fought, or how clever they were, there really wasn't a single hope for the Votadini. A Batavi cavalry outflanked them, another was heading from Canovium to cut them off to the south, thousands of soldiers motivated to protect their food supplies. Macrcellius was down to the south somewhere with the painfully slow, but heavily defended, bullion wagon that they might accidentally come across. Although Magnus had pressed the importance of defending it, there were several hundred elite soldiers in the guard train. They wouldn't have too much trouble defending it from the raiders, so all of their escape routes were cut off. They might not know it yet, but they were hopelessly trapped. It was more of a corral than a battlefield. In the more than twenty years since he'd been given his first command, he'd never lost a fight and looking down over the countryside, he couldn't think of anything he'd overlooked.

Being so far removed from the fight, as well as trusting enough in his plan and the men that the outcome was pretty much assured, he felt rather strangely aloof and detached. With the Areani, Elen's brother and Andragathius carrying out his orders and plan, knowingly or not, he'd arranged his pieces on the ludus board, but the feeling was as though he'd set counters off and was watching them move of their own accord.

Idly, he wondered if God felt something similar when from heaven he looked down as armies of empires clashed and tens of thousands of men turned the ground to mud with their blood.

And even if, as he intended, the men of the Twentieth would proclaim him emperor in a few days, he judged himself safe from Gratian's ire as well. He would decline, of course, gracefully, humbly, and would make sure his embarrassment would be reported back to Mediolanum.

And that would be the very first step.

Then he would have plenty of time to work on how best to do

the same with the Sixth at Eboracum and the auxiliaries on the Wall. Plenty of time to sift through his commanders one by one, working out which ones would stand at his side.

Plenty of time.

His hands were so sweaty on the staff he had to hand the draco back.

And then he threw up.

* * *

Two wagons full of stuff was all the bastard barbarians had taken from the villa. Two wagons of goods that fifty or more simple, yet innocent, people had died for. Two wagons for them to cross the sea and risk their lives under the noses of the Twentieth Legion for. It all seemed so pointless.

Anything metal had been thrown in, smithy tools and horse tack, all the legs of curing meat they could find, and wheels of cheese. Half a dozen farm children, both boys and girls, were trussed hand and foot and bounced about in the back with the rest of the goods. They'd tossed an amphora in over the side, but had had no idea it should be stored on its point, and so it had smashed and now everything was covered in olive oil. It still dripped through the boards as they trudged away up a rough track.

Kenon had been brought up on tales of conquest, of emperors and generals stripping the wealth of entire kingdoms to take back to Rome, where in celebration triumphal arches were built and ornately carved and painted columns erected. What the bastards had come so far, risked so much and killed so many for was worth next to nothing. Even the gold, as glorious as it looked in the light, wasn't close to what Father stored in the strong room of Segontium's principia. It didn't come close to adding up, and so he feared there was something even worse to come.

The dozen or so horses they'd stolen had been poorly harnessed and one was in obvious pain as it twisted and staggered along, kicking in protest at an angle as it pulled the leading wagon. Either they had wildly different ways of doing things on the other side of the Wall and just had no idea about Roman leatherwork, or perhaps they really were as stupid as Kenon thought.

The horses obviously didn't have too long left to live as they wouldn't be getting in the tiny boats, but sick of seeing it suffer, as well as fearing the raiders being in a bad mood if it should try and bolt and tip the wagon, he offered to set it right. He was rewarded with a slap hard enough to split his lip.

He welcomed the taste of blood as it was what he deserved, but was also revolted by it as it reminded him that he was still covered in the blood of the poor girl he'd been forced to kill. It had dried and the feel of it pulling tight on the back of his hands disgusted him to the point that he wanted to rip his skin off his bones.

Compared to the speed they'd paddled up the Dee, the wagons creaked along infuriatingly slowly, but still bumped enough to dislodge one of the rough boats that had been carelessly thrown on top. Kenon was summoned to carry it and along with the worst of the deserters, picked it up, turned it upside down and rested the frame on a shoulder, the seat plank under his chin. It stank, but he'd got used to much worse smells in the last few weeks.

Just animal hide and a frame, it wasn't heavy, and at least with his head inside, he didn't have to look at the barbarians…but with no northern idiots to distract him from his desperate anger. He wanted to destroy every last one of the raiders. But more than that, the teeth-gnashing anger that seethed in his heart yearned to set everything that would burn alight, to wither all of the crops in every field, to knock down the walls of every fortress and turn every house in every town to ash. He wanted to be the bringer of Revelations, to scream so loud his voice would be recognised by the faithful as a trumpet of the apocalypse…

No amount of pain or suffering would satiate him, not until the last little girl alive had screamed the last of her life away and the world had become perfectly lifeless and still. Only then would the scream in his head stop... but he knew that would end his death as well. So he tried to negotiate a path through his blinding rage to try and see if there was any way he could survive this.

There was nothing though.

With a degree of self-contempt that shocked the small part of him that was still the spoiled and privileged little boy he'd always been, he thought it would be for the best if he was just taken to the post and burned, as had been done to many Christians in time of the purges. He couldn't imagine anything else to better purge the horror of what he'd done to the girl.

After a while, the bastard in front mockingly asked, "What are you so sad for after such a victory?"

Kenon didn't welcome the intrusion into his morbid introspection, so didn't give him the dignity of a reply.

"Did you see that bitch run off through the fields with her dead baby?" he asked. "She lives. Padarn ordered it so. And soon she'll find a soldier to tell her story to. To tell your name to! What do you think will happen when word gets out about what you did to her?"

And so he'd been betrayed to an even deeper degree than he'd thought. He'd assumed that when the raiders had had enough fun with her, she'd be sent to join her daughter in the afterlife. But if she lived...She'd recognised him, knew him to be the son of Octavius, and he'd killed her baby right in front of her. Her story would get to the men of the Twentieth, to Magnus...to Father. A reward for his capture would be posted, and as soon as they found him, they'd nail him up for the crows like they'd do to the deserters if they were to get caught.

Although it would be a perfectly reasonable thing to do to someone like him, it wasn't something he'd volunteer for. And the thought made him dizzy.

Despite being just a couple of miles away from a villa that should have been his, there was no way back to his old life from here. He was as foreign here as any of the barbarians.

"Think it wasn't worth it for what we got? It's not about the slaves or gold, you idiot. It's all about status. *Prestige*. I doubt you have any idea what that is, though, do you? They're things *real* men care about." He tugged the boat forward again, so hard Kenon was almost knocked off his feet. He didn't care.

"See, Padarn has enemies back up north. Men from other tribes, Picts and Scotti, all rough bastards, and they're always fighting for land and livestock. And so when Padarn goes back with Roman gold from raiding Britannia, people will come from all over to pay him honour. The first to dare raid Britannia since the Conspiracy. A living hero, he will be!"

And so all the expedition had been for was a barbarian's bragging rights.

"And the son of the governor as a slave. As his *willing* slave. Do you know what kind of status that will give him? He'll be remembered forever!"

The brute could feel that Kenon's pace had slowed. "Thought you were staying down here, did you?

The bastard tugged the boat so the rim of the coracle thumped painfully into the back of Kenon's neck. "But we found all the gold thanks to you, so you are in Padarn's favour. Maybe he'll let you sleep in his bed now, not on the floor, when he's finished with you."

And so he'd live out the rest of his probably short days as Padarn's slave. Padarn had made it so he was trapped above the Wall as securely as though he was kept in chains, as if he had any hope of staying alive, he could never set foot in Britannia.

It was an utterly crushing prospect, but after what he'd done to the little girl, nothing less than he really deserved.

It was late in the evening by the time they camped. Long past the point of utter exhaustion, Kenon slumped gratefully to his knees. There was no respite from his suffering though. The boy he'd thrown the rock at had spent the day fermenting his hatred and Padarn granted his wish for payback. A couple of men held Kenon while the boy punched him in the face a few times. The pain from a small fist was nowhere near what he wanted, needed, yearned for, and although he was bleeding from his nose and a split lip, he was disappointed when the boy stopped.

While everybody else feasted merrily on the edible spoils, all Kenon was given to eat was a few scraps of bread. His jaw hurt so much he couldn't chew, so like a baby before its teeth had come through, he only managed the soft inner part.

Padarn wasn't in as festive a mood as his men though. Kenon could understand that. Being the target of a Roman army would be a nervous position to be in. He'd want to keep running through the night.

They were on the move before dawn, walking as fast as the wagons could go towards the direction of the rising sun. He wondered why they were heading east and not north, but didn't really care.

Carrying the boat, as light as it was, still caused his shoulders to scuff and his back to ache, and from a gnawing hunger, he was feeling light-headed, so when there was a commotion ahead and the deserter dropped the boat, Kenon fell with it.

They'd managed to work out how to harness the horse properly, but a wagon wheel had broken. Kenon was sure the Votadini hadn't brought a spare with them from the farm, or even just a couple of spokes to fix it. Even if someone could ride back to the farm workshop for a new one, all the tools and spares they'd need were now all ash.

And then a rider tore off ahead at breakneck speed, leaving shouts of anger in his wake. "Kill him!" Padarn boomed in anger and outrage.

It was the Areani who'd gone. Even though he'd betrayed him so deeply, Kenon still felt cruelly abandoned. His last connection to his former life gone, so much for the man's promise to his grandmother...the grandmother who hadn't ever wanted to meet him.

A few of Padarn's men hurriedly got their stolen horses ready and charged after him. In the ruckus, no one paid Kenon any attention, even though he was close to the tree line. They didn't need to. They knew he had nowhere to run to...and he'd been starved for days so he wouldn't get far, even if he was fool enough to bolt.

He looked at the broken wheel. It hadn't broken by accident. A couple of thick spokes had clearly been cut through. Thinking about why the Areani would have done that caused a shiver of apprehension to turn his skin to goosebumps. Yet another betrayal to add to the long list. And if it wasn't Kenon, his Grandmother or Padarn the Areani was working for, then who was it? Magnus was the only name left?

He didn't know how it could have been set, or what was about to happen, but he was sure they were in a trap...but instead of scattering and trying any way they could to get back north alive, the dumb barbarians milled about the wagon wanting to protect their loot. They might not have known how to load one properly, or how to harness horses to it, but he couldn't help but be ruefully impressed with their ingenuity. While some men cut down a small tree, others tethered the rest of the horses to the front of the stricken wagon. Using the remains of the wheel and the freshly felled trunk, they fashioned a kind of a sled. With six horses pulling, it moved very noisily as it scraped along, but moved just as fast as when it had four wheels.

Padarn was either unconcerned or oblivious to the situation he now found himself in, and Kenon certainly wasn't going to get hit in the head for opening his mouth to warn him, so they carried on. About midday, a relieved cheer spread through the raiders. Kenon put the boat down and saw they'd come to a small river. The flimsy boats were pushed in and quickly loaded up with the proceeds from the raided farm and village. The harnesses were taken off the horses, but instead of being cut free, their throats were slit. Seeing the glorious beasts shudder to their knees, tossing their necks in heart-breaking death throes, soaking the killers in thick splashes of blood, brought all the raw pain of the day before back and Kenon's legs gave way in sympathy with the dying animals. They only died because the barbarians didn't want to leave anything useful for the Romans.

As Kenon paddled his full boat downstream, he noticed how much lower it was sitting in the water and couldn't believe it would stay afloat in the sea on their way back north. He was going to drown for a couple of cheese wheels. Gasping for his last breath alone, miles from the nearest friendly soul, seemed a horrible way to die. Even worse than having his skull caved in by a group of children. As the boat began to pick up a bit of speed, he supposed either was better than being crucified in front of an audience... With the Areani sabotaging the wagon that was what he had the unnerving sensation he was paddling straight towards.

The stream was narrow and not fast flowing, so it was hard work to keep going at the pace the others wanted to go at. Around a couple of tight turns, where the soft clay banks rose up higher than the height of a man, Kenon knew something was wrong. So did the others, and they all stopped paddling to sit silent as the boats slowed to the unhurried flow of the stream. Around another bend Kenon's boat bumped into the ones ahead, all stuck by the tree that had fallen across the river.

The others were about to get out to try and move it, but Kenon's attention was caught by the sharpened stakes sticking out of the bank, mostly covered by the undergrowth. He was still deciding if it would be in his best interest to point them out or not when, in the midst of a chorus of panicked screams, a boat behind was dragged up the bank so fast the men tossed out of it cartwheeled in the air before splashing into the muddy water. The boat disappeared over the top of the bank in the blink of an eye as though some monster from the Book of Revelations had grabbed it out.

Kenon screamed in fear, but a loud cracking noise drowned him out. He looked up to see a tree falling right on top of him. Instinctively, he cried out a warning, but there was nothing anyone could do. It seemed to take forever for it to come down. As it smashed into him, its thin outer branches felt like the end of Father's whip, the thicker ones like the butt of Bassus'spear. And then he was flailing in the muddy water, desperate for breath. He was pinned down, about to die like a cornered barbarian. He couldn't tell if the screams he heard were his own or those of the raiders dying with him.

Lying face down on the ground, wrists once again bound tightly behind him, Kenon was held as securely as an animal for sale on a market stall. With torn clothes, covered in filth after being fished out of the silty stream, face beaten, he knew he didn't look any different from the other captured men, so was probably about to be killed as one.

There was surely no benefit in announcing himself as a Roman deserter, so he stayed where he was.

He saw the remains of some of the flimsy boats that had been ripped out of the river with hooks on ropes. They'd been pulled by horses. It seemed so simple now, but he remembered the horror of seeing them dragged out like children's toys. He couldn't imagine how the army could have got to them so quickly...unless the Areani had something to do with it. But that would mean he'd had everything planned since before they went over the Wall... and that was too much to think about.

At first, it was a relief to hear Latin spoken. In a proper accent too, but it only took a heartbeat for the memory of the girl he'd killed to come slamming back. Governor's son or not, the last moments of life for a murdering deserter were going to be unpleasant in the extreme. The prospect of dying slowly on a cross, in full view of mocking onlookers, filled him with such dread that he felt his bladder empty. Being a slave, even Padarn's, was infinitely preferable to being crucified. "I want to be a slave!" he wailed. "Please!"

"I'm sure we can sort something out," the Areani said. Being so helpless at the feet of a man who'd betrayed him to such an unfathomable degree, Kenon was very conflicted. He wanted to rip the bastard's eyes out for what he'd done, yet at the same time he wanted to beg forgiveness for whatever had made the Areani hate him so much that he would do such a thing. He'd do anything so that they could be as they were in those days just after they'd crossed the Wall.

He didn't know why the Areani untied his hands and bundled him on a horse while the other raiders were kept bound and forced to walk. Being ridden to his execution didn't seem like any sort of privilege though. Perhaps they wanted to put him on parade, to humiliate him as much as they could before they put him to death.

By evening, desperately exhausted and reduced to a whimpering wreck from the fear of what was coming, he saw the thick walls of Deva ahead. Instead of looking at the thick perimeter walls with the sense of welcome protection they offered to those inside, Kenon saw them as an impenetrable barrier, like the Wall, intended to keep the likes of him out. In despair, he realised he already didn't consider himself a Roman any more. And with another gut-wrenching realisation, he knew that in a few hours…long drawn out, mind-breaking agony filled hours… he wouldn't be considered among the living either.

A pair cohort was out to greet them and the hundred and sixty of them all stood in perfect rows, a stark contrast to the wild disarray of the barbarians. All in impeccable armour, they stared at the captives in utter, and understandable, contempt. Including Kenon. At the head of them, he recognized the wide shoulders and thick legs of Magnus and his heart threatened to seize. Beside him, some workmen were preparing something on the ground. When the horse took him closer, he saw it was crosses. The nails being driven into the cross member to hold it together felt like they were being hammered into his heart.

"Slave," he whimpered. "I want to be a slave."

Arms and legs drained of all strength, when the Areani pulled him out of the saddle, all he could do was roll himself into a ball near Magnus' feet. He tried to lift his bruised wrists to show how poorly he'd been treated by Padarn's men, but knew that whatever bruises his body was covered with, nothing would take away from the fact that he'd gone north with the intention of bringing a barbarian army to Britannia. There could only be one punishment for that. The workmen had almost got it ready.

Without ceremony, almost as though it was a routine everyone understood, the first of the deserters was dragged to one of the crosses. He used to stand at muster with the men now kicking him to the ground, used to march and eat with those now tying his wrists to either end of the crossbar.

With some scuffling, as even bound, Padarn was almost a match for a couple of soldiers, the Votadini leader was forced to his knees next to Kenon. Even though the beast had his hands bound, Kenon didn't feel safe next to him.

Magnus still didn't say anything, but gave the signal for the man with the hammer and nails to attach the deserter to the cross a little more securely than with just ropes. The man had been quite impressively brave up until that point. Resigned to his fate, or expecting some mercy from Magnus, Kenon didn't know. The sharp spike of iron smashing through the palm of his hands made him scream like some animal caught in a trap. But the way Magnus was standing there with so much satisfaction, seemed to Kenon as though he'd wanted this to happen.

The man cried even more as the cross was hoisted vertical and his weight pulled on the nails. But when the post fell into its slot and suddenly dropped down a foot or so, his screams came not from a man, but from the depths of the inferno.

The deserter was living Kenon's worst fear…and now he could see and hear the effect of the cross, it seemed even worse than he'd imagined. Even Padarn's face had turned pale. And knowing it would soon be his fate, the last vestige of self-restraint fled Kenon's control and he tried to shuffle on his knees towards Magnus' feet. The Areani's foot on his back stopped him. "Slave," he begged. "I'll be a good slave."

"Next!" Magnus shouted and Kenon, thinking the command was for him, cried out for mercy.

It was no relief that it was the second deserter they pulled to the wood he was going to die on.

Magnus stepped towards Padarn. "So your plan was for a lightning raid up the Dee, steal horses so you could carry your loot and drag your boats overland to the other river to the east. And there, you'd be away on the tide before the legion even got back to Deva. I have to admit, I am impressed. Such a plan shows understanding of the land and of your enemy's movements, and predicted their response. You had insiders with you to give you detailed advice, which you followed to choose your targets. Very clever. You almost had everything perfect."

Kenon couldn't understand why the Dux was complimenting the old Votadini, but it seemed he couldn't think too much at all. The first deserter was screaming so loudly, a ragged note of such agony, it seemed to Kenon that his sanity was beginning to unravel.

"You made just one fatal miscalculation though," Magnus said with a cruel smile.

"Did I?" Padarn growled.

"It seems the only thing you didn't account for was that you were attacking Magnus Maximus."

Some of the men around them laughed, but Padarn didn't respond.

Since they'd left the rough hillfort north of the Wall, everything had seemed like the chaos of madmen, the Votadini no more organised than a pack of dogs, so it was a surprise to realise that destroying the farm had been a calculated plan.

"It doesn't have to be a *fatal* mistake, though," Magnus continued. "Right now, you have two possible outcomes ahead of you. You stand at an important fork in the road. As you have no doubt heard my reputation, I am a fair and merciful man, so I will allow you to choose which. The first...All of your surviving men will die in front of you, one by one, like the deserters from my army will do in a day or so. Some will die today, a few tomorrow. Some of the tougher ones may last until the day after. As you can see, I don't have too many crosses, so for all of them to perish in this way, it could take a couple of weeks. I will tie you in a place where you can listen to their cries and curses and watch the crows peck out their eyes. And then, finally, after the last one is dead, I will do the same to you. My slaves might need a new chamber pot, and your skull would do for that. Or..." He paused to let the second deserter's agonised screams ring out as the nails were hammered through his hands.

Kenon had a feeling that the second option wouldn't be the best choice of the two.

"Or your future, and that of your men, can be very different. For the second choice, I will give you weapons, horses, training, gold..."

Kenon almost gasped in joy, but Padarn's huff sounded disparaging.

"A client king is still a king," Magnus added. "And when you return to your lands, you will be much richer than when you left. That was your plan, wasn't it...just achieved in a slightly different way. We will make trade agreements and we can arrange ways to help you defend against the Attacoti, Picts and Scotti, who, I understand, are your enemies just as much as they are Rome's. If you swear allegiance to me, your men will form a detachment of foederati and in time their children will become citizens. And your son..."

At the mention of his baby, Padarn pulled against his ropes.

"I am fair, but I am also a bastard when I need to be," Magnus smiled. "So to help you make the best decision, let me explain the first option in a little more detail for you, so you get a fuller understanding of what will happen. If you make the wrong choice, while your men are taking their turns on the crosses, I will take a detachment north and wipe out every single woman and child I find within fifty miles of the Wall. With so many men dying slowly here, I assume they'll be pretty poorly defended and will be easy pickings."

Kenon couldn't understand why Padarn wasn't begging Magnus to make his people foederati. It was so much more than he could wish for.

The cross of the second deserter was hoisted up and Kenon cringed as the man who'd left his legion to lead enemies against them cried out desperately over the sullen crowd for mercy. None was given.

"Pleeeease..." he managed to gasp once more but as the cross fell into the slot dug in the ground his heart-rending wails became incoherent.

The cross was meant to be a slow death. It could be a day or so before he found relief from his suffering, but it would be the Lord who granted it, not Magnus.

"Your silence saddens me," Magnus said to Padarn. "In that case then, would you choose which of your men we put up first?"

Kenon groaned at how the big man remained sullenly silent.

"I offer your leader a deal," Magnus shouted at the kneeling barbarians.

Kenon twisted around and saw that although there were a fair many of them, there were noticeably less than when they'd come on the tide up the Dee. He suspected the missing ones were more likely dead in the stream than heading north, free.

"But he would rather watch you all die in front of him," Magnus continued. "Slowly. So be it. So, who will be first?"

Even though Kenon was shaking and was half delirious with fear, he was still aware enough to understand how clever Magnus was. Instead of choosing one of the tough, burly men, he pointed at one of the youngest, one who'd been guarding the boats as the adults raided. The boy was already in floods of tears from seeing the others get nailed to the crosses, and as he was dragged forwards, he began crying out to Padarn. Some of his kinsmen shouted out as well. Kenon didn't understand the rough language, but the sentiment was clear; they were pleading for their lives. The boy's hands were pulled out and tied securely to the crossbeam and the man with the hammer pressed the end of the nail against the skin of his palm and raised the hammer, ready to strike it through.

Finally, Padarn shouted something to his men.

"Do you want to be Roman?" the Areani translated to Magnus. "He used a derogatory term for Roman," he added helpfully.

The Votadini boy desperately shouted what sounded like enthusiastic agreement, as did a few others. They'd probably become more vocal supporters of making a deal with Rome the nearer it got to their turn for the cross.

Magnus waved for the man with the hammer to wait, pointed at Padarn, then down to a spot in front of his feet. "Here."

A look of absolute hatred and disgust in his eyes, to the sounds of one of the crucified deserters begging for the release of death, Padarn shuffled ungainly to Magnus in absolute supplication. Andragathius stepped forward to stand at Magnus' side, his sword drawn and angled straight at Padarn's throat. "Swear your allegiance to me on the life of your son, and he will be spared Roman steel," Magnus said.

Kenon had heard those words before, when the Areani and Padarn had been talking in Padarn's hut, but he couldn't believe that the Areani had concocted such a mad plan to raid just to get his revenge on his father. There had to be more to it than that.

It was the Areani that Padarn looked at, not Magnus, glaring at him, understanding the full depth of the betrayal. "For my *only* son and my men, I swear loyalty," he growled. "But I swear vengeance on the man I used to call my son. Cut my hand! I wish to make it a blood oath!"

A nod from Magnus and a soldier cut the ropes from around Padarn's wrists and in an action that looked like complete madness to Kenon, he reached out to grab at the soldier's blade. The soldier snatched it away, slashing deep cuts into Padarn's palm and fingers. He held his fist out, letting his blood drip to the grass. "It is witnessed," he said, holding his bleeding fingers to the sky. To Magnus, he said, "I agree. The Votadini are now foederati."

"Good decision," Magnus beamed. He undid the clasp of his cloak and ceremoniously draped it around Padarn's shoulders, then signalled for him to get to his feet.

Bright red cloak of the highest quality wool and most expensive dyes over the filthy animal skins and torn trousers looked ridiculous as Padarn got to his feet. Kenon wondered if the Votadini thought the cloak was a trophy, or felt more like a yoke.

"It is done!" Magnus shouted. "Take the Votadini to the barracks. Give them food, take them to the baths and give them new clothes. They are our allies now, not our enemies. Any harm done to them, that man answers to me!"

With two men of the Twentieth to each still bound Votadini, the raiders were led away. The young boy was let up unharmed and he hobbled off rubbing his hands together as though he felt the pain from the nails...and Kenon was left with the uneasy feeling that he'd been an unwitting player in some spectacle.

XXIV

Deva, Britannia Secunda

He should have been calm, revelling in his complete and decisive victory, the leader of the powerful Votadini tribe now his sworn subject, but his heart was thumping in his chest harder than the hammer that had fixed the deserters to the crosses.

Ask him how many he'd killed with his own hand, and he could answer to maybe the nearest ten or so. Ask how many he'd ordered to be sent to their deaths, and he wouldn't be able to give anywhere close to an exact answer. But there was a huge difference in killing a man in a fight, crowded in with screaming and dying men, and setting one to a cross then having to stand and listen to his pitiful screams. A flick of Magnus' finger is all he would have to do for the man to be taken down and granted mercy, and he knew enough about soldiers to know that he'd grovel at his feet with such gratitude to be spared such an awful death and that he'd probably be his most loyal man for the rest of his days.

The deserter's death was worth a lot more than his life though.

An act of mercy might make Magnus appear weak, and he couldn't afford that. Not now. To die in such a gruesome way was the prescribed punishment for a deserter, and the two nailed up weren't simply deserters; they'd come back as part of a barbarian raiding party and had played their part in sailing up the river and killing farmers. As much as it turned his stomach to listen to them, they would stay up there until nature took its course. In a day or two. Long after they'd screamed themselves to silence.

The nails weren't strictly necessary, but he'd wanted them to scream.

Looking just as wretched as those suffering in the process of their executions was the boy who was soon to be brother-in-law. Filthier than the most destitute beggar, by rights the pathetic little bastard should be up on the third cross. Son of the Governor or not, he'd gone north with the intention of raising an army to come against him. Or at least the dumb idiot thought it was what he'd done.

While he would not do the boy any harm, he could at least use him to wrest a concession or two from his dear bride.

He pointed at the free cross laid out invitingly on the ground. "And now you!" he said to the wretch. He had to fight to keep a straight face as Kenon's pathetic wails joined those already on the crosses.

On cue, Elen pushed her way through the men crowded close around Magnus, and he signalled them to raise their spears and let her approach. "Magnus! Please, I beg of you..." she wept.

She grabbed his arm, fingers pressing into his skin. "I *beg* you. He is my brother. He will be *your* brother soon. Mercy. I beg for clemency. Whip him, scourge him, if you must, but don't *crucify* him! Mercy!"

"He went north to bring enemies against me," he said solemnly, but loud enough for those in the crowd to hear. "It must be done!"

"*Please*!" she begged. "I will do anything?"

Magnus pretended to think for a moment. "Anything?"

"Yes!"

"I will grant your wish for mercy..."

"Thank you! Thank you!"

"On one condition."

Suddenly distrustful, she pulled away from him. "Which is?"

"We marry tomorrow."

"So soon!" she gasped...and he smiled as she raced to think of a way to postpone it. "My father can't get here until..."

He leaned closer. Those watching might have thought he was whispering some sweet endearment, but over the cries of the crucified, he said, "I must ride the momentum of the victory, like their boats rode the tide."

"No..." she started.

"Maybe when your father arrives he can pull what's left of your brother down from the cross?"

They both knew it was a hollow threat, but reluctantly she nodded her agreement.

"I want a moment with him," Magnus told her. "Don't worry, I will not harm him."

The Areani took one of Kenon's arms, the huge Batavi the other, and walked him away from the onlookers, set him on some grass where the cries of the deserters weren't quite so disturbing and no one in the crowd could hear.

Only just managing to resist the urge to kick him back to Segontium, Magnus leaned over him. "I know exactly what you intended to do," he growled. "Bringing a foreign army against me is the highest treason. Even your own father would put the nails through your hands for that."

The Areani had spoken of the horrors the boy had suffered at the hands of the Votadini and Magnus was sure that once the boy had recovered to be able to think clearly again, he wouldn't be happy that the Barbarians weren't being punished in a way he deemed suitable. If he'd had a cruel heart before, the need for vengeance remaining unrealised for long enough could consume a man's heart and easily make a monster out of him.

Magnus knew it well.

Allowing a weak, vindictive man anywhere near power was asking for trouble, and these days that was far from the empire needed, but he knew he was in no position to break a promise to the old woman, and so the idiot stayed curled up at his feet.

"If you even *think* of standing against me again, those screams you can hear, the ones that I hope will haunt your dreams tonight, they will be *yours*. I will crucify you. In front of everyone. Do you understand?"

"Yes, sir. Yes, sir," the boy cried.

Making him fear a pain that was worse than death was easy, but Magnus had a better way of assuring the boy's loyalty. Rejected by his father, betrayed by the Areani, he had no one to truly respect. He could change that. "But in the end the raid was ineffectual and seeing as I am Magnus Maximus, I made it work to my benefit, so I end up being grateful to you. So, instead of nailing you up, I offer to hail you as a hero for surviving Votadini capture. How does that sound? If you fight for me, under my personal command, doing *everything* I ask of you, I will reward you. Does that sound like an acceptable arrangement?"

The boy nodded, but swallowed the wrong way and choked on his own saliva. "There was a girl…" he gasped. "A woman knows me…"

The Areani nodded and Magnus let him speak. "They made him kill a young girl so they could find the gold at the farm. She knows him as the Governor's son."

"Of course she does," Magnus said as he rolled his eyes. "Find her and have her brought to me. I wonder if she is any good with a whip." Elen had said he could scourge him, perhaps he'd take her up on her offer.

There was one more thing to do before he dismissed the men and he walked further away from the sounds that wouldn't be the appropriate background for the next little act, over to the crowd of people from the vicus who had come to see what the commotion was about.

The First Spear, happy to have something important to do for the hero of the hour, had found the man Magnus wanted. "Legionary Flavius Claudius Constantinus!" he announced so loudly he frightened the young woman. The lad Magnus had shared roast mutton with at Canovium a few days before stepped nervously forwards, pummeled his chest with a fist and then held his arm out straight in salute.

Magnus wanted to talk in a soft voice to his wife, but she was so small he had to bend over. "Your fine husband here has told me the tragic news about how you lost a daughter recently."

On the verge of tears, she nodded.

"I am so very sorry about that. But I wonder if you can help me. Those Votadini bastards destroyed a village not far from here. The only ones to survive are a couple of young girls that they took with them. I think the best place for them would be with a loving family. Now, you don't have to, and I will understand if you decline, but I wonder if you could look after them for me. I will pay for everything you need for their upkeep and education, of course."

The girl looked up at Magnus with her puffy, blood-shot eyes. Andragathius towered beside her and the sight of the Batavi made him smile. Earlier that day he'd managed to capture a band of barbarians with just forty of his own men and now he held two terrified little girls in his arms. He knelt slowly and gently set them down. Surrounded by dozens of scary-looking soldiers, the girls saw the timid woman and clung tightly to her. In a motherly instinct, the girl put her arms around them, then feeling their soft hair, and how frightened they were, she sank to a knee and held them properly, hushing them, and telling them not to fear.

If anyone watching didn't know how staged it was, hopefully they'd have seen a heart-warming scene with a Dux Britanniarum who seemed to deeply care for people. A scene he hoped would get told and retold through the barracks, bathhouses and brothels all night. Along with those talking about how he so viciously punished the deserters, and was strong enough to take on the responsibility of setting up the Votadini as foederati, hopefully a few of them would have the idea that a leader like that was one worth following. And would put voice to that at his wedding tomorrow.

XXV

Magnus walked slowly down the hill from Deva to the harbour. It was just after dawn and apart from songs of the birds, it felt calm, still and full of possibilities. It felt like the many days he'd woken with the sun knowing a battle was about to begin, one where the outcome was not assured, wondering if this would be the last sunrise he'd get to see.

No one would be fighting today, but by the time the sun had set, many things would be as different as though a real battle had taken place. The ludus counters re-arranged, hopefully into a much stronger position for the part of the plan that would come next.

As the Dux Britanniarum, he had the emperor over him as the ultimate authority. As the usurper, he had the old woman. Magnus wasn't sure the ire of which he feared most.

The ship had arrived from Segontium the evening before, but for reasons known only to her, Elen's grandmother had chosen to stay aboard and not watch what he'd done with the deserters and her grandson. As Magnus wobbled over the boarding plank, he hoped how he'd treated Kenon would please her.

The slight movement of the ship bobbing up and down did nothing to waylay the growing feeling of nausea and he felt sympathy for Andragathius who'd been too ill to speak as soon as he'd got on the ship they'd crossed on from Gaul. Magnus was glad that despite the bile building up, he could still speak. He expected that the words he was about to say and hear would be some of the most important of his life.

He listened to the faint creaking of the timbers and the mooring ropes pulling taut as the current of the river pulled against it, and the faint slapping of the small harbour waves against the hull. Ships, even more than horses, always made him think of the distant shores he'd dreamed of as a boy. There weren't many shores further away from his boyhood hacienda in Hispania than Deva. And there probably weren't many women in the empire with the powers of the one waiting for him in the captain's cabin.

If the old woman were to make herself known, instead of dwelling in the shadows, she'd be a real rival to Justina. Maybe she already was.

He'd only visited her in her rough vicus house before and had thought the exotic scents she'd perfumed her room with were to mask the odours wafting in from the muddy street outside. Mixed with a slight fishy smell, the stench in the small cabin was the same and he realised it was her own foul smells she was trying to cover. They were not those of a healthy person. "You are unwell?" he asked.

The nodding motion made her chin sink into the hefty collar of flesh around her neck. "Oh, I know that my days are running out," she sighed. "I can feel my last one coming like the coolness that nips the nape of your neck when the sun is setting. But fear not, my Elen will take over from me. All of my connections, all my ears, all the nameless little helpers I have scattered over the empire, all will be hers. And all of my gold. And believe me, she is more ready for the role than she thinks. I dare say that if there was someone in Rome in whose head she wanted to put a dream, she could manage that now."

At the thought of being married to a girl with the old woman's power, a shiver of a cold dread trickled up his back.

She had a stick that she held onto as though her life depended on it. Her gaze turned distant and she wondered if she was seeing some distant future unfold in her second sight. Or maybe it was just wind.

Her rheumy eyes seemed to clear for a moment as she looked him straight in the eye. "You have come for my blessing for your endeavour."

Magnus supposed he had. Having the old woman's resources behind him would be a formidable advantage. Or beside him, in the form of her granddaughter. And although he was sure her co-operation would come with some complicated conditions, he would much rather have her as an ally than an enemy.

"This I would say to you, a warning for the future, as it forever forks in front of us. Just as you offered our new friend Padarn. Listen well. A greedy poor man means nothing to the world, but a powerful man driven by greed...As the empire stands now, there can be nothing more dangerous, unless, of course, you add a touch of madness."

Nero, he thought. She was worried that Kenon would take after him if he was allowed sufficient power.

"Now, you Magnus Maximus, are not mad, strange dreams that drag you across the empire aside..."

She just couldn't help herself teasing him. He hoped it wouldn't be a trait her granddaughter had inherited. And only then did he realise that although the old woman's chair was far from a throne, she sat while he stood. The last time he'd been in such a position, he'd been before the emperor.

"But if you are greedy enough to abuse whatever power you manage to amass, rather than using it to set the empire on a more secure course, then I truly fear what world your children will have to live in. In dark dreams, I see Goths in Rome. That might not spell doom for the people of this island, but it will be close to it. If you manage to take the purple, and I mean *if*, as today is only the very start of your journey, you must remain satisfied with your part in the triumvirate. Ruling in balance with Theo and the young Valentinian is the only way that promises any security. Your cousin may well be outraged at the method of your ascension, but if you prove yourself fitter in the purple than Gratian, which might not be that much of a challenge for a man like you, he will not move against you. Be greedy though, and I fear everything will be at risk. Everything," she said again for added emphasis.

She tried to shuffle into a more comfortable position in the chair, but gave up and sighed. It sounded to Magnus like a soldier trying to hide how badly injured he was. He would be rid of her sooner rather than later. He'd take his chances with the girl over the old woman any day.

"With Elen at your side, you may go far. Follow her advice and you will not go far wrong. At your *side*, though. To look at her, she may seem like nothing but a little slip of a girl, but her power, although it is hidden, is formidable."

Magnus did not doubt that.

"I did not intend my last words to you to be a threat, but I will leave you with a warning I feel I must speak. To say it formally, not just to have it implied. Listen well, man who would be emperor, for on these words, maybe your life will depend. If you even think about raising a finger to harm a hair on that girl's head, your life ends that same day. Whatever that means for the empire. I don't know how to go about initiating curses from beyond the pyre, but if you don't keep your word on this, I will do everything I know to find out. Or," she said with that cheeky smile and gleam in her eyes. "Or maybe it will simply be that my men in your retinue will act swiftly against you."

She laid her stick across her lap and clapped her fat hands together. With the big self-satisfied smile on her face, she looked a bit like a happy baby. "Oh, that feels better to have such words out in the open, doesn't it? All I ask is that you do right by your wife, your son and the empire."

"My son?" Magnus asked, unsure if he'd heard her right.

"Oh, you will have daughters, believe me, the bloodline of the old family will not be broken. Strong ones, they will be too. But a man like you, I am more than sure fate will smile upon with a son. And through you, the Theodosian dynasty will continue. I will not meet him, but I see him as I speak...and I will tell you this; your boy shall be the greatest treasure you will ever know. More even than the colour you seek."

Wondering if she was in the vision of an augur, no matter that these days such a thing was punishable by death, he summoned the courage to ask, "And what will become of me?"

A smile spread slowly across her face.

"I see the future, Magnus Maximus, so be assured that the words I tell are a truth to trust."

With a deep chill that set the skin on his arms to goosebumps, she seemed to be looking through him, rather than at him.

"In days far distant from this, there will come to be histories and there will come to be legends. Your name will be in both."

Magnus had no idea what she meant. But surely all emperors would be part of history, just like any man of such a station who could afford to have his name chiselled into stone. Any boy in the army could name all of Rome's rulers since the days of her kings. But if he would be successful against Gratian or not, her meaning wasn't clear. He wasn't confident enough to ask her for more though.

"But I didn't travel all this way to speak only ill words," she added. "I also have gifts to help you and my granddaughter on your journey together."

She tapped her stick on the floorboards and a few moments later a well-dressed man came to join them in the small cabin. Magnus was instantly wary that he'd been listening to the traitorous things he and the old woman had been discussing, but it was too late to do anything about it now.

"Aed Brosc, son of Eochaid, king of the Deisi. The man who will arrange the settlement of your people on my land, in exchange for the defence of it...should you be... otherwise engaged. I ask that he will be treated better than his father was."

Magnus nodded his respect to the king.

"The two of you will talk to Elen to make arrangements that all parties will find acceptable. Oh, I almost forgot. How silly of me. Octavius, sadly, will soon be meeting his end. For Elen's sake, it will seem natural, but you know how it is with these *wild* tribes and the need of sons to avenge the murders of their fathers. You will accept it as natural, a result of his advanced age, and you will not investigate or attempt to persecute the perpetrators."

"He will not suffer," Aed said. "Not like my father did by his hand."

Magnus was about to protest, but knew that what Octavius had done to the last king could not go unanswered by the new one, so reluctantly deemed it a fair agreement. Yet at how he was casually agreeing to let the old woman kill a man as powerful as the Governor of Britannia made him shiver again.

Another tap of the stick on the floor and a plain woman with sun-bleached hair and a weathered face came in.

"A king and a slave," the old woman chuckled. "And this fine lady is the wife of one of the most important men in my retinue. And now yours."

She was the wife of the Areani, the one captured in the slave raid and had sought for a decade.

A cold sweat flushed over Magnus. Of course she would have found out about the deal he'd made with the Areani. But he was still alive, so she hadn't been that annoyed at having the raiders run loose.

"We still seek the daughter and be assured, it is an active search. But now I would have some time alone with my granddaughter before the ceremony. You may leave."

She said it almost pleasantly, but was unmistakably the command of a superior to a subordinate. It reminded him of many years ago, talking with Theodosius, being dismissed without a thought, as a man far superior in rank had better things to do. He tempered the outrage it stirred up in him, and forced a smile.

"I wish you well Magnus Maximus, I truly do. A lot depends on you and the decisions you make from this point onwards. Not least the empire itself."

Magnus let the other two go ahead. Two small but important keys on his journey. But before he was through the door, the old woman tapped her stick on the floorboards and pointing a gnarled finger at him, added, "This may be the last time we speak together, but it mustn't be the last time you consider my words."

* * *

Delicately, reverentially, almost lost in the concentration it took, Elen plaited the hair of her doll.

"My little sister had one just like it," Eugenius said.

"All girls do," Elen said. "And we leave them behind, as we do our childhoods, the day we get married."

"I never imagined such a thing could be so meaningful," he mused.

In the barracks, she supposed there wasn't too much talk about the rituals of young girls. "She's the symbol of my childhood. She has shared my bed since the day I was born. I whispered every one of my fears to her, she was there with me every time Father felt the need to…discipline me, and this should be my last moment with her."

"What is her name?" Eugenius asked.

"Tacita."

"The silent one," he smiled. "Quite an apt name for a doll."

When she was younger she'd tried to keep Tacita dressed as she imagined Helen, the mother of Constantine, had looked. Elen shared the name, but Tacita had the style and Mother would get tiny new clothes made on special occasions.

She rubbed her thumb over the cracks in the little face. The craftsman had done a good job with the repair, but the poor doll would forever live with the scars from when Kenon had tossed her against the wall. Terrified that the next time he found her, he'd do even worse the next time, she'd lied to him and said she'd been broken beyond repair, but had pleaded with Father to let Tacita live in the safe room of the principia. It was the most secure place in the whole fort, and guards didn't mind letting a young girl play among the army's gold.

But still, she'd always been terrified that Kenon would get to her one day. And she'd always hated that she wasn't strong or powerful enough to protect her.

She was now.

Eugenius was much more meaningful to her than Tacita could ever be. And she would not be leaving him before going to Magnus. Still working on the tiny braids, she said, "I am going to tell him about us."

"Why?" Eugenius asked. "Your Grandmother told us to keep it a strict secret. If he knows, there will be a target on me."

"I don't want you to be my weakness. I want you to be my strength. I will not live in fear of any man any longer."

"You're just going to tell him straight to his face?"

"Yes."

"When?"

"When he can't say no."

Getting a bride ready for the ceremony was women's work and Tacita done, she slipped into Eugenius' arms last time as just his wife. It was a long hug that was hard to pull away from, and she tried not to cry when the kiss ended.

And Tacita wouldn't sit locked away from Kenon on the legion's gold any more. Her new throne would be the heavy metal head of Gordd-ap-Guwia.

* * *

The tradition that the new wife entered the man's family house went further back in time than anyone knew, so the amphitheatre was an unusual choice to host a wedding, especially as everyone, Elen included, had to walk past the crucified deserters to get in.

Magnus had long joked that he'd spent his life married to the army, so perhaps the amphitheatre was a fitting place to have it after all.

It was also the only building big enough for the ceremony to be witnessed properly by all of the men of the Twentieth Legion. That was much more important than following convention. Marrying Elen needed to be a spectacle.

With her as his wife, he was about to become richer than he'd ever dared dream. But it was her power, as secret and hidden as it was, that would be the real strength. With a few men dotted through the crowd, he was about to get a demonstration of it.

In her yellow dress, hair tied up in intricate patterns, the six braids signifying the rape of the Sabines, a story many hundreds of years old, she looked beautiful. So beautiful that he worried the scene was a little too close to the drugged state he still couldn't forget. And he almost burst out laughing to think that all of this was thanks to an old woman who'd managed to slip herbs into his food to make him dream of finding the most beautiful girl in the world.

He knew this to be real though. In his dream, he hadn't felt any fear, and his stomach hadn't threatened to turn itself inside out.

The legion legate, prefect and the full complement of tribunes of the Twentieth stood on the rows behind him in their gleaming uniforms.

To the other side, Andragathius loomed with a couple of his men, and behind his sister, Kenon, still only barely coherent after his ordeal, swayed slightly on legs that after a day of good rest were still uncertain. Magnus hoped the lashing he would soon be receiving from the farm owner's wife, as she took her pain and rage out on his back, would beat some much needed humility into him. Even so, he couldn't help thinking of the boy as much more of a hindrance than an asset.

Marcellinus came to stand at his side, fat pouches swelling with coin in his hands. He'd ridden ahead of the lumbering bullion wagon and had plenty of coin to hand out. As well as paying the wages that were several months past due, Magnus would add another month of pay on top.

Respect was best earned, but popularity could be bought.

The sandy arena floor was usually a place for practising to fight and to snap into attack formation at the blow of a whistle, and the occasional blood sport for entertainment if some criminal needed to be dispatched. It was now crowded with formal rows of men, and every stone bench in the surrounding rows was crammed full of soldiers, all proud to be witnessing the special occasion of the marriage of the new Dux Britanniarum, a man who seemed to care for each of them individually and who'd captured the whole band of Votadini. So much polished bronze reflecting the sun, Magnus had to squint to look at them. They looked magnificent and it was almost bewildering to think that one day they could be his army fighting against the emperor.

It wasn't exactly the Colosseum, but, with a flutter of nerves, he knew this was the moment his journey there would start.

Patting him gently on the chest to get his attention, Elen stood on tiptoes and said, "There is something I must tell you."

"Yes?" he asked as all thoughts about leading glorious battles dispelled. He knew her well enough now to be on his guard.

"Grandmother warned me to silence about this, but she also convinced me to be myself, to act as I see fit."

"Carry on," he said, a weight of foreboding settling on his heart. He was sure she was about to destroy everything he'd spent weeks preparing for.

"I give you my word on the lives of the children I will bear you, I will do my every duty as your diligent wife, and in time, I am sure we will come to share the love of our children together. But I must tell you that I will never love you as a man. In the depths of my heart, there is another."

And just like that, the bitch brought it all crashing down.

"Who?" Magnus growled and suddenly it was as if five thousand soldiers weren't watching them, that the whole amphitheatre was empty.

"I will be yours in all the ways of the flesh, and I will make sure, on my life, there will never be a doubt about your progeny. In matters of the heart though, I will always be his."

"One of your guards?" Magnus asked, and from the sight of her pursing her lips, he knew his suspicions to be true. "The one who's been whispering to you all the secrets of a soldier's mind?"

She rested a hand on his chest and he wondered if she could feel his thumping heart through the three layers of armour. "Husband of mine, rightfully you owe him gratitude. Because of his counsel, which I passed on to you, every man of the Twentieth is about to fill this place with chants of your name. But hear me now, I swear to you, if harm comes to him, that same day shall be your last."

The words, spoken so politely, yet full of threat, could have come from the mouth of her grandmother, and it made Magnus freeze. "If any were to find out, I would be humiliated," he growled. "They will contest the lineage of my son!"

"Husband..."

"It will be a *sin*!"

"None shall know. Agree it. Swear on your life that he will not be harmed, or I will call off this ceremony."

As she looked up at him, eyes full of feigned innocence, he realised she couldn't have chosen any better time or place to say such a thing. Even after everything of the last weeks, he'd still not realised just how much of a master manipulator she was. She'd caught him at exactly the right moment and had him dangling like a thread, utterly unable to deny her. Or to give her any less than everything she wanted. If he was to call the wedding off, with the whole Twentieth Legion watching with rapt anticipation, all the momentum he'd built up over the last weeks would be lost, his journey to the purple over before it had even begun.

Through gritted teeth, he forced a smile and said, "Very well," while holding onto the thought that maybe it could be sorted out later.

"Swear it," she snapped a little louder than he liked, "On the life of your unborn son."

"Which son?" he asked, confused.

"The one I shall conceive tonight."

He looked out over the crowd of five thousand expectant faces and wondered once again how a young girl could possibly have so much power over him.

Anyone watching them whisper into each other's ear would have thought them talking sweetnesses. Who among them could have imagined he was agreeing to such a crushing humiliation? "I swear," he growled. "But if any are to find out about it…"

"I understand the risk," she said.

"Are your grandmother's men in the crowd?" he asked.

"*My* men," she said in a way that made it feel like ice water was trickling down his back. "You'll see."

He had no choice but to trust her.

At a signal from Andragathius, a handful of his men stepped forwards and embraced Magnus as though he was a close friend of equal standing. At first it felt outrageous, but he forced himself to let them. Then hands were on him, pulling, lifting, and as his feet left the ground, instinct kicked in and he thought it was a fight for his life so he struggled desperately to get his sword. But they hoisted him up onto the back of a shield, and he cursed himself for being such a fool again. Held aloft in sight of the men, the roar of ascent rose again. From the rows of seats, men flooded onto the sand and quickly became a heaving mass, the outstretched arms reaching towards him desperate to touch him as though he was Christ himself come again.

He waved in appreciation of their enthusiasm and let the men have their fill, trying to note the ones staring with stony expressions for later. At some other signal, the shield was lowered and Magnus found himself at the far end of the amphitheatre, shoulders clapped and hand shaken by men who'd otherwise never dare to act familiarly with him.

Andragathius' men then made space between the soldiers down the middle of the amphitheatre, and as the soldiers stepped back a path opened between him and his way back to Elen, like the sea for Moses.

It was time.

His way was lined with the Twentieth Legion's blood-red standards fluttering in the breeze, he began to walk. The whole place had the atmosphere of a forest after a summer thunderstorm. Fresh. Invigorated. And then it came. "Aug –ust- us!" a man shouted from somewhere in the crowd and the scale of events unfurling like a fern in spring, struck him as hard as someone had slammed into him with a shield. A painful surge of foreboding flowed right to the tips of his fingers. There was no way back now.

It had begun.

"Aug –ust- us!" the man shouted again at the top of his voice and by the third time he was joined by others. A few more steps and it became a chorus, then the ones not paid by Elen's grandmother shouted out with them until there were so many men bellowing a storm of voices reverberated around the amphitheatre. He'd refuse it of course, he was nowhere near ready to take an army against Gratian. Yet.

Not even half way back and the whole amphitheatre was roaring with chants of Aug –ust- us! As he walked slowly back, he felt as though he was still on the shield high above the men's heads. They were making a glorious noise.

"Aug –ust- us!"

He knew it to be the sound of him entering history.

THE END

AUTHOR'S NOTE

If you enjoyed Usurpers and would like to play a little part in its success, as well as that of the coming sequels, perhaps you could do me a little, but lovely, favour. Nothing benefits an indie author who has to compete with the tens of millions of other books on Amazon than a rating. Or even better, a review. It doesn't have to be a treatise, just a few words would be fine.

Also, if you sign up for my infrequent newsletter via my website you can get a free short book, Blood of the Druids. Set seventeen years before Brethren, and is based on the true story of the Battle of Mona.

www.robbpritchard.co.uk

ACKNOWLEDGEMENTS

To my wonderful girlfriend, Jana Goetzova, for all of the support and for not getting to mad at me when I need to scribble ideas down at 3am. It's such an honour to be your second favourite writer...

For the invaluable developmental edit, Hal Duncan, author of the unbelievably amazing *Vellum and Ink*. A man I credit with teaching me how to write.

Joseph C for convincing me that the first draft was worth editing.

Elaine Borges-Ibanez for the proofreding.

Callum Nelson and all at the incredible Park in the Past near Wrexham (https://parkinthepast.org.uk). An amazing idea, an amazing place. Well worth a visit. I will be spending plenty of time here over the next summers with these experts and enthusiasts.

Shahaf Galil for helping with an incredible opportunity I couldn't have afforded otherwise.

Marina Kosenkova, my best friend, for helping me with my inability to distinguish between past and passed.

Chloe Adams for giving me the very first feedback and the assurance that the six months it took to write and edit this book hadn't been a complete waste. And to my little team of ARC readers.

Kristina Spiel for finding some spare moments to help with that bane of writers, the dreaded blurb.

For the most in-depth account of the life of Magnus Maximus, I recommend Maxwell Craven's *Magnus Maximus: The Neglected Roman Emperor* and his British Legacy. From the dozens of sources I pulled information from, I found his work to be by far the most authoritative. He also helped with some specific information that found its way into Usurpers, for which I am very grateful.

For historical advice and the brilliant FB page on the fort of Caerhun, (Canovium) in North Wales, David from facebook.com/Caerhun.

For once again going way beyond the call of duty for the artwork, I owe massive thanks to Sasa Juric for the work he did on that gorgeous cover.

Marion Blockley Ironbridge Coracle Trust for her invaluable knowledge about ancient sea and river faring craft.

And lastly, but definitely not least, to my awesome Mum, Carol Pritchard, typo finder extraordinaire!

Printed in Great Britain
by Amazon